Breaking the Rules

CAROLINE LASSALLE

Breaking the Rules

VIKING

For Camilla

VIKING
Viking Penguin Inc.
40 West 23rd Street
New York, New York 10010, U.S.A.

First American Edition

Published in 1987

LIBRARY OF CONGRESS CATALOGING IN PUBLICATION DATA

Breaking the rules.
I. Title.
PR6053.A859B7   1987   823'.914   86-40228
ISBN 0-670-81522-5

Printed in the United States of America by
Haddon Craftsmen, Scranton, Pennsylvania
Set in Sabon

Contents

Celia 1977   1

CHARLOTTE 1952   10

Celia 1978   100

ELEANOR 1957   106

Celia 1979   131

LAURA 1962   135

Celia 1980   179

IDA 1967   182

Celia 1981   253

ANDREA 1972   256

Celia 1982   275

Acknowledgements

I should like to offer my warmest thanks to W, for impeccable research on various subjects, and to Ben Turok for his account of an execution in Pretoria Central Prison.

Breaking the Rules

Celia 1977

The five women were dead.

Cold would strike suddenly, at the exact moment when the courtyard wall effaced the sun. Then she would leave the veranda, taking the table and chair with her. Inside the house were only a bed, an electric heater and her landlady's old wardrobe: eight feet tall and six feet wide; columned, pinnacled, railed, mirror-fronted, its raised panels embossed with acanthus leaves. Bare bulbs dangled on knotted flex from the ceilings. There was a sickening yet alluring smell of paint.

She tilted back her chair against the wall. On the table in front of her were three books. Two of them – George Gissing's *Isabel Clarendon* and *The Road to Xanadu* by John Livingston Lowes – she had brought with her from England. The third – *Pale Grey for Guilt* by John D. MacDonald – she had found in a stationer's shop that morning.

She was reading the Gissing. 'The past,' she had just read, 'is no part of our existing self; we are free of it; it is buried. That release is the pay time owes us for doing his work.'

She closed the book. The five women were dead. She swallowed a gulp of red wine. Next to the tumbler was a packet of cigarettes. She lit one; she had been turning the matchbox over and over in her left hand. Now, although the tiled floor was littered with cigarette stubs, she replaced the dead match neatly in the box.

She turned her head. A bow-legged orange cat, crouching at the far end of the veranda, bounded off across the courtyard, then up the fig tree and onto the wall. The women were dead. She carried that with her all the time: the crammed-in, forced-down, crushed and crumpled load.

She remembered how her mother had packed a suitcase: each garment folded round one sheet of tissue paper, then wrapped in another. (Did tissue paper still exist? She had not seen any for years.) There were no such parcels – in childhood she had regarded them, with dislike, as sham presents – in this agglomeration, which she was now free, which she now had time to unpack.

Freedom and time: the words weren't soothing: they unsettled her;

I

she couldn't trust them. They might be heavy with prospects or quite weightless: loosed from gravity by the imminence of some annihilating blow. The five women were dead. She looked up. As the sun sank, the leaves of the lemon tree darkened but its fruit paled.

*

During her first weeks on the island she had stowed the mess away, out of mind. She concentrated on escape from the hotel, where plastic chair-covers sucked at her skin and clammy music seeped out of the walls. During dinner a big drunk Swede moved from table to table. At each he asked, 'Why you no love me?' Tears left snail's traces on his mauve cheeks.

'I don't love anyone,' Celia murmured, so that only he could hear. His eyes focussed, then blurred again. He stumbled off. After this he avoided her table though he still halted by the elderly married couples and the parties of widows on Winter Sunshine Holidays: *'Why you no love me?'*

Embarrassed, whether they showed it by frowning or sniggering, they looked more stupid than usual: they always looked stupid. Age wiped away sexual distinctions, and left a sheep's face behind.

At the hotel she understood women's longer life-span. Inactivity had softened and weakened the wethers, but the ewes – lambs long gone from the sheepfold – were inured to uselessness. It had toughened them. Now they were blunt as rams. These were years of revenge for past diffidence and timidity. They wore trouser-suits, and the hair at their napes was grimly sheared. Neatness sufficed; concessions were repudiated. 'All that' was over, and their laughs were loud and careless. She remembered a film of a holiday camp where women of this age competed for the title of 'The Knobbliest Knees'.

She ate breakfast early, before the flock jostled in. But, disinclined to go out alone in the evening, she had booked half-board, and observed them at dinner, glancing up from her paperback and her – always tedious – plate.

She had found good food in the town, at a workman's restaurant where, behind her book, she lunched on garlicky lamb stew, stuffed vegetables, or boiled white beans with olive oil and parsley. The waiter brought half a round loaf with a yellow, ridged crust, a quartered lemon, and two raw purple onions, sprouting green. These were free; and almost free was the black wine that tasted of dust and sugared iron.

The sheep, she knew, could not have borne such food ('strong',

'oily', 'funny') or such surroundings ('nothing nicely served'). Naturally – though against nature – hotel meals were well-presented and
insipid: sheep customers must safely graze.

Sometimes the sheep were herded in coaches to new pastures, but
usually they strayed round the town's shops. Her own walks were
different. They had a purpose. She was looking for a house: one she
could bear to live in.

The town was built on a hill. The hotel was at the top, off a noisy
bypass named after an archbishop. At the bottom of the hill was the
sea.

On and around the bypass, builders knocked down thirty-year-old
houses with tiled roofs and big verandas, and put up concrete cubes.
On each completed cube they placed a solar heater: a grey cylinder
under a square tank on stilts.

Seen from the hotel window, these cube-topped cubes seemed
scattered at random on waste ground, but each was planted in a fenced
plot. When she passed them on foot they became miniature prisons:
vertical metal strips barred the doors; closed horizontal shutters, like
blinds, sealed the windows. Walls embellished with crazy paving or
with pink and grey pebbles stuck in rough cement evoked a precise
image: a chain-gang in a quarry, breaking stones. She turned down
towards the sea.

In shops, postcards of the sea-front still recorded a skyline of erratic
charm, dominated by bell towers and a silvered dome in the next
parallel street; for on the front itself the Metropolitan Hotel was the
only building of three storeys. Ionic columns flanked its entrance,
which was sheltered by a faded blue awning. Over this, six tall
windows, coroneted with plaster wreaths, each led onto its own small
bosomy balcony, while on the top floor a single deep veranda receded
behind a close rank of pillars.

There were pillars all along this sea-front: of stone, stucco or
mud-brick. Hellenism was the rule though, here and there, obeisances
were paid to other cultures: a few yards of castellation; a Gothic arch;
a pointed gable shielding an empty conventual niche.

Nearly every roof was terracotta-tiled: tiles between dome and bell
tower, tiles on a gable, tiles above the Metropolitan's top storey. Tiles
backed a pediment; they sloped over a timbered outwork that rested
on stone supports curved like dolphins. Only one crooked shack, its
mud face painted a bold pink, had a corrugated iron lid of the same
grey as its kebab oven, from which a column – here of smoke – rose
straight into the quiescent air.

But this was now only a postcard world. Pillars, tiles, pediments had

3

vanished; even the Metropolitan had been pulled down. Dome and bell towers were hidden by concrete. Concrete rose or was rising all along the front.

Walking east and west between bypass and sea-front, she gradually defined a territory. Its upper limit was a road of old mud-brick houses, most of which were turned into mechanics' shops. It was noisy and dusty; posted along it, sets of traffic lights marked bleak straight avenues leading to the bypass.

The lower limit was the street of the domed church. The street was narrow and lively; its buildings were varied. But the shops sold hideous souvenirs, and it was shadowed by the sea-front buildings, which, on this side, were pock-marked with mean rear windows.

To the west – if she were standing with her back to the sea – the frontier was just above the old harbour. (Four miles further west, beyond an industrial area, was a new one, designed for container vessels.) Here, on the grimy stone face of a disused brandy factory, a large plaque showed a young person of mysterious sex: non-committal breasts, a neat growth of vine leaves submerging the lower hips, a bandeau concealing the hair. This figure, right ankle lightly crossed over left knee, sat on a hooped barrel which floated among solid, bolster-like clouds. Its right hand raised a goblet; its left held a spear. Its expression was calm, remote. In spite – or partly because – of its vine-leaf bikini, it seemed too decorous to be a hanger-on of Bacchus. Studying it, she became aware that the customers of a café were watching her; at once she moved on.

The territory's fourth boundary was the Public Gardens, between the sea-front and a tourist region stretching six miles east along the coast. The entrance to the Gardens faced the sea; long and narrow they extended nearly to the territory's upper limit.

They were crowded with old acacias, bluegums, cypresses, and with other trees whose bare branches resembled nests of snakes. There were also palms, ranging from plump squat pineapples to tall poles with rusty falls of beard. Patches of lawn were inaccessible behind neatly trimmed hedges that erupted haphazardly into topiary: an approximate ball, an aspirant acorn, a rabbit's head with three unequal ears.

At the junctions of paths, busts of civic heroes – two wore glasses – stood on fluted pillars. Seats had curved arms; benches rested on *art-nouveau* supports. In the playground, small iron rockers were occupied by children in knitted hats. Walking faster, she reached the museum and the zoo, which she called the Houses of the Dead and the Living.

The House of the Dead was a corrugated-iron hut with a bright green door. Inside, glass-topped boxes on stands lined the walls, and an upright glass case stood at the centre.

In the boxes, on beds of jaundiced taffeta, butterflies had faded to the colour of moths. Legs, beaks and glass eyes were uncertainly connected to small birds, lurching sideways, and to larger ones, lying supine. Clutches of mothballs, like frosted eggs, surrounded them. Against each bird was propped a name-card, handwritten – now almost invisibly – in both Greek and English.

The island's taxidermist – surely dead by this time – had dealt more confidently with the larger subjects in the upright case: a fox, a hare, a small deer. An exception – and the only item without a name-card – was a flattish pouch of yellow fur. Although drawn to a point in front, it was noseless, mouthless, and had neither eyes nor ears. A bony peeling tail extended behind it, with two long feet like bunches of damp string.

In the House of the Dead, the air was dusty. Celia's throat and nostrils became dry; her ears seemed blocked; she felt that she was going to choke.

She crossed the path to the House of the Living. By the gate, in a small wire-fronted box, a mina called out – martyr-witness – to each visitor. Celia remembered how St Paul's Rocks, when Darwin and Fitzroy landed there, had been covered with birds, and how the party from the Beagle found sticks and beat some of them to death. Even then, the others did not fly away. It was, as Darwin noted, their first encounter with man.

On the left, inside the gate, was the elephant. In front of its enclosure, one Sunday – when the zoo was always full of dressed-up families – she met a receptionist from the hotel who pushed a pram while her shorter husband held the hand of a small boy in smart tweed trousers. The receptionist told Celia how, a year before, this elephant had trodden on its keeper's head. 'Squished just like a tomato,' she explained with relish, though piously she cast up her eyes. The elephant did not look fierce, just depressed, shifting from tomato-squishing foot to foot, swaying its trunk, fidgeting as if its grainy skin itched, but now Celia noticed that people watched it with particular interest.

Beyond were birds. An eagle hunched near the top of one truncated pine tree, and a griffon vulture huddled in another. Doves sounded gentle, though she had heard that they had peevish natures. Pheasants – Golden, Silver, Lady Amherst's – enacted Lawrentian scenes: self-conscious showy males strutted before drab submissive females.

After these pens, and behind a larger enclosure where pelicans,

5

cranes and ducks shared a pond, was a narrow semi-circular detour. She hung back from this, especially when – often, on weekdays – the zoo was almost empty, but she always forced herself along it in the end.

Half way, terror waited. She had seen lions before, but had never undergone the knowledge of their power till here, just where the small path rounded, she was overtopped by this great pair: idols of clouded amber in what seemed a fragile cage. Some morning – the bars splayed open with a single shrug – the mat-maned flat-faced male would thud to the path. She – immobilized as in dreams – would be felled by one swat of an emblematic paw.

Each time, she imagined it; each time, whether they paced or lolled, the lions' absolute indifference shamed her. She hurried past. Emerging from the detour she faced a muddle of monkeys. Impartially they busied themselves with their own and each other's bodies, though one grey female often crouched apart, sucking her nipple while she heaped her head with straw.

Beyond the monkeys, three camels stared across at the elephant. Celia's tour was complete. By the gate the mina shrieked. *St Paul's Rocks had been covered with a warm, pulsing layer of birds.*

If she had planted a pin in the exact centre of a map of the territory, it would have pierced the town market, the *agora*. 'Agoraphobia' – the dread of space – had, she supposed, derived from an open market. This one was in a building: square, solid, of the same stone as that of the old brandy factory.

Inside, along the walls, garlic plaits and heavy baskets – which crackled at a touch and smelt of compost – dangled over sloping wooden stalls of produce: lush green whiskers; polychromatic sacs of innocent flesh. Down the centre, other flesh was laid out on marble slabs: bleeding wounds, dark tumours ready to burst their skins, fat-coated secretions on splintered lengths of bone. Whole pigs and sheep hung from iron hooks, their clotted noses just above the ground.

Behind this main hall, in the fish market, a stone counter was dotted with small tumuli – of red and grey minnows, of pink and purple tentacles and pulp – and large sombre-faced groupers were sawn into slices. In an adjoining room old peasants, dressed in mourning, sold pallid cheeses, hard sausages, and olives of various sullen colours which, adamantine, creased or swollen, were ladled in heavy spoons from tubs of brine.

In front of the market building, on a raised oblong of uneven paving, men – never women – drank coffee under small trees. A cripple knelt to polish shoes, and a blind lottery-ticket seller, calling monotonously, felt his way between the tables.

It was in the narrow streets around the market that she found stone and mud-brick houses like those on the postcards of the former sea-front.

Here she could observe detail: fanlights above heavy double doors; playful ironwork decorating balconies and guarding windows; door-knockers of brass or iron, varying in size and finish, but all shaped like women's hands. Here also was decay. Exterior walls were crumbling. Tiles were missing from roofs, slates from shutters, struts from balconies. Many of the doorknockers were black with tarnish.

Passing, she would, if a window or door were open, look inside. Nearly always, a courtyard flared green beyond the rooms. Often the interior was converted into a workshop or small factory, with raw patches on the walls, and cracks and gaps in the patterned floor-tiles. Inhabited houses, though cleaner, were frequently almost as dilapidated. Poverty – one reason for this – was not necessarily the decisive one. She felt that paint and maintenance were grudged. Houses which had been repaired had been degraded. A clumsy cement balcony replaced an iron one. Shutters were supplanted by the hateful horizontal blinds. A new door had a boomerang-shaped handle and was made of nubbly amber glass, fronted with glittering gilt bars. Old houses were not esteemed. She sensed that their owners' real desire was to demolish them.

It was in a street near the market that one morning she saw a notice stuck to a double door: ENOIKIAZETAI – TO BE LET. She stepped back to assimilate tiled roof, uneven walls, a fanlight, faded grey paint on door and shutters. She paused. Although she was studying Greek each evening in her room – she never went into the hotel lounge – she could speak only a few words. But the owner of the house might well speak English. Many islanders did, and the notice was in both languages. She advanced, and lifted a – small, tapering, only slightly tarnished – brass hand. She knocked, waited, knocked again.

The house was on the corner of another street; very narrow, almost an alley. In the courtyard wall that ran down it was a door, just behind the house. The wall was overgrown by a fig's bare crooked branches. Beyond these she could see the bushy tops of citrus trees.

No one came to the front door. On the other side of the house was one of many small shops in this district. She approached it, then hesitated on the step.

There were provisions from floor – heaped with sacks of beans and lentils, and crates of green-stuff – to ceiling, just above a row of brandy

7

bottles. A customer leant against the counter, talking to the shop-keeper. Both were men in early middle-age. They stared at her as she pointed towards the house next door. 'To let?' she asked in a very loud clear voice.

The shopkeeper did not speak English, but his customer was keen to interpret. Yes, the house was to let. At once she was beckoned into the shop and was offered the single rush-seated chair by the counter. Would she like coffee? She had heard that it was rude to refuse refreshments on such occasions. She nodded and smiled, and the shopkeeper shouted across the road to a man in a café.

Now questions had to be answered. Yes, she was from England. Yes, she wanted to stay on the island. No, she did not want a new house; she wanted an old one. At this both men closed their eyes, tilted up their chins and turned down the corners of their mouths.

The *kyria* to whom the house belonged had, she was told, moved out only the day before, to live with a married daughter in a beautiful new flat near the bypass. Now the man from the café arrived with a small saucerless cup of black coffee and a glass of cold water on a round tin tray. Then, as she sipped, the shopkeeper inaugurated a long, emotion-al telephone conversation, interrupted eventually for a question: could she come back that afternoon? She could; this, too, was reported at length, but at last the receiver was replaced. The *kyria*, she learnt, would meet her at the house at four. Hopeful, walking rapidly, she returned to the hotel.

Its entrance was blocked by trouser-suited figures. She stood aside for the party to descend steps that were shiny with wetness. (In this town, steps, paths, pavements were constantly mopped, hosed, doused.) A woman a few paces ahead of the others slipped and would have fallen heavily if Celia had not leapt forward and grasped her arm.

Bone pressed through shrouds of sleeve, of skin. The woman's mouth gaped open. Regaining balance, she closed it, and Celia, withdrawing her hand, heard the click of false teeth. 'Why, thank you,' the woman said. 'Thanks ever so much, I'm sure.'

'Oh, that's all right.' Now the whole flock was jostling forward, expressing solicitude, exclaiming about the dangerous steps. And Celia – politely, fixedly smiling – dodged round them, and up – treading carefully on those wet steps – into the hotel, where, breathing deeply, she rubbed her right hand – violently, repeatedly – against her skirt, as if to wipe off filth or blood.

*

Sharply chilled, she realized that the sun was gone. As she stood up, her arm brushed *The Road to Xanadu*, which fell, open, to the floor. She picked it up. Smoothing a crumpled page, she read:

> *Is that a DEATH? and are there two?*
> *Is DEATH that woman's mate?*

She clapped the book shut. As she put it down on the table, she glanced from its subtitle, *A Study in the Ways of the Imagination*, to her empty glass, which she now went into the kitchen to refill. She wanted to be distracted from what loomed in her mind. Up they rose now, in a single wave, and then, dying, down they fell, dropping away from each other like cut sheaves: one, two, three, four, five.

CHARLOTTE 1952

She spent the day after Jeremy's party in her room with the door locked. People occasionally rattled the handle. One of these was Lissa for, after rattling, she called 'Charlotte', and when Charlotte did not answer called again.

Lissa might think she was ill if she remained silent. She wished that women, like men, had 'oaks' to 'sport' when they wanted to remain undisturbed. (Why didn't they? Had the cost of installing double doors deterred the college authorities? More probably the thought of 'oaks for women' had simply not occurred to them; just as, although men had two rooms, they had automatically given women one.) 'Charlotte,' Lissa called a third time.

'Please go away. I want to be alone,' Charlotte said in an unnatural voice. Mentally she added, 'as they say'. 'I want to be alone' sounded intense, as if she were imitating Greta Garbo. Anyway, the calling and rattling stopped; a moment later Lissa's heels – high ones – clicked off. Charlotte looked at her watch. The time was quarter to twelve. Lissa was probably going to a Sunday-morning sherry party.

As usual Charlotte had woken early. Today she had tried but been unable to fall asleep again. Soon she had put on both bars of the electric fire, in spite of the extravagance. On Sunday the scouts did not come to clean the rooms (they swept and dusted, but did not make beds as men's scouts did), and though extra coal was left on Saturday, Charlotte was in no mood – in no condition – to clear the grate and to lay and light a new fire. She shivered; her teeth chattered. (Yet, though she was so chill, her forehead was sweaty.) She wanted to feel thoroughly warm: a state of well-being never accomplished with the sole aid of the coal fire.

It had probably snowed all night; certainly for most of the morning. The snow was scarcely dinted on the road and pavement – there was little traffic, especially on Sunday, in this part of North Oxford – and it was thick on the grey slate roof of the red-brick college buildings. The brick seemed horribly bright, but the white woodwork of the windows looked grubby, as people's teeth – even Lissa's – always looked against snow.

Although more seemed held in reserve in the heavy sky, the fall was stopping; only a few tentative flakes floated past. After Lissa had gone, she wondered whether a walk might be a good idea, but instantly decided that it wouldn't. She would wait until dark. In the harsh light reflected from the snow, she could not face people, or even buildings. She could not, in fact, face Oxford. Before coming up, five terms ago, she would never have imagined such a reaction to a place where she had believed she would experience perfect liberty.

*

Certain limitations had been evident from the first. For instance, there were books to sign. Whereas an Oxford man had to dine in hall a certain number of times each term, a woman had to sign a book at breakfast. She must sign another book if she intended to be out between eight and eleven in the evening. Should she wish to stay out till midnight she must queue in the morning outside the office of the Principal's secretary for a signed permission, and to be out of college after midnight, except in the case of summer 'commem' balls, was absolutely prohibited. However, within these limits, time did not have to be accounted for; there was no need to lie about one's whereabouts.

It was a pity women dons were so much like schoolmistresses. (In men's colleges, undergraduates were more tactfully treated.) Charlotte felt they would have liked to insist on attendance at lectures, but they lacked this power, and – just as for men – only the weekly essay and the weekly tutorial were obligatory: reasonable enough. Charlotte's sense of restriction had a different cause. 'Reading English' was not what she had hoped.

She had experienced a premonition of this at her first interview with her tutor, Miss Denison, who was an authority on Dryden's poetic diction. (Later Charlotte was unsurprised to learn that Miss Denison preferred *All for Love*, Dryden's play about Antony and Cleopatra, to Shakespeare's treatment of the same subject.)

Miss Denison had what are called 'fine' features: a thin aquiline nose, almost invisible lips, and the round eyeballs of a marble statue. She wore no make-up. (Many women dons were nun-like. Some were monkish: Charlotte thought of Miss Dale, the stout crop-haired scientist who shared Miss Denison's North Oxford flat. Others, such as Miss Wynde, the Vice-Principal and Senior English Tutor, were subtly less austere; attuned to the vicarage rather than the cloister.)

II

'Nur,' Miss Denison began. (Where other people said 'Hmm' or 'Er' Miss Dension said 'Nur'. It was pronounced to rhyme with 'cur'; the 'r' was silent, the 'u' dragged out on a descending scale.) 'Nur,' she repeated. 'Perhaps you would care to give me some indication of your literary preferences?'

Charlotte's mind at once emptied, but after a moment a massive shape loomed up in it: 'I . . . I very much admire Dostoyevsky.'

'*Dostoyevsky?*' The tone was that of Lady Bracknell ('A *handbag?*'). Up went Miss Denison's eyebrows; they were perfect semicircles though Charlotte doubted if she plucked them. A little shudder was succeeded by a definite shrug. 'Dostoyevsky?' This time the offending name was pronounced with less emphasis. 'Nur. I am afraid that I am not well acquainted with him. I once embarked – with some trepidation, let it be said – upon *Crime and Punishment*. I reached the point at which a labourer beats a horse.' *On its meek eyes*, Charlotte remembered. 'Nur. It was . . . too . . . much . . .' Miss Denison dismissed this excess with deliberation. Now her voice quickened. 'I desisted immediately, and made no further approaches to the morbid Slav.' She paused. Then she said, 'Of course, ac-tu-ally, I was enquiring about *English* literature.'

Words from childhood recurred to Charlotte: *Who's your favourite author?* She struggled. 'I like Shakespeare,' she said. This sounded weak. 'And Dickens.'

'Nur. One would rather expect the year's only English Scholar to appreciate Shakespeare – though one might feel that he can hardly figure as a *personal* preference. And *Dickens* . . . yes, I see!' It was clear that Miss Denison did not care for Dickens. 'Not a very *original* choice, if I may say so. And you are aware, of course, that he falls outside the syllabus?'

Yes, Charlotte was aware of it. Although she had not thought about it before she came up, 1830 – the final year of the syllabus – might have – perhaps had – been chosen to exclude Dickens yet include Jane Austen; once, but no longer, Charlotte's 'favourite author'. (Miss Denison, inevitably, would prove to be a 'Janeite', combining this first-name familiarity with formal references to 'Miss Austen'. She also used 'nice' in its 'true' sense: a 'nice distinction', and so on. *Nur! Denizen of the shallows!*)

As with Miss Denison, so she found it with Oxford English as a whole, though any implication of unity conveyed by the word 'whole' was misleading.

Better informed now than when she had plumped for Oxford on the basis of *Brideshead Revisited* – which hardly mentioned work – she wished that she had chosen Cambridge. There, the moralist – object of Oxford mockery – who dominated the English school was a force; she could at least have battled against his influence. He had no Oxford counterpart; to have 'battled against' Oxford's most famous English don would have been like wrestling with one of its damp autumn mists.

He wrote *belles lettres* (Charlotte's mother found them charming): elegant but ungrammatical essays on minor poets and novelists whose modesty he admired. Although he was inaudible, it was 'the thing' to see him lecture; he drooped and wove gracefully on the rostrum.

Lecturers with *chic* were few. They tended to 'deliver' epigrams or to be notably 'queer' in manner. One or two – such as the man who spent each Michaelmas term proving that Virgil had prophesied the birth of Christ – seemed possessed. But the belletrist was unique; he was loved because he was a lord: it was remarkable that a lord should bother with literature. His rank explained both his bad grammar – grammar was beneath him – and his patronage of humble authors: literary equivalents of the deserving poor.

Yet, on the critical menu of the English school, the lord's confections were refreshing: sorbets relieving a pedantically weighty *table d'hôte*. Nothing from Cambridge (let alone any other place) was offered, even *à la carte* on the 'general' summer reading list. Oxford cuisine was so stodgy that it stuck in Charlotte's throat (or, in the lord's case, so insubstantial that it melted in her mouth in a moment). *Nur!* The cooking smells tainted even her own reading. Weren't Dostoyevsky and Lawrence a bit 'intense'? Wasn't Dickens – though jolly – rather crude? (Surely it was absurd to speculate about his 'darker side'?) Such attitudes made her (literally) shelve the books that moved her, intermittently conscious that she did so to preserve them. And as, at school, she had picked up a worm on a twig and chased others with it to conceal her own disgust, so here, as her alibi, she had 'adopted' Pope.

> *Avoid extremes, and shun the fault of such*
> *Who still are pleased too little and too much.*

Nur! It was with extreme perversity that she had made Pope hers. And was there not a danger that, like Mephistopheles with Faust, he might make her his? Secretly, sporadically, extraordinarily slowly, Charlotte was writing a poem in heroic couplets.

In the basement of the English school, the study of Anglo-Saxon ground on, inexorable as Grimm's Law. An obsolete mill, its purpose was to make ingestible a few stony chronicles, some crusts of verse, and *Beowulf*, a giant's dish of cold, almost petrified pease-pudding.

Anglo-Saxon occupied about a third of her work-time. Charlotte sat staring gloomily at a page of *Beowulf*. She hated Anglo-Saxon more and more. Even the shorter pieces, 'The Wanderer' and 'The Seafarer', which were meant to be so poignant, failed to move her.

She liked Middle English, but of course, between Anglo-Saxon and Middle English, a splendid event had occurred: the French invasion. She blessed William the Conqueror. If he had not arrived, people might still be speaking that thick guttural language she now had to learn in order to read 1,650 lines of *Beowulf*, which as far as she was concerned was wholly depressing. The hearties carousing in the meadhall were as dreary as Grendel and his ghastly old mother. *Beowulf* smelt of fish.

Obviously she would have to learn the text as an actor learns a part (forgetting it as soon as the play closes). She felt sure that a few months after 'schools' she would find Anglo-Saxon as impenetrable as Sanskrit:

felahrōr feran on Frēan wāēre.

Under this she had written its translation: 'very eager to go into the Lord's keeping.' (Was anyone, ever?)

Sometimes she wondered if, after leaving Oxford, she would ever look again at anything written before the terminal year: 1830. But time would dispel the dust that Oxford shed so thickly (Oxford sometimes reminded her of M. R. James's ghosts, with their strange ability to influence the physical world, climbing trees or taking possession of crumpled sheets). Shakespeare, Milton, Wordsworth would re-emerge – like sprayed mosaics – refreshed by life. Meanwhile she had begun to wish that she had read some other subject.

If only she had read Philosophy! But that would have been impossible. She could never have controlled its ponderous team-mates, Politics and Economics, in the troika of Modern Greats; and Philosophy could not be read on its own. Anyway, Oxford Philosophy was not intended to provide what Charlotte wanted: explanations; it concerned itself with the precise use of language. To have discussed this topic in the English school might have been useful; there, however, it was never mentioned.

At least, as she was not 'reading' Philosophy, she did not have to shelve it. On her bedside table, as her mother kept a missal, she kept Kant. Kant was pure; he was also outrageous.

To tell a falsehood to a murderer, who asked us whether our friend, of whom he was in pursuit, had not taken refuge in our house, would be a crime.

What a sentence (though *that* crime might be, at least partly, the translator's)! What a scene: panting murderer; anxious friend, listening for the outcome in a cupboard perhaps; and – she saw him clearly, answering the door at midnight, in his dressing-gown – the philosopher: so absolutely not one's idea of the perfect host. Traitor because of his definition of moral perfection, how would he feel when, having indicated the cupboard, he saw the murderer's razor rip his friend's throat? But feelings were not meant to count; that was the point. Of course she couldn't accept it. Yet that loftiness, that inhuman – superhuman? – nobility fascinated her.

Kant had also written, 'Two things fill the mind with ever new and increasing admiration and awe, the more often and more steadily we reflect on them: *the starry heavens above and the moral law within.*'

*

For a short time, in her third year at the convent, she had puffed at religion as if it were a balloon that would inflate until suddenly it took flight, transporting her – carried on sky tides like the umbrella-borne boy in *Struwwelpeter* – to the empyrean.

She did not make these attempts during the official rites, Mass and Benediction, but in the period after supper known as evening recreation. Then, having asked permission from the nun in charge – and what nun would have refused it? – she would 'make a visit'. Putting on her black lace veil – it fastened with elastic under her back hair and, never washed, smelt musty – she would go to the chapel, quiet at this time – one nun in the front pew – and dim: one weak light, apart from the sanctuary lamp. Kneeling in these suitable conditions, she tried to release the soul which, she had been told, was distinct from, though temporarily confined in, her body.

The elastic of her veil was tight, and the hassock under her knees hard.. She picked at her rosary beads, made of olive wood from the Garden of Gethsemane and blessed for her by the school chaplain. (If someone else used the rosary, it would be necessary to have it blessed again.)

Fingering the five sets of beads on the chain while saying the reiterated prayers that went with them (one Our Father; ten Hail Marys; one Glory Be) was meant to free the mind to meditate on Five

Mysteries, Joyful, Sorrowful or Glorious: one chose before one started.

It resembled knitting. Some people can knit stitches, read the pattern (ten plain, two purl), and talk, all at the same time. Charlotte was not one of them. She did not want to knit, and she felt more and more sure that she did not want to say the rosary. The scent of incense, rich at first, mixed with the smell of her veil and turned sickly, and the solitude was polluted by the black bulk of nun ahead. She wanted to escape from the chapel, but the chapel itself was an escape. Apart from the imagined balloon trip – didn't she blow hard enough, or was there a flaw in the rubber? – she had another reason for the evening 'visits'.

To Charlotte, children had always been xenophobes. She was the stranger, and they hunted her through bushes, crowded round her chanting rude rhymes, or ran away shouting, 'We don't want to play with you.' She used long words; she couldn't catch a person or a ball. She didn't join in properly, but watched like a grown-up.

She had wondered if this would change when she went to the convent, but it didn't. Here, too, catching was important; so was something new called 'gym'. She couldn't walk along a narrow board; she couldn't raise herself from the ground by transferring her weight to her arms; she charged again and again at the vaulting-horse, but was never able to surmount it. Girls laughed.

Outside the convent, grown-up people varied: some were polite; others said, 'Run along now.' In the convent, at first, all seemed fearsome in their shrouds and their chains of office: heavy crosses, huge rosaries, jailers' keys. It was surprising – a relief or a disappointment? – to discover the pettiness beneath these Gothic props.

At her first English lesson, the class-mistress (it was common to say 'form' or 'form-mistress') asked, 'Who is your favourite author?'

'Jane Austen, Sister.'

'No, I mean really – not pretence.'

'But it's true, Sister.' Charlotte was surprised. When she was eight her mother had first read Jane Austen's books aloud to her. Now that she was ten she read them to herself. She enjoyed the stories, and the jokes were funny.

'Goodness me – aren't we affected!' Charlotte would always remember that nun's face: grey-eyed, sallow against the white pie-frill. The class laughed.

The nun in the library said, 'You take out too many books. That's a silly way of showing off, you know. It's quite clear that you don't have the time to read them.'

'But I do read them, Sister.' Again she was surprised; she had always read quickly.

The nun put the books Charlotte had returned in her desk, and said, 'Before you take out any more, just write down what those were about.'

The nun gave her pencil and paper. Soon Charlotte asked for more paper. Perhaps she wrote too much. She was never asked to do it again, but every time she changed her books she was conscious of the nun's dislike. This one was Irish, with a black moustache.

There were stories the nuns told. A saint began to be holy in childhood when her priest brother threw a handkerchief she had embroidered for his birthday on the fire. ('It was her first lesson in the vanity of earthly things.') A navvy, given a bunch of violets, ate them. ('That was all Beauty meant to him, poor man!') A little boy, asked whom he loved best in the world, didn't say 'Mummy' or 'Daddy' or even 'Nanny'. He said 'Me'. ('Why are you smiling in that silly way, Charlotte? That's a terrible story, and a very sad one, too.')

Detecting pride in her, the nuns did their best to eradicate it. Not education but expurgation – deleting undesirable material – was their aim. In her first year Charlotte won the English, History and Latin prizes. When, in her second year, she received none, she was certain this had been contrived. The nuns damped the desire to shine; like God, they preferred girls veiled. They believed Pascal: 'Admiration spoils all from infancy. Ah! How well said! Ah! How well done! How well behaved he is.' If they read on – 'The children of Port-Royal, who do not receive this stimulus of envy and glory, fall into carelessness' – they considered carelessness, though to be deplored, a smaller sin than ambition. Charlotte developed an enthusiasm for Lucifer, Son of the Morning, who, because of ambition, had plummeted like a hawk from heaven.

Body, as well as mind, had to be suppressed, concealed. To be naked, even when alone, was immodest, and common too. Baths – undergone a few years earlier in calico cloaks – were now exempted from this rule but, like changes of underclothes, took place only once a week. Cleanliness – attention to the body – was not stressed; neatness – a curb on it – was. Comfort-seeking – snuggling down in bed or lolling in a chair – was rebuked; crossed legs were forbidden. Full advantage was taken of wartime rationing to provide unappetizing meals.

In another way, however, war had contravened the convent's ethos; the move from austere London premises to a country mansion had set school life at odds with its environment. There were silky red and purple wallpapers in the dormitories, and canopied four-posters – assigned to girls who were sisters – soared above the interloping iron cots. Prohibition of physical – as opposed to spiritual – self-examination was flouted by huge gilt-framed mirrors, bolted to the walls. A Kneller countess, *décolletée* and ringleted, hung in the refectory. The ceiling of the ballroom – where, at dancing-class, they learnt the Irish Jig over and over again – was painted with a Judgement of Paris, and the walls of the main staircase were a jigsaw of pictures. Worldly couples with dogs and horses, nymphs scrutinized by satyrs, lavish arrangements of flowers, fruit and slaughtered game, gave place on upper floors to dark, heavily varnished Italian ruins and English dells.

Charlotte believed that, if it had been known, her joy in all this would have been condemned; somehow she would have been deprived of it. The nuns could scarcely have blindfolded her; might they have made her use the back stairs to mortify herself? ('Mortification', a favourite convent notion, was meant to be 'offered up'.) But this, she recognized, was far-fetched; in fact – as with Jane Austen – she would simply have been mocked for affectation.

Her mother had introduced her to pictures as well as to literature, giving her a book on paintings from the National Gallery for her ninth birthday. Charlotte still wondered why a spectator had muttered 'Poor child!' for she had been delighted with the book and now, three years later, knew it so well that she could find any picture in it instantly. She also collected postcards of works of art – most of them sent to her by her mother – which other girls found funny-looking. One of these was Augustus John's portrait of Madame Suggia, haughty and stern, commanding her cello. 'What a hag!' exclaimed Fiona Douglas-Maxwell, a member of Charlotte's class, picking up the postcard, glancing at it, and sending it sailing across the room.

Charlotte first noticed Pandora Warren, a girl of sixteen, because hers was an exact replica of Madame Suggia's noble profile. Pandora did not play the cello, but she played the piano: absolutely brilliantly, as all the girls agreed.

Pandora walked with long strides, swinging her arms from the shoulder, with her elbows jutting and her toes pointing outwards. ('Elbows at twenty to and twenty past; toes at ten to and ten past,' said Fiona.) Her head was usually flung back, but occasionally she tossed it. Then her hair flopped in short but poetic locks which – height of the exotic – were prematurely grey. Other girls – not Charlotte! – found Pandora funny-looking.

'Charlotte's cracked on Pandora! Charlotte's cracked on Pandora!' chanted Fiona.

'I'm not!'

'Oh yes, you are. Typical! No one else would choose such a weird crack. Twenty to and twenty past! Ten to and ten past! Charlotte's cracked on Pandora!'

Charlotte was always on the look-out for Pandora. She watched her in chapel and at assemblies. Whenever possible, she stood outside the curtained alcove where Pandora practised. (Here, though this was not her object, she began to enjoy music, which was the only art her mother did not care for.) Pandora, emerging from behind the curtain, strode past Charlotte ignoring her, till one day she halted: 'I say, look here, you,' she said, 'I wish you'd stop following me about.'

Charlotte turned and ran. On that same day she was summoned by Reverend Mother for a blowing-up. A poem she had written about Lucifer had been found during a routine search of desks. The poem was unmistakably a tribute, though she had ended each verse with the words, 'Or so he thought.' She raised this in her defence, adding, 'After all, Reverend Mother, Milton wrote about the devil in *Paradise Lost.*'

'Milton, although a Protestant, was a great poet. Not an insignificant twelve-year-old girl.'

The school stood in a landscaped park. Late that evening, when the others in the dormitory were asleep, Charlotte got up and dressed. She left the house by a side door, crossed gravel penitentially weeded by girls, stepped carefully on the slats of the ha-ha. In the park she took off her shoes and socks and put them down at the edge of the drive. The coarse grass felt unnervingly alive under her bare feet. She stretched out her hands to touch the night, which was balmy.

Although there was no moon, the river glimmered. She could hear, half a mile away, the rush of water into the pool where the games mistress, Miss Hester Brickley, taught the girls to swim. Miss Brickley did not go in herself. She stood on the low diving-board in her gym tunic, holding a rope fastened round the learner's waist. To Miss Brickley's surprise, Charlotte took to swimming 'like a duck to water – huh, huh.' Swimming was a recent innovation: parents had finally overruled Reverend Mother's objection to the immodesty of bathing-dresses: heavy black one-piece garments with a skirt covering the tops of the thighs.

Now Charlotte's feet were getting used to the grass, becoming fond of it. She lay down flat on her back. Absence of moon made the stars whiter. Absence of accustomed things revealed a core of value in herself. When she read Kant he confirmed what she had known then: *'the starry heavens above . . . the moral law within.'*

She became aware that the grass was damp, and that an insect had bitten her shin. She scratched the bite, and stood up, feeling at ease. Things would be better from now on, she thought. However a patrolling nun had discovered her absence.

At the interrogation next day she had no answer to the question, 'Why?' Punishments – known as 'penances' at the convent – were imposed: weeding the gravel, and two weeks' forfeit of the daily boiled sweet, of 'story books' and of 'second rising', the extra half-hour's sleep allowed on Saturday morning.

Weeding with a small trowel, she tinkered with a poem to Pandora. Soon she rolled this in her mouth more smoothly than she had ever rolled the daily sweet, which she could never resist crunching. While others read their story books, she wrote her poem, under the cover of an exercise book. At Saturday Mass – attended, because of second rising, only by nuns and Children of Mary – her lips moved, muttering the poem. (She also put blotting-paper in her shoes because this was meant to induce fainting, but it didn't work.)

The poem was her triumph over the penances; all the same, it presented problems.

> Again I kiss thy lips so full
> And press my body 'gainst thine own.
> I love thee with adoring love
> And beg thee to be mine alone.

'Again' was, of course, inaccurate, and Pandora's lips were rather thin. Charlotte also found it hard to visualize kissing, let alone pressing her. Yet, while the first two lines – inaccurate – sounded like real poetry, the third and fourth – true – seemed dull. It was a pity that poetry and truth did not match.

She was often conscious of this difficulty as she composed the seven stanzas – seven was a lucky number – which she finally placed on the striped Viyella pyjamas under Pandora's pillow.

So that no one would see her, she did this after the tea-bell, and was late for the meal. 'No jam for you today, Charlotte,' said the refectory nun. The words, like a splash of petrol, made a low fire inside her blaze up. 'Damn,' she said, not loudly, but the nun heard.

From her little frown, Charlotte saw that she first thought the word was 'Jam!' When she realized that it was something far worse her face went stiff. Then, quite unexpectedly, it sagged; she turned away as if she had heard nothing. Charlotte suddenly understood that a deadly enemy may falter: not from kindness – never that! – but from exhaustion or from weakness. Other girls, who had heard and seen, whispered. Excitement pounded in Charlotte's head like hooves.

The pounding persisted. What would Pandora think of the poem? Surely she would admire it. What would she do? Surely, with that noble profile, that absolutely brilliant piano-playing, she would never tell tales to a nun. Although Charlotte had not signed the poem she felt certain that Pandora would know who had written it.

During afternoon recreation next day – it was raining, and they were in the classroom – a small girl brought a message that Biddy Bing wanted to see Charlotte in the Blue Ribbons' room.

Blue Ribbons were the convent equivalent of prefects. Across their swelling bosoms – most of them were seventeen-year-olds – they wore broad bands of pale-blue watered silk, trimmed with silver fringe.

Biddy Bing's mother was on the stage, and she herself acted absolutely brilliantly, as all the girls agreed. She was the protagonist – male or female – in every school play, and her hair was the exact pale colour of her face. All this was romantic, and lots of girls were cracked on her, but Charlotte couldn't imagine having Biddy for a crack. She had a docile, modest look, and her features were flat which added to the puddingy effect of so much cream: if one had touched her cheek, it might have dented, like a mousse.

Biddy was alone in the Blue Ribbons' room, sitting in one of their straight-backed armchairs. She had Charlotte's poem to Pandora in her hand.

'Did you write this?'

'Yes.'

'Well, you should be ashamed of it. It's very silly.' Biddy read the poem aloud. Naturally she read well, and Charlotte had never heard a poem sound worse.

Biddy paused once, after the words, 'And beg thee to be mine alone.' She raised her eyebrows, said, 'What can you mean by *that*?' and went on reading. When she had finished, she said, 'I shan't tear this up. Pandora wants me to tell you that if you ever pester her again – hanging about outside the music room, and so on – she'll show it to Reverend Mother. She felt she really ought to anyway, but it's too silly and embarrassing. So you have one more chance. You're very lucky. You can go now.'

Opening the door, Charlotte glanced back. A smile had settled on Biddy's face like a cat on a cushion. In the classroom, where recreation was about to end, a girl called Bella Waddell said, 'Did Biddy blow you up? Why?'

Charlotte rushed at her and grabbed her hair. She found a large tussock of it in her hand. Bella, after one shriek, huddled on the floor, moaning and holding her head. Girls crowded round, staring down at her. Charlotte wished it were Fiona Douglas-Maxwell on the floor; Bella was actually the nicest girl in the class.

Charlotte ran out onto the landing. The rail of the main staircase was on her left. She looked over. Down in the hall, Reverend Mother was talking to another nun. Charlotte dashed back into the classroom, seized a large wire waste-paper basket, and swept a pile of red catechisms into it, from a shelf. Out on the landing again, she tipped them over the banister onto the two nuns.

*

When war broke out, Charlotte – like the convent – had been evacuated from London. Her mother stored their furniture – later destroyed during the blitz – and they moved to Thornbury, a small country town, where they stayed at the Manor House Hotel. On the envelopes she addressed to her mother from school, Charlotte left out 'Hotel', hoping nuns and girls would believe she lived in a manor house. The convent was very snobbish; Charlotte had a famous surname, which – though, like Milton, Protestant – was her one advantage. 'To think that a girl of such good family could behave as you have,' Reverend Mother said at their parting interview.

'I simply don't understand all this,' said Charlotte's mother, after her own interview with Reverend Mother. The journey home was uncomfortable, the train crowded with soldiers. The war in Europe had recently ended. At school the girls had been told, and there had been prayers of thanksgiving for victory, but Charlotte, absorbed in Pandora, had taken little notice.

'I shall have to look for another boarding-school.' Her mother sighed. 'All girls go to them nowadays. Anyway, you must make friends of your own age, and there are no possible day schools: nothing in miles except the High School.'

'If you send me to another boarding-school, I'll behave so badly that they'll expel me on the first day.'

'I simply don't understand it.' But a few weeks later Charlotte's mother heard of Miss Hale. Retired from school-teaching, she was known as a private tutor who achieved good results from poor material. Most of her pupils were backward boys; it was necessary for boys to pass exams.

When they met, Miss Hale reminded Charlotte's mother of a

governess she had liked as a girl. 'Of course governesses don't exist any more, though they seemed all right to me. In any case, this arrangement would only be temporary. I must look for a good school where you can make friends of your own age.'

'No, no!' said Charlotte.

That autumn – after two bombs of a new kind had beaten the Japs – Charlotte started lessons with Miss Hale. School Certificate was their – still distant – goal. 'Everyone takes it nowadays,' said Charlotte's mother, 'though I can't really see what use it is. When one marries, interests are much more important than certificates.'

Marriage was the only future Charlotte's mother had visualized for herself; it was the only one she envisaged for Charlotte. In her room at the hotel were various relics of matrimony: photographs, drawings, a few pieces of engraved silver. Among many other books was a history of Charlotte's father's family.

The founder of this family was conjectured to have arrived in England with William of Normandy; the first on record pleased Henry IV by killing the leader of a peasant uprising. A chronicler reported that 'when this caitiff insolently sought to bandy words with his liege lord the king, that worthy knight, justly incensed, raised up his sword and with one blow struck his head from off his body. Then was there great rejoicing, and the king quoth to that knight, "Now shalt thou be well rewarded for the brave service thou hast done us this day."'

The knight's descendants inherited his flair for getting on with royalty, and had the knack of backing winners in contests for the throne. They were political, lying low only under Mary Tudor and Cromwell, whose aims and ardour, in both cases, they found uncongenial.

There is a Holbein portrait of the first Baron, instrument of Henry VIII in the dissolution of the monasteries. Like his master, he is sparsely bearded and has tiny eyes. His son, in the miniature by Isaac Oliver, is charming; he has a fox's face, and wears one earring. Although his intimacy with Queen Elizabeth never became dangerous, she made him an earl.

Painted by Van Dyck, with small spaniels and wearing an enormous wig, the first Duke transformed accumulated *objets d'art* into a great collection. The family patronized ideas as well as art; they protected an atheist philosopher, who became their librarian and tutored two generations of their sons. However the fifth Duke – cod-eyed in the Reynolds portrait – forbade his wife to visit his own cousin, Edward. There was no *affaire*, which for her was unusual; but in any case the Duke, whose mistress lived in their house *à trois*, was not upset by that

23

sort of thing. His objection to Edward was that he was a scientist of genius or, as the Duke put it, 'Edward is not a gentleman. He works.'

For many of the Duke's descendants, work was a necessity. Inevitably it became sanctioned, provided it took military form. For over a century young shoots and collateral branches smote Asia and Africa, making them safe for the tradesmen they despised.

Both Charlotte's parents were born in India: her father when his father's regiment was stationed there, and her mother the daughter of an indigo planter.

As a child, Charlotte heard it said that her mother's family had 'lived like rajas' in Bengal, and she imagined her grandfather on an elephant caparisoned with jewels. Leaving Scotland as a youth with three guineas in his pocket, he acquired a vast estate on which brothers and cousins joined him. At forty-four, he married startlingly – an Italian Catholic in her twenties – and died of fever three years later. His widow brought Charlotte's mother, their only child, to his country, or at least to London. Fond of warmth, cards and good cooking, she drew the line at Scotland. She settled in a Knightsbridge hotel, attending Harrods on weekdays and the Brompton Oratory on Sunday.

Charlotte, reading 'Mowgli's Song against People', associated it with her grandfather's tomb, imagining a marble angel toppled among creepers.

> *I will let loose against you the fleet-footed vines –*
> *I will call in the jungle to stamp out your lines!*
> *The roofs shall fade before it,*
> *The house-beams shall fall,*
> *And the* Karela, *the bitter* Karela
> *Shall cover it all.*

'The *Karela*,' Charlotte muttered. 'The bitter *Karela*.' She liked the word 'bitter'. Her favourite Christmas carol was 'We Three Kings' because of the verse about myrrh. (*Myrrh is mine. Its bitter perfume / Breathes an air of gathering gloom. / Sorrowing, sighing, weeping, dying, / Sealed in the stone-cold tomb.*) But in spite of the jewelled elephant, the marble angel and the bitter *Karela* – which she imagined with poisonous purple flowers – she preferred to hear about her father's family. Her mother's was *middle-class*, and Charlotte idealized aristocracy. Her heroes were Byron – dashing off his poems and dying carelessly for a cause – and Charles I, martyred by a warty killjoy. Although her mother said it was 'a bad painting', Charlotte was devoted to that picture of a long-haired boy, questioned by grim Roundheads, which is called, '*And when did you last see your father?*'

Charlotte could not remember her own father, killed in a car accident when she was three. Her mother's accounts delineated a good soldier, who had loved the army – 'his men adored him' – had been fond of games and had dismissed most other things with simple jokes. Any contra-indications were at once corrected.

'Your father always read a great deal.'

'*Did* he? What?'

'Oh, anything that was going: history, biography, novels – though he thought a lot of modern stuff was bosh.'

The word 'bosh' sounded forced on her lips, but she seemed to like its effect, for she repeated it: 'He said, "A lot of these new chaps write awful bosh." '

'What "new chaps"?'

'Oh, I don't know. Aldous Huxley. . .'

'Why?'

But her mother said, 'I gave up after *Eyeless in Gaza*. That dog falling out of an aeroplane – so unnecessary.'

On another occasion: 'Of course your father was a brilliant mathematician.'

'*Was* he?'

'Yes, but at school they divided into what were called "sets" for subjects. He went into the top one for Maths, when he got there, and stayed in it, doing the same work each year, till he left.'

'How *awful*! Did he mind terribly?'

'Oh, I don't think so. He was *very* happy at school.'

Such recollections built not a bridge but a barrier between Charlotte and her father as, in photographs, his uniform and moustache did. Of course her mother meant to enhance, not to defame him; yet she had an unpredictable streak. Sometimes, when she had neuralgia and turbaned her head in a garnet scarf, her face, above her carapace of tweed, wore an erratic expression.

Other people had memories of when they were three years old. Charlotte, with none before four, had to depend on her mother's stories.

At three she had been upset when Alison, her nanny, ran away with her father's soldier-servant – it was common to say 'batman' – and even more upset when her dog, Ricky, died. (Alison? Ricky? She didn't recognize the wedge-faced woman or the wire-haired terrier in the snapshot; any more than she recognized herself, picking flowers and wearing white, white socks.) At three she had read aloud from a newspaper, 'George Vee dies,' and had added, 'Poor George Vee. Who is he?' Her mother described her response to Ricky's death and to George V's, but not to her father's, and she could not ask.

At three, after the pantomime, *Cinderella*, she had said, 'I'd have married one of the Ugly Sisters – much more in*tresting*.' Telling this, her mother laughed, with a note of doubt. But it was with unmixed approval that she recalled how neat Charlotte had been. 'You were always tidying your toy-cupboard – it was sweet. And you were always washing your hands. If you couldn't, you'd get upset. And you knew the name of every flower in the garden – so many wild ones, too.' Her mother sighed. 'It was remarkable.'

Charlotte supposed it had been, particularly as now she was untidy, and knew the names of hardly any flowers, though her mother constantly picked, bought, arranged and drew them. On walks, her mother kept stopping to examine wild flowers while Charlotte yawned and fidgeted. Stopping killed the whole point of walking, which was to take over the body as novels took over the mind.

Charlotte calculated that during the six years after she was expelled from school, she read more than five thousand novels. Two a day added up to 4,382 (1948 was a leap year), and two a day was probably an underestimate.

Her mother had read few new novels since Huxley's dog fell from heaven. She did not belong to a library, though, as well as taking *The Times*, the *Connoisseur*, *Country Life* and the *Tablet*, she often bought books. There were always several competing for her attention, which, easily attracted, was less easily held. Once, on her bedside table, Charlotte noticed, apart from her missal, Blake's *Job*, *Four Victorian Ladies of Wiltshire*, a life of Gerard Manley Hopkins, *Conversation Pieces*, some newly discovered poems by John Clare, and *Sense and Sensibility*; there was a bookmark in each. Caring about condition as well as contents, she deplored the way Charlotte left books open, face down ('cracking their poor spines'), and the 'thumbed' aspect of library books repelled her. Charlotte enjoyed some – though by no means all – of her mother's books, but they could not sate her appetite for fiction, any more than her mother's sweet ration – always added to her own – could satisfy her desire for sugar.

The Thornbury public library opened twice a week; a borrower might take out three books at a time. This was not enough for Charlotte, who read a novel of average length in an hour. She also joined W. H. Smith's subscription library; here she met local ladies.

'Oh, good morning, Charlotte.'

'Morning, Mrs Dyer.'

Once, after Mrs Dyer and her husband had been to tea at the hotel,

Charlotte's mother mentioned that a Victorian murderess, 'the Reading Baby Farmer,' had also been called Mrs Dyer. Questioned, she explained that a Baby Farmer was someone who took charge of babies for money, and then killed them: 'Really most unpleasant.'

'Not back at school yet?' People like Mrs Dyer often asked this question. Although Charlotte had now been taught by Miss Hale for two years, her mother never acknowledged that the arrangement was permanent.

'No,' Charlotte answered, as usual.

'And how is your mother?'

'Oh, all right.'

'Are you changing her books? How nice!'

'No. Mine.'

It was surprising that Charlotte should have heard about 'the Reading Baby Farmer' from her mother, who never looked at reports of murder trials in the paper or understood how people could enjoy detective stories ('So tedious, and always so badly written'). Now, when Charlotte referred to Mrs Dyer as 'the Baby Farmer', her mother would smile, though with a trace of guilt.

'I should have thought most of the books here were too old for you. Only fifteen, aren't you?'

'Yes.'

'Do you find many you can enjoy.'

'The trouble is there's so much rubbish here. The public library's better really.'

Obviously the Baby Farmer had just come from Recuperine, the hairdresser. Her grey hair was set in stiff ridges, with the ends in a tight roll, and her face was red from the dryer.

'Oh, you use the free library? I'd be afraid of catching something. New Poor though we are – ha ha – we still keep up our Smith's subscription. Though of course there's so little time for reading nowadays. One seems to spend all day at the sink.'

People who referred to themselves as 'the New Poor' constantly talked about the washing-up. It was a ghost that haunted every meal. Visitors must always offer to help to exorcize it, though their offers would always be refused.

'Only yesterday I was saying to Lady Jackson – she *quite* agreed – that the washing-up is so much the worst thing. Worse than the cooking – we eat very plainly – and of course the garden is worth every ounce of effort. But then there are Mac's walks – the dear old fellow can still cover a lot of ground.'

Mrs Dyer usually spoke of her husband as 'the Captain' (an

appalling habit, according to Charlotte's mother, even apart from the fact that his First-War temporary rank was incorrectly retained). Anyway, surely his name was Edgar, not Mac? But now the Baby Farmer stooped to pat a small black rag-rug on the floor. One end of it twitched; the other was attached to a tartan lead. Charlotte stepped back.

'Not fond of dogs? Isn't she a queer girl, Mac? And of course I don't grudge you your walkies, do I, boy? I suppose we're lucky to have a daily woman, though I don't know how long *that* will last. She's over sixty – still quite willing, but awfully slow. The girls who used to go into service are all making tea in government offices . . .'

Why did she wear dead white powder, like talc, on her red face? Perhaps it was Johnson's Baby Powder – just right for a Baby Farmer.

'. . . Or they're forced to stay on at school instead of being allowed to leave at fourteen, as they'd like to. Why, just the other day I heard about some wretched boy, longing to go on the land like his father, but kept cooped up in a classroom. Such a shame . . .'

The flush from the dryer was fading, but the Baby Farmer's nose – under the white powder – and her cheeks were still red.

'No freedom, but everything free – that's the motto! Free medicine doled out to people who used to think twice before they went to the doctor. Now they block up the surgery over the least little thing. It was packed the other day when I looked in to have a word with poor Dr Wilcox about my toe.'

The red effect, healthy at a distance, came from hundreds of tiny veins. The Baby Farmer's face looked as if it had been scratched by sparrows.

'. . . Nannied from the cradle to the grave! Although the new council-houses are such eyesores, apparently they're positively palatial inside. Mr Cottrell – the MP, you know – was telling the Captain that the Socialists' latest scheme is to put in extra downstairs lavatories. Two lavatories in a council-house – no wonder Conservatives are making a fuss! And meanwhile, of course, the bath is never used.'

It was surprising when her teeth were so huge – perhaps Baby Farmers ate their stock – that she could also show so much pink gum.

'But I can see, Charlotte, from that yawn of yours – you should cover your mouth, dear – that all this is a bit *beyond* you. Like some of the books you call *rubbish*, I expect. But I'm sure your dear mother would appreciate the truth of what I'm saying – though of course, living in a hotel, she doesn't have to face quite the same difficulties as most of us. Not that hotel life would suit me. Poor Mac would hate it –

wouldn't you, boy? – and I'd miss my garden far too much. I often wonder how your mother can bear to be without one, loving flowers as she does. Do tell her I hope she'll be able to come to tea just as soon as the umtibotia' – could that be it? – 'is out. And you too, of course, Charlotte, by all means, if you wouldn't find it too dull . . .'

If she went, she would. It always was. But the Baby Farmer baked nice scones.

*

'Provincial life is a hotbed of disease,' Charlotte said at breakfast one morning.'

'What *do* you mean?' Her mother sounded irritable. She was staring at an unopened envelope – typed but not brown, so probably from her lawyer – but Charlotte was glad of the question. She had prepared an answer, polishing it up in bed the night before.

'Symptoms: weekday palpitations, Sunday coma. Diagnosis: boredom. Prognosis: fatal.'

'What nonsense, Charlotte. The provinces are no more boring than anywhere else.'

'They must be. In books, they are. Trollope, Jane Austen . . . and just look at *Madame Bovary*.'

'Where on earth did you find *that*? Most unsuitable.'

She should have remembered how her mother, who usually didn't notice what she read (she had never heard of most of the novels Charlotte borrowed from the library), sometimes jibbed at a French book. Once, out of the blue, she had specifically proscribed *Twenty Years After or the Vicomte de Bragelonne* by Dumas, and when Charlotte had tracked it down, skimming its musty pages in a second-hand bookshop, it had seemed dull; it was certainly not shocking. Afterwards she learnt that, as a girl, her mother had been warned off it by her own mother, and – how unlike Charlotte! – had avoided it ever since. Perhaps the same thing had happened with *Madame Bovary*.

'But it's a *classic*,' Charlotte said. She hurried on with her speech. 'The disease is spread rapidly by carriers in all parts of the countryside – people like the notorious Baby Farmer, Mrs Dyer.'

This morning her mother didn't smile at 'Baby Farmer'. She said, 'It's not my fault, Charlotte, that you have no friends of your own age. That was one of my main reasons for sending you to boarding-school.'

'I don't *want* friends of my own age.' This was true. She was glad that the children of her mother's contemporaries were grown-up and

29

had left home. They were older than Charlotte because her mother had already been ancient – thirty-nine and married for twelve years – when Charlotte was born.

'Well, what *do* you want?' her mother asked, picking up the typed envelope, and looking at it with horror.

Charlotte believed that the answer to this lay with all those noble connections of her father's – of hers! – whom she had never met. Among them she felt sure that, as in Aldous Huxley's *Crome Yellow*, a marvellous life went on: brilliant, witty, cultivated. ('Cultured' was a word her mother had condemned as 'BBC', adding, 'Only pearls are cultured; second-rate ones, at that.')

'Everyone here is so *middle-class*,' Charlotte said.

As she spoke, her mother snatched up a knife from the breakfast-table; she edged its blade under the flap of the typed envelope. (She never ripped envelopes open with her hands, as Charlotte did, though as soon as the war ended she stopped re-using them with gummed economy labels: 'So ugly!') Now, having slit the flap, she pulled out the letter inside, held it up and began to read it. All this was done with haste, as Charlotte sometimes grabbed a boring textbook, fearing that otherwise she would never bring herself to tackle it at all.

Through the paper, Charlotte could see the printed heading: *Mackenzie, Ross and Co.* The letter was from the lawyer; there was now no question of further discussion of provincial life. She slid the library book that lay open, face down, at her feet, onto her lap. (Her mother's attitude to reading at meals varied with her mood and with whether or not she was doing it herself.)

This particular book impressed Charlotte with its sophistication and the grandeur of its style. Most novels ended with marriage, but this one started years afterwards: Arabella was now nearly thirty, and Marcus had married her when she was very young, rescuing her from illness and a dreadful home life. Poor Arabella had found out that her first love, a 'very pale gold' undergraduate, was having an affair with her mother, a person with 'the brittle tinkle of crystal lustres'. This discovery killed Arabella's appetite, and she became 'painfully thin'. (Was it 'painful' to be very thin? Charlotte wondered if she would ever find out.) 'Passing a looking-glass, Arabella would swiftly avert her eyes from the image of her own despair, from cheeks and sockets hollowed like stones caressed too persistently by the sea.'

Marcus had saved Arabella, but now she bored him. 'Bored, he closed his lips like a neutral frontier suddenly turned hostile, and it was as if a transparent blind descended over his normally brilliant eyes.' Now he was interested in a girl called Lalage. 'Contrasting with the resolved authority of Arabella's beauty, Lalage's features, as yet uncrystallized, seemed instinct with entrancingly unpredictable moods and weathers.'

Lalage had been a music student, until Marcus heard her play. 'When her hands ceased their strife with the keys – regarding her, he had been reminded of a wrestling quattrocento angel – his single sharp though compassionate glance sufficed.' Lalage gave up the harpsichord. Although Marcus was not a musician – he was some unspecified kind of business man; and a millionaire – he knew about music. 'In the arts, as in the gratification of the senses, he was intuitively expert in technique, in assessing the correspondence between actuality and ideal.'

The book was absolutely brilliant, of course, yet not entirely satisfactory. Charlotte expected to be fascinated by the hero of a novel, and though both Lalage and Arabella were fascinated by Marcus she was not; she couldn't picture him, and his being a business man was unromantic. Nor could she see herself – another expectation – as either of the women; half way through the book she was still not sure which was the heroine. She despised Lalage for giving up music so easily, though 'with a sudden desolate look of total dispossession', and Arabella – anyway too old – sat and suffered too much. She was doing it now. In a *peignoir* (some sort of garment: unfamiliar words never bothered Charlotte; she glided over them), on a *chaise-longue* (some sort of sofa), she was brooding over things that Marcus had once taught her. 'Vivid pricks of nostalgia, a shower of tiny diamond-shafted arrows, were waking nerves, numbed, she had imagined, irrevocably, into painful animation.'

'It is legalized robbery!' Charlotte started, and looked up. Her mother's voice and face were distraught. 'Ross' was having his usual effect on her.

When Charlotte's father was run over by an uninsured, drunken driver, his pay had been his only income. (He had inherited nothing from his father, whose small capital, on a friend's advice, had been disastrously invested.) As he had not been killed in active service, the War Office was not bound to pension his widow, but it granted her seventy pounds a year, with a further sixteen for Charlotte. What they actually lived on was money from India, bequeathed by Charlotte's Scottish grandfather. Her Italian grandmother had died shortly before Charlotte's birth.

The time when the family had 'lived like rajas' was over long ago. Ever since her grandfather's death the income from India had decreased. Chemical dyes displaced indigo, and the huge zemindari estate was planted with other less profitable crops. Two more partners died, and the last member of the family left the country, after appointing a Eurasian manager, Mr Tombs. (Each Christmas, from Bengal, Mr Tombs sent Charlotte's mother a frosted card, picturing robins, holly or a stage-coach in snow.) Decline continued, gradual and steady, till, at the end of the Second War, came the prospect of Indian Independence and expropriation of the estate. Compensation, considered inadequate by the compensated, was negotiated, and divided among descendants of the original partners. Charlotte's mother's portion was invested in safe stocks which paid small dividends.

A talent for business had not passed to Charlotte's mother's generation of the family. Scottish cousins were doctors, schoolmasters, an engineer. These distant acquaintances, met and written to only in connection with Indian affairs, were little more fitted than she to accomplish an advantageous settlement, and less dependent on it: the task was left to the family lawyers, Mackenzie, Ross.

This firm, like the family, had once been successful in India. Under the management of Mr Ross, son of one of the deceased founders, the resemblance continued in decline.

After being expelled from school, Charlotte grew conscious of her mother's anxiety about money; she became accustomed to it, as one person does to another's illness. This fever of her mother's, often dormant, turned hectic whenever a letter came from Mr Ross. Charlotte gave his face – seen once, during a visit to London – to Nicholas Nickleby's baleful uncle, Ralph.

'Don't you think you should go out there to conduct the negotiations yourself?' the only cousin – a doctor – who was on good terms with Mr Ross had suggested to him.

'To India? Good God, no. Went once, as a young man. Couldn't stand the place. Swore I'd never set foot in it again. Really, in many ways, this Independence will be a merciful release.'

'For India?'

'Good God, no. For me.'

To this cousin, Mr Ross had then confided his chief interest: the development of a new variety of gladiolus. As gladioli were the only flowers, apart from calceolarias, that Charlotte's mother disliked, botany would have formed no bond between them. In any case they never discussed it. Possibly Mr Ross, a bachelor, disapproved of all women; certainly he considered Charlotte's mother impractical, extravagant and 'la-di-da'. He had used this last word when, after her husband's death, she rented a flat in Kensington: 'Very la-di-da! Wimbledon would be more appropriate to your income.'

Charlotte's mother, who thought Kensington a concession to impoverishment – she would have preferred Knightsbridge – had been enraged by the sheer preposterousness of this. She still often recalled it. 'Wimbledon!' she would exclaim at some stage in most discussions of the man she always referred to as 'Ross'. Ross, she was convinced, took pleasure in making sure that she received as little income and paid as much tax as possible. Ross was a double agent, employed by her but working for her oppressors: Independent India and the Inland Revenue.

When she was upset the two merged in her mind. 'Legalized robbery!' she repeated now. 'That's what it is, though they talk of compensation. Compensation – a pittance! And how can they tax my income as unearned when my father died earning it? If Mr Churchill had been re-elected this would never have happened. Why, he said himself, "I refuse to preside over the dissolution of the British Empire." He would never have handed over. And Ross does nothing.'

Charlotte could understand her mother minding that they had less money; she was sorry herself, but what was the use of going on about it? She returned to her book.

'Marcus had invariably eschewed the obvious. He had taught her to match only her shoes and handbags – never her dresses – to her eyes.'

'We abolished suttee and the Juggernaut car. They are dying like flies since we pulled out. Why, they used to call us the Heaven-born.'

'He had taught her to appreciate the drama of contrasts in both colour and texture, to discover voluptuous satisfaction in a skirt of coarse bronze linen worn with a plain silk shirt the colour of a wheatfield.'

'I once played tennis with an Indian, and he kept hitting his balls just over the net.'

'Why had her *vinaigrette* never attained the pungently bewitching quality of his? Scrupulously she had followed his method, impregnating a *crouton* with garlic, just as he did, blending identical proportions of olive oil and *vinaigre de vin*, using the – only admissible – particular variety of Dijon mustard which he ordered especially from a dark redolent little shop in Soho. Yet obstinately the essence – like his own? – eluded –'

'It's so rude to read when I'm talking to you.' Her mother was now standing, ready to leave the dining-room. As Charlotte, guilty, leapt up, she added, 'What on earth are you so absorbed in?'

It was easier to hand over the book than to describe it. Her mother turned a few pages, and then paused; not, Charlotte hoped with sudden alarm, where Marcus first brought Arabella to ecstasy. ('The

33

wave crested; it fragmented; now she was dissolving in foam.' So that was what 'it' was like; roughly, at least, for the description did not make it very clear.) But her mother gave back the book, looking uninterested rather than disapproving. All she said was, 'Lal-a-gy – what a pretentious name!'

'Lal-a-gy? Oh, is *that* how you pronounce it?' In her mind Charlotte had been rhyming Lalage with barrage. 'Why pretentious?' she asked, following her mother out of the room.

Her mother didn't answer. On the stairs she said, 'Gandhi went to Buckingham Palace in a loin-cloth – such cheek!'

Charlotte ground her teeth at 'cheek'. Reaching the landing they diverged: Charlotte up more Tudor stairs, her mother through an arch into the Georgian part of the hotel.

Its name, the Manor House, was the invention of its proprietor, Mrs Meade. It consisted of two double-fronted High-Street houses, of different periods, which now communicated on each floor.

Charlotte's mother had heard of the hotel at a London party, shortly before the war, from a shipmate of the late Commander Meade. When he told her where it was, she remembered that, struck by the town's aesthetic composition, she had once cut an aerial view of it from a magazine.

Y-shaped, Thornbury was bounded by two rivers. These, with outlying water-meadows always flooded in winter, had prevented development. A Norman abbey, solid and noble, dominated Church Street, long, narrow, and ending at an ancient cross. Here the High Street branched to the left and Market Street to the right, each following and contained by the course of a river. These three main streets, interlaced with antique alleys, formed a compact town where almost every house was pre-Victorian.

Her mother had been looking for a wartime refuge for Charlotte. (She would never, as she often said, have left London on her own account.) This remote country town was an improbable target for bombs, and it also appealed to her rigorous eye. She was immediately attracted to the Georgian part of the hotel which most people considered less beautiful than the Tudor.

In her room, Charlotte, overpowered by a sudden languor, flopped onto the unmade bed. Sue, the current chambermaid, would not reach the top floor for at least an hour. Charlotte stared at the ceiling, furtively enjoying the effect of uneven brown beams against white plaster.

During the war, visiting a neighbouring village with her mother, she had stopped at the gate of a thatched, half-timbered cottage.

Numerous pink roses grew round its tiny leaded windows and black nail-studded door. 'Oh,' said Charlotte, 'isn't it lovely! Don't you wish *we* could live there?'

Her mother looked horrified. 'Good heavens, no!' she said. 'So badly proportioned – poky little rooms with low ceilings and great clumsy oak beams. How much I dislike oak – so dark and coarse. Anyway the whole thing reminds me of a chocolate box.'

Charlotte was puzzled. 'But it's so *old*. I thought you liked old things. And it looks so cosy.'

'*Cosy?* What a ghastly word!'

'Why ghastly?'

'So sentimental.'

Now, as she lolled, beam-watching, on her bed, it occurred to Charlotte that 'sentimentality' provided a key to most of the words her mother abominated. 'Tender' was a particular *bête noire*, but the majority ended in 'ee', 'ie' or 'y'. As well as 'cosy', her mother hated 'wee', 'bonny' and 'tiny' (though 'tiny' was acceptable as a term of abuse), and she never bought Christmas cards with 'Merry' printed in them. ('Happy' – like 'pretty', it was a word too commonplace to be sentimental – might scrape past behind a Piero della Francesca, but she far preferred 'Best Wishes'.)

It was, of course, only in the case of favourable words that ee-ie-y suffixes were sentimental. 'Ghastly', 'ugly', 'silly' and 'poky' (like derogatory 'tiny') were unexceptionable. So were those hideous (but unsentimental) words – 'bosh', 'cheek', 'rot' – which jarred on Charlotte, and which she associated with her mother's tweeds and short hair.

That Roman face, mitigated by huge timid eyes, and the pliant figure stiffened by an upright stance seemed to demand soft dresses and coiled tresses. These Charlotte's mother would have damned – 'instanter', as she sometimes said – as 'arty', an adjective that often overlapped with 'sentimental': in connection, for example, with Pre-Raphaelite painting, and with any manifestation of 'folk'; weaving, pottery, dancing, music, lore.

Charlotte was aware of her own arty and sentimental tendencies. She liked not only thatched cottages, but also Staffordshire figures ('daubed', as her mother put it, with orange and black), and she cried over books and films.

She had only once seen her mother cry; in response to an accident Charlotte had caused by knocking a blue and white vase which had been her grandmother's off the mantelpiece in her mother's room. It shattered in the fireplace, and her mother covered her face with her hands; her shoulders rose and fell, and her breath creaked. It took a moment for Charlotte to understand what was happening. 'I'm sorry. I'm so sorry,' she said.

Was her mother mourning the vase's beauty or its history? Her eventual words did not make this clear. "All for nothing.' Her voice was high-pitched and peculiar. 'All for nothing.'

'What do you mean?'

'You wouldn't understand.'

'After all,' Charlotte said, 'It was only a *thing*.'

Her mother raised her face – it was crumpled and grey; her nose stood out – with a movement and then a look of contempt. In a louder voice Charlotte repeated, 'Only a *thing*.' Then she said, 'At least when *I* cry, it's because of people. Or animals,' she added, thinking of *Black Beauty*.

'Not *real* ones,' her mother said. 'Made-up ones. In novels. Even in *films*.'

The Regal Cinema, of maroon brick, set back from the road, at the top of the High Street, was Thornbury's only ugly building. The programme changed three times a week, on Sunday, Monday and Thursday. Most of the films, especially the Sunday ones, were several years old.

Visits to the cinema depended on whether the film was 'suitable' for Charlotte; her mother was a more active censor of films than of books. Suitable American films were Musical, Historical, Cowboy-and-Indian or Comedy. When, misinterpreting the dates and photographs in the glass case outside the Regal, her mother took Charlotte to *The Belle of New York*, and it turned out to be *Of Mice and Men*, she insisted on their leaving at once; she did the same, ignoring Charlotte's hissed explanations, when, expecting *Sun Valley Serenade*, she imagined the trailer for *King's Row* to be the film itself. Although going to the cinema often, she never became familiar with its customs; there was a 'second feature' instead of 'shorts' at least once in every three programmes, but it always puzzled and agitated her.

She and Charlotte saw all the films of the 'Bathing Beauty', Esther Williams, and the 'Brazilian Bombshell', Carmen Miranda, who danced with a tower of fruit on her head. Charlotte's mother had a strange affection for them both: 'That swimming girl looks so silly and good-tempered, and that fruit woman is so absolutely ridiculous.'

She seldom felt that a film deserved critical comment. She went 'to amuse Charlotte' and often dozed off when the action was at its peak. She found occasional English films 'not bad'; for instance, *Great Expectations* and *In Which We Serve*. *Henry V* – they went by bus to

Leckingham, the large Regency town nine miles away, to see it – was the only film Charlotte ever heard her call 'good'.

Henry V was Charlotte's favourite film, too, though she liked *Rebecca* almost as much. Heroes were harder to find in films than in novels. George Sanders and Leslie Howard both had charm, but the first was too frivolous and there was something soft about the second; handsome, sinister James Mason was fascinating, but only Laurence Olivier was ideal. However, awareness of his marriage to the perfect beauty, Vivien Leigh, tended to spoil Charlotte's daydreams about him. (They were obviously ideally happy, so Vivien Leigh had to die – in the centre of the stage – before Charlotte could replace her.)

Most film-stars were hopeless hero material. Some were too big and coarse (Clark Gable with his awful ears and moustache); others were too young and mawkish (short, freckled Mickey Rooney and Donald O'Connor). She hated it when an attractive heroine sacrificed an interesting career to marry some hulking or diminutive lout. Once, when a brilliant young actress gave up the stage for a gangling farmer from 'back home', Charlotte cried with rage, instead of – as usually – from sentimentality.

An odd and shameful thing happened to Charlotte in the cinema. Although she rarely discovered a hero, although musicals embarrassed her (she found it so false when actors broke into a song or dance, 'doing turns' like circus animals, that she would blush in the dark), although love scenes were usually so 'soppy' . . . yet the climactic music, the concluding embrace or expiry (it made no difference), the very words 'The End' filled her eyes with tears which, as the lights came on, trickled down her cheeks.

Her mother's astonishment was unfailing: 'How *can* you, Charlotte, when it's such rot?' Here the detested word seemed apt; Charlotte recognized that crying at films was rubbishy. But surely crying at books was acceptable?

'Hasn't a book ever made you cry?' she once asked her mother, who paused to think before answering, 'Perhaps, when I was a child.' Then her face emptied, and Charlotte felt sure that her thoughts had been dragged back to the cruel ayah, Teresa (brought to England from India, and wonderful at sewing and ironing), who had poisoned her childhood. She would never say what Teresa had done, only that she had been cruel, and Charlotte imagined gruesome tortures. Thinking of these while looking at a photograph of her mother as a child was another thing that made Charlotte cry. The longer she stared at the enormous eyes in the photograph, the more hopeless their suffering seemed till suddenly her tears dried up and she felt a kind of revulsion. 'Why didn't you tell your mother about Teresa?' she asked crossly.

'A child never does.'

Yet, at first, when other children bullied her, Charlotte had informed her mother. If she had not been reproved for 'telling tales', she was sure she would always have done so. 'A child never does' reinforced her view that she had never really been one.

Now, in her Tudor room, the bedsprings twanged as she gave a violent shrug; the phrase 'telling tales' still chafed her. Now she saw it as 'military', her new term for, among other things, philistinism, moustaches and 'obeying orders', which was even worse than 'telling tales'. Both phrases were like 'bosh', like tweeds: part of an unbecoming uniform that her mother wore with unquestioning loyalty.

Loyalty! That too had a 'military' flavour, and loyalty was her mother's vice. Loyalty was what made her portraits of Charlotte's father so unsatisfactory.

Although she found Victorian story-paintings absurd, her verbal pictures of him might have borne such titles as *Playing the Game*, *A Little Joke*, *His Not to Reason Why*, and though, on canvas, crude colours disgusted her, to have 'shaded him in' would have seemed to her disloyal. Hers was an official gallery; in it, pastels of Charlotte's grandmother appeared similarly untrue to life. And, though she saw them seldom, and corresponded with them only by Christmas card (she hated writing letters: this, she said was partly 'Ross's fault', partly the result of answering condolences on Charlotte's father's death), her depiction of old friends – Margery, Ethel, Frances, Elaine – was rigidly iconic.

Since the war she had taken Charlotte on several visits to London. They stayed at the Knightsbridge hotel where Charlotte's grandmother had lived for thirty-four years, and where ancient waiters and maids recognized her mother with muted cries.

This hotel was furnished like a private house. There were 18th-century glass-paintings on the walls, and oriental vases and ornaments were scattered about the rooms and passages. Charlotte sniffed the air, which had a cinnamon density; at any moment it might crumble into powdered spice.

During one of these visits, Margery came to dinner. Gradually Charlotte realized that her mother, too, was bored by the insolent bus conductor, the missing half-pound of sausages, the error in Harvey Nichols' account. When at last the commissionaire, in claret with gold braid, closed the door of a taxi on this guest in her black dress, diamond regimental brooch and short silver-fox cape, Charlotte sighed with delight. 'Almost as dull as the Baby Farmer, isn't she?' she said.

Her mother turned on her. (In Shakespeare she would have drawn a sword.) 'How can you be so disgusting? Margery is one of my oldest friends.'

Cloudy dark-red rage filled the upper part of Charlotte's mind. Underneath was something raw and messy. As the page-boy, in claret with little gold buttons, dragged shut the criss-cross grille of the lift, she identified it as pain.

'Margery leads a very lonely life,' her mother said upstairs in the passage; she was carrying their bedroom key which clinked against its heavy metal tag. Charlotte was not surprised that someone as boring as Margery was lonely. Outside their door a stone Buddha sat on a lacquered table. As her mother turned the key, Charlotte ran her hand over its head; the sensation was pleasurable, sacrilegious, strikingly cold.

Why wouldn't her mother allow her – no one else – behind the scenes after the performance? (It was one! She knew that her mother had been bored by Margery.) Why wouldn't her mother acknowledge to her – to no one else – the conspiracy? (If none existed, the portraits would look genuine, the words would not jar, the uniform would be becoming.) But she would not. So her loyalties were in fact betrayals –

'Of her only child!' The words sounded melodramatic when Charlotte, lounging on her bed at the Manor House, said them aloud to herself, but they were true. Now, a year later, she still resented her mother's having taken sides with Margery. 'That dreary old bitch,' Charlotte muttered.

As on that evening with Margery, so this morning at breakfast, her mother had not smiled when Charlotte mentioned the 'Baby Farmer'. Absent had been that always fresh sensation when the stale joke was shared: a thrust of joy that she and her mother were united. *Against the world*, as she put it to herself, for that was what she wanted. But the desire was hopeless. Why, her mother even stood up for – took sides with – Mrs Meade: not a friend at all, let alone an old one.

Just after Charlotte was expelled from school, Mrs Meade, approaching from the opposite direction, had come up close to her in a passage, brought her bulldog face near, and said, low, 'How unhappy you are making your poor mother, Charlotte. I call it a bad show. If you were mine . . .' Mrs Meade's eyes, behind the gold *pince-nez* had a gloating look. The passage was dark. (It was in the Tudor section.) Charlotte turned and fled.

She had been impelled by disgust, not by fear, but had Mrs Meade realized that? Ever since, Charlotte had felt a horror of her. Yet ever since – unexpectedly – Mrs Meade had seemed to avoid her. Charlotte never mentioned the episode in the passage to her mother; she could not have mentioned it to anyone.

Mrs Meade usually wore a black suit and a white tailored shirt with a small black bow fixed under its collar. 'Except for her skirt, she looks like a man in evening dress. She should wear trousers. Then people might mistake her for a smart head-waiter. Ha ha.'

When Charlotte made this comment, her mother said, 'How unkind you are. Poor Mrs Meade!'

It was funny that her mother and Mrs Meade called each other 'poor'. Was it because they were both widows? Her mother, of course – in Mrs Meade's opinion – was additionally unfortunate in being encumbered with Charlotte. *If you were mine . . .* Why was it 'unkind' to expose the absurdity of this woman's disguise? No one who stayed at the Manor House could fail to penetrate it.

Mrs Meade's appearance of efficiency – her *uniform* – was a disguise; like her hotel, with its invented name, it existed 'through the looking-glass'. The 'permanent staff, attentive at all times to guests' requirements' of the Manor House brochure, was a trickle of neglectful drifters. As for the "appetizing meals', nothing tasted of anything, and everything of nothing. The hotel's 'old-world charm' – it was surprising that Mrs Meade had not written 'olde-worlde' – was actually an advanced state of decay.

Charlotte's mother, on a recent rare visit to the lounge – she usually sat in her own room – had remarked with a startled look at the beige upholstery visible through worn patches in the cretonne covers, that the room looked 'rather run-down'. But a moment later she was distracted by the Campbell Taylor reproductions hanging from the picture rail. There were three of them, almost identical: women in long dresses, doing nothing in front of draperies. Charlotte's mother did not admire Campbell Taylor's work, but she liked to tell Charlotte how, at seventeen, she had met him when staying with her mother at a hotel (Charlotte's mother said 'an hotel') in Brussels. A clergyman as well as a painter, he had begged her not to join an expedition to the Musée Wiertz, because Wiertz's pictures were 'not fitting for a young girl's eyes.' What amazed Charlotte was that she had not gone.

Remembering Campbell Taylor, Charlotte's mother had forgotten the run-down lounge. In any case, where formerly she had blamed the war for the hotel's deficiencies, now she blamed the Socialists. Charlotte supposed they would stay at the Manor House for ever. Her mother, in spite of her good taste and knowledge of 'exactly how things should be done,' put up with it for 'poor' Mrs Meade's sake, and also in preference to finding a house or flat.

During her marriage she had moved eight times in fifteen years, and when, after Charlotte's father's death, she had settled in London, the war had uprooted her and a bomb had destroyed her furniture. She was also daunted by the prospect of cookery, something she had never attempted. 'That was why we always had such good cooks. They knew I depended on them. Now, of course, there are none.'

'I could learn to cook,' Charlotte said. 'We could rent a furnished flat in London.'

Her mother evidently considered the first suggestion too ridiculous for comment. (Thinking it over, Charlotte had to agree; she actually felt no desire to learn cooking.) 'London!' her mother exclaimed. 'So impossibly expensive nowadays, and so filthy and crowded. Quite different from what it used to be.'

London! Charlotte thought of people with hard exotic faces, of the green leather armchairs in Harrods' Banking Hall, of prostitutes on corners, of the stone Buddha in the Knightsbridge hotel; of someone famous for something, behind every front door. 'If only we'd stayed in our flat,' she said.

'During the war? It was out of the question. You were a child. I wouldn't have left, of course, if I'd been alone. Then none of our things would have been destroyed.' (The block of mansion flats had survived the blitz undamaged.)

Although she realized that her mother would never move back to London, Charlotte still often proposed it. She had meant to do so that morning at breakfast. Her speech on the provincial disease would have culminated in the words, 'The only possible cure is – escape!' But Ross had intervened.

Now, with a last yawn, she stood up. She collected her homework, and set off for an unfrequented room that overlooked the weedy garden. Because it contained a desk and, in a revolving bookcase, a few pre-war novels, the two 'Steps' books by H. V. Morton, and some old copies of the *National Geographic*, Mrs Meade called this room 'the library'. Heading for it, Charlotte, as usual, felt more cheerful. Working, she would forget London, forget the provincial disease. Just as she knew that she did not really want to learn cooking, she knew that she did not really want to leave Miss Hale.

*

When nun-numbed Charlotte met dullard-downcast Miss Hale, the result – as so often in the game, 'Consequences' – was startling.

Charlotte went four times a week to the small terrace house in which pale calm Miss Hale lived with a red harassed sister. (They reminded Charlotte of Mary and Martha in the Bible; she had always warmed to Christ's preference for Mary.) In an upstairs room, Charlotte, sitting next to Miss Hale at a square wooden table, faced a window. Outside, close to the glass, grew an apple tree. The influence on her mind of Miss Hale's noble passion for learning was to Charlotte inextricable from seasons recorded on apple boughs.

When she passed School Certificate (with Distinction in English), her mother wished she could spend a year being 'finished' in France – as she herself had been in 1909 – and could then 'come out', meet 'people' (which meant young men) and 'do a season'. The full programme – especially the giving of a dance – was far too expensive, but perhaps a reduced version might be contrived. Charlotte, abetted by Miss Hale, had another purpose; she was determined to go to Oxford.

Although Miss Hale had been to the University of London (Holloway College), she and Charlotte talked only of Oxford and Cambridge. Miss Hale believed that Oxford was 'better for arts', as Cambridge was 'better for science'; the glamour of *Brideshead Revisited* decided the issue for Charlotte.

Her mother visualized a women's college as an institution where earnest, unattractive ageing schoolgirls 'swotted', played games and constantly drank cocoa. She could not understand why Charlotte, having rejected school at the right age, should desire it, in this bizarre form, at the wrong one. Observing a loud-voiced, shiny-nosed girl at the next table in a tea-shop, she murmured, 'A typical undergrad*uette!*' The girl was with a fat, fuzzy-haired young man. Charlotte's mother believed that though 'undergraduettes' could scarcely fail to 'meet people', only this sort of person would want to meet them.

'I can't imagine why you think she's an undergraduate,' Charlotte said.

Frowning, her mother nodded. 'I'm certain of it.'

This certainty was founded on memoirs and biographies set in the first third of the century. Reading them, Charlotte admitted – though only to herself – that their subjects were not unlike the 'overgrown schoolgirls' her mother deprecated.

Keenly they pedalled off to early lectures, taken down in full by racing pencils, and slogged at essays which – at last perfected – they copied out in their best writing. But they also had awfully jolly times in college. There were play-readings, debates and river picnics, as well as tennis, hockey and even cricket. Sometimes they stayed up till midnight, talking about religion; they were all religious, and their intense friendships had a holy quality, too. Why did they make Charlotte think of sanitary towels?

In only one book did a man – a 'fiancé' – surface in this female pool. 'It is his purity I love,' the author wrote in her diary. But he soon vanished: carried off, drowned in the current of the Great War. Pure though he was, he had seemed an intruder.

When Charlotte realized that the Oxford of *Brideshead* – whimsical, doomed Sebastian; strange, fascinating Anthony Blanche – was contemporary with that of many of these books, she felt astonished. Evelyn Waugh, of course, never mentioned women undergraduates, just as most of these women authors never mentioned men. But surely things had changed since those days? Surely women no longer lived apart? It was Cynthia who reassured her.

Charlotte was sixteen when her mother's old friend Frances died, and Frances's daughter, Cynthia, came to see them. On this first visit Cynthia stayed at the Manor House, but on later ones at the grander – and fully licensed – Royal George.

Cynthia now had rooms in Chelsea. Previously she had been at an art school in Oxford, which she had left without taking her diploma. Frances's illness was the reason, though Charlotte's mother doubted whether, in any case – 'So little stamina!' – she would have persevered. She lived in the income from a trust, doled out, she complained, by 'mouldy' trustees, who never let her touch a penny of her capital. Although often broke, she had no job, for she could not get up before midday: 'It's my insomnia, you see. I only fall asleep at dawn.'

There was even more medicine than make-up on her dressing-table. Insomnia was only one symptom of what she believed to be a fatal illness, obtusely undiagnosed ('Doctors are all utterly useless, of course!'). This hypochondria was one of the aspects of Cynthia that Charlotte's mother found 'wearing'.

Although visiting the cinema with her was to be avoided because she talked all through the programme, Charlotte liked to spend time alone with Cynthia at the Manor House or the Royal George. Away from Charlotte's mother, Cynthia could be fascinating.

She used orange 'pancake' make-up, which ended at the jawline, and in a clear light her neck was grey. Her bruise-coloured eyelids glistened with vaseline, and she wore three coats of Post Office Red or Damson lipstick. She thumbed her nose at her reflection in mirrors, waggling fingers with bitten nails, varnished Post Office Red or Damson; usually not the one that matched her lipstick.

People stared at her in the street, noticing her likeness to Garbo, or just admiring her. She was conspicuously beautiful. If Charlotte said so, she crossed her eyes, puffed out her cheeks and then popped them, or crooned one of her fragments of song:

I get too hungry for dinner at eight.
That's why the lady is a tramp.

This made no sense to Charlotte. Tramps were men who roamed the roads; fewer and less threatening, her mother said, than they had been before the war.

Me and my dog are lost in the fog.
Will some kind gentleman see us home?

Charlotte could not see the point of this, either; especially as Cynthia never revealed whether anyone had been charitable enough to volunteer.

I marched up the stairs like a good girl should.
He followed me up the stairs like I knew he would.
Tumti, tumti, tumti. Tumti, tumti, tee.
Now listen while I tell you what that fellow did to me.

She didn't tell, but she told Charlotte more and more about her time at Oxford.

'We were tight as ticks. He had me on the kitchen table.'
'Oh. Wasn't that uncomfortable.'
'I didn't notice.'
'Oh . . .'

'We were drunk as owls. He went into the garden, and found a raspberry cane to beat me with.'
'Oh – how awful!'
'No, I enjoyed it.'
'Oh . . .'

'We were pissed as newts. He asked me to do it in a macintosh.'
'Didn't you laugh?'
'No. Rubber's a well-known fetish.'
'Oh . . .'

Most of these encounters had been with the ex-servicemen who came up to Oxford after the war. Some of them were now in romantic occupations: they were actors, journalists, broadcasters; one of them had actually had a novel published.

44

'Did you know anyone from the women's colleges?' Charlotte asked. They were in her room at the Manor House. Cynthia was sketching on a block of expensive paper: imaginary faces; men's and dogs'.

'What?' Even when she heard, Cynthia had a way of saying 'What?' so that remarks had to be repeated. This was another thing Charlotte's mother found 'wearing'.

'Did you know anyone from the women's colleges?'

'Oh yes. There was Delia Vaughan. She used to write for *Cherwell*. Terribly well-dressed and hard-boiled. Roddy Fen fell madly in love with her. He knelt at her feet, sobbing, in the Randolph bar.'

'What did she do then?'

'What? Oh, she walked out. As I say, she was terribly hard-boiled. Someone told me she got a job on *Vogue*. Roddy once borrowed ten pounds from me, and never paid it back. I was rather keen on him, but he turned out to be an awful swine.'

Men Cynthia was keen on often seemed to turn out like this. Now she tore her sheet of drawings off the block, crumpled it, and threw it towards but not into the waste-paper basket. Then she yawned, picked up *Dubliners* from Charlotte's bedside table, and turned a few pages. Putting it down, she said, '*Ulysses* is absolutely filthy, of course.' She yawned again, and stretched. When, as now, she was not wearing scent (*My Sin*), she smelt like the inside of an old lady's handbag.

'Did you know any other women?'

'What?'

'Did you know any other girls who were undergraduates?'

'There was Dolly Nelson. Awfully pretty. She acted. She was in that Sartre thing. She wasn't the Lizzie; she was the other one.'

'Lizzie?'

'Lesbian.'

'Oh.' Charlotte had a sudden picture of Pandora Warren, striding along.

'Peter Kenyon produced it in a teeny cellar. The play was meant to be claustrophobic, you see.'

'There can't have been much of an audience if the cellar was so teeny.'

'It was absolutely packed, though. That was the point. Because it was so difficult to get in, it was awfully smart to go. *I* went. It was freezing. Very damp.'

'What happened to Dolly Nelson?'

'Haven't a clue. She probably got married. As I say, she was awfully pretty. Very feminine – like you.'

'*Am* I?'

45

'Oh yes. You're awfully feminine, ducky.'

'Like those twittering old fools in *Cranford*?'

'No.' Cynthia laughed.

'Or a martyred Victorian heroine? Agnes in *David Copperfield*, pointing upwards all the time?'

'No, you idiot.'

'Like Becky Sharpe, then? Fatal and fascinating – ha ha. Funny joke!'

'No, I don't mean that.'

'Of course not. What *do* you mean?'

'What?' Cynthia was picking at the chipped varnish on one of her nails. Either she hadn't heard or she was too lazy to formulate an answer. Perhaps a different approach might work.

'Would you say *you* were terribly feminine, Cynthia?'

'*Me?* Don't be ridiculous, ducky. I can't be bothered with all that. *I get too hungry for dinner at eight . . .*'

From the tone of her '*Me?*', it seemed that Cynthia not only 'couldn't be bothered' with being feminine, but decisively – almost derisively – rejected it. Why? Although the examples of femininity she had picked from literature ('real life' seldom provided adequate illustrations for her ideas) appeared to differ markedly from each other, Charlotte now discerned a shared quality in them. The Cranford ladies were infested with affectations: of gentility, of timidity, of delicacy. Even if Dickens believed Agnes sincere, Charlotte felt sure she was a hypocrite. (No one could genuinely be so self-sacrificing.) As for Becky Sharpe, though – brave and clever – she was the best of the bunch, her 'fatal fascination' was rooted in calculation and deceit.

They were all false . . . Hamlet had expressed this view of women very scathingly. Yet surely it was 'attractive' to be feminine? Cynthia was always classifying people according to their attractiveness, and Charlotte herself – especially when lying in or on her bed – spent long stretches of time wondering if she were attractive. Her mother's valuation was higher than her own.

'This Oxford business would be such a waste of your looks,' she had complained on a visit to the National Gallery, pointing out the resemblance between Charlotte and beautiful Susanne Fourment in Rubens's *Le Chapeau de Paille*. (In spite of the picture's name, the hat – Charlotte's mother pointed this out, too – was not made of straw at all; its texture was plushy.) Charlotte could see the likeness. An aquiline nose, sharpened at the tip; eyes which, because of their big pupils, seemed navy blue; rusty, uncontrollable hair; skin exposing every vacillation of the blood: Charlotte had all these, though she lacked Susanne Fourment's high, full bosom.

Once, coming into her room when she was wearing only a night-dress, her mother had placed both forefingers under Charlotte's collar-bone, and prodded upwards. '*It* should be like this,' she said, and then – retracting her fingers, so that 'it' subsided slightly – 'not like that.' Her mother's lofty over-all assessment of Charlotte's 'looks' was balanced by an accurate disparagement of detail. She had spoken in the same detached tone one evening when Charlotte, glancing up from her book, saw that her mother, head tilted sideways, was watching her. 'You know, Charlotte,' she said, 'you have an extraordinarily weak mouth.' Then she raised the *Connoisseur* – open in her lap – to form a barrier between them. Charlotte had hurried to the bathroom mirror. Yes, the outline of her lips was vague; her mouth – like 'it' – drooped a little.

Susanne Fourment's mouth was not weak; it was ripe. Like her bosom, it seemed swollen with self-confidence. But the crucial difference between her and Charlotte lay in their expressions. Susanne's was tempting, mischievous: she had what Charlotte's mother referred to as 'a come-hither look'; what Cynthia called 'bedroom eyes'. Conversely, Charlotte, in even the most flattering photographs, appeared distant. This did not mean provocatively remote or aloof. It meant stranded. As on a rock in the North Sea.

'Cynthia . . .'

'What?' Cynthia was brushing flakes of Post Office Red varnish off her skirt onto the floor.

'Is being feminine the same as having sex appeal?'

'What?' Cynthia began to scratch at her thumb-nail.

'*Cynthia!*'

'Yes? Cynthia looked up.

'Do you think I've got sex appeal?'

'Don't ask *me*, ducky. Ask a man.'

*

Would she ever know any man well enough to ask him such a question? She doubted it very much.

She had stood by the cooker for years, stirring her fictional-historical-daydream mixture: Mr Rochester, Steerforth, Henry Crawford; Byron and Charles II (whose father she had renounced, some time ago, as pompous); James Mason in *The Seventh Veil* and Laurence Olivier in anything (though she wished he had not gone blond for Hamlet). The mixture bubbled hotly, but there was something disgusting about it: in a stew-pot, vegetables had dissolved into mush; in a dye vat, variegated clothes had all turned grey.

She concentrated on Oxford Entrance, which she took in a room at the High School, with a High School teacher invigilating.

A few weeks before, her mother had said, yet again, 'How do you think I can possibly afford this Oxford business?' and Charlotte, as usual, had answered, 'If I get a place, I'll get a grant.'

They were on one of their walks; down a muddy lane just outside the town, and then across fields that would later be flooded. Her mother bent to examine a plant.

'How I hate flowers. They're so *boring*,' Charlotte said, and then, 'Anyway, I shall win a scholarship.'

Her mother stood up. She said, 'You seem to have a lot of confidence in yourself. I've got a strange feeling that you'll never do quite as well as you expect.'

The telegram announcing Charlotte's Open Scholarship came in December. Her mother said the news was 'very good'. Mrs Meade said she would never have believed it. Miss Hale, her face flushed, said it was what she had always expected, and repeated a favourite prediction that one day Charlotte would become a critic. Charlotte did not think she wanted to do this, but she knew she was being paid a compliment. She guessed that to be a critic had once been Miss Hale's ambition.

Now, before she went up, there were nine months to fill. She continued to read novels, and whenever possible, went over to Leckingham. This was the local music centre. (In the county town, nothing happened except choral festivals.)

Charlotte's mother, although she herself did not enjoy music, encouraged Charlotte's interest in it, awakened by Pandora. Charlotte's first independent outings were to concerts.

'Why don't you take piano lessons?' her mother once suggested.

'Oh no, I'm far too old.'

Her mother laughed. 'Too old! How absurd you are.'

'Too old ever to be really good.'

'Oh well, if you mean professional . . .'

'A real talent would have broken out years ago.'

'You make it sound like measles. But even if you can't be a Paderewski, you could learn to play well, and you might enjoy it.'

'No, no.' To Charlotte, 'amateur' – defined by her mother as 'doing something for love instead of for money' – was a term of abuse; it implied frivolity. That was why, though they were not only botanically accurate – as she was told – but beautiful – as she saw – she did not take her mother's paintings seriously.

They were water-colours of flowers and plants. Charlotte's mother drew with strength as well as delicacy, and her colours were exact and pure. (Hers was the visual equivalent of absolute pitch. Matching something, she did not need to have it with her; she carried its colour in her head.) But there was more. Twining frond and stem in entanglements of her own devising; licensing a petal's fall or tendril's curl beyond the ruled square which bordered each of her pictures; extracting from the total composition a single leaf or seed-pod to anatomize, magnified, in a corner: she was bold. And when she took these liberties she brought them off . . . just as a real artist would.

'It's marvellous,' said Charlotte, gazing at a subject even she could identify: a sprig of two acorns, an empty calyx and nine oak-leaves. In the generous space within the customary ruled square, it was positioned high on the left, and Charlotte recognized that this was the only, the ordained place for it. 'Marvellous,' she repeated. 'Oh why didn't you become an artist?'

'If it is . . . what you say, then perhaps' – her mother gave an airy laugh – 'I am.' But Charlotte, unable to accept this, was silent. Although it was a pity and a waste, her mother was an amateur.

'I'm surprised,' her mother said, 'that as you're not an expert on music and painting, you go to concerts and exhibitions. Isn't that rather *amateur*?'

'Oh no. Quite different.' Charlotte was determined to justify her ignorant pleasures. 'Artists,' she announced, 'require an audience.'

She was part of one at her first meeting with Arthur. She arrived early, he after the orchestra though, tuning up, it was still in a state of nature. There were grunts and bellows from the wind instruments as he stepped over her feet. He sat down on her right to a sudden thrilling bird-call. Glancing sideways she recognized him.

She had seen him once before; here in Leckingham, at the bus terminus. Dusk was falling; in the seedy light it had been a miniature storm when he, tall and black-haired, passed at speed. His footsteps almost thundered; she felt a lightning-flash of that sense of 'the hero' which real life so consistently failed to provide.

Once, Pandora had personified 'the hero'. That didn't count, because Pandora was a girl. Yet the jolt Charlotte felt at the bus station reminded her of that earlier electrification.

On the Town Hall platform, nature yielded to applause – for the first violin, for the conductor – and then to silence. Now it was the turn of art. As Beethoven's 'Egmont' Overture began, the man next to

Charlotte spread his hands on his knees. He wore green corduroy trousers, which were bohemian, unlike brown, which could be considered rural.

Beethoven was Charlotte's favourite composer. When he battered her into submission she felt she was responding to his greatness; though during the symphonies she sometimes felt that one more reiteration might provoke resistance. Conversely, in an overture, he lacked the scope to enforce surrender. Several times she glanced sideways. Her neighbour's hands were pale against his emerald knees.

She ignored Vaughan-Williams's *Fantasia on a theme of Thomas Tallis*. She wondered if the man next to her were enjoying it. After moderate applause the audience shifted and murmured; it was hungry for the soloist.

Once a girl prodigy, this pianist was now nearly thirty. She was well known for playing two concertos – the second always Grieg's – at every concert, and even better known for playing each in a different dress. She was a draw; the Town Hall was full.

Rather than what Charlotte thought of as a musical face – the features squashed together under a swollen forehead – hers was a pretty one, neatly set out. For Mozart in C (K503), she had chosen pale blue. The dress, with a wide sash and heart-shaped neckline, was girlish. Charlotte, without turning her head, glanced sideways: the man was leaning back; legs crossed, arms folded, eyes shut.

In her prodigy days, the pianist had been praised for the freshness of her Mozart. To Charlotte, hearing her this evening for the first time, it seemed that she rattled off fast passages like an efficient typist, and fingered slow ones till – pawed fruit – they leaked their juices. Surely . . . but Charlotte did not trust her ears; questioned, she would not have risked the opinion that Mozart was pure and this was not.

However, though the audience's response was ardent – the pianist curtsied gracefully instead of bowing – Charlotte's neighbour scarcely clapped at all; he even muttered 'Oh dear!' She felt licensed merely to give herself a few slow handshakes. Then, as the applause died down, he turned to her, saying: 'I wonder what sort of get-up she'll wear for the old Grieg.'

Unused to being spoken to by strangers, especially men, Charlotte laughed nervously; when she answered it was with a drawl: 'Yes, I wonder. Changing her dress is rather affected, isn't it?'

'Idiotic! Just imagine a man doing it.'

'That would certainly be hilarious.'

'What?' But a moment later he laughed and said, 'True!' He paused. 'How about a coffee?'

Many of the audience were now standing. Charlotte always wondered what to do during the interval: whether to stay in her seat or wander along the corridors. She never went into the gloomy council-chamber where people jostled round a long table at which elderly women in green overalls manipulated metal urns and thick white cups and saucers.

'Er,' was the only answer she could manage, but she stood up. She stepped left, into the aisle – she always tried to book an aisle seat so that she would not have to climb over people – and moved towards a door. Tentative in crowds, apt continually to mumble, 'Excuse me', she was surprised by the speed with which he impelled her into the council-chamber, and then, while she waited by a maroon-curtained window, fetched coffee. As at the bus terminus, his advance had force.

'I put one sugar in,' he said. (He pronounced 'one' as 'wan'; as if it rhymed with 'don' instead of 'son'.) 'So don't stir it, if you don't take sugar.'

'Oh, I do.' Indeed she usually took two spoonfuls. Now she wriggled the strap of her bag over her left wrist to the crook of her elbow in order to transfer the cup and saucer to her left hand. With her right now free, she picked up the teaspoon, and stirred the grit at the bottom of the pale filmy liquid.

'Mind if I light up?'

'Light up?' She glanced towards a huge shallow brown-veined basin – containing low-watt bulbs – which hung on chains from the centre of the ceiling.

'Smoke.'

'Oh. Not at all!' Would he offer her a cigarette, and if he did would she accept it? Apart from one of Cynthia's, lit with difficulty and soon stubbed out, it would be her first. It would be difficult to handle it in conjunction with her cup and saucer. However it was a pipe, followed by a tobacco-pouch, that he pulled from the pocket of his almost carrot-coloured tweed jacket.

When, after a lot of tapping, wadding and sucking – which had a frothy sound – smoke came out of the pipe, the smell was strong but not nasty. Charlotte's mother disliked pipes; they reminded her of a wartime broadcast by a writer she detested, J. B. Priestley. '"I am a pipe-and-slipper man,"' she would quote, and add, 'Ugh!'

'Do you often come to concerts alone?'

'Yes. My mother's not fond of music.'

'Nor's my wife.'

'Oh! Mmm, yes, I always come over on my own.'

'Over?'

'From Thornbury.'

'Nice, sleepy little place.'

She was about to agree about the sleepiness, when he asked her name and told her his, which was Arthur Simpkin. Simpkin, Charlotte remembered, was the name of the cat in *The Tailor of Gloucester* by Beatrix Potter. 'Have you any children?' she asked.

'No, thank goodness.'

She warmed to this. 'You don't like them?'

'By the end of the day I've seen quite enough of kids. I teach English – at the Grammar School.'

She added the Grammar School and the word 'kids' to 'a', instead of 'some', coffee. There had also been 'wan' for 'one' (though apart from that he didn't seem to have an accent). All the same, he was as handsome, close to, as she had thought him at the terminus: very dark and rather hawkish. She preferred men to be dark, and thought they should have aquiline noses, though she envied women with straight ones.

'I'm going to read English,' she said. 'At Oxford. I go up this autumn.'

'Up to Oxford, what?' The 'what' was jocular, slightly caustic; he stressed the 'h' sound. 'How old are you then?'

'Seventeen.'

'I thought you were more.' She was used to people thinking her older than she was. It had something to do with her manner, her voice, and also, she thought, her nose. 'Do you plan to teach?' he asked.

'Oh *no*!' Then she blushed with embarrassment.

He laughed. 'I suppose you want to write.'

'Why do you suppose that?'

'Doesn't everyone who "reads" English want to?' ('Reads' was also jocular-caustic.) He tapped the bowl of his pipe against the chocolate-brown window-sill. 'Those who can, do. Those who can't, teach.'

She had heard this before, but he made it sound extraordinarily glum and bitter. Wanting to cheer him, she smiled straight into his face. When he smiled back – he did seem cheered – she looked away. A buzzer sounded; the interval was over.

Now there was a Haydn symphony: the 'Maria Theresa', named after an empress of Austria. Charlotte had reservations about Haydn, who had written a loud chord into his 'Surprise' Symphony, to awaken sleepers in the audience, and whose 'Farewell' Symphony, in which the members of the orchestra stopped playing, one after another, until only two violins were left, had been a hint to his patron, Prince Esterhazy, that the court musicians wanted a holiday. These jokes seemed frivolous, and so did the fact that Haydn had written 125 symphonies. Surely that was too many, especially when compared with Beethoven's nine? This was a composer she could take or leave with a clear conscience. During the 'Maria Theresa' she left him. She thought about Arthur Simpkin.

That he was married was fascinating. 'A married man' had an attractive, dangerous sound. 'Those who can't, teach,' on the other hand, depressed her. (It was true of course: no one would *choose* to teach.) But perhaps Arthur Simpkin – both his names were a pity – might yet escape to write a book. His age did not necessarily disqualify him. After all, Virginia Woolf had published her first novel at thirty-seven, and surely he was too vigorous to be more than about thirty-two? She remembered how he had impelled her into the council-chamber and how when she had first seen him he had made her think of a storm. He possessed, she decided, an 'elemental' quality; the word, evocative of the Brontë family, exhilarated her.

'Very enjoyable,' he said, leaning towards her, at the end of the Haydn, and she speeded up her clapping to match his. Now it was time for the last item on the programme: the Grieg Piano Concerto.

The pianist wore an off-the-shoulder dress, sumptuous and sweeping, of green velvet; darker than Arthur Simpkin's corduroys. She had changed not only her dress, but also her hair, now piled on her head instead of curling round her neck. Charlotte and Arthur Simpkin turned to each other and smiled, raising their eyebrows in shared disdain. *Crash* –

How splendid it must be to charge from top to bottom of the keyboard, firing that fusillade of chords. Although 'the old Grieg' was 'hackneyed' – even Charlotte's mother, not musically knowledgeable, had used that word when she saw that it was on the programme – it, unlike the Haydn, had a taking-over quality, like novel-reading and walking (when uninterrupted by flower-spotting). Off it went with its passengers, though Charlotte could not tell if their driver, the pianist, were doing well or badly.

It must be well, presumably, for the Grieg was the pianist's speciality. Yet that might conversely imply that her feeling for it had become worn. Why, anyway, did she *always* play it? And why did she wear showy clothes and change her dress and hair-do between concertos? Was it because, no longer the 'girl prodigy' she had to replace that rôle with another?

Her proper course – to develop her musical talent – would, of course, involve no rôle-playing at all. But, say – here Charlotte felt a chill at her nape – she lacked the potential for such development? If that were so, her only way to carry on was through her 'trappings': those 'props' people thought of when they heard her name, and which she could not have used if she had been a man.

Arthur Simpkin's remark could be seen as something more than a joke. For the pianist was vulgar because she traded on being a woman; a pretty one. What would happen when she stopped being pretty?

Already there was a little soft pad under her chin. (Charlotte quickly ran her hand over her own firm neck. Aware of a glance from Arthur Simpkin she tilted her head back; she felt that this made her nose look smaller.) One day, the pianist's trappings would become more than vulgar; they would be laughable. Then she would have to stop performing. What would she do instead? Would she marry and – if not too old – have children? What a come-down! Charlotte again felt a chill.

It was interesting that Arthur Simpkin – like Charlotte herself, but unlike most other people – did not pretend to be fond of children. It must make teaching very tiresome. However, by the time they went to a grammar school – she wished he taught at Leckingham College, a public school, though not a very good one – 'kids' were no longer children in the worst sense. That ended when the teens began.

Arthur Simpkin had thought her more than seventeen. She wondered how old his wife was. The thirties seemed far older for a woman than for a man, though a few women in their thirties were well-preserved, even glamorous, like the sophisticated *Vogue* model, Barbara Goalen. Perhaps Mrs Simpkin was like that? What did she do when her husband – a word that always made Charlotte think of old clothes hoarded in cupboards – went to concerts? It would be awful to be called 'Mrs Simpkin'. Charlotte smiled.

The applause was very loud. Charlotte realized that she had 'left' as much of the Grieg as of the Haydn. 'A very meretricious performance,' said Arthur Simpkin. She nodded vigorously. Again, like him, she hardly clapped at all. They left the Town Hall together. Outside, though she had plenty of time, she said, 'I must hurry for my bus.'

'I'll walk with you,' he said. 'I catch a bus too.' She matched her steps to his, which were faster and longer. 'Are you coming to the *lieder* recital next week?' he asked.

She had not intended to. Musical instruments seemed to her at a much higher stage of evolution than the human voice, which she wasn't very fond of, though *lieder* singers were greatly preferable to choirs. (She had once – never again! – been to the Three Choirs Festival, where everything she loathed – the godly, the Victorian, the provincial – took sound, as opposed to shape, and was magnified into a dreadful booming: cathedrals, though architecturally worthy, echoed so!) Now she said, 'Yes, I want to, but I haven't booked yet.

'I'll get tickets if you like.' When she started to say, 'But', he raised a hand. 'You can pay me at the concert. I'll meet you on the steps.'

That was how, in January, it began.

For two months, during which they met only at concerts, Charlotte suffered from what she thought of as symptoms. She wished she knew a doctor who could explain the lurching, thumping and panting, the flushes or shivers – sometimes simultaneous – which occurred just before she and Arthur met and when they were together. The resemblance to illness was remarkable, but luckily the symptoms were uncomfortable rather than painful, and were not disfiguring, though she always tried to catch sight of him first, so that she could get over her invariable blush before he saw her.

Between their meetings, she returned to her fantasy cooker, her dye vat. Now, however, the food was fresh, and the dye was a clear scarlet. (This, when occasionally suffused with blue, produced a luscious melancholy purple.)

Then, just before she got into the bus to Thornbury, on one of those March evenings that are trailers – unnaturally heightened; more momentous than the film itself – of summer, he said, 'My wife's going to her father's this weekend. I'll be all on my lonesome.' He made a comic, rueful face. 'I wondered if you'd like to come and hear some records on Saturday evening.'

'That would be awfully nice.' She felt truly sick, but also wildly happy. As the bus started she was already inventing an excuse to give her mother: a new pianist's first recital in an obscure hall.

The house – which her mother would have called 'a little red-brick villa' – was on a bus route. When she reached it, and as she pushed the doorbell, she felt convinced that Betty, Arthur's wife – as the result of a sudden change of plan – would open the door. Charlotte would have to pretend that she had come to the wrong address, and mention some fictitious surname; but the only name she could think of was Simpkin. However, it was Arthur, wearing soft brown shoes – almost slippers – and a scarf tucked into the neck of a Viyella shirt, who appeared, and showed her into the room on the left of the dark narrow hall.

The coal fire was bright. Dim yellow light came from a standard lamp with a crackle-parchment shade. In the bay of the window, under closed curtains of cinnamon and fawn – the unequal horizontal stripes blurring into each other – three beige cushions were aligned on a divan, covered in spinach-green hopsack, with a clumsy flounce. Beige rugs, flecked with grey, lay on the shiny floorboards; one in front of the divan, the other in front of the fire, between two wooden armchairs, their lime upholstery protected by crocheted coffee-coloured anti-macassars. By the wall opposite the fire was a yellowish dining-table with outward-slanting legs, and with four matching chairs pushed close under its four sides. At its centre a shallow bowl of dull-green pottery stood, empty, on a crocheted mat. Two long-necked gourds made of the same pottery – their orifices, too small to hold flowers, proclaiming them to be ornaments – flanked, on the mantelpiece, a shut-in, washed-out Utrillo street. (Charlotte always found it hard to believe that, as she had read somewhere, this painter had been 'a debauchee'.) The only other picture hung above the table: Van Gogh's portrait of a dull young man with a moustache.

Gloom and terror possessed her. She glanced desperately from the pitch-pine shelves on one side of the mantelpiece, which contained many books, to those on the other, behind a gramophone, which held records, some in mock-leather albums, others neatly stacked in their brown envelopes. Longing to be back at the Manor House, reading, she crossed to the fire.

'Feel like a coffee?'

She didn't, said she did.

After the coffee, in glossy brown mugs, came music. He was adept at dealing with the records, slipping them in and out of their envelopes and on and off the gramophone. Strauss's *Thus Spake Zarathustra*, Elgar's *Introduction and Allegro*, the Brahms Second Piano Concerto: it was all heady, stomach-hollowing stuff. Gradually, though besieged by symptoms, she felt better. It was when he had put on the last side of the Brahms that he came and squatted by her chair, and gazed. His face came nearer till it was like a close-up in a film. Seen thus, his mouth seemed a little too small and neatly shaped. It was almost prim, she thought, just before he put it on top of hers.

*

Sometimes they went into the country, but usually they met at what Charlotte did not tell him she thought of as the Villa Simpkin. His wife was often away that spring and summer; her widower father was dying of cancer. Arthur asked Charlotte never to wear 'perfume' when she came to the house because Betty (who never used it) had a keen sense of smell. He always carefully folded the hopsack cover of the divan when he took it off, and then covered the mattress with a large towel.

56

She walks – the lady of my delight –
A shepherdess of sheep.
Her flocks are thoughts. She keeps them white;
She guards them from the steep.

Although her mother was fond of this poem by Alice Meynell, Charlotte scorned it. 'A shepherdess of *sheep!*' she said. 'What else? Lions? Bears?'

'Well, perhaps goats in Mediterranean countries,' her mother answered vaguely.

'Hunh!' Apart from this specific objection, the poem's idea was enraging. Thoughts should not be white and guarded, but vivid and reckless; they should be encouraged to stray on any 'steep' available. It was tiresome to be reminded of this cowardly poem by the fact that she now had to put a 'guard' on her own thoughts. Otherwise she might have formulated a view of sex as disappointing, even distasteful. Such thoughts – unsophisticated, middle-class, Victorian – were impermissible; indeed they were unthinkable.

Although she had been bad at games, she was determined to be good at this. Perhaps she would suddenly acquire the knack, as she had with swimming, but she didn't 'take to it' as she had taken to that ('like a duck to water – huh, huh').

She was pleased when Arthur called her body beautiful. His, with its straight hips, big shoulders, muscled arms and legs, was handsome; apart from the appendage which, whenever possible, she tried – as with the male statues in museums – to disregard. It was sad for women that their own bodies – continuous, like rivers – were more aesthetic than men's.

At the beginning, he had taken off only her twin-set and brassière. The first time he did this, on a hilltop, he said her pearls were exactly the same colour as her breasts. Clouds were towing shadows over the fields that day, and the strong breeze stiffened her nipples. When he touched them, she had a strange wish that he would do this 'through a veil', but the wish was absurd, and she suppressed it.

Being undressed by him made her feel doll-like; she learnt to bundle off her clothes herself, as fast as possible. In novels, romantic dinners and conversations led up to sex, but if she and Arthur had been free to dine out, she would have preferred to get the sex over first; she wondered why it was always supposed to be 'the climax'.

'Climax', in a different – though related – sense, was a word of Arthur's. 'Did you have a climax?' he would ask when his activities were over. At first she had not known what to say, and he had looked offended or even embarked on further activities. Then she remembered a description of sex in *Eyeless in Gaza* (it came just before the dog fell from the sky), and found that if she groaned and rolled her head from side to side – like a cinema heroine, in childbirth or a high fever – it convinced him that everything was all right. That saved time and trouble for both of them.

Even so, activities were protracted. She discovered that if she were active, he became less so; like traffic, she kept moving. This was necessary anyway, if she were to be 'good in bed' (a favourite expression of Cynthia's, never – alas – explained in detail).

She found it odd that she was still a virgin. Arthur's and her activities seemed as peculiar, as 'impure' – that was how a nun would have put it – as 'the deed' – this was what Charlotte called it in her mind – sounded. More so, in a way, because the deed had a purpose: 'reproduction'. But that, of course, was something absolutely to be avoided; was indeed, for her, the chief argument against doing the deed. Surely it was for Arthur, too, even though he said his main reason was 'principle' (by which he meant scruples about her 'youth', etcetera)? And he had another reason, which he never acknowledged, but which she sensed: his squeamishness.

When, absent from Arthur, she thought of sex, she pictured his large white handkerchief, she smelt his Palmolive soap. He and Betty did (or had done: he put it in the past tense; he said their sex-life was over) just the same things as he and Charlotte. 'After all,' he said, 'we didn't want children, and contraceptives are so sordid.' But she believed his squeamishness lay deeper than this distaste for methods of birth-control. She had an intuition that he felt *the deed itself* was unhygienic.

He was a vegetarian. On the morning of their wedding-day, Betty had eaten her last bacon breakfast. Saying the word 'bacon', squeamish Arthur would grimace. The same finical look accompanied other comments on Betty, who had a way of blowing her nose, once and decisively, just before she fell asleep ('She never misses'), who pretended she had finished *War and Peace* ('Her bookmark's still halfway through Volume One'), who had a large mole on her right cheekbone. ('It doesn't have a hair growing out of it, thank goodness! But anyway I've always hated moles.')

Charlotte would have preferred profounder criticisms of Betty, but she decided that these were superficial because Betty was. Yet this too was frustrating. How could she believe herself triumphant if Betty lacked stature? All the same, throughout that spring and early summer, the thought of Betty – his wife; her rival – could palliate Arthur's activities, and revive her conviction that she loved him.

Surely she did? Simpkin symptoms had stopped soon after Simpkin sex started, but she always looked forward to seeing him. They had absorbing conversations.

His taste in books was the converse of her mother's: he valued range and naturalness, where she esteemed proportion and polish. Having heard his opinion, Charlotte would elicit hers. He revered Wordsworth ('Such a *silly* man'), D. H. Lawrence ('Disgusting, and so dull'), Dostoyevsky ('Insane, of course; he was an epileptic') and Dickens ('Not a novelist, a caricaturist – and so mawkish').

Charlotte, converted to many of Arthur's opinions, was still annoyed by his disdain for all her library books.

She invariably carried a book with her. (The prospect of being stranded without one – say the bus broke down! – unnerved her.) Arthur would take it from her with his squeamish fingers: 'Reading another cheap novel?'

The word 'cheap' maddened her: 'It's *not* "cheap". It was awfully well reviewed. *The Times* said it was very sensitive.' (She now read the arts columns, though not the news, in her mother's paper.)

'Lady novelists are always called "sensitive".'

'What do you mean, "lady"? You never talk about "gentleman novelists".'

'There aren't any,' he said. 'Except perhaps Charles Morgan.' Reluctantly she laughed.

He introduced her to philosophy; he was especially attached to Kant and Schopenhauer. Charlotte read Bertrand Russell's *A History of Western Philosophy*, except for Book Two ('Catholic Philosophy') which she knew Arthur would not want to discuss.

That he was an atheist delighted her, but she was shocked that he was a socialist. Socialism – though it was fascinating to meet someone who voted Labour – was menacing.

She told him about the Indian estate. 'Of course it's legalized robbery,' she said.

He laughed. 'Your grandfather pinched the land from the Indians in the first place!'

She was angry, and she thought the word 'pinched' vulgar. 'We brought them a hundred years of peace.'

'They didn't want *your* peace.'

'So now they're dying like flies. Anyway just look at what's happened here in England. The Socialists are destroying all individual freedom.'

He laughed again. 'We seem pretty free to me. As far as I'm concerned, this government's not "socialist" at all. It's done too little, rather than too much.'

He actually admired Bev*a*n; not the (comparatively) reasonable Bev*i*n, who had stood up to the Russians, but the dreadful 'Nye' who said that Tories were 'lower than vermin'. 'I agree,' said Arthur. Arthur of course held these views because he came from the working-class. His father had been a factory worker, and he himself had been educated on scholarships. Even though he had escaped, he was still biassed by his background.

Early that summer, Charlotte and her mother visited London, staying as usual at the Knightsbridge hotel. Charlotte spent half an hour with the famous dancing-teacher, Madame Vacani, who showed her how to sink down, back straight but head inclined, and then rise and advance, moving sideways, to repeat the process. Next day she put on a pale-blue pleated dress and a dark-blue hat with a pale-blue bow, and went with her mother in a hired chauffeur-driven car to Buckingham Palace. There, in a huge room, her name was called out, and she curtsied four times: to the King, to the Queen, to Princess Elizabeth and to Princess Margaret. Then she drank a cup of tea and ate a Lyons cake in a smaller room, full of girls she did not know.

Arthur thought it was ridiculous. 'It's not even,' he said, 'as if you were going to mix with that sort of person.'

'What "sort of person"?' She was annoyed.

'*Aristocrats*, and so on.'

After all, *she* was an aristocrat; well, partly. 'What makes you say that?'

'Well, you don't know any, and you haven't got the money.' He added, 'Anyway, you're far too good for them,' but she was not appeased. She believed that, somewhere, the *Crome Yellow* world awaited her. Perhaps she would enter it at Oxford.

Yet, though she deplored Arthur's politics, his working-class origin was the aspect of their relationship that made her feel most emancipated. How it would have shocked her mother . . .

Like Betty, her mother was a source of sustenance. The affair (though it wasn't *quite* an affair) with Arthur was fed not only by how it would have shocked her, but by the need to conceal it from her. Charlotte had not guessed herself to be a natural conspirator till she noticed how she relished this deception, how inspired she was at inventing pretexts – such as a course of lectures on musical appreciation – for visits to Leckingham. However, her mother was not difficult to deceive. Although this was fortunate, difficulty might have put an edge on Charlotte's appetite which, increasingly, nothing seemed able to tempt.

One Saturday afternoon in mid-July, when Betty was at her father's, Charlotte – unable to command the energy to be active, even to groan or head-roll – lay, unscented, smelling Arthur's Palmolive, on the Simpkin divan, eyes closed, arms straight by her sides, toes tidily pointed. 'Force me to feel,' she said in a loud whisper. These involuntary words surprised her, and she opened her eyes.

Arthur had turned away from her. Head lowered, he was pressing his palms against the wall. She was reminded of the schoolmaster in *Our Mutual Friend* (Arthur had urged her to persevere; eventually the book had astonished her), hammering on the tombstones with his naked hands. She had felt pity for that schoolmaster but she felt none for this lump of statuary. Why didn't he know – for heaven's sake, he was old enough – some way to revive the hectic feelings of the 'symptoms' period?

After a moment she said, 'I was only joking.' When, immediately, he turned towards her, she received the feeblest conceivable stimulus – hardly a fillip – from the fact that she could still delude him.

Later that afternoon she said, 'Cynthia's coming next week.' She had told Arthur all about Cynthia.

Otherwise naked, he had put on his socks, which looked silly. (Why didn't he leave them until last?) He wrinkled his nose.

'What are you making that face for?'

'She never sounds very appetizing, your friend Cynthia.'

'She's *beautiful*.'

'I'm not sure *I'd* think so.'

'Unless you're blind, you would.'

'You'd better introduce us. That's the only way of finding out.'

'I might. Then you'd have to admit it.' She was wondering what Cynthia would think of Arthur. Would she find him good-looking? 'I couldn't bring her to a concert. She's not interested in music.'

'You could tell her I'm a musical acquaintance, though. She wouldn't mention me to your mother, would she?'

'Oh no. Not if I asked her not to.' Could she do this without telling Cynthia about her affair with Arthur?

'Perhaps we could all meet for a coffee.'

'Cynthia's not very fond of coffee. She likes drinks.'

'How about a public house, then?' He grimaced.

Charlotte had never been in one. (Why didn't he call it a 'pub'?) She said, 'Yes. Why not?'

*

She went to meet Cynthia in Leckingham on the following Friday. Although Cynthia's train from London was not due till noon, Charlotte caught the nine o'clock bus from Thornbury, arriving in Leckingham twenty-five minutes later.

She went to the stop for the local double-decker which passed the Villa Simpkin. Usually, of course, she took this bus to visit Arthur, but several times recently she had made the journey when she knew he would be at school; as now. It was the last week of term.

She alighted at her customary stop, five houses beyond the Villa Simpkin. Turning back she crossed the road to the wooden bus-shelter directly opposite the Simpkins' gate, and sat down on the bench inside it.

Here she had often waited, alone, for a bus back into town. Arthur never sat there with her, in case 'the neighbours' should observe them. Charlotte resented this for two reasons. She felt that after a 'tryst' he should have chanced it. Also, she found the idea of inquisitive neighbours vulgar; reminiscent of drab novels of suburban life. (Charlotte preferred the word 'vulgar' to her mother's word, 'common', which seemed rather crude nowadays. As for Arthur's word, 'cheap', she winced with irritation at the thought of it.)

This was a heavy morning; the sky, not actually clouded, was low and pale. The sun's rays seemed not transparent, but chalky. Although it was still only July, the leaves of the trees in the poky gardens had a fatigued end-of-summer tint. Charlotte, in a fresh, blue-striped cotton dress, wearing plenty of make-up and Coty *Muguet* scent, had Elizabeth Taylor's *Palladian* open in her lap but was not reading it. Instead she gazed at the Villa Simpkin. An approaching bus slowed, when the driver noticed her, but she waved it on.

Surely Betty must come out sometimes. She couldn't spend all her time toiling in the house, even though she kept it so clean and tidy. The thought of this domestic efficiency did not enliven Charlotte. It made Betty seem formidable, but in a boring way. Before marriage, Betty had worked in a laboratory. Did she do her household drudgery in a crisp white coat? Two scientific terms remained with Charlotte from her single year's Chemistry at the convent: 'Bunsen burner' and 'Petrie dish'. Perhaps Betty (after measuring her ingredients in test-tubes) cooked her nut roast over the first before arranging it on the second?

At that moment a thick white ray struck the Simpkins' highly polished brass doorknocker (which represented the Lincoln Imp). Charlotte blinked. Instantly, as in a fairy tale, the door flew open. A little schoolgirl emerged.

The door clicked shut; the schoolgirl came down the steps and down the path. She opened the gate; she closed it behind her. Before crossing the road she looked right, left, and right again, as recommended in the Highway Code.

She had short straight hair. She wore the Peter Pan collar of her white blouse outside her fawn cardigan, and her green skirt came exactly to her knees. On her feet were fawn ankle-socks and flat-heeled chocolate-brown sandals with thick straps, and she carried a beige shopping-bag appliquéd with felt flowers. Who was this girl? What had she been doing at the Villa Simpkin? It was as she started to cross the road that Charlotte sensed something awry.

When she was six, Charlotte had been taken to the circus at Olympia. A jolly tune was played, and into the ring tumbled a troop of children. But no: they weren't children; they had big heads and grown-up faces. She had clutched at her mother, who explained that they were 'midgets'. Afterwards Charlotte had bad dreams about them.

The person crossing the road was not a midget, but nor was she a schoolgirl. She was a small woman, ridiculously dressed. (Her skirt was several inches shorter than the fashion. How awful her hair looked! Why did she wear ankle-socks and children's sandals?) She entered the bus shelter and sat down next to Charlotte, who gave her a short keen glance. Matt mouse-coloured beads like oak-apples matched the hair. She wore no make-up. A protruding mole topped her right cheekbone.

'I've always hated moles.' With the recollection of Arthur's words came knowledge, instantly confirmed by the familiar – and repellent – smell of Palmolive. Perhaps Betty – her appearance wholly consistent with her reported dislike of scent – felt equally revolted by the aroma of *Muguet*. Now Charlotte noticed that Betty's skirt was made of the same spinach hopsack as the divan-cover Arthur always folded with such care.

He had deceived her! She had not known that she was running against a cripple, competing with such an absurd rival. Fortunately there had been no spectators at the race, for how they would have despised her. She shifted on the bench. *Palladian* slid from her lap to the ground.

As she stooped to retrieve it, so did Betty. Charlotte reached it first, but their heads almost collided. Straightening up, each looked full into the other's face.

Betty smiled.

Automatically Charlotte stretched her lips in response. At the same time, a weight dragged at her stomach, and fire raced from her neck to her forehead.

As Betty's face resumed its previous aspect, the intrinsic quality of the vanished smile became more, rather than less, evident; so with the quality of light in darkness, and that of water in a desert place.

Betty's mouth did not droop. Since deep trenches ran from her nostrils to her lips, effort alone must be what maintained its straight pale line. Sentinel hollows reinforced this impression: determination leashed in the cheeks so that they should not subside. Finally, in spite of the dark erosions under them, the eyes – grey – had a willed, clear blankness. Yet when Betty smiled, Charlotte had seen that she had once possessed the power to be happy; her smile was a memento of it.

Charlotte had heard the story of a traveller in Turkey who, robbed of his wallet, went out to sell some of his blood. Later the body, diaphanous and grey, was found floating in the Bosphorus. Words linking that corpse with – unsmiling – Betty now came into Charlotte's mind: 'Her father's dying'; 'She doesn't care for music'; 'Her last bacon breakfast'; 'I – we – never wanted children.'

Betty stood up. Charlotte, seeing a bus coming, did the same, but then hung back. When Betty turned inside, Charlotte jumped on, and climbed the stairs.

She did not want to look at Betty any longer. She wished she had never come in search of her. Anyway, she always went upstairs in double-decker buses. Sitting downstairs was not only a sign of decrepitude. It also revealed an unaesthetic approach (indifference to the view) and a lack of curiosity (one saw so much more from above). Betty, of course, was not young. (That was what made her clothes so particularly absurd.) She – obviously – had no taste. She looked too dull to feel curiosity. *Betty's smile*: remembering it, Charlotte dragged her hands down over her face, from forehead to chin, as if to remove a layer of cobwebs.

How soft her face was! She inhaled the scent on her wrists. Suddenly she felt dazzled by the blue and white stripes of her dress. She drilled lightly on the floor with her high heels. Seeing Betty had, in some sense, given her an advantage over Arthur.

She and Cynthia were to meet him – so she and he had arranged – in three days' time. She wondered again how Cynthia would react to him; Charlotte was not sure what reaction she wanted. It would be intolerable if Cynthia did not think him attractive. On the other hand, she no longer wanted him – as she would have at one time – to receive unstinted praise.

*

The bus had reached the outskirts of Thornbury before she said to Cynthia, 'You haven't seen *Orphée*, have you?'

'Seen what?'

'*Orphée.*' Charlotte intensified her French accent, though there was no reason why this should be helpful, for Cynthia pronounced French exactly as if it were English. 'The Cocteau film,' she added.

'Oh. No, I haven't actually *seen* it, though people say it's absolutely marvellous.' Cynthia's friends, like Arthur, thought most French films were marvellous: far superior to English – let alone American – ones. It would be a pity really to see *Orphée* with such an exceptionally unsatisfactory cinema companion as Cynthia.

'It's on in Leckingham for three days next week. I thought we might go on Tuesday.'

'What?'

'I thought we might go to *Orphée* on Tuesday.'

'Oh, Yes.'

Looking out of the window, Charlotte said, 'We could have a drink first with a man I know slightly – I sometimes see him at concerts.'

Cynthia started to sing. *'They say that falling in love is wonderful.'*

'Oh do shut up, Cynthia.' People were turning to look at them.

'Just wonderful – that's what they say.'

'*Please.* Anyway, he's only a musical acquaintance.'

'Cool down, ducky. Why should I care? What's his name?'

'Er. Arthur Simpkin.'

When Cynthia laughed, Charlotte joined in.

'By all means let's have drinkies with *Arthur Simpkin*. Have you arranged it?' Cynthia seemed more enthusiastic about this prospect, Charlotte noticed, than about seeing 'marvellous' *Orphée*.

'I said we might possibly drop into the Swan at about six.'

'I'm sure you're up to something, ducky.'

'Oh Cynthia, what nonsense.'

'You're so *feminine*, Charlotte. Does your mother know about *Arthur Simpkin*?'

'Oh, I never mention *anything* to her. She fusses so.'

'Your secret is safe with me, ducky.'

'Oh *Cynthia*!'

'Is he married?'

'Mmm. I believe he is. Why?'

'Tra-la-la.'

'I promise there's nothing in it.'

'Is he good-looking?'

Charlotte's first impulse was to say that she hadn't noticed, but she sensed that this would sound unconvincing. The bus was drawing up at the terminus. She said, 'Not bad, I suppose.'

*

After tea on the following Thursday afternoon, Charlotte was in her room, copying a poem into her latest anthology. (Not prepared to admit that what she recorded might be ordinary, she rejected the term, 'commonplace-book'.)

The anthology was a large expensive notebook, its cardboard binding attractively covered in patterned paper. She had bought seven of these notebooks in the past few years, and had thrown away six of them. An anthology had to be perfect, by which Charlotte meant that it must perfectly express her. Of course, when she altered, it must alter too.

Long ago, Swinburne had suddenly seemed too purple, and Christina Rossetti's 'Bride Song' downright embarrassing. Later she had wondered what had drawn her to Aldous Huxley's 'The Cicadas', and had decided that Stevenson's 'Requiem' was a little trite. She had also become doubtful about poems that were 'too' good, by which she meant too well-known and generally admired. Wasn't it rather obvious to copy out a Shakespeare sonnet or a Keats ode? Anyway, she had recently 'gone off' Keats. Although Byron was an inferior poet, she saw why he had thought Keats namby-pamby ('*I stood tiptoe upon a little hill*').

Banishing disowned items raised problems of presentation. Deletions looked so ugly. Worse, the crossed-out passages were reminders of a past she wished to obliterate. If she detached whole sheets, the corresponding pages dropped out, and the binding loosened. This loss of solidity suggested vacillation and impermanence; to buy a new book became essential. Starting an anthology, Charlotte would feel sure that this would be the definitive one, suppressing the memory that she had felt the same about earlier volumes.

Today she was wondering whether to discard Meredith's 'Lucifer in Starlight'.

> *Soaring through wider zones that prick'd his scars*
> *With memory of the old revolt from Awe,*
> *He reach'd a middle height, and at the stars,*
> *Which are the brain of heaven, he look'd, and sank.*
> *Around the ancient track march'd, rank on rank,*
> *The army of unalterable law.*

In a way she wanted to be rid of it, but it dragged at her feelings. She decided that to leave it out would be dishonest.

Her mind wandered to the meeting, the day before yesterday, in the 'lounge-bar' of the Swan: Leckingham's third best hotel; centrally positioned; chosen as a compromise between pub and café. The occasion had not been lively, though Arthur's eyes had opened wide at his first sight of Cynthia, as tall as he on her stilt heels, her tortoiseshell hair hanging over the collar of a magnificent black velvet overcoat. Yet Charlotte felt (she would not know till they met alone next week, after Cynthia left) that – ruthlessly observant – he must also have noticed how dandruff from Cynthia's lank, rather greasy hair lay thick on the black collar; and when Cynthia removed her coat – he should have helped her out of it – her dusty black blouse and checked skirt with a cigarette burn near the hem must have disappointed him. Had he also observed the dark hairs on Cynthia's bare legs? (High-heeled shoes, in Charlotte's opinion, should not be worn without stockings.)

Cynthia had to explain to Arthur that her request for 'pinkers' referred to a Pink Gin. (Charlotte drank dry sherry, and Arthur half a pint of Bitter.) Conversation was stilted; not surprisingly, as it was chiefly about *Orphée* (which only Arthur had seen) and the end of his school term that day. Charlotte felt a desire for escape, and went to the Ladies' Room where she spent five minutes re-doing her face. When she returned, Cynthia and Arthur seemed to be making some sort of conversation, but became silent as she approached. She felt relief when it was time to go to *Orphée*.

In the cinema, Cynthia kept asking her to repeat the subtitles ('I missed that one'), and several times expressed bewilderment ('What on earth are they doing with that mirror?'). She commented often on the good looks of Orpheus ('Someone told me he's Cocteau's boy-friend. What a waste!') and of Death ('I wonder what I'd look like with that hair-do'). She also saw 'amazing' resemblances between various members of the cast and people she knew ('He's the absolute *image* of Charlie Parkinson, ducky – you remember I told you about him and the bottle of vermouth').

Arthur had walked with them to the cinema – only a short distance from the Swan – and they had arrived just as *Orphée* was starting, so Charlotte did not hear Cynthia's opinion of him till afterwards: 'Not bad-looking at all. Mouth a bit too small. And, of course NQOCD.' (This stood for 'Not Quite Our Class, Dear' an expression Charlotte thought vulgar.) Cynthia added, 'Never trust a man who drinks half pints.' That was all. Charlotte had been disappointed, but at least Cynthia made no more embarrassing jokes about her and Arthur.

She looked at her watch. The time was six o'clock. Cynthia had said she would be back early in the evening. Yesterday morning she had suddenly announced that, as the result of a telephone call, she would have to 'dash over to Oxford' and spend the night there. She had been unusually uncommunicative. Probably she was meeting a man. Charlotte wondered again what Arthur had thought of her. She would find out on Monday afternoon – Cynthia was going back to London on Sunday – when she and Arthur were meeting for a country walk. Now Charlotte composed an ideal weather forecast: torrential rain, clearing at lunchtime. This would mean that they would be able to go out, but not to lie on the grass. She sighed, and returned to the anthology. Her latest discovery was a poem of Auden's. She re-read her favourite verse.

> *Moving along the track which is himself*
> *He loves what he hopes will last, which gone,*
> *Begins the difficult work of mourning.*
> *And as foreign settlers to strange country come,*
> *By mispronunciation of native words*
> *And intermarriage create a new race*
> *And a new language, so may the soul*
> *Be weaned at last to independent delight.*

It was astonishing; he even got away with the word 'soul'. Could the poem be true? Might one, some day, achieve 'independent delight'? Nothing, surely, could be better; nothing, surely, more difficult. The door opened, and Cynthia came in.

She was wearing a grey flannel skirt and a short-sleeved green jersey. Cynthia never wore cotton dresses, Charlotte's favourite clothes. Of course she felt the cold more than Charlotte did, because she was so thin.

'Did you have a good time?' Charlotte asked.

Cynthia shrugged. She was smiling in a secretive way, but she did not keep her secret long. 'Well, so much for Arthur!' she said. She flopped onto the bed, kicking her feet up in one of her deliberately ungainly gestures.

Charlotte was startled by a rush of symptoms. 'Arthur?' she said.

'Yes, old Simp. He asked me not to tell you. He thought you'd be shocked, being such a pure little girlie. He doesn't know you at all well, does he, ducky?'

'Oh,' Charlotte said. 'No.'

'You give that good-as-gold impression because you're so *feminine*, you see.'

68

'Oh, do shut up about that.'

'Temper, temper!'

Charlotte, controlling herself, produced a bleating laugh. 'How on earth did you get involved with *Arthur*? You've only just met him.'

'It was when you went to the lav at the Swan. I made a date with him.'

'*You* suggested it?

Cynthia laughed. '*I get too hungry for dinner at eight* . . . He's really awfully handsome, you know.'

'Oh.' Charlotte looked out of the window at some chimneys. 'And was it fun?' she asked.

'Not much. He's got a good bod, but he doesn't know how to use it.'

So, Charlotte thought, it was Arthur's fault that *she* didn't enjoy it. She smiled at Cynthia. 'Where did you go?'

'Oh, over to Oxford. We stayed at my old landlady's. A night of lurve, ha ha.'

'Are you going to see him again?'

'Oh no. I shouldn't think so.'

*

Charlotte and Arthur met, as they had done on other occasions, at the bus stop in Girne Hill, a village half way between Leckingham and Thornbury. It was raining – a warm steady drizzle – and they went into a tea-room called The Oak Tree to wait and see if the weather would clear. As soon as the waitress left to fetch their tea, Charlotte said, 'So you went to bed with Cynthia?'

He was lighting his awful pipe. 'I asked her not to tell you.'

'That was thoughtful.'

'Anyway, it didn't mean a thing.' He made one of his faces. 'It wouldn't do her any harm to bathe a bit more often.'

Smiling, Charlotte said, 'I gather she didn't find it particularly amusing either.'

'You can be a right bitch,' he said.

Standing up, after a quick glance at her watch – a bus to Thornbury was due in ten minutes – she found his words a perfect pretext for departure. Outside the café, she felt relieved, though it was a pity, in a way, that the scene could not have been postponed until just before she went to Oxford. She also regretted leaving Arthur with a bad impression of her; she would have liked him to pine a little.

*

Admiration spoils all . . . this stimulus of envy and glory. Charlotte was sure that wasn't true. She was convinced that if she had been applauded unceasingly throughout her life – by her mother, by grown-ups and children, by the nuns, by Arthur, and now by the dons of her college – she would not have been spoilt, but improved. Pascal was wrong.

He was her enemy, yet his *Pensées* kept reappearing in the pile of books on her bedside table. She read him much more often than she read Kant, even though his self-seeking wager was so inferior to Kant's pure imperative. (It was a sham, anyway; not a true wager at all. Where was risk when the 'gambler' had nothing to lose?) Charlotte also disliked his sectarian polemics, his Miracle of the Holy Thorn and the fetish 'testament' he wore round his neck.

Oxford, in one respect at least, represented true freedom. She no longer had to go to church. At home she had done so, dreading confrontation not only with her mother, but with the parish priest, Father O'Shaughnessy. In the religious context she regarded him with such aversion that it startled her, when she met him walking in the town, to see a pleasant-looking man with a large copper dog.

Appropriately, the route to the Thornbury church was along a dull stretch of road, edged with ugly pollard willows beyond which lay the flat fields that were always flooded in winter. (Sometimes the road was also flooded and became impassable, but this – much hoped for by Charlotte – was rare.) At the end of the road, a steep hill, bordered by a scruffy wood, led to the church. In the small hideous brick building, Charlotte classified the contents of prayers under three headings: flattery, self-pity and begging-letters (proportions varied). She noticed that few of the congregation attempted to follow the Latin service. Most muttered their rosaries, only interrupted by the bells which told them when to bow down, and when to rise and file up to the altar.

Each Sunday, at the early mass – which she preferred because there was no sermon – Charlotte joined this file. However, she never went to confession, telling her mother that she disliked Father O'Shaughnessy and preferred to confess in Leckingham. At first this had been a pretext for visits to the cinema; later for meetings with Arthur.

At Oxford, deception was unnecessary. The Monsignor in charge of the Catholic chaplaincy was interested in only those undergraduates who were very rich or who, like himself, came from 'old Catholic' families. There were none such in the women's colleges. In any case the Monsignor appeared not to care for women, apart from pious aristocratic ladies whose large country houses he frequented. So Charlotte was left in peace. That was one of two burdens which

70

Oxford lifted from her shoulders. The removal of the second was an even greater relief.

Before she came up she had been troubled by a nagging preoccupation: might her fellow undergraduates hate and persecute her as 'people of her own age' had done when she was a child? This fear proved unfounded. Growing up had miraculously transformed those savage animals. She should have foreseen this; instead it was a joyful surprise. She quickly made two friends.

*

'I shall sing,' Lissa said, leaving at seven for a six o'clock sherry party.

To sing – for your supper – was to charm a man into buying you dinner, and Lissa was a *diva*.

'When you get back, you must come and tell me all,' said Charlotte.

'What if you're asleep?'

'You can wake me.' Charlotte was ashamed of her sleeping habits.

She woke long before Lissa in the morning. Daily, at breakfast, after signing her own name in the book, she forged Lissa's signature. All the same, getting up early seemed discreditable: either hearty – reminiscent of merry peasants – or grim, like birds pursuing worms. As for 'early nights', could anything sound more decrepit? But, just as Lissa recharged during the day for the evening's *Grand Prix*, so Charlotte ran down. Usually her battery was quite flat by nine pm.

She felt dread when she was entered for the race, but she liked to hear reports from Lissa. Often, however, at the actual moment when she was prodded awake, and the overhead light glared into her gummy eyes, keenness was in abeyance; she produced a fretful moan.

'You told me to wake you,' Lissa said. She smelt of scent and drink, compounded by body heat.

'Yes, I know.' Charlotte shielded her eyes with her hand, and made an effort. 'Was it fun?'

'Mmm. Rather blissy.'

'Was Alexander there?'

'Alexander? Oh yes, he was there. He asked about you.'

'*Did* he?' Now she was fully awake. 'Did you do some propaganda?'

There was a pact between them. When either, out on her own, met a man who interested the other, she would speak flatteringly of her to him. Charlotte believed she took this duty more seriously than Lissa did, but Lissa went out more often, so probably their scores were even. Lissa, of course, needed propaganda less . . .

'Yes,' Lissa said now. 'I told him you'd gone out to dinner.'

71

'Oh. Had he asked what I was doing?'

'Mmm. Well he asked about you. He said, "And how's your friend, Charlotte?"'

'And you said I'd gone out to dinner.'

'Yes. I said you were frightfully well and rushing about like mad. That was when I brought it in.'

'Did he ask who I'd gone out with?'

'Mmm? I don't *think* so. Anyway it was awfully good propaganda for him to think of you being out with some mysterious man.'

'Yes.' After a pause, Charlotte said, 'And who else was there?'

Lissa kicked off her black court shoes. She drew her feet up onto the bed and covered them with the bottom of the eiderdown. Revved up, she started to relive the race. 'Jeremy was there,' she began, 'but so was Edward. It was tricky. Especially about dinner . . .'

When Lissa, with a sudden yawn, had gone, switching off the light at the door, Charlotte was not at all sleepy; though, if Lissa had not woken her, she would have slept till morning. Now she turned on the bedside light, hurled herself out of bed – the room was icy – and pounded over to the dressing-table. Opening the second drawer, she groped under a cardigan for the bar of nut milk chocolate she had hidden there; then she rushed back to bed, tearing off the paper as she went. She started on the chocolate as soon as she was under the bedclothes; the hazelnuts made a loud crunching noise. Half way through the bar, she transferred it to her left hand; with her right she edged Kant's *Critique* from among the books on her bedside table.

Inside the back cover were two folded sheets of thin paper: a Debrett proof sent to her mother for corrections or additions. (As usual, there were none.) Here, summarized in tiny print, were the ramifications of Charlotte's father's family. On the second page – under COLLATERAL BRANCHES LIVING – was her own name: 'issue living, Charlotte, *b* 1932'. She looked at this until she had finished the chocolate. Then, feeling reassured, she replaced the proof in the book, the book on the table. She switched off the light, pulled up the bedclothes with a nearly numb hand, and licked the last traces of chocolate off her teeth.

As she had foreseen, she was at once ashamed, in spite of a fact she treasured: after a hard day's work, one great philosopher had been accustomed to devour quantities of cream cakes. (Was it Kant? She didn't think so, though she wished it were. Had it, perhaps, been Schopenhauer?)

Charlotte ate moderately of the college meals. This was not difficult; though substantial, they were not titillating. But a treat or binge or be-ah-no – as Lord Curzon had once pronounced the word 'beano', unfamiliar to him – was different; usually taking the form of a bar or two of chocolate or half a Fuller's Walnut Cake, eaten – fast – when she was alone in her room.

Occasionally, when the smell of dinner in hall seemed particularly inauspicious, she and Lissa – each paying for herself – went out to the over ambitiously named Café de Paris, where a mixed grill cost five shillings and sixpence. The Café de P was too grand for patrons of the British Restaurant at the bus station or of a place with communal benches called the Stowaway, but its attempts to attract the better-off misfired. The dim lights seemed not romantic but proof of parsimony, and evening dress made the waiters look more, rather than less, decayed. But the mixed grill was good: a chop, a square of pâté, a kidney, a slice of liver, a rasher of bacon and half a tomato; the accompanying potatoes were not chips, but sautéed. Charlotte never told Lissa that she sometimes felt she could have eaten two mixed grills. In a man this would have shown a healthy appetite; in a woman it could only be deplored.

At the convent Charlotte had been told that 'one doesn't *love* food'; she was still unconvinced. That philosopher, she was sure, had loved his cream cakes. But did Lissa love food? Certainly her desire for mixed grills was less ardent, less urgent, less frequent than Charlotte's. Charlotte took into account that Lissa's appetite for good food was more often satisfied than her own, because men more often bought Lissa meals at restaurants, but she knew this was not the decisive factor. To Lissa, being attractive was more important than other forms of gratification: she preferred to spend money on clothes and make-up than on food, and almost every day she dashed into some chemist's shop to check her weight. She did not have to struggle, as Charlotte did – often in vain – to keep feminine commandments: they were her natural law. Lissa would never have eaten that bar of chocolate. Of course, no one knew that Charlotte had done so . . .

She did not transgress openly. For instance she would never have ordered two mixed grills, just as she would never have eaten alone at the Café de P.

To eat a solitary five-and-sixpenny meal would be unfeminine: secondarily because it would appear greedy – a woman should not be keen enough on food to eat a restaurant meal alone – but primarily as evidence of inability to find a man to pay for it. On the same grounds, of course, eating with another woman was suspect, but Lissa was so famously attractive that she – and by association, Charlotte – could get away with it occasionally. Yet, even for Lissa, and even in the

73

unfrequented Café de P, it would have been unwise to take the risk too often.

At least, when women ate in college, men – only admitted to the buildings between one and seven pm – had no idea of their where-abouts. So, tonight, it had been safe for Lissa to do that propaganda: to tell Alexander, untruthfully, that Charlotte was dining out. (Lissa said that she had told him; Charlotte felt almost sure she had.)

Charlotte would now have liked to eat a second bar of chocolate, but she was glad she had not got one. According to the chart in *Vogue Beauty Book* she was twelve pounds overweight. It would have been more if she had classified her 'frame' as Small or Medium, instead of as Large, which might be inaccurate, for her wrists and ankles were exactly the same size as Lissa's, as she had discovered one evening when they had compared all their measurements. It was at bust, waist and hips that they differed. Charlotte could not wear Lissa's clothes though, when they had full skirts, Lissa could wear hers, taking them in at the waist.

*

Lissa was very keen on clothes. Shopping for them was a pursuit which she took far more seriously than writing essays. 'What do *you* think?' she continually asked Charlotte in shops, though she trusted no woman's judgement. (In these circumstances, scepticism was justified, for, marooned in a showroom or confined in a tiny fitting-room, Charlotte praised everything: 'Gorgeous! Blissful! Yes, of *course* it suits you!')

When Charlotte shopped for herself, she would try on three or four dresses, and usually left with one of them, even when unsatisfied with her choice. Lissa, who tried on every garment in her size, often bought nothing. *Insufficient correspondence with the archetype*, Charlotte would think, sitting, half stupefied, on a small uncomfortable chair.

It was better in college, when, having cleared a space, she could loll on Lissa's bed. Clothes were heaped on all the furniture, and the floor teemed with shoes. Dunes of powder lapped the lidless jars on the dressing-table. Preparing to go out, for Lissa, was a total commitment. This was one reason why she was always late, unlike Charlotte who, when she had bathed, dressed and done her face, always had spare time in which to worry about the coming ordeal.

It was lying on Lissa's bed that Charlotte had formulated the theory of the archetype in Lissa's head. If her appearance did not correspond to it exactly, Lissa would laboriously revise. Or often she would begin again, stripping off her dress and creaming the make-up from her face. Engrossed, she peered short-sightedly – she never wore glasses – into the mirror, and pouted appealingly.

> *She pouts her lips as if she wants to kiss her*
> *Own image in the mirror, this Narcissa.*

Yet Charlotte knew that this couplet of hers was unfair. Lissa, peering and pouting, was not self-loving. She was summoning all her powers to put herself in the position of An Other, An Observer, and – of course – A Man.

'If only I *could* see myself as others see me.'

'That's impossible,' Charlotte said. 'One only sees one's real self, as they say, in unexpected mirrors. And then only in a flash before one recognizes who it is and changes it.'

'How do you mean – changes it?'

'Adjusts it mentally . . . makes it fit with how one wants to look. But even in the first flash one doesn't really see what other people see. Because the mirror image is reversed. As they say.'

'Mmm.' A moment later, Lissa snatched up her hand-mirror. Quickly, as if taking a snapshot, she angled it to catch the reflection of her reflection in the dressing-table mirror.

'Trying to trap yourself?'

Lissa laughed, but perfunctorily, not considering the subject one for jokes.

At first, Charlotte had been puzzled that Lissa enacted her ritual of preparation not only before big parties or evenings with favourite men, but every time she went out. Now Charlotte had reached the conclusion that Lissa felt any chance encounter might be one that would change her life, or, rather, as a result of which a man would change it.

'Life urges men forward, and drags women back,' said Charlotte in a gloomy mood.

Lissa looked astonished. 'I think women are much more free than men.'

'More *free?*'

'Yes. People don't keep forcing them to *do* things. They can choose the sort of life they want to lead.'

Lissa meant that men had to choose among jobs, while women could simply choose among men. In her case this was true: many men wanted to be chosen by Lissa. Leading aspirants were Jeremy, an easy-going Etonian, Edward, an ambitious Wykehamist, and Tim who, though from a minor public school, was very rich as well as literary (a keen admirer of Charlotte's least favourite author, Ernest Hemingway). Would Lissa choose one of these three or someone quite different? Charlotte did not know, but sensed that Lissa would not choose Tim, who came from Australia and would be returning there.

> *'Look at those stars! The Southern Cross,' said Tim.*
> *'The wrong side of the world,' she answered him.*

So Charlotte encapsulated it, but felt that Tim's rejection would probably be more tactful: Lissa might avoid having to put it into words at all. She was considerate of men's feelings: one of many qualities they appreciated in her.

Lissa's body, not tall, was long-legged, straight-backed, small-breasted. Her head – strong bony little nose, long narrow eyes and mouth, uneven but white teeth, colourless but clear skin, mousy but very soft hair – was neither sedative nor unnerving. An intelligent man felt it discerning – even though he was one of a large company – to be attracted by her, rather than by very pretty girls, whom he tended to dismiss as silly, while the words 'a classic beauty' summoned up an image that was cold, monotonous, curiously old-fashioned, almost dowdy.

Brilliant women could appear masculine, witty women alarming; silent women were dull, yet men disliked women who 'held forth'. Lissa seldom expressed views of her own, but always responded vivaciously to those of a male companion. Interpreting this as evidence of her exceptionally sensitive intelligence, he would feel proud of his ability to elicit it, even though so many others shared the talent.

> *Each suitor his dream self can realize,*
> *Reflected, rosy, in those mirror eyes.*

The subject of what men found in Lissa led to that of what she looked for in them. What would Lissa eventually require from *the* man?

He would not be dim; that was certain. 'Dimness' – in the sense in which Lissa and Charlotte used this word – was unforgivable.

To use clichés was dim, but there was a simple way to correct a lapse. Should a cliché, like a toad in a fairy tale, fall from one's lips, it must immediately be followed by the words 'as they say': 'It's a lovely day – as they say.' Or 'I sometimes feel life's a bit pointless – as they say.' Or, 'I wonder if I'm in love – as they say.' In the second and third of these examples the phrase also protected the speaker against a possible accusation of being 'intense'. Intensity was dim: it was dim, for instance (and 'hearty', too), to be keen on games – which must never be referred to as 'sport' – just as it was dim to work hard or, at least, to be observed to do so.

Subjects could also be classified according to dimness. All scientific subjects, with the possible exception of Maths, were dim. Reading 'Greats' (Classics) was the antithesis of dim, for a man, though intimidating in a woman, as was Law, which was suitable, if not quite splendid, for a man. Modern Greats (PPE), another 'masculine' subject, was too new not to bear traces of dimness, but these were fading, and History was acceptable for members of either sex. Modern Languages were charming for women, and appropriate for men aspiring to Diplomacy. English, a woman's subject, was decidedly dim for men, while Geography was dim for anyone. It did not even demand the brilliance – was a dim brilliance possible? – admitted to be necessary for a rigorous scientific subject like Physics. Lissa read Geography: if she had known about dimness before she came up, she would certainly have chosen something else. Lissa was almost, but not quite, as preoccupied with dimness as with her overriding interest: class. The man would have to be a gentleman.

He would have been to a public school (preferably one of the three or four most prominent; ideally Eton), and a rigid disciplinary code would govern his dress and speech. To have been at a grammar school; to wear a blazer, a brown suit, or – worst of all – a college scarf; to say 'perfume' instead of 'scent' or to pronounce the first syllable of 'envelope' to rhyme with 'pen': any of these marked a man not as an outlaw – which sounded romantic – but as an outcast. Lissa, brought up among perfumed women and blazered men, espoused this code with fanatic zeal. She reminded Charlotte of a Catholic convert.

A few years ago, an appeal to the Pope that the Assumption should be declared a dogma – it had since become one – had circulated outside Thornbury parish church. Of course Charlotte had not signed it; but, more interestingly, nor had her mother, who, though convinced that the Blessed Virgin had been taken up physically into heaven, disliked the idea of any change in the Church's doctrines. Converts in the congregation – motivated, in Charlotte's opinion, by eagerness to prove their credulity boundless – had been active in promoting the petition. Lissa's ardour for class was of this extreme character.

For instance, having heard or read, on what she considered good authority, that abbreviations were vulgar, she always, when addressing an arnvelope, wrote the word 'Esquire' in full. She also spoke of 'luncheon' and had once referred to catching an 'omnibus'; laughter deterred her from retaining this antique usage. Charlotte's own snobbery was more relaxed (like the faith of a 'born' Catholic). She didn't for instance, insist on 'looking-glass'. What a mouthful! And she could hardly have written of Lissa's 'looking-glass eyes'.

To achieve smartness at Oxford, one needed money, as well as 'birth', or – provided one followed the code – instead of it. Charlotte felt sure that Lissa's man would be rich. ('Wealthy' was as inadmissible a word as 'perfume'.) In addition he would be attractive. Acknowledging that, if he were old or ugly, a rich amusing duke would stand no chance with Lissa, Charlotte felt proud of being fair. But the pride was uneasy: surely she should not feel proud of being 'fair' to her best friend? Charlotte was almost always certain that Lissa held this title though occasionally, in the company of Vicky Bray, she wavered.

*

During the summer term, just before an afternoon storm, Vicky rushed into Charlotte's room in her bathing-dress; urged, Charlotte had put on her own. The storm, flashy and loud, began as they ran downstairs. When they reached the back lawn, the rain broke like a waterfall, and they started to cavort, quite regardless of the many windows that overlooked the garden. Leaping up and down, they waved their arms. Soon they were soaked. Vicky sang the Hallelujah Chorus, and Charlotte shouted lines of poetry.

'O, the wild joy of living,' she yelled, 'the leaping from rock up to rock, and the cool silver shock of the plunge in the pool's living water.' She was blinded by rain and by her dripping hair.

How odd, she thought afterwards, that she had not given a thought to watchers at the window: male ones, possibly, since it was during visiting hours. As she and Vicky ran indoors, panting and laughing, she had felt purged, pure. It occurred to her that it would have been impossible to have danced like that, in the storm, with Lissa. Lissa would have been concerned only with the overlooking windows, with the possibility that to a man – the man? – she might look ridiculous. Charlotte and Vicky had undoubtedly looked ridiculous, galumphing like percherons; shouting, singing, sopping wet.

Another religious metaphor for Lissa arose. Nuns were required to be – a special technical usage – 'recollected', implying a perpetual guard on movements, eyes, speech, even thoughts. Lissa's dedicated self-consciousness was a worldly equivalent. She would not have danced in the storm, as she would not have gone into Oxford wearing, as Vicky often did, old trousers and a shabby sweater, her hair dragged back by an elastic hand. Lissa, who thought women more free than men, was certainly less free than Vicky.

'Somehow I can never quite see the *point* of Vicky,' Lissa remarked. That both were friends of Charlotte's did not bring them closer to each other.

Vicky was reading Law, and intended to be a barrister. She had no worries about whether her subject was 'suitable' for a woman, and was not concerned about dimness. Tall, with a curvy figure, symmetrical features and white, regular teeth, she had many admirers, who tended to be 'hearties' and/or Rhodes Scholars. In 'colonials', especially Americans, she evoked nostalgia, recalling robust salubrious native belles.

Where Lissa believed that to give her body to a man was an act charged with significance, Vicky felt that not to do so was stingy: 'After all, except the first time, it doesn't hurt at all.'

This attitude seemed negative to Charlotte; she preferred Lissa's. With Tim, Lissa had apparently soon enjoyed sex as much as women in novels did; and now, with Jeremy, she felt the same pleasure. Charlotte, however, had still not done the deed.

'Women who don't,' said Vicky, 'get all bitter and twisted, like these ghastly dons.'

Charlotte thought there might be some truth in this, but surely decades must pass before one was in danger of resembling Miss Denison or Miss Wynde? Charlotte felt certain that she would have taken the plunge long before she reached that stage.

Vicky advised her to do it with a faithful admirer whom Lissa did not care for, always referring to him by his surname. Now Charlotte, too, called him 'Thompson'. It was a pedestrian name.

Although good-looking – very blond – Thompson was poor, hardworking, and not at all smart; his public school had been minimal rather than minor. He reciprocated Lissa's lack of enthusiasm.

Charlotte was fascinated that Thompson seemed immune to Lissa, whom he had actually described as 'vapid'. For a moment, this had thrilled Charlotte, but then she had wondered if it were not an indication of dimness. Yet – handsome, clever, sometimes quietly amusing, and without any trace of accent – surely he did not deserve the dreadful epithet? He and Charlotte both loved films, and he was teaching her to appreciate jazz.

Jiving with Thompson, Charlotte, for the first time, enjoyed dancing. Lissa hated jiving. Moving on her own, she felt quite lost. She preferred to be held and guided, which conversely made Charlotte uneasy and stiff. Anyway, Lissa wasn't sure that jiving was acceptable. Mightn't it perhaps be dim?

Lissa never actually described Thompson himself as dim, but

she called him 'loyal' which seemed perilously close. 'Very loyal,
Thompson,' she would say, and Charlotte could never help giggling.
'What does she mean – "loyal"?' Vicky asked Charlotte. 'In
any case, loyalty's a very fine quality. And why do you call him
"Thompson" like that? I think he's smashing.'

Vicky's keen advocacy was reassuring. 'The trouble is,' Charlotte
said, 'that he doesn't make me feel any symptoms.'

'What do you mean – "symptoms"?'

'Like I used to feel with Arthur, at the beginning. Though it's odd to
remember it. Now, when I think of him, I just feel a mild dislike.'

Charlotte had told both Lissa and Vicky about Arthur. Lissa was
fascinated until Charlotte mentioned his working-class origins, which
shocked her; at once she had dismissed the affair as sordid. Vicky
disapproved too, but for a different reason: because Arthur was a
married man.

'Alexander makes me feel more symptoms than Thompson,' said
Charlotte.

Vicky snorted; she considered Alexander – Lissa's candidate for
Charlotte – a snob.

Charlotte sighed. She and Vicky were sitting in front of Vicky's fire,
drinking what Vicky – whose father was in the navy – called 'ship's
cocoa'. Made with water – Vicky had run out of milk – it was lavishly
sugared, and had a lump of butter dissolved in it. Charlotte found it
delicious, though guiltily, for she knew Lissa would have despised
it, because it was fattening, and also simply because it was cocoa.
Even if they did not drink *ship's* cocoa in what Charlotte and Lissa –
though not Vicky – called 'the cocoa cells', cocoa's associations were
appalling.

Charlotte thought of her mother, who had recently been ill.
Although she said it was nothing serious, she was having tests of
some kind. This had prevented her visiting Charlotte at Oxford
recently.

Since meeting Lissa, Charlotte's mother had revised her opinion of
women undergraduates. 'Lissa rather reminds me of Becky Sharpe,'
she said, but in an indulgent tone. (Charlotte felt that her mother
would have preferred a daughter like Lissa – so unmistakably focussed
on marriage as destiny – to one like herself.) Charlotte now reflected
that if, instead of meeting Lissa, her mother had penetrated into the
cocoa cells, she would have found that their inhabitants markedly
resembled her original stereotype.

*

Even if poor, the cell-mates did not have to wear such dingy colours. Why were they all either very thin or very fat, with spots and greasy hair? They weren't fresh: often, when you passed one of them in a passage, you smelt her sweat, and their rooms had a frowsty, subterranean atmosphere. Although they went to all the lectures recommended by their tutors, none of them seemed to be very clever: there wasn't a single Scholar or Exhibitioner among them. Many of them were members of the Student Christian Movement. They had crushes on each other, and on various dons.

One cell-mate in Charlotte's year, Clare Farmer, kept every note she had ever received from her tutor, Miss Wynde. The notes were tied up with pink ribbon in a cross-stitched handkerchief sachet. They all began, 'Dear Miss Farmer'. Nowadays, men's tutors often called them by their first names. This never happened with women. One of the few ways in which women dons distinguished their undergraduates from schoolgirls, it in fact perpetuated a schoolroom distance between teacher and pupil.

Dear Miss Farmer,
I find that I am obliged to postpone your tutorial on Tuesday from 2 pm to 3 pm.
Yours sincerely,
L. H. Wynde

Charlotte visualized Clare fastening the pink ribbon round this letter, perhaps pressing a kiss on it, before putting it in the cross-stitched sachet. (She would first have replaced it in its envelope, not wanting to lose a single 'Miss Farmer' in Miss Wynde's tiny, beloved handwriting.)

Charlotte's own encounters with Miss Wynde had been unsatisfactory. During her second term, Miss Wynde had tutored her on the Lake poets. They clashed when Miss Wynde responded sharply to a casual sneer of Charlotte's about Georgian verse. Much of it, Miss Wynde declared, was 'quite delightful'. After this, although she knew so much about Wordsworth and Coleridge – and too much about Southey – Charlotte ceased to respect her.

A different kind of encounter had taken place over a disciplinary matter.

To spend a night out of college undetected was quite possible. Many people considered it less risky than climbing in. This had been Lissa's opinion during her affair with Tim, in whose laxly-conducted lodgings she sometimes stayed. One evening, however, mistakenly believing that she would be out only for dinner, Lissa had 'signed out', forgetting

81

later that she had done so. When the porter checked the book at midnight, he saw that she had not 'signed in'. After knocking at her door, he found her room empty. Staying out for the night was grounds for being permanently sent down. Miss Wynde, as Vice-Principal, was responsible for an investigation.

Lissa's story was that she had signed out very early: at six pm. Returning just before eight – which was when the porter came on duty – she had forgotten that she had done so. After several hours' work, she had fallen asleep – and had spent the night – in Charlotte's armchair.

In Miss Wynde's sitting-room, a bower of chintz and vases of chrysanthemums, dotted with silver-framed photographs of grim women with sentimental mouths, Charlotte had confirmed every word of Lissa's story, which Miss Wynde, though hostile, had been unable to refute. Lying with passion, Charlotte felt herself to be serving a higher truth. So much for Kant!

And so much for Miss Wynde. It astonished Charlotte that anyone could have a crush on her. Presumably Clare would recover. Perhaps she would marry: some cell-mates did, though their Oxford lives seemed so devoid of men.

Men had been the only subject Charlotte and Lissa, oblivious of listeners, had discussed during one particular lunch in hall. Afterwards, Vicky had told Charlotte that the cocoa-cell view of her and Lissa ('How do they get a view?' Charlotte asked. 'From a periscope?') was disapproving. Vicky herself sounded censorious: 'They think you're snobbish, affected, frivolous and insensitive.'

'I *see!*' Charlotte exclaimed. Then she laughed, but her laugh was forced. 'How preposterous,' she said. Later, when Vicky had gone, she repeated the words: 'How preposterous,' but she still felt uneasy.

Could there be something in it? Why hadn't she asked Vicky for her opinion? Had she been afraid of Vicky's famous frankness? (Frankness, in Lissa's view, was a very tedious quality.) Had she been afraid that Vicky might confirm those four adjectives which, though Charlotte had only heard them once, she remembered perfectly.

Snobbish? Oh, surely she wasn't. Her mother, perhaps; but not *she*. Possibly she had some attitudes . . . but all that was just fun, just – really – a game one played. (Since it was only a game, mightn't one conceivably be spending rather too much time on it?)

Affected? She supposed she could see what the ghastly cell-mates meant, in *their* terms, but what they called affectation was again just fun and games: the way one talked, the words one used. Anyway – she felt an onrush of vigour and confidence she hadn't been quite able to summon when denying 'snobbish' – why should one never exaggerate, never show panache? 'I wouldn't mind . . . Yes, it was quite nice . . . An enjoyable evening': how she loathed that miserable middle-class flatness; she felt, indeed, justified in being 'snobbish' about it. How much livelier, more exhilarating – for both speaker and listener – it was when one said, 'I'd adore to . . . It was utter bliss . . . I had a simply divine time.' To hell with those mincing future schoolmistresses, sub-Denisons! Nur, nur, *nur!*

Frivolous? Charlotte blushed with anger. She felt sure she would get as good a degree as anyone in the cocoa-cells. There wasn't a potential First among them: certainly among those in the English school. She, she felt sure, could have got a First. Mightn't she still do so: if she tried, if she did not prefer other (*frivolous*) concerns? Anyway she had read more than any of them, and her perceptions were more subtle than theirs. Perceptions? After this burst of self-aggrandisement, the final word of the cell-mates' indictment dropped – stone into well: down, down, down, then plop! into her consciousness: *insensitive.*

Insensitive? Why, if there were one thing she wasn't, it was *that!* Yet indignation failed to blot out a sudden picture of herself, dressed-up, made-up, chattering and laughing with Lissa about gorgeous times and blissful men, regardless of listeners, spectators – peering up, she thought viciously, through their periscopes – at the performance. And a performance, of course, it was. If the spectators only knew the effort, the doubt, the unease – for her – of every blissful occasion . . . Yet the idea of their knowing was worse – far worse – than their regarding her as *insensitive.*

The cell-mates could think what they liked: mean, envious creatures (envious of her!). Why were they such carpers? She had not been rude to any of them. Admittedly she did not pay them much attention, but they had their own friends: unsnobbish, unaffected, serious, sensitive, *boring.*

When she told Lissa about the cell-mates' comments, Lissa said, 'Well, what do you expect. They're so utterly dank and dim. I must say, your friend Vicky knows the most extraordinary people.'

'The most ordinary ones, you mean.'

For Lissa, the dim, dank cell-mates were the enemy. For Vicky, the enemy was the two chinless Chelts. Both were History Scholars, from Cheltenham *Ladies'* College, as that school with the hideous green uniforms felt it necessary to label itself.

They seldom spoke to other women in the college. They looked different, too: smart or tarty? Charlotte could not decide. They wore a lot of rouge on their hard, sallow little faces, and skimpy clothes on their skinny bodies: clinging suits in the daytime, and horrible short evening dresses; nothing romantic. Most of their clothes were checked. Charlotte, a devotee of stripes, hated checks, and thought a limp red tartan evening dress, worn by the cleverer, richer Chelt, was the nastiest dress she had ever seen.

'Off on a vacuous-vike hunt!' Vicky observed to Charlotte one evening, as the Chelts, like two small painted dogs, trotted out of the college. The chinless Chelts devoted their time at Oxford to chasing viscounts. In vain! Obstinately the viscounts preferred silly debutantes from London. 'Just as well,' said Vicky. 'Those vacuous vikes are even more chinless than the Chelts. Imagine the result if they mated!'

But the Chelts puzzled Charlotte. One of them was the daughter of a millionaire connoisseur, the other of a famous playwright. Surely, thought Charlotte, in *that* world, they must meet people far more fascinating than vacuous vikes. For Charlotte had now learnt that the aristocracy bore no resemblance to those *Crome Yellow* figures she had dreamed of for so many years. Petulant, pink-faced youths, obsessed with an obsolete animal – the horse – she had met several of them as a result of the formation of the foursome.

The foursome consisted of Lissa and Jeremy, Charlotte and Jeremy's friend, Alexander. Subtle denigrator of 'loyal' Thompson, Lissa had long encouraged Charlotte to be interested in Alexander.

Tim, back in Australia since last summer, when he had gone down (gone down, and gone down under), had taken Lissa seriously; he was still committed to her. This was reassuring, but not challenging, as Jeremy's lightness was. Jeremy was so easy, so charming: cat-like he could have slid through the smallest crack in any fence. Almost everything he said was a joke; this both worried and fascinated Lissa.

But what about Alexander and Charlotte? Did Alexander really admire Charlotte as much as Lissa said he did? At first, Charlotte's and Alexander's meetings had all been at after-lunch coffee in Lissa's room. Surely, said Charlotte, since he came to Lissa's room, not to hers, it was logical to presume that he was interested not in her but in Lissa? Lissa said no, adding, 'One can always tell.' (Was that true? Charlotte felt unsure that *she* could.)

According to Lissa, Alexander thought Charlotte 'frightfully intelligent' and 'awfully attractive'. Why then didn't he say so to her? And why did he never take her out on her own, away from the foursome, as Jeremy took Lissa?

Perhaps, Charlotte told herself, the trouble was that she was sceptical about the very idea of being admired. With Arthur, that had been different; but, with Arthur, there had been no competition, so Arthur proved nothing.

Charlotte knew that the way she denigrated herself was silly, but she seemed unable to stop doing it. If a man told her she looked nice, she would say, 'Oh no, I look awful,' or if he admired a dress she was wearing, she would say, 'Oh no, it's terribly old.' A similar thing happened when she was offered a cigarette, or another drink, or a second helping of food. Whether she wanted it or not – and she usually wanted it – she would say, 'Oh no – *really*.' Either people believed her, which was frustrating, or she had to be persuaded: just like one of the coy old ladies in *Cranford*. With Thompson, she didn't do this so much, but – especially to begin with – she did it a lot with Alexander.

Was *he* 'frightfully intelligent' and 'awfully attractive'? Surely MPs had to be intelligent? Alexander wanted to be a Conservative MP. He was good-looking, though there was something snoutish about the tip of his nose, and his laugh sometimes rose high, bringing the word 'squeal' to her mind. It was a pity that both these associations were with pigs.

'Lissa and Jeremy': that sounded natural to Charlotte, but 'Charlotte and Alexander' did not.

The foursome seldom went to plays or films. (Charlotte's outings of this kind were with Thompson, 'loyal' Thompson. Sometimes she felt guilty about making use of him but, after all, he chose to keep on seeing her.) Lissa was not fond of the cinema, or the theatre. She preferred to go out to dinner, and to 'chat'. At this she sparkled. Although she was not witty – and was not always very quick at seeing the point of funny stories (which she did not care for) – she laughed a lot, and she invented charming things to do.

In the summer term Jeremy and Alexander had often walked Lissa and Charlotte back to college. Opposite Keble, a building they all considered ridiculous, was the Engineering Department.

They climbed over the fence which separated this building from the University Parks, and crouched down outside a brightly lit window. Here they engaged in the pastime Lissa had invented and which was called 'Watching the Scientists'. Inside the building, engineers – 'funny little men' – would be doing the most absurd things: fiddling with strange machines, using improbable instruments, and scribbling calculations on sheets of paper. Shaken by fits of laughter, the foursome clutched at each other. Lissa was always between Jeremy and Alexander. Charlotte was next to Alexander, at the end of the row.

When winter came, they sat in Jeremy's or Alexander's rooms –

usually Jeremy's, which were nicer – talking, and drinking gin and tonic or brandy and ginger ale. These were rich drinks. Most undergraduates could not afford to offer visitors anything but sherry, or sometimes wine.

Out with Thompson, Charlotte asked for the cheapest things: beer or tomato juice. Somehow it seemed jollier to drink half a pint of bitter, though tomato juice tasted nicer.

Gin, disguised by tonic water, or brandy, masked with ginger ale, tasted much better than beer. However, for Charlotte, the revelation was that the taste did not matter. What mattered was the effect: the way that drinks set her free. After she had drunk two brandy and ginger ales, she stopped apologizing for herself, and she accepted compliments, as well as cigarettes, second helpings and more drinks. It was as if she had put on invisible armour.

In male company she tended to be quiet. (This was not the case when she was with Thompson. But, in a sense, being with Thompson was like being with another woman: she felt so sure of him that she did not have to make an effort.) However, with drinks, words – like the drinks – flowed. She found she could even be amusing: about dons, about cocoa cells, about varieties of dimness. It was this discovery that dictated what she did before Jeremy's party.

*

A London advertising agency was trying to popularize a nasty new Italian vermouth. The best way to do this, it was decided, was to suggest that fashionable young people drank it.

A party was planned at which this would be seen to happen. Oxford was agreed to be an ideal setting. It was a concentrate of youth, with a smarter, dizzier aura than Cambridge had.

Jeremy, who knew 'everybody' and had splendid rooms in the Magdalen New Building, was employed as host. Invitations were dispatched. Acceptances came from a duke's heir, three viscounts (a treat for the chinless Chelts, also invited), several 'hons', and other undergraduates whose surnames, in connection with commercial products, were *household words*, as they say. Indeed 'they' did say so, for with this very phrase the man from the agency – referred to by Jeremy as 'Adman' – expressed approval of the guest list.

Adman had at first proposed to supply a lot of the aperitif (christened by Jeremy 'the Red Menace'), as well as soda, tonic water (with which the Red Menace tasted less sweet and therefore less nasty), ice, lemons, canapés, and three waiters. However, Jeremy had persuaded him also to provide gin, by remarking that, after all, it was with gin that most people drank vermouth: 'Martinis, you know.'

At the mention of this famous competitor, Adman first winced, then capitulated. 'So,' Jeremy said afterwards to Alexander, Lissa and Charlotte, 'at least there'll be *something* drinkable: gin and tonic. Pity I couldn't persuade Adman that smarties add vermouth to brandy and whisky, too. But there comes a point . . .' Undimly, he left the sentence unfinished. (Dim people always finished their sentences, even when everyone knew what was coming.)

Anyway there would be gin. Despite this, on the afternoon of the party, Charlotte bought a quarter bottle from a grocer's shop in the Cornmarket. It was a sudden inspiration. Feeling the customary dread, she had wondered why she should not put on her invisible armour in advance of the party, instead of having to acquire it – laboriously – after she arrived.

*

She had bathed and brushed her teeth. Now, back in her room, she rubbed Odo-Ro-No cream into her armpits, from which, the day before, she had removed hair with Veet. (After removing hair, one had to wait a day before using Odo-Ro-No, or it stung, though not as much as the other deodorant: a red liquid called Arrid.) Some girls shaved their armpits, but this was said to make the hair bristly, and also to encourage its growth. Lissa was the only girl Charlotte knew who, even when she was going to wear a strapless evening-dress, did not depilate her armpits. Lissa had read in a magazine that French women never did, and that this added to their sex-appeal. (Charlotte, however, would have felt uneasy if she had not done hers.)

Now, after scattering herself with Yardley's Lavender Talc, she drank some gin: about a third of the quarter-bottle, diluted with Orange Squash. (This was a drink she would never have consumed publicly. Gin and Orange was very dim: the invariable choice of unsophisticated girls, making a first hesitant advance from sherry. However, downed in one swallow, it gave her a marvellous jolt; like a blissful electric shock, if one could imagine such a thing.)

She began to dress, putting on the newer and more constricting of her two pink corsets, a precious pair of 15-denier nylons, a pink bra, and her best 'set': matching, lace-trimmed, white nylon petticoat and pants. Now she must do her face; before putting on her dress, for she did not want to spill powder on it.

It was a pity her skin was so fine; it didn't 'take' make-up as thicker

87

skin, like Lissa's, did. But anyway she could disguise its pink-and-whiteness with a layer of beige 'pancake' make-up, applied on a damp sponge. She only used 'pancake' – said to clog the pores – on special occasions, though it achieved a delightful effect: monochromatic, like Lissa's natural complexion, and matt. But, even after using 'pancake', she took further precautions to ensure that her nose would not shine. (A shiny nose looked awful. Even Charlotte's mother, who wore no other make-up, put vanishing cream and powder on her nose, and all cell-mates' noses shone.) Charlotte now covered her face with powder, fluffing it on thickly with a swansdown puff, and then dusting off loose traces with cotton-wool.

Next she did her eyebrows, with a dark-brown pencil. (Black made one look hard.) Then she spat on a little brush before rubbing it over her cake of (dark-brown) mascara. She applied two coats of mascara, pausing after each to let it dry, and then blinking her lashes against a piece of cotton-wool to make sure she would not get little marks, like insects' footprints, under her eyes. Her eyelashes were long; it was a pity they were so pale. Lissa's – shorter, but thick and dark – were much more attractive.

Her eyes were nearly ready. She had only to smear on a little eye-shadow: blue, of course, to match her eyes. Now there was just her mouth to do. Before that she would have her second – her final – gin. She drank just under half of what was left in the quarter-bottle, swallowing it down with orange, as she had done before, though, this time, the jolt did not have the same thrilling power.

Lipstick – and scent, of course – and then her dress and shoes: that was all. As usual, she had plenty of time to spare. She wondered if ever, in her life, she would be naturally late for any occasion. Although not anxious to arrive at the party, she knew that soon, in Lissa's room, she would be on edge, constantly glancing at her watch while she tried to respond to questions about which necklace, which pair of shoes, what colour lipstick Lissa ought to wear. It seemed extraordinary that Lissa, who always looked so marvellous whatever she wore, should take so much trouble. Yet, if she had not, she would have been a different person; perhaps not such a fascinating one.

The task of putting on lipstick suddenly seemed daunting, enormous. But in the mirror she was pleased to see that her eyes had an exceptional sparkle, and her face glowed. ·The glow was, in fact, almost a flush, but a further layer of powder might look patchy. Leaning her elbow on the dressing-table, she first carefully outlined, then filled in her lips with Bermuda Coral. She blotted her mouth and then powdered it, before repeating the whole process.

At last! She always felt released when she had finished doing her face. How easy life must have been when women wore no make-up (though, of course, they must have looked awful with their shiny, insipid faces). Abundantly, she splashed her wrists and neck with Coty *L'Aimant*, to which she had progressed from *Muguet*.

The dress she was wearing tonight was her favourite, her most sophisticated. It was black, of course: taffeta, with lime-coloured straps showing through fine net over her shoulders. Now: shoes and evening-bag; the latter first, for it was in one of the drawers of the dressing-table, and – as posters had stressed during the war – one should avoid unnecessary journeys. Into the bag – black satin, with a criss-cross diamanté pattern – she transferred, from her daytime bag, gilt powder-compact, small comb, and a pound note; she added a handkerchief and her coral lipstick.

She must put away the gin bottle, which stood on the dressing-table. (Although women were not forbidden to have drink in their rooms – was this perhaps because dons did not conceive of their doing so? – she would not want anyone to see it.) She picked it up. But then, instead of putting it away, she quickly unscrewed the top, raised the bottle to her mouth and, tilting back her head, swallowed what was left in it: glug, glug, glug. Water came into her eyes. As she pushed the bottle into a drawer, she felt a strange sensation, like a punch in the stomach: a jolt different in kind from previous ones.

She dragged her coat from the wardrobe and hung it over her arm. She stepped into her best black court shoes. The heels seemed higher than usual, and she wobbled for a moment. She pressed her hand against the wardrobe door to regain her balance.

'*God for Harry! England and St George!*' she declaimed, imitating the way Laurence Olivier had extended the word 'George'. Then, with the gesture of a general urging his troops into battle, she set off to Lissa's room.

*

Charlotte and Lissa reached the party, which had begun at six, just after seven. Jeremy's rooms were crowded. The loud steady hum of conversation was broken by brays, barks and yelps of laughter. As always at Oxford, there were more men than women. Across the room, Charlotte saw one of the chinless Chelts – in checks – but did not know if the man she was talking to was a viscount; though he looked vacuous enough to be one.

Charlotte hated the moment on the brink of every party before one sank into its icy seething current. (For Lissa, the experience was probably a smooth dive into a warm pool.) This evening, however – thanks, she guessed, to the invisible armour – she felt slightly less terrified than usual. Jeremy came towards them, holding a glass containing pale-pink liquid. His normally vague and amiable expression seemed particularly vague and amiable tonight.

'Seems to be going quite well,' he said. 'Adman is pleased. There he is, holding forth to Eddie Devereux. Eddie's looking quite desperate, poor him. Charlotte, do you feel like tackling Adman?'

'Absolutely not,' she answered boldly.

'Sad. Poor Eddie. Goodness how sad! Anyway, must get you a drink at once. I'm fearfully tight. Before the party, Alexander and I spent *hours* testing the Red Menace, to see how little one need use to produce a convincing colour. One feels Adman might be upset if one just drank gin and tonic. Anyway, it takes awfully little to produce a blush of rose.' He pointed to his glass. 'You shall see for yourselves.' He headed for a table behind which a waiter was mixing drinks. A second waiter came past, holding a large plate of canapés. Lissa took two: 'Never drink on an empty tummy, as they say.'

Charlotte, though unusually unhungry, took a little square of toast, smeared with pink paste. Toast and paste had merged; both were soft and damp. She wondered where Alexander was.

When Jeremy returned with drinks, Charlotte took hers with a feeling of lightness. He offered her a cigarette. She slung the chain of her bag over her arm. Drink in one hand, cigarette in the other, she faced the party. The waiter with the canapés came past again, and Lissa took one, but Charlotte swallowed a big mouthful of her drink instead. She could just taste gin under the quinine tang of the tonic which, in its turn, battled bravely through the sweet blur of the Red Menace.

'Paul de Vigne's dying to meet you,' Jeremy was saying to Lissa. Paul – sometimes kindly nicknamed 'Divine' – de Vigne was, Charlotte knew, a rich old man who visited Oxford often. He was famous for queerness. Could he really be dying to meet Lissa?

Charlotte realized that the moment was approaching when she would have to cope on her own: to launch herself on the party and – as they say – sink or swim. Looking round the room, she saw several people she knew, but they were all busy talking and laughing; or perhaps gabbling and giggling was a better description. What was the secret they all shared, and which only she did not know?

In Lissa's room, after putting on the invisible armour, she had felt she would be able to cope with anything. Sitting on Lissa's bed, talking and laughing – gabbling and giggling – she had been exceptionally animated, as Lissa had noticed. 'You're tremendously cheerful this evening,' she had said, looking puzzled, for usually, before a party, Charlotte was quiet and rather morose.

'*Mmm*,' Charlotte said. 'Looking forward to the marty – I mean party – madly.'

However, as time passed – Lissa took even longer to get ready than Charlotte had anticipated, and the taxi they ordered was slow in coming – the flow of confidence seemed to evaporate, drop by drop, till she was almost her usual – desiccated – self again; though not quite. For even now, dithering on the brink of the party, she felt bolder, if not much happier, than usual.

Finishing her drink, she sensed that Jeremy and Lissa were about to move away. But, 'A drink, Charlotte?' Jeremy asked. (It was rude to say, 'Another drink?', even if someone had already had ten, which of course she hadn't; as far as Jeremy knew, she had only had one.)

She saw that Lissa's glass was still half full, but, 'Yes, please,' she said. Jeremy went off to fetch it, and she was left alone with Lissa for a few more undemanding minutes.

Lissa's eyes, however, were roaming wildly. To talk to another woman at a party was almost as bad as standing by oneself; absolutely non-Lissa. Charlotte looked round the room again. She still couldn't see Alexander.

Jeremy was back, saying, 'Charlotte, I really insist on introducing Adman. Be heroic. Poor old Eddie simply must be rescued.'

Why couldn't Jeremy and Lissa rescue him? But wouldn't even the company of Adman be preferable to being stranded on her own? Following Lissa, who drifted after Jeremy – Jeremy was one of those who can effortlessly part a crowd – Charlotte felt hot and rather tired.

In a corner, both Adman – small, sharp-faced and oldish (well over thirty) – and Eddie – tall, fair and droopy – looked eager for distraction. As soon as Jeremy started to introduce Adman to Lissa and Charlotte, Eddie vanished, murmuring inaudibly. Adman's eyes lingered on Lissa, but she and Jeremy were moving off.

Charlotte took a gulp of her new drink. 'Lovely party,' she said. A camera flashed somewhere.

Adman – whose name was Barry Frith – said, 'We're getting some good pics, anyway.'

'Pics?'

'Photographs,' he said impatiently, frowning at her. He seemed aware of her for the first time, and not enthusiastic. 'Is that Jeremy's girl-friend?'

91

'Lissa? Well yes, in a way.'

'Ho ho!' Charlotte had never heard anyone say 'Ho ho!' before, though she had read it in historical novels. 'What sort of way would *that* be, I wonder?'

'I meant' – she spoke coldly, closing ranks – 'that they go out together quite often. They aren't engaged or anything.'

'Or anything. I'm glad to hear they aren't *anything*.' He sniggered. Then he said, 'Have you got a title?'

Shocked by this vulgar question, she shook her head. Now he looked openly bored. Taking her – again empty – glass from her hand – almost snatching it – he said, 'Here, let me get you a refill. We can't have the world's greatest aperitif going to waste when a lady's glass is empty.' He pushed off; he had to: people didn't make way for him as they did for Jeremy.

How hot the room was! She felt quite dizzy, and leant back against the wall. Across the room – the crowd was thinning – she saw Adman put down her empty glass on the drinks table, and move away. She was lighting a cigarette – it was difficult to make contact between cigarette and match – when hands clasped her arm.

'Charlotte! Been looking for you everywhere. Found you at last. Absolutely splendid.'

It was Alexander. A lock of hair had escaped from the dressing he used to keep it down, and bounced above his right eye. His face, usually –like her own – pink and white, was red (she hoped her 'pancake' was still doing its work), and his tie was crooked. Lissa would have straightened it; Charlotte would normally have felt that this amounted to 'making advances' to him. How absurd! She resolved to make the gesture, and was shifting her cigarette to her left hand, when he said, 'Why, Charlotte, you haven't got a drinkikins! Where's your glass?'

'Oh, I'm not sure.' She couldn't tell him what had happened, which reflected badly on her as well as on Adman. (Such a thing could never have happened to Lissa.)

'I'll get you another. Lovely gin and tonic, with just a dash of the Red Menace.' It was nice to realize that in no circumstances would Alexander – a *gentleman* – behave as Adman had done.

When she took her first swallow of the drink he brought back, something twanged in her head, like a bedspring. As the echoes of this died away, she became aware of a different sensation. An octopus (it sounded gruesome, but this one was friendly, a pet octopus – a French decadent had taken a lobster for walks on a lead, so why couldn't there be a pet octopus?) – had settled in her stomach, where it was spreading

92

its tentacles. Two wriggled downwards, one into each of her legs; two wriggled outwards, into her arms; another weaved up her spine, through her neck, and then spread into the huge smile she gave to darling Alexander.

'Seen Jeremy and Lissa anywhere?' he asked.

'Yes. Before. Somewhere round. Went speak someone called Paul.' She was talking like a telegram.

'Ah, Paul de Vigne. Saw him moment ago. Devine de Vigne. Come up view the gilded youth.' Alexander was talking telegram too; obviously it was a new fashion. 'Thought we four might go out to dinner,' he went on. 'All this over soon.'

'Jeremy and Lissa having dinner with de Vigne. Heard Jeremy say.'

'Oh!' His tone and look were downcast. He swallowed his drink. 'One more,' he said, 'before gin runs out.'

She gulped down hers. 'All right,' she said.

While Alexander was away, a friend of Jeremy's called Johnny Farleigh, came over; he was known for cheerfulness. 'Hullo, Charlotte.'

'Oh, hullo, Johnny.' Detaching herself from the wall, she found herself swaying forward, and leant back again. Johnny was looking at her with an – unusual – frown.

'I say, Charlotte, are you feeling all right?'

'All right?' she repeated. 'Perfectly all right. Why not all right?'

'You just look – well, a little odd.'

'Odd. What d'you mean *odd*?' She felt cross. At that moment, Alexander returned. Johnny looked relieved, she thought, but suddenly her picture of his face blurred.

'Oh well, must dash.' Then he said to Alexander, 'You're looking after Charlotte, aren't you?'

'Looking after Charlotte? Course I'm looking after Charlotte. Just been gettin' her a drink. Couldn't look after her better.'

Johnny – clear again – was again frowning. 'Must rush,' he said. 'I'm late for dinner. Goodbye Charlotte. Goodbye Alexander.'

'Always so damn cheerful, that chap. Rather gets on my nerves.'

'Yes,' she said. 'See what you mean. He's always so cheerful. Could get on one's nerves.'

'Agree with you absolutely. Always so cheerful.'

How handsome Alexander was! Rather misty, like a Lenare photograph. He had looked red earlier, but now he was pale, and awfully handsome.

'People going,' he said. 'All going.' Glancing round, she saw that this was true. Many had gone; others were leaving; few remained. The

93

waiters were clearing up. The one behind the drinks table was talking to Adman, who looked annoyed. Charlotte had seen only one photographer. She giggled. Perhaps Adman felt that Jeremy should have stayed to the end.

'Pity about Lissa and Jeremy. Great pity,' said Alexander. 'Had hoped we could go out to dinner.'

'Well, we still could.' She felt uncharacteristically bold. This must be how Lissa always felt. Miraculously she had discovered Lissa's secret. In future, she would always feel like this. She stared into Alexander's eyes; she usually avoided men's eyes.

He beamed vaguely. 'Mmm. Well, yes. Why not? Let's go.' There was no one to thank or to say goodbye to. Adman stood alone by the drinks table. She wasn't going to speak to *him*, and Alexander did not do so either.

Walking downstairs, ahead of Alexander, she held onto the banister. Usually people who did this were old or 'making an entrance' like Bette Davis in *Mr Skeffington*.

At the bottom of the stairs, Alexander stood still. 'Where are we going?' she said.

'Going? Oh yes. Dindins. Mmm. Plenty of time. Perhaps one drink in my rooms. Steel us to face the chilly night.'

Chilly the night was, snow falling thick on their heads, on the big collar of Charlotte's coat and the shoulders of Alexander's beige cavalry twill. Grass crunched under their feet. They went through the archway to Cloisters; rather dwarfish after the New Building.

In Alexander's rooms, they sat on the sofa. The sitting-room was cold, and rather untidy. He lit the gas fire, and opened a bottle of red wine; the cork broke, and he had to push it in. There were little flecks of cork in her glass. She tried to hook them all out with her finger, but when she drank, she found cork in her mouth. Alexander was sitting rather slumped, saying nothing. Remembering a favourite passage about wine in *Brideshead*, she tried to invent one of her own. 'Like a darling Persian kitten,' she said.

Alexander shook his head as if insects were buzzing round it. 'Persian kitten?'

'The *wine*. Like a Persian kitten. Soft. Not *furry* of course. Though more furry than gin. Gin's more like a dog than a kitten. Woof, woof,' she barked, to make her meaning clear.

'Mmm. Never thought of it like that. Gin – woof, woof. Suppose wine would be meow, meow – what?'

'No, not meow. Purr, purr.'

94

'Purr, purr. Trouble is I can't stand cats.' Laughing, they collapsed towards each other. He smelt of violet hair oil, which Charlotte hated.

*

After Charlotte and Alexander did the deed, it was Alexander who cried.

She awoke first, and extricated herself. He lay on his back on the sofa, snoring. Only his position and his colour were reminiscent of 'The Death of Chatterton'. Attempting to make him look more lovable – after doing the deed with him, she really ought to love him – she picked up his trousers from the floor, and draped them over the middle of his body. She looked at her watch, which said ten to four.

She would be sent down. But then, staring at the hands of the watch in horror, she realized that it was actually twenty past ten. Relief was so huge that for several seconds she felt happy. Then she felt sick. The terrible yellow overhead light glared down on Alexander. She went over to his desk, and turned on the reading-lamp. Then she switched off the centre light.

She was still wearing her bra and petticoat, and her corset was in a roll around her waist. She tugged it down, and then put on her stockings and pants, which were on the floor. So was her dress. It was very crumpled, and the net at the back was torn where Alexander had wrenched at the hook and eye. Net was impossible to mend invisibly. She supposed she could remove the net, and wear the dress with only the lime-coloured straps over her shoulders. But it was the net that had given this dress its particular charm.

She went over to the mirror that hung above the mantelpiece. Propped against it was a little stack of invitations. (It was dim to spread invitations out along the mantelpiece, and even dimmer to keep outdated ones, however smart the parties they commemorated.) She thumbed through the cards, they were for parties in London and Oxford, and a dance in Norfolk.

She looked awful in the mirror. Her nose shone horribly; her eyes stared; her mascara had run; her hair was a mess. She spat on her handkerchief, and scrubbed at the mascara; she put on powder and lipstick, and she combed her hair.

'Alexander!' He didn't move, and went on snoring. 'Alexander!' She went over to the sofa, and shook his arm. He stopped snoring, and looked better with his mouth shut. She shook his arm again. He raised a hand, and clasped hers. 'Alexander, wake up!' she said more gently.

95

'Lissa. Oh, Lissa!'

'It's not Lissa. It's *Charlotte*. Wake up!'

His eyes opened. They looked bleary. 'Thought you were Lissa.'

'How odd! We're not a bit alike.'

'No, no. Of course not. Not in the least. Awfully sorry. Suppose I was dreaming of her. But you do understand . . . she and I . . .' During a pause after this, he seemed to be recovering his memory. 'She and I,' he repeated. 'Never anything of this kind.'

'Oh I know. Of course not.'

'Sorry about all this.'

'Oh, not at all.'

'Yes, well. But we had fun, didn't we – the four of us, I mean. Going out, and so on.'

'Oh yes, tremendous fun.'

'Love her. Love her so much. Do anything just to be with her. Told her often, but it's no use. She doesn't love me. I can't seem to get over it though.' That was when he cried.

'Alexander, I'm afraid you really must tidy up, and take me to the porter's lodge, and order me a taxi, if you wouldn't mind too *fearfully*.'

'Oh, oh, oh.' Then, 'Yes, of course. *Awfully* sorry.'

*

Not at all hungry, she ate nothing all day. Extremely thirsty, she drank a lot of water. At lunchtime, when she knew the pantry down the corridor would be empty, she made herself a pot of weak tea. She sipped it cautiously, and kept it, as they say, down. She realized that she was undergoing what she had always believed to be an exclusively male experience: a hangover. She blushed with shame.

It was half past five – quite dark – when she crept out for her walk. Lissa's light was off, and at this time on Sunday the college was quiet, apart from those occasional echoes – like the clash of distant cymbals – that, except in the depth of night, resound in the bare corridors of institutions.

Outside, the silence was dense: deep-pile carpeting on the ground; soft down starting to fall again from the sky. Charlotte wore gloves, and a scarf over her head. In the pocket of her coat was last night's empty gin bottle.

Next door to the college, two rich elderly sisters – its active patrons – lived in a grey Gothic house. Each Michaelmas term, they invited the year's new clutch of scholars – one Scholarship was endowed by them

– to an evening gathering. Slides were shown of a visit to Dr Albert
Schweizer's leper colony. The elder, bolder sister not only operated the
projector but delivered the commentary. Synchronization was imper-
fect. On the evening Charlotte attended, the words, 'And here is dear
Dr Schweizer at his organ' had accompanied the picture of a large
African woman, stirring porridge. The entertainment was followed by
weak coffee and small malleable biscuits. Charlotte, tossing the gin
bottle over the sisters' hedge, smiled, with relief at disposing of it, and
also at the recollection that the ladies were strictly teetotal. But – since
yesterday – so, of course, was she.

It had been a day of pledges. The teetotaller was one of four drably
clad recruits whom Sergeant-major Charlotte had been haranguing
since she woke. The others were a quiet frequenter of the cocoa cells
(hadn't the cell-mates defined the former Charlotte with startling
precision), an obsessive swot – *Beowulf* in her back-pack – and
Thompson's affectionate, though sexually unyielding, 'steady'.

All the same, the recruits – however strongly exhorted and abused –
seemed capable only of marking time. Although they moved their feet
as if marching, unfortunately they did not advance a single step.
However, this was not altogether surprising, for they had nowhere to
go.

Charlotte turned left into Parks Road. Sobriety, she reflected, was
not a destination; it was a self-committal to detention. Gallant but
glum, the teetotaller plunged her arms into a straitjacket of social
immobility. The jacket was rough; soon the skin beneath it would
become raw.

Now, ahead on her left, lights gleamed faintly through the snow.
Even on Sunday evening 'the scientists' were at work. Outside this
building, four fools had crouched last summer.

Yet, summoned up in defiance of the foursome, the cell-frequenter
was already in decline. She flinched from shared honesty in a stuffy
room, and gagged on her pinkish dose of puckered cocoa. No, Vicky's
company, Charlotte realized, was the closest she could come to 'taking
a cure' for Lissa. The diet would be austere: simple, though nutritious.
A certain aroma, a certain flavour – however deceptive – would be
missed.

The swot was surely the most promising of the recruits. Yet
mind-building had not liberated Miss Denison or Miss Wynde; it had
left them muscle-bound. And the objective made the exercise seem
sweaty, though a 'good degree' could lead to a 'good job'. It was a pity
she was unable to envisage one she wanted. Thompson, of course,
would spur her on. They would read together in his darkish room.

His devotion would continue to survive – even to be enhanced by her continence: now strongly reinforced. Hadn't she always suspected – though rejecting Vicky's evidence – that doing the deed would not necessarily result in – as they, as Arthur would say – 'climax'? Now she wondered why, when obviously so desirable, this climax was so often described in terms of natural catastrophe: tidal wave, tempest, earthquake, flood? Passionless, pleasureless, it was odd that her first time had not – unlike both Lissa's and Vicky's – been painful. (Pain would at least have been an experience.) Probably she had been anaesthetized by gin. She remembered that, before chloroform was invented, surgeons had administered spirits to prospective amputees. Anyway the operation was over; it had been so 'minor' that she felt it could not possibly have made her pregnant.

She felt better now: as if encased in a soft yet protective cocoon of snow.

Down the whole length of Parks Road, she passed only one huddled, hatted man. At the corner of Broad Street she hesitated. On the left, Holywell led to Magdalen. She did not want to go that way. She crossed the road, going down Catte Street to where, with her back to All Souls, she could admire her favourite building, the Radcliffe Camera. Tonight there was chaste icing on the luscious honeyed cake.

Suddenly, inside her chrysalis, she felt a stirring of love for this empty city. Was it possible that what the place had to offer was not company but solitude. She remembered how, long ago, she had copied out that poem of Auden's. *Weaned at last to independent delight.* She had stopped compiling anthologies when she came up to Oxford.

She crossed the High, and walked down Magpie Lane. Merton Street was deserted, but not quite silent. She stood still. Behind a lighted window in Oriel, someone was plucking a stringed instrument; not a guitar. Although the idea was romantic, almost stagy, it sounded like a lute.

Moving slowly towards Christ Church, she noted that the player was not skilled. The hand faltered; yet, if it had not, the music might have sounded false.

Ahead of her loomed the black bulk of Christ Church library. Time began to strike loudly from Old Tom, the Christ Church clock. As she vibrated with the first chime, she lay down on the cobbles: two, three, four, five, six. *The starry heavens above*; but she could see no stars tonight. *The moral law within*; softly, tentatively, the little snowflakes fell onto her face.

She shivered. She scrambled to her feet. Vigorously she brushed her coat with her leather-covered palms. Briskly she set off in the direction of Carfax. Stepping off the pavement, in the High, she did not see it – lights dimmed by snow in the air – or hear it – sound muffled by snow on the ground. Travelling fast, the car struck her when she was half way across the road.

Celia 1978

The hall had formerly been bisected by a hinged double door of opaque glass, framed in chocolate-painted wood, as had the room on the right, where she slept. In the permanently closed – and still divided – room on the left, containing empty tea-chests, suitcases and old newspapers, these disused partitions were propped against a wall.

Now the hall was twenty-five paces long. As, reaching the front door, she wheeled for the return journey towards the veranda, ash fell from her cigarette. Often in the morning she noticed a grey broken trail, sometimes with wine splashes beside it, marking her evening route.

In winter she brought the landlady's old pine table, four rush-seated chairs, and a metal divan, covered with a striped rug, into the hall. She wrote and ate at the table; she read lying on the divan, propped against cushions she had covered in cream and yellow corduroy. (Thalia, who came to clean the house once a week, had raised her eyebrows at the big careless stitches.)

She had enclosed the electric bulbs hanging from the ceiling in paper globes though, abhorring overhead lights, she seldom switched them on; she had converted two unglazed earthenware jars into lamps, one standing on the table, the other by the divan on a stool which was actually a fish-trap of cane bound with twisted bark.

Now, for the summer, all these objects, except the lamp on the stool, had been transferred to the veranda. Now, down the length of the hall, there were only the shelves.

*

She had ordered the bricks and planks from Thalia's husband, Andreas, who was a builder. Andreas and Thalia looked surprised at the way Celia wanted them set up against the walls, and more surprised when their contents arrived.

After dealing with Customs, Celia arranged for the twenty-two packing-cases to be delivered to the house. A small crowd formed outside the front door to watch the lorry driver, helped by Andreas, unload them.

In England the packers had printed the contents of each case on the lid. 'Books,' Kyria Christofidou, a neighbour who spoke some English, read aloud, as the first tea-chest was heaved down.

'Books?' said the lorry driver.

'*Biblia*,' said Kyria Christofidou. The driver, and everyone else, looked bored immediately. But when, as each case was carried into the house, the *Kyria* repeated the same word, a chorus started.

'Books! *Biblia*!' Everyone was chanting it when the giant roller of mirth struck them. Theatrically, yet spontaneously, they rocked, staggered, leant against each other. (Meanwhile, a single case marked 'Misc. Household Objects' – an inscription probably beyond the translator's powers – passed into the house unnoticed.)

'Books! *Biblia!*' So many packing-cases, expensively shipped from England, and holding nothing but *biblia*: it was laughable. But – and as suddenly as it had started, the laughter stopped – it was also disappointing . . . and odd. Looking uneasy, even slightly depressed, people began to drift away. Since that day, Celia had been called – so Thalia told her – *e daskala*: 'the schoolmistress'.

*

Now, cigarette in one hand, glass of wine in the other, she paused between the two lines of shelves, conscious of stillness; though, even on this hot night when not a tremor of air swayed the paper globes above her head, the house – so thick-walled, so high-ceilinged – was cool. But if ever she commented on its coolness to an islander, he or she invariably made that particular gesture – head jerked back, corners of the mouth turned down, eyelids flicked shut – which expressed rejection and disdain. And should she venture to call the house beautiful – its high wooden ceilings, the fanlight over the door, the wrought-iron window guards, the *trompe l'oeil* tiles on the hall floor (flowers, ribboned poles and angled blocks, in cream, black and terracotta) – the response would become irritable, even angry. *Was she mocking?* But no; she was merely stupid.

*

Even if new houses and flats were not *particularly* cool, each had its small veranda, decorated with a rubber-plant; leaves polished, earthenware pot concealed by a wrapping of silver foil. Onto this veranda, in the evening, the family could squeeze and, backs to the street, watch the television set that stood indoors. Anyway, all concrete buildings were superior to one built of mud-brick and roofed with tiles, just as modern roses – salmon, orange, mauve – planted in front of a house where passers-by could see them were better than old trees hidden away in a courtyard. Besides, courtyards had unpleasant associations; they were reminiscent of villages. *Peasants'* houses had courtyards.

Islanders found it extraordinary that she lived in the old house not because she was poor, but by choice. She wore a large sapphire ring, and she never asked the prices of the goods she bought, on monthly account, from Niko's shop next door. Also she paid high rent; everyone in the neighbourhood knew how much: it was too much for an old house. In addition she had paid to have the inside of the house and the walls of the courtyard painted white. (Why all white? White was dull, and it became dirty quickly.) She had bought an electric water heater for the kitchen and bathroom (both out of doors; leading off the veranda in the old-fashioned way), and had installed a new water-closet. (Yet she had bought, second-hand, a shabby refrigerator and stove.) Silliest of all, she had engaged the workmen who were demolishing a stone house further down the street, to bring the old stones and lay them unevenly in the earth around the fruit trees, so that now the courtyard looked more peasant than before. It was folly to spend money on someone else's property, but if she were determined to be foolish she could have had modern crazy paving for the same price. Thalia had told her so, and she had answered that she liked the old stones better.

*

She heard sounds from the street outside: a man and a woman talking. The man's voice was simply loud; the woman's sounded like pebbles being dropped into a tin bucket. As she had expected, their footsteps passed the house, and their voices died away. It was too late for visitors. Anyway, people no longer called on her.

*

Pavlos: Hullo, Anna. How are you?
Anna: Hullo, Pavlos. I am well. Where are you going?
Pavlos: I am taking my evening walk.
Anna: But why do you walk alone?

102

Pavlos: I like it. I get out of the town, away from the cars and the
people. Why are you laughing, Anna?
Anna: But don't you like company, Pavlos?
Pavlos: Oh yes. Yes of course I enjoy company. Company pleases
me very much. But I see people – people of every kind – all
day. So I like to take my evening walk alone. A short time
alone does one good.
Anna: But what do you do alone? Do you talk to your dog?
Pavlos: Yes – why not? I talk and sing to my dog, Mourgo.

Celia's Greek textbook was interspersed with such short dialogues,
most of them between recurrent characters. Only Pavlos, the single –
hesitant, apologetic, strictly vespertine – loner in its gregarious world,
did not reappear.

Inevitably there were times when work and other exigencies en-
forced solitude (though usually, nowadays, the housewife whose
children were at school, the postman on his motor-scooter, even the
goatherd under a carob tree, had a transistor radio to relieve the
oppressiveness). Yet Celia, who was free to do as she chose, refused
invitations to weddings, christenings, name-day parties, morning
coffee with neighbours. Xenophobia was not the explanation; for nor
did she associate with other English people living on the island. When
she had first moved into the house *Anglides* had often knocked,
unanswered, at her door. Neighbours who told her of these visits
looked puzzled, for they knew she had been in.

She was always in. She had no television, and listened only to the
news – once a day – on her radio. She was always in, except – like
Pavlos, but without the pretext of his dog, Mourgo – when she went
for walks alone. Even these walks – apart from brief shopping
expeditions – were at strange hours: very early in the morning, or after
dark.

*

In other places, at night, she had imagined exotic people behind the
curtains drawn across lighted windows: illicit lovers, tormented
artists, murderers plotting or executing their crimes. Here, she could
picture only happy families . . .

Her glass was empty; her cigarette had burnt down to the filter, and
smelt disgusting. She went outside, to the table on the veranda, where
she put down the glass, and squashed the cigarette stub in an ashtray.
To keep out tiny insects – not repelled by the mosquito coil burning in
a saucer on the floor – she had placed a matchbox on top of a half-full

wine bottle. About to remove this, in order to replenish her glass, she became aware of a strange shrill noise, and paused.

The sound was repeated. It came from the far end of the courtyard. Certainly not human, could it be the cry of some night bird? Although piercing, it was not menacing, and she was about to investigate when, looking down at her bare feet, she remembered the slow night journeys of the island's slugs. These were yellow and pulpy: treading on one in the kitchen, a week before, she had screamed, and then run to the bathroom to wash her foot. Afterwards, before scooping up the slug in a dustpan, she had poured salt on it. Oozing slime, it had shrivelled at once, though for a few seconds its blind head continued to move from side to side.

She put on her sandals, which were lying on the doorstep. The high plaintive call continued. (Might the bird be injured or trapped?) She walked to the end of the low veranda wall, and into the courtyard. From the area of stones surrounding the trees, a narrow path led through a bed of zinnias – planted by Thalia in the spring – to the washing-line, which hung in front of the courtyard's rear wall (behind which was a small, neglected lemon grove).

The zinnias – as tall as she was – brushed against her. She peered ahead in the moonlight. The sound was very close now. Against the whitewashed wall was something small and dark. But it was not a bird; it was a kitten.

*

On her walks she often encountered thin little cats; long-legged, with small heads and pointed ears. Only once had she met one that did not shrink or run from her. Plump, snowy-chested, brightly patterned in black and orange, when she spoke to it – she always spoke to cats – it trotted up, and rubbed against her ankles. But, as she bent to stroke its thick soft fur, her overriding emotion was fear that it might, on some other occasion, trust some less friendly stranger. On the whole, islanders were not fond of animals. Dogs were lean and chained. It was unlucky to kill kittens, but not to leave them – often in plastic bags – on patches of waste ground.

*

She could hardly credit the kitten's lightness. As soon as she picked it up, it stopped crying, and clung to her dress. By the time she reached the veranda she could feel a minute vibration: it had begun to purr.

When she put it on the table, it started to cry again at once. It was a tabby: yellow, streaked with grey, and so thin that its eyes protruded. She felt sure it must be starving. She put it on the floor, because she was afraid it might fall off the table. (How could it have come over the wall? Might its mother, carrying it, have dropped it? More probably, it had been dumped in the courtyard by an islander.) She fetched a saucer of milk, which she put down in front of it, but it did not know how to lap. She remembered that there was an eye-dropper in the bathroom cupboard, and went to fetch it. What else could she do?

ELEANOR 1957

'This house is full of witches,' Julian had said. 'Do they flit about at night, like bats, on their broomsticks?'

'How fey you're being,' Eleanor answered. 'Score two on the pseudometer.'

The pseudometer ('It scans with thermometer, not alligator, of course.' 'But of course,' said Julian) was her invention; points were awarded from one to ten, which was known as pseudomax. Julian's invention, the hormonic scale, worked differently. Plus ten was ultra-masc, and minus ten, ultra-fem; between pluses and minuses, logically enough, came neut.

Using these two instruments, Eleanor and Julian measured the characteristics of everyone except Eleanor's husband, Peter – from motives of delicacy – and her son, Teddy, who, at eighteen months, was too young.

Alone in the flat – except for sleeping Teddy – on a howling March evening, twitchy Eleanor, thinking of a nest – coven – of witches, would ordinarily have felt chilled. But now she was quite unmoved by the thought of the old women on the other three floors of the house. Taking her former slimming-pills again today had changed things.

*

She had taken the Dexedrin pills first, a year before. Dr Green had prescribed them to help her lose the weight she had gained during her pregnancy.

'You girls and your slimming fads!' He chuckled, stubbing out a wet-tipped cigarette in the full ashtray on his desk. 'Anyway, I'm sure you'll find these pills will do the trick. They'll curb your appetite, and stop you feeling depressed. That bit of weight should soon drop off. Avoid all starchy foods. Take one tablet when you wake, and another at noon. Don't take them later in the day, or you may find difficulty in sleeping.'

She had followed these instructions, and in two and a half months she lost twenty-five pounds. When she stopped taking the pills, she still had two weeks' supply, which had remained, forgotten, at the back of her make-up drawer until this morning.

*

Getting up in the morning, which she never used to find difficult, was nowadays a labour that must be undertaken because of Teddy (apart from whom, of course, it would not have been one). Teddy must be cleaned, dressed, fed, taken out, watched, and prevented from damaging himself as well as any objects he encountered. She could not 'turn her face to the wall', a phrase that often came into her mind, and which reminded her of a new trick of Teddy's. When she was sitting in a chair for a few minutes, reading or just thinking, he would clamber onto her, seize her chin between his hands, and turn her face towards him. Instinctively she felt anger and – immediately afterwards – guilt: *unnatural mother!*

Yet she loved him, had done so ever since that first quiver of disappointment she had felt on hearing that he was a boy. (Just the opposite of her own mother who had said that, after her birth, she had exclaimed, 'All that for a girl!')

During her pregnancy she had thought she would feel more at ease with a daughter. She had imagined a gifted one who would become an artist: painter, writer, composer; Eleanor didn't mind. She would help the girl, Edwina, to surmount obstacles till she achieved independence; then she and Eleanor would be friends. Edwina would, of course, have love affairs, but would not be trapped into marriage; unless to a man who would devote himself to her interests. Art-dealer, publisher, impresario; he would be whichever was appropriate.

However the child was Edward, not Edwina. His lavish prospects at once contracted. If he were to be an artist, dreadful battles must be fought. No one cared what a girl did: for Edwina, this indifference would have been the enemy Eleanor would have helped her to defeat. But for a boy, everyone would be plotting success at something pedestrian: law, politics, medicine, education.

All the same, she would help him as best she could. As soon as possible – in another year, perhaps? – she would start teaching him to read. (Thomas Babington Macaulay, 1800–59: *From the time that he was three years old, he read incessantly, for the most part lying on the rug before the fire, with his book on the ground, and a piece of bread and butter in his hand.* What a delightful picture!)

'Of course I shan't force him in any way,' she told Peter. 'I'll just give him the opportunity to enjoy a better life as soon as possible.' With a little laugh she produced a quotation from Logan Pearsall Smith: *'Most people say that life is the thing, but I prefer reading.* After all,' she added, 'there's no reason why he shouldn't learn young, if he wants to, is there?'

'Well no, I suppose not. Except of course that, when he goes to school, the teachers may not like it if he's at a different stage from the other children.'

'*Teachers!* Bloody teachers! The bloody teachers "may not like it." Why on earth not?'

'Well, they may think it's a bit unnatural.'

'*Unnatural!* What's "natural" about reading, anyway? It's not a "natural" activity. It's just the opposite. It's *civilized.*' (Eleanor liked to declare, though she did not do so now – Peter had heard it too often – that she greatly preferred Art to Nature.) 'The truth is,' she went on, 'that those ghastly prigs and eunuchs who go into the teaching trade can't bear any kind of excellence. Say "prodigy" or even "precocious" to them, and at once they seethe with hate because they're so utterly mediocre themselves. They're actually jealous of their bright pupils. Just as the "nice normal little kiddies" – silly halfwits! – are. Teachers! *Yawns!* I've never met such numbskulls.'

Peter, of course, was a lecturer, not a teacher, though Eleanor privately felt that lecturing at a provincial university was on the borderline of 'teaching'. Attacking teachers, was she attacking him, without admitting it? Nonsense! And, after all, she herself had taught for two years. When they first arrived, for Peter to take up an assistant lectureship – he was now a lecturer – she had taken a job at the local high school for girls.

*

If only she had been teaching the sixth form, instead of eleven-year-olds, she was sure it would have been less nasty. (It would have been better still if she could have taught at a special school for gifted children. Why were there no such schools in England?) As it was, to keep order she had needed unceasingly to exert the full force of her will against the class. The girls talked in silly, unnatural voices, and she suspected them of imitating the gestures she made when she was trying to explain a point. She often had difficulties, for she seemed unable to convey to her pupils things which she herself understood perfectly. (As she put it to herself, she had the food, but was unable to cook it suitably. She could have prepared *Sole Meunière* with *Pommes Anna*, but was incapable of fish and chips.)

Only one child had responded to her; of course, an unusually bright one. If only she could have devoted herself to this girl and left the drab majority to fend for itself (or to be dealt with by her dreary colleagues); but that was impossible. Nonetheless, she gave as much time and attention as she could to her 'cygnet', which she imagined sailing away down the river while the rest – stupid chickens – stayed clucking in the farmyard. The aptness of this comparison with Hans Andersen's 'Ugly Duckling' became evident at an interview with the headmistress, who said that she heard that the cygnet – *she* didn't call her that, of course – was having 'rather a bad time.'

'A bad time?'

'She's being bullied a bit apparently.' The woman hesitated; her tone was not unkind. 'For being *Mrs Posh's pet.*'

'Mrs Posh?'

'Yes, well . . .' The headmistress sounded embarrassed. She seemed to be trying to be tactful. 'I think that's a – very silly – nickname the children have given you, because of your . . . very *educated* voice. And I realize that it's difficult, especially for an inexperienced teacher, to avoid having favourites, but we must all try to avoid it, mustn't we?'

So the children, just like those hateful little fowls, had attacked the cygnet because they were its inferiors. But Eleanor realized that she must now treat the cygnet as if it were just one of the chickens. As a result, she felt as uneasy with it as with them.

If Teddy were able to read when he went to school, would he be a poor cygnet, attacked by pecky-peck chicks?

*

Pregnancy had released her. At that time, compared with *farmyard maintenance*, staying at home had seemed an idyll.

The university was in the centre of a growing town. New suburbs spread northward into the country. But on the south side, between a ragged stretch of garages and small factories and a canal, Eleanor found a small area of shabby 18th- and early 19th-century houses.

Their flat was here, in a crescent of four-storey houses, each of which had once been lived in by a single family. Now they were divided into flats, or let as rooms; two of them were boarding-houses. The crescent was quiet. Built on a raised stone terrace, approached by narrow flights of steps with iron railings, it overlooked a small neglected park. Most of the residents were elderly.

'Bit seedy, isn't it?' had been Peter's first comment. But, as Eleanor pointed out, the end house on the left, where she had found a second-floor flat, was quite spruce; the outside woodwork had definitely been repainted since the war.

Each storey of the house was a flat. On the ground floor lived the landlady; brisk, abrupt; a doctor's widow with three cats. Appropriately, the first floor, with its pagoda-roofed veranda (this, with wrought-iron screens marking the divisions between houses, ran the full length of the crescent) was occupied by two old sisters with an Eastern connection. (Eleanor, on her way up to the next storey, glimpsed fretted wood, a brass gong, a gilt-mounted watercolour of an un-English sunset.) A tall old lady with a vague smile, drifting scarves and gunmetal stockings, lived on the top floor.

'Doesn't the lady upstairs have to go through our hall to reach her flat?' was the first question Peter asked the landlady. (Typically bourgeois, thought Eleanor. *Yawns!*)

'Well, yes. But Miss Warburton seldom goes out. Never, in the evening. She's a very quiet person. Artistic, you know.'

'Oh I see,' Peter said, but glumly.

The flat on the second floor consisted of a big living-room, two medium-sized bedrooms, and a smaller room ('Your study, darling,' Eleanor said to Peter), which contained a huge flat-topped kneehole desk and a bookcase. There were large pieces of essential furniture – beds, chairs, tables, wardrobes – in all the rooms, and two gas fires, one in the living-room, the other in the 'study'. A regal bathroom held a very long bath with ball-and-claw feet, a proportionately large wash-basin, and a mahogany-seated lavatory on a platform. In what the landlady called the kitchenette, a deep alcove at the end of the passage, were a gas cooker, a sink – under a window overlooking the garden – a square wooden table, a Bentwood chair, and a hanging cupboard.

It was not the flat that Peter, on his own, would have chosen. But he had already learnt, with regret, that he was too junior to hope for one in a new staff block near the university – this news had delighted Eleanor – and when he lingered in the study, examining the desk and gas fire, she felt she would achieve her purpose. She could imagine – as Peter definitely could not – the flat garnished with pictures, shelves of books, new curtains, the kelim rugs on which she had already spent some of a small inheritance (her parents were both dead), and various little treasures. On the mantelpiece she visualized, one at each end, her two Sheffield urns, which were topped with acorns; the plating on them was so worn that the rose-brown copper underneath showed through. Peter had said that it would be nice, when they could afford it, to have these urns replated; repressing her shudder, she had let the remark pass. Now she thought of the tea things – unmatched pieces of china – she was collecting. When Peter had noticed the price of one cup and saucer, he had been astonished. 'But surely,' he said, 'for that price we could buy some nice bone china.'

'Oh, that cup and saucer are Worcester: more expensive than most of the others. Anyway, doing it this way is more fun.' She added, 'It's what's known as a harlequin set.'

'Oh, is it?' He had sounded cheered that it could be called a set at all.

His older sister, Wynefrede, thought the flat awful: 'So old-fashioned and difficult to clean. Why, it's the sort of place most of my women are longing to get out of.' Wynefrede gave the laugh Eleanor was sure she considered 'musical' (possibly intended – if so, mistakenly – to rob her remark of its offensiveness). Wynefrede was a social worker, the only one Eleanor had ever met, and not – as she had expected – a socialist, but a Young Conservative (surely due for superannuation?). Eleanor felt certain that she had chosen her career entirely from a desire to bully people.

Wynefrede said that a sound way of assessing if a woman were 'coping' was to examine the condition of her cooker. Eleanor imagined herself as one of Wynefrede's 'women', and pictured Wynefrede stooping to look inside her oven. She saw herself putting her foot in the centre of Wynefrede's flat, low-slung bottom, and pushing her inside, as Hansel and Gretel had pushed the witch. But a wretched 'woman' would, of course, be conscious of the fact that her income depended on Wynefrede's recommendations. Anyway, there wasn't room in a modern oven for a person; even for someone 'petite', which was how Wynefrede liked to describe herself. But sometimes just the thought of an oven (like that of the words, 'nice bone china') could put Eleanor in a rage. Conversely, the thought of Wynefrede's disapproval made her feel particularly contented with the flat. She had been happiest in it during her pregnancy.

*

No one went into the garden except an old man whom the landlady paid to cut the grass once a fortnight. That summer, Eleanor spent hours lolling there, in a deck-chair, under a tree, working her way through Proust.

She herself was planning a novella, about an unhappy love affair (what other subject was there?). It would be subtle, yet crystalline. But, each time she finished a page she tore it up. Reminded of the literary clerk in Camus' *The Plague*, who never advanced beyond one sentence, which he revised again and again, she decided that she would leave the novella to mature in her head, like the baby in her womb. (Perhaps it wasn't possible to produce a book and a baby at the same time.) She embarked on Gibbon, but progress was slow. Volume One lay open in her lap while she looked up into sun-blanched tremulous leaves, or watched cats fighting and mating – it was often hard to tell which – in the bushes.

Hungry or thirsty, she would lumber to her feet. (Curiously, despite its ungainliness, she felt unprecedentedly comfortable in her body.) Indoors was a crepuscular coolness, smelling of cats and fish on the ground floor, of dust and joss-sticks on the first. Their flat seemed to her to have no odour, but Peter sometimes stood sniffing by the stairs up to Miss Warburton's, saying he smelt gas; Eleanor felt sure that he imagined it.

During the summer vacation, Peter sometimes worked in his study, but usually in the college library, which she preferred. She enjoyed the emptiness of the flat, as she sat on the Bentwood chair in the kitchenette, eating pickles, fresh bread thickly spread with butter, and Welsh rabbit with a lot of mustard. Each morning she went down to a small cluster of local shops to renew her supplies of these foods, which she ate in vast quantities. Eating, she read novels; Gibbon was reserved for the garden.

When Peter came home, he didn't complain about cold food, partly because of the hot weather, but chiefly because of her 'condition'. This was a pleasure in itself, for she disliked cooking the food he enjoyed: 'meat and two veg', but especially potatoes (boiled, mashed, fried, roast or baked; he didn't care), and puddings. She had now found a mixture of diced vegetables, tinned in salad cream, which he liked with corned beef. She gave him this meal often.

Another pleasure of pregnancy was the licence to forget her appearance. She wore her three maternity dresses in turn. She believed that the weight she was putting on was due to the baby.

There was a delightful release from social contacts. None of Peter's colleagues lived in their neighbourhood; few of them owned cars, and the wives of those who did seldom knew how to drive. Eleanor had initially felt surprise that academics – even though they were provincial ones – chose such exclusively domesticated mates. Now a wife arrived by bus with the present of a baby's dress; she offered the pattern for it to Eleanor, who could not help looking startled. Eleanor had never sewn or knitted a garment in her life, and did not intend to start now. On guard against being 'Mrs Posh', she gave effusive thanks, but the woman did not visit her again.

Another wife, Mrs Graves, whose husband was the Senior Lecturer in Peter's department, brought a book on Natural Childbirth to a departmental 'social evening' at which men stood in one part of the room, discussing their work, and women sat in another babbling about domesticities and diseases. (Before her pregnancy, Eleanor, on principle, had joined the men, but now she could not be bothered.)

Mrs Graves, who had three children under eight, talked as though being a mother was a profession, for which giving birth was the qualification: Natural Childbirth led to good exam results. On Eleanor's monthly visit to Dr Greene she asked him about it, and he said it was a fad. After all, as a doctor, he presumably knew. She was relieved not to have to do the exercises. It was nicer to recline in her deck-chair, looking at the leaves and the angry or ardent cats, reading a single noble sentence from *The Decline and Fall*, dallying with the idea of her novella. She hardly ever thought about the baby.

Having it was more painful than she had expected, but towards the end of the process she took blissful gulps of chloroform. As a result she pushed too hard; stitches were needed. But the baby was pretty, even just after it was born; which she had not expected, especially in the case of a boy. It had violet eyes, though they soon faded to blue.

Some women had their babies at home. She would have disliked that: not only because something might go wrong but because she would never have been looked after as she was in hospital (Peter was hopeless, domestically). In the hospital they had not let her move from bed for ten days, though in some places, Eleanor had heard, they were now forcing women up after only a day or two, and making them change and bath their babies. The matron of this hospital, thank goodness, was old-fashioned. Eleanor would not have minded being a mother in the days when women – though not the working-class – stayed in bed for a whole month.

Hospital life had a pleasantly impersonal quality; she was free to think and read. The chatter of the other three women in the ward did not disturb her. (It was better to share with three women, than with one, who would undoubtedly have nagged at her to talk.) Every four hours (except at two in the morning, when she had supposed – until she came home – that the babies 'slept through'), a nurse brought the baby to be fed.

To her astonishment she enjoyed breast-feeding, which she continued for six months; she did not even object to the feed at two in the morning. When the baby started to suck, she felt a pang in the womb.

(After a few minutes she usually picked up a book.) A baby was not as difficult as she had imagined. Teddy slept a lot. She didn't even mind changing his nappy, though she felt sure that, if she had been obliged to change some other baby's, she would have vomited.

It was when Teddy was six months old that Peter, who had spoken several times of the amusing new lecturer in Classics, first brought Julian, unexpectedly, to the flat.

She had finished giving Teddy his six pm feed. She sat in an armchair in the living-room; he dozed in her lap. She was wearing one of her old maternity dresses. (She had found, when she came out of hospital, that her normal clothes did not fit. To her surprise, the extra weight she had gained had not been merely that of Teddy.)

Peter brought Julian, who was very handsome, into the living-room. Julian gazed at Eleanor and Teddy. Then, arms upstretched – tilted back from the elbows, the fingers extended – as in a Nativity painting of an astonished shepherd, he reverently exclaimed, 'Ah – *motherhood!*'

'That's right. Old Mother Hood: parent of Little Red Riding,' Eleanor said at once, in Mrs Posh's voice.

He burst out laughing, and became her only friend.

*

Peter had been keen for her to make friends with Deirdre, the wife of Norman Bollard, a lecturer in Economics. Deirdre had produced a daughter – always referred to as Baby Linda – six weeks before Eleanor had Teddy. Peter felt that, in these circumstances, the two women would have something in common. This showed, Eleanor thought, how little he knew her.

Deirdre had a heavy fringe and wore dirndl skirts; she was interested in what she called 'mothercraft'. When not talking about this – in connection with Baby Linda – she spoke of recipes dependent on cornflour and margarine, or of how many minutes Norman – a great gangling bore – liked his eggs boiled. Deirdre usually referred to Norman simply as 'he', as if he were the only man in the world. (Which of course, for her, he was. What a thought! *Yawns!*)

It irritated Peter when Eleanor called Deirdre 'Dreardre' and Norman 'the Norm'. It amused Julian, who had not met the Bollards ('Or did I glimpse the Norm once, bowed over the *Listener* in the SCR?'), and for whom they became a legend.

The Bollards were too earnest to be good material for the pseudo-meter; it was more fun to grade them on the hormonic scale.

'I think the Norm's neut,' said Eleanor.

'Oh nonsense. What about Baby Linda?'

'Well, perhaps plus two. And Dreardre plus one.'

'Old Mother Craft? She *must* be minus.'

'I think all that's really a substitute for Meccano. You should see her moustache.'

'A moustache on a woman is considered a sign of beauty in Spain.'

'Dreardre's wouldn't be.'

Wynefrede, in contrast to the Bollards, made the pseudometer rocket (her name, her 'petite-ness' – pseudomax, surely? – and the fresh flowers she simply couldn't do without), but was harder to grade on the hormonic scale. Her bossiness demanded a plus mark, but her trilling laugh, her dainty ways, seemed to establish her in the minuses. 'And those poor little legs,' Eleanor added. 'Even though she's so *petite*, I can never think how they bear her weight.'

Eleanor and Julian had this sort of conversation in Peter's absence, when Julian dropped in to see her in the afternoon or early evening. When all three of them were together, it was different.

*

They sat round the living-room table. Julian had provided two bottles of red wine. They had eaten Eleanor's casserole of skirt of beef. This contained garlic and a bottle of stout; when she had tried it out the week before, Peter had come into the kitchen just as she was pouring in the Guinness.

'What on earth are you doing, Eleanor? Beer in the food? I've never heard of *that* before. Of course I know that, in France, they *cook with wine*' – he sounded puritanical about this – 'but I've never heard of cooking with *beer*.'

She had tried to reassure him. All the same, he had approached the dish with doubt, poking at it with his fork – which always maddened her – and eating less of it than he would have done if he had not known about the suspect ingredient, though he made up for this with mashed potato.

Tonight, however, after Julian expressed enthusiasm for the casserole, Peter had eaten it with relish. Even the substitution of rice for potatoes, which usually made him unhappy, did not seem to disturb him. Julian was an excellent gastronomic influence on Peter. In Julian's company, Peter devoured foods which would at other times have aroused his fear and revulsion.

'Women aren't creative,' Julian was saying now, 'but they can be marvellous interpreters. Acting . . . singing . . . dancing . . . playing musical instruments – though possibly the *very* greatest instrumentalists are male.'

'Don't you think you're being too generous?' Eleanor said. 'After all, Shakespeare wrote his women's parts for boys. Perhaps they acted them better than women do. Perhaps Donna Elvira should ideally be sung by a counter-tenor.'

'How her eyes flash!' Julian exclaimed.

'Yes,' said Peter. 'To think that Norman Bollard told me that Deirdre thinks she's "nice, but very quiet and shy."'

'Oh no!' Julian laughed. 'I can't believe it. "Nice"! Our Eleanor! Our serpent of old Nile . . . or perhaps she's even one of the asps. As for "quiet and shy," she's a positive Ella Gabbler!'

It was understandable, thought Eleanor, that Dreardre, whom she could never be bothered to talk to, found her quiet; and it was charitable – more likely, stupid – of her to attribute this to shyness. In fact, Eleanor was often quiet. Alone with Peter, the effort frequently didn't seem worth while. Yet with Julian she always chattered away like mad.

'What about novelists?' she said now. 'What about Jane Austen, the Brontës, George Eliot, Colette?'

'Jane Austen? I admit she's lively, but what bores she writes about. As far as I'm concerned, the Brontës just produced turgid sexual fantasies. George Eliot was an old windbag. Colette is charming, of course, but so slight. In fact I sometimes wonder if, apart from the *giants* – Tolstoy, Flaubert, Stendhal – the novel isn't essentially trivial. But I agree that there *are* women novelists. How about painters and composers, though?'

There was a good French woman painter, but all Eleanor could remember about her was that she had been Utrillo's mother. As for composers, she could summon up only Dame Ethel Smyth.

'And *thinkers*?' asked Julian. 'Philosophers, scientists?'

'Madame Curie,' said Eleanor, but the words were drowned by his, 'Absolutely none!'

'None at all,' echoed Peter. Then he said, 'Don't look so crusty, darling. Men create *things*, but women create life. Women *live*!'

'*Living*?' she almost shouted, then added, lower: '*We leave that to our servants.*'

Both men were laughing. 'That *must* be a quotation,' said Julian. 'Who said it?'

'Someone called Villiers de L'Isle-Adam,' she said. 'A *man*, inevitably.'

She saw that Julian was looking, with surprise, at her hands, and she realized that she was clenching and unclenching them. She was also grinding her teeth: a dreadful habit, recently acquired. She reached for her packet of ten Craven A.

'How about some coffee?' Peter said.

We leave that to our servants. But it was with a sense of relief that she went to make it. Putting on the kettle she saw that her hands were shaking. She took the jug from the cupboard. As she started to measure ground coffee into it, Julian came down the passage; she saw him reflected in the window over the sink. He put his hands on her shoulders. She had to make an effort not to lean back and rub her hair – she had washed it that afternoon – against his cheek.

'Did I tell you,' she said, 'that when Wynefrede's on her own, she has two proper courses for dinner every single day. She says that living alone's no excuse for lowering one's standards. Just the opposite, in fact. Oh, one must keep up one's standards! Eight on the pseudometer, I think. She lays the table nicely, with a vase of those fresh flowers of hers on it, and she never reads at meals because then one doesn't appreciate the food. Pseudomax!'

'What do these gourmet feasts consists of?'

'Oh, one lamb chop or one fillet of plaice, with one large potato or two small ones, and a green or yellow vegetable – she took a course in nutrition for that job of hers. Probably something like a baked apple or pudding, or "sweet" as she calls it. Small helpings – no, she says "portions". She says, "I'm rather a small eater, you know," and I do indeed, after watching her toy with my cooking!'

'Darling, what a divinely cold eye you always cast.' Julian's hands were still on her shoulders.

'On Sunday, she cooks herself a teeny joint. Lamb one week, beef the next. (She thinks pork's indigestible.) And she makes it last three days. Hot on Sunday, cold on Monday, Shepherd's Pie on Tuesday. Sometimes I think the pseudometer may break.' Eleanor's voice was trembling.

'Tell me, sweetie, are you feeling all right? I think Peter and I were being rather boorish, in there. Of course I know that *your* novel, when you write it, will be something *quite* extraordinary.'

'Oh no, essentially trivial!'

'Silly girl! I was just rambling on. I never believe a word I'm saying.' He began to massage her shoulder. A glow suffused her body, as well as her face which she kept turned away.

Picking up the kettle carefully, in order not to dislodge his hands, she poured boiling water onto the coffee in the jug.

She stirred it. 'Caught you in the act!' She jumped at the sound of Peter's voice. 'Making passes at my wife again, Julian?'

'Oh definitely. Mad in pursuit, as ever.' Casually removing his hands, he didn't sound at all embarrassed. He must be very experienced, she decided.

She put three cups and saucers on the tray: the gold-flowered Worcester for Julian, pink Staffordshire roses for Peter, a blue and white Chinese tea-bowl for herself. (Julian appreciated her 'harlequin set'; she had been pleased when he said so to Peter, who admired his taste.)

'Let me carry that tray,' said Julian. As they returned to the living-room she wondered if Peter knew anything about Julian's sex-life. If he knew, he probably wouldn't tell her, because men always ganged up against women. Women's occasional temporary alliances against men were different. Men liked to feel that they were united by bonds of brotherhood, but who had ever heard – except in terms of nuns – of sisterhood? It would be an improbable addition to the Hood family.

*

Being with Julian was always fun: an interruption in such silly days of living. (*We leave that to our servants.*) Factory work was, she had heard, repetitive, yet nut after nut, bolt after bolt went – clean and new – into the world, never to be seen again. At home, the same objects – remorselessly deteriorating as they endlessly cycled – always returned, requiring attention, to the same pair of hands.

Most women didn't seem to feel the horror of it. Dreardre had once mentioned that a pile of warm-smelling freshly ironed clothes gave her 'a lovely sense of achievement!' Eleanor never ironed.

She sent sheets and towels to the laundry, and Peter's newer shirts were all nylon. They didn't look too bad, as long as he didn't wear a vest that showed through underneath.

'But I get cold.'

'Wear a jersey, darling.'

'That can be too hot.'

'Darling, one must suffer to be beautiful.'

He complained that his older – non-nylon – shirts and his handkerchiefs – why couldn't he use tissues? – looked crumpled. She told him that the creases – as she found with her own clothes, and Teddy's – soon shook out. 'Anyway,' she said, 'academics should look a trifle dishevelled. It shows they're sincere.'

During the previous year, she had gone alone to London, on a day return, for a matinee of *Look Back in Anger*, to find out what all the fuss was about. It was a Saturday, and she told Peter he must look after Teddy, whether he liked the idea or not. (In the event, Peter and Teddy spent the day with the Bollards, being waited on by Dreardre.) Eleanor had enjoyed going to London by herself. She took a taxi from the station to Hatchard's, where she looked at the new books till it was time for an early lunch: tomato sandwiches and iced mint tea at Fortnum's.

In the theatre, from first to last, she was possessed by hatred of the sneering, whining layabout, Jimmy Porter. She sympathized with his wife: poor Alison couldn't help being upper middle-class; Porter seemed to think it was her fault. But why was she so passive? Why did she spend her time *ironing* while Porter read the paper and nagged and bullied her? Why didn't she stand up to him, as her friend Helena did? But then Helena surrendered to his – incomprehensible – charm. With what result? *She* replaced Alison at the ironing-board.

Eleanor had returned from *Look Back in Anger* with her determination never to iron reinforced. But other tasks had to be coped with.

One found one could manage by doing things in a special order, which must always be the same. And there must be a verbal accompaniment. This too must never vary.

It was strange that one had read a description of this in, of all places, *The Wind in the Willows*. It was where the Rat distributed weapons for the battle of Toad Hall: 'Here's-a-sword-for-the-Rat, here's-a-sword-for-the-Mole, here's-a-sword-for-the-Toad, here's-a-sword-for-the-Badger! Here's-a-pistol-for-the-Rat, here's-a-pistol-for-the-Mole, here's-a-pistol-for-the-Toad, here's-a-pistol-for-the-Badger!'

When one laid the table, one said: 'Here's-a-little-knife-for-Eleanor, here's-a-little-knife-for-Peter! Here's-a-big-knife-for-Eleanor, here's-a-big-knife-for-Peter! Here's-a-little-spoon-for-Eleanor, here's-a-little-spoon-for-Peter! Here's-a-little-fork-for-Eleanor, here's-a-little-fork-for-Peter! Here's-a-big-fork-for-Eleanor, here's-a-big-fork-for-Peter!'

It was important to get things in the correct order – arranged from right to left – because otherwise one had to gather up all the cutlery, and start again. The name for the whole procedure – the doing and saying – was 'Making One's Lists'.

One had to 'Make One's Lists' with more and more things, nowadays: making beds, washing up, putting things away.

Teddy – who so resented her silences, especially if she were reading – seemed to like 'One's Lists'. Perhaps he thought she was talking to him. There had been a day when one was 'Making One's Lists' with the washing-up: 'Here's-a-plate-in-the-rack, here's-a-plate-in-the-rack! Here's-a-cup-on-the-draining-board, here's-a-cup-on-the-draining-board! Here's-a-saucer –'

'Da da da,' shouted Teddy. She swung round, and there was Peter. Shocked, she dropped the saucer (Peter's pink Staffordshire roses; not one of her favourites) on the floor. He had *caught one at it*.

'Oh,' he said. 'So sorry if I startled you, darling.'

She crouched to pick up the broken china. When she looked up, Peter – laughing – was swinging Teddy in the air. He had thought she was talking to Teddy. (But what would he have thought if Teddy hadn't been there?) She felt afraid. 'Making One's Lists' had been interrupted, and this boded ill. They wouldn't work now. It was Peter's presence that made her ask herself what she meant by 'work'. She couldn't answer. One mustn't ask or answer. It would only make things worse.

She said, 'Have you had a good day?'

'Oh yes. Fine.' Peter sounded surprised. He knew Eleanor considered such conversation banal ('*Yawns!*'). Once, when he had asked about *her* day, she had said, 'Oh, please *don't*. If anything interesting happened to me – ha ha – I'd be bursting with the glad tidings.' He had sighed, and turned his drooping head away. That had been one of the times – formerly quite frequent; now very rare – when she thought, *Poor old Peter*. She had approached him, and had run her hand over his hair. Surprised, he had grinned, but like a nervous dog.

At the beginning of her marriage, the thought of *poor old Peter*, if it did not 'galvanize', could at least activate her. But nowadays she usually felt '*Yawns!*', or worse. There was so much one had to do at night before one went to bed. There were many objects in the living-room to put at the correct angles – in the correct relationships – to each other. Often, by the time one had finished, Peter was asleep.

It wasn't her fault, Eleanor felt, that Peter fell asleep. When he was awake, she never refused. That would have been against her principles.

*

After Teddy's nap, and after she had strapped him into his pushchair, and wheeled him round and round the little park where budding green always looked spurious, came the worst time of the day. Peter's adjective, 'seedy', which she had rejected for the crescent, seemed precise when applied to the late afternoon of a 'young mother': milk spilt and a spoon hammered on the tray of the high chair; crumbs round Teddy's mouth and on the floor; jam-stained bib; banana smeared on clutching hands; daylight inadequate, but electricity garish; dull evening ahead and silly day behind.

When Teddy had finished tea, she wiped his face and hands; he did not like this. She unstrapped him from the high chair, and put him in his play-pen, with his bear and his bricks. Usually, for a few minutes, he would seem content, but would then start to whimper. She put down the book she had snatched up, and went over to the pen.

At one stage he had been delighted when she rattled the row of beads, set between the bars. Now he found this tedious. (*'Yawns!'* She could understand that.) She must lean over, pick up the bear and make it walk towards him, or arrange a tower of bricks for him to knock down with one blow. But these were delaying tactics. The moment soon arrived when she must reach down, and raise him from captivity. At this time of day he felt particularly heavy.

Recently, at tea with Eileen Graves – Ken Graves was Senior Lecturer in Politics, and could influence Peter's career – there had been a moment when a saucepan of milk boiled over. Eileen, hurrying to the rescue, had transferred the small baby – number four – she was holding, into Eleanor's arms. The baby was very light, as Teddy had once been. Eleanor sat holding it rather stiffly on her lap. Suddenly, and quite involuntarily, she lowered her cheek onto its soft head. The feeling – there was also a smell of Baby Powder and of baby – produced an odd dragging pain under her ribcage. Quickly, she raised her head. As soon as possible she handed the baby – it was so light! – back to Eileen who, looking at her quizzically, asked 'Are you aching?'

'Aching?'

'Yes. For another baby.'

'Oh, *no!*' Eleanor said. When Eileen laughed, and gave her another look, she felt irritated, but did not show it.

Eleanor was never going to have another baby. As people said when they reminisced about the war, she had 'done her bit'. Everywoman – used in a general sense, like Everyman – should do it once; but that was enough.

When Peter talked of more children, she used delaying tactics – as with Teddy in his playpen – and, of course, contraception. She said, 'Let's wait a bit longer', rather than that she was never going to have another; which she did not say to Eileen Graves. Instead, she smiled, for the sake of Peter's career in Politics.

Peter could not be called a politician – as a lecturer in Economics could be called an economist – because Politics had nothing to do with politics. But he seemed to love his strange abstractions. He also enjoyed the academic life: he was keen on his research, and liked lecturing.

Perhaps she herself might not have disliked lecturing, as opposed to teaching. Lecturers did not have that awful interaction with their students which teachers had with their pupils. Lecturers just stood up and speechified. Eleanor knew she would not have been able to lecture from notes, as Peter did; she would have had to write down every word. But, once her lectures were written, she could have delivered them again and again. Although Peter thought this 'mentally slovenly', many lecturers – like vicars with tattered sets of sermons – gave identical lectures every year. She could see no objection: after all, the students were different each time. Anyway, Peter changed his lectures every year, as well as toiling at his thesis. It was probably very praiseworthy; though Eleanor felt more sympathy with Julian, who said lecturing was a 'chore', and was not writing a thesis. 'I've no intention,' he said, 'of adding to those mountains of academic waste-paper. I could only write about Horace, and it would kill my devotion to him.' He smiled, and murmured, '*O fons Bandusiae!*'

When Julian spoke of academic waste-paper, or the chore of lectures, Eleanor laughed, but Peter frowned. Afterwards, Peter told her that Julian's lectures were said to be outstanding, and that he took a lot of trouble with his students. 'Although, of course,' he added, 'there aren't very many of them. Classics is rather a dead-end subject nowadays.'

There was a sheen of complacency on these words. Politics, apparently – even though it had nothing to do with politics – was not a 'dead-end subject'. However Julian, with his private income, did not have to worry as Peter would have had to if he had been a classicist.

Undeniably, Peter was hard-working and conscientious. Was it unfair to wonder sometimes if he were so often late in the evening in order to avoid the play hour?

Released from his pen, Teddy was a tornado. She must be patient. This was known to be a difficult age. He would improve. (Thomas Babington Macaulay: *From the time that he was three years old, he read incessantly . . .*) But how wrong she had been to imagine that small babies were the most difficult. Teddy had been easy to manage then. Now, when she picked him up and put him in her lap, he fought free. He did not nestle down, as he had done on the first occasion Julian visited them:

'Ah – *motherhood!*'

*

It had been a few days after first meeting Julian that she had obtained the Dexedrin pills from Dr Greene, and had started to wean Teddy. Perhaps it was her happy mood that had made the weaning so easy.

At the time she had attributed her happiness to Julian. Now she conjectured that the pills might have been partly responsible for it.

At four o'clock this afternoon she had taken the third pill of the day.

Ever since this morning when, opening her make-up drawer further than usual – with a particularly vicious jerk – she had chanced upon the pills and taken one on impulse, everything had been easy: especially so this evening, after the third pill. Teddy had loved it when, barking like a dog, she crawled round the floor with him, and lay on her back, holding him in the air above her. (He did not seem as heavy as usual.) When she put him down, she rolled over, and leant on one elbow, laughing, and dabbing at the dimple in his chin. The time passed quickly. Afterwards, when she bathed him, she did not care how much water he splashed on the floor.

When she had put him in his cot, he fell asleep almost at once. Now, with the March wind rattling the windows, she felt wide awake. She remembered Dr Greene telling her that the pills had this effect. There was no reason for her to go to bed early, though Peter was out (but she would like to seem to be asleep on his return).

This evening he was at a Faculty of Arts meeting. (Why was Politics an Art? Peter sometimes – pompously – referred to it as Political Science.) She looked at her watch. Eight o'clock: that was when the meeting started. Before it, Peter had gone for what Eileen called 'a bite of supper' with the Graveses. Apparently Ken Graves wanted to discuss one or two points connected with the meeting. She would have thought they could have done that at the university, during the day; but anyway it was convenient for Peter not to have to make the double bus-journey home, and delightful for her not to have to boil, mash, fry, roast or bake potatoes, especially as she did not feel hungry. She had eaten nothing all day.

She was smoking her third packet of ten Craven A. Peter – who did not smoke – often told her that ten a day were quite enough ('Listen to that cough of yours'), but she never smoked less than twenty. Thank heaven for her own little income; though it became smaller each year, because she kept on selling shares.

She lit a cigarette. Usually she would have left the living-room at least three times during the past hour: to check, each time, if the door of Teddy's room were ajar, if the bathroom light were out, if the kitchen tap were turned off. (These habits resembled 'Making One's Lists'. Even when one knew, for instance, that one had turned off the tap, one had to make quite sure. One couldn't be too careful.) Tonight, however, she cared about none of these things.

Usually, also, in her present circumstances, she would have felt on edge.

Lately, she had suffered from night terrors: worse than any fears she had experienced as a child. Nowadays she sometimes thought that the happiest aspect of marriage was that she did not have to sleep in a room alone.

The spotted stomach of a tabby cat: creamy, with uneven darker patches. The cat must obviously be lying on its back. Surely nothing could be more agreeable than the soft, spotted fur of a cat? But now the spotted area was receding rapidly. (It was moving away from her; not she from it.)

Now she saw that it was not a cat's stomach, but a country; the creaminess was parched earth, and the dark patches were scrubby bushes. And suddenly, from very far away, from very high up, she saw herself. The country was all round her. She stood among the dark bushes and bleached earth, which were endless.

When she awoke, shouting or screaming, from this recurrent dream, Peter was always very kind.

Even before bedtime, she never felt at her best when she was alone in the flat after dark. Usually, remembering Julian's remark, 'This house is full of witches,' she would have shivered; but not tonight. Perhaps the only witch was she, Eleanor thought now, and laughed aloud.

Lord Chesterfield had considered laughter vulgar. Even during the present century, upper-class people, when photographed, never laughed, never gestured, seldom even smiled. They did not look at the camera or, if members of a group, at their companions. All this was the antithesis of Julian, she reflected; his fluidity, his spontaneity were the converse of that hateful rigidity. His exuberant gestures, his shiny smile – his teeth were very white – and his frequent, rather high laugh: all these were evidence that he was free. So, of course, was his money. She wondered why he bothered to lecture at a provincial university, and also why he was domesticated.

Julian's 'Georgian artisan's cottage', as the estate agent had described it ('Am I a Georgian artisan, do you think, darling?' Julian had once asked her) was exquisite. Eleanor thought of it as a jewel-box: a rich setting in which beautiful objects were perfectly arranged and maintained. A charwoman came every morning, and a gardener once a week, but Julian seemed to devote much time – as Eleanor would never have done – to the house: polishing objects which the char-woman was not allowed to touch, and snipping at the refulgent garden. He was also a dedicated cook. Where Eleanor trusted to a tablespoon and a pint milk-bottle, he weighed solids on a machine, and measured liquids in a jug, marked with tiny divisions. Where she liked to do her cooking in one spurt, he followed complicated recipes with various stages that often involved long periods of waiting.

She wished that Julian would drop in now, but knew he would not. He never called at this time. He visited them in the evening only when he came to dinner, or fetched them to have dinner with him, in his cottage, or sometimes in a restaurant. (She enjoyed sitting in a restaurant between Julian and Peter, both good-looking: Julian dark and Peter fair.) If only they had possessed a telephone, she could have rung up, and invited Julian round. And then . . .

She imagined that making love with Julian would be different in kind from making love with Peter, though she did not specify details. There would be a kiss, and then they would be in a bed. But what bed?

She had not been into Julian's bedroom, but had passed its open door on her way to his bathroom. His bed was bigger than a single, but smaller than a double. It had a curved, gilded back-rest, and a stiff, heavy, ecclesiastical-looking counterpane: deep red, and gold-embroidered. It would be uncomfortable to lie on, and removing it did not fit into the scene where she and Julian *sank onto* a bed, as people did when they were *carried away*. A picture of Julian physically carrying her she dismissed at once. He was only an inch or two taller than she, and his build was so slight that they probably weighed about the same. No, but *carried away*, in the metaphorical sense: that was what she was determined to be.

The alternative to Julian's bed, of course, was the 'marital couch'. She visualized Teddy asleep and Peter away for the night; but where would Peter have gone, and why? Perhaps his father had had a stroke or a heart attack; that would be ideal. If it happened, Peter – a devoted son – would rush to Bournemouth immediately.

In such circumstances, Julian might well call in the evening, to cheer her up. But, in such circumstances (though the stroke or heart attack would not, of course, prove fatal) mightn't it (and she and Julian would not yet know that Peter's father would recover) be in rather bad taste to . . . ? What would Julian feel?

She could never precisely define Julian's attitude to Peter. It definitely wasn't '*Yawns!*'. It was friendly. His tone was different, when he spoke to Peter, from when he spoke to her, when it was teasing. (That, of course, was because of the sexual element.)

Sometimes she tried to imagine being married to Julian, but never succeeded. Why should he want a wife? Certainly not for domestic purposes. And she could not imagine him as a father. He was nice to Teddy, but quickly sated with his company. (She did not blame him for this. Why, she herself was often bored by Teddy. As for other people's children: *yawns!* She could never distinguish between them or remember their names, let alone their ages.) The solution was obvious. Marriage was 'out'. She and Julian would simply have a tremendous affair.

She lit another cigarette, and looked at her watch again. The time was twenty-five past eight. Her heart was beating in an odd irregular way. Now, the splendid idea occurred to her. Peter would not be back before eleven. Why shouldn't she visit Julian this evening, and see how the situation would develop? She knew the answer to this question: because of Teddy.

When Eleanor and Peter went out, they arranged in advance for one of Peter's students to baby-sit. There was no one in the house whom they could ask. The old sisters' lights were always out by eight pm. Miss Warburton was too vague. (When Eleanor met her – rarely; it was true that she seldom went out – on the landing, her smile seemed sightless.) As for the landlady, her manner was so abrupt that Eleanor would not have dared to ask her.

Dreardre Bollard never employed baby-sitters. She only went out when she could take Baby Linda with her. She liked to quote her favourite authority, a Dr Bowlby, who said that leaving a child under three was 'a major operation, only to be undertaken for good and sufficient reason, and, when undertaken, to be planned with great care.' Eleanor suggested that Dr Bowlby referred to going away on a trip, not out for an evening, but Dreardre said the principle was the same. Eleanor believed that, even with regard to a trip, Dr Bowlby's view was ridiculous. She thought of people of past generations who had been left with relations, or with nannies, while their parents jaunted off for months, and who had turned out perfectly well: far more interesting, she was sure, than Baby Linda would ever be.

Why shouldn't she leave Teddy on his own, for once? It was not as if the house were empty, or as if anyone would want to burgle the crescent, or as if he ever awoke at this time of the evening; she could not remember the last occasion when he had done so. Propping her cigarette on the lip of the ashtray, she went along to his room. Tiptoeing in, she saw him, in the light from the passage, fast asleep: flushed, with one arm flung up behind his head.

In her own room, she worked out a timetable. It would take about half an hour to reach Julian's cottage: though in the town, it was on their side of it. She would be there soon after nine. She could stay until half-past ten, when Julian would drive her home. If he were out, it would be 'a sign' (and she would have plenty of time to walk home). As she thought about all this, she changed her underclothes, but not her outer ones (in case Peter arrived back just after her). She put on make-up and what was left – quite a lot – of her bottle of Chanel 5. Peter had given it to her. He said it was his favourite scent, but she thought it was the only one he knew.

She took her coat from the hook on the landing, and checked that the key of the front door was in the pocket. At the top of the stairs, she thought she smelt a whiff of the gas that Peter imagined escaped from Miss Warburton's flat. She sniffed, but now all she could smell was Chanel 5. Quietly she went downstairs. The old sisters' flat was in darkness, but on the ground floor, a line of light showed under the landlady's sitting-room door. Silently she opened the front door, and closed it softly behind her.

Hurrying down the steps from the terrace to the pavement, and then – on the opposite side of the road to the shadowy park – down the hill, she had a floating feeling; as if the only thing that held her down was the weight of her uneven heart-beat. The great gusts of wind that shook the trees seemed to bear her along.

Down on the main road, with its deserted garages and warehouses – very few cars passed – she thought that she would normally have been afraid. Once she heard footsteps behind her, and increased her pace, not daring to look round, but after a few minutes she heard the footsteps turn into a side street and die away.

What would she say when Julian opened the door? She decided that she would play it by ear, as he sometimes played Noël Coward. He was in. When she reached the corner of the row of neat little houses, the first thing she saw was his white car. There were lights on, and she could hear a soprano. He loved Italian opera. Perhaps he had visitors, listening to records.

She rang the bell, and waited for what seemed a minute or two, her heart keeping up that fast, irregular beat. The music continued, very loud. Perhaps he had not heard her. She rang again. This time, after a few seconds, there were footsteps in the passage.

He had a door-chain, which always surprised her; she did not know anyone else who had one. He peered over it, then looked astonished. 'Eleanor!' he exclaimed. He undid the chain. 'Come in.' He was looking past her. 'Where's Peter?' Then, 'You're alone? Is something wrong?'

'No,' she said, and then, 'Have you got visitors?'

'Not a soul. I was just listening to some music. A quiet evening at home. Well, not *very* quiet.' As the soprano soared, he laughed. He pressed himself against the wall of the narrow passage to let her past. 'You must explain this mysterious visit. There's really nothing wrong, you say?'

'No,' she said. 'Well, not *really*.'

In his little drawing-room, the chair he had been sitting in – next to the record-player – was dented. The cover of *Traviata* was on the floor beside it. The other chair and the yellow velvet sofa were immaculately smooth. 'Sorry to have interrupted your concert,' she said.

'Not at all. Let me turn it off.' Extremely carefully, he lifted the stylus from the record. Then he switched off the machine. In the silence she felt suddenly embarrassed.

'A drink?' he asked. 'And do sit down.' She sat on the sofa. 'Whisky? Brandy? A glass of port?'

'Oh port, please.'

'What on earth have you done with Peter and Teddy?' He took a bottle and two glasses from a corner cupboard which had a brass railing and a marble top.

'Peter's at a meeting. I got one of the old ladies to baby-sit.' She couldn't admit that she had left Teddy alone.

'One of the witches? Good heavens! That's a new development. I hope the poor child doesn't wake up. *Life-long* traumas I should think, if he does.'

'Oh, I'm sure he won't. He never does.'

Julian put her drink on a little table next to her, beside the figure of a harlequin (Nymphenburg, he had said). Smiling, he looked down at her, his eyebrows raised. 'Well now, tell me all. You're looking so pale and wide-eyed, darling. Like Maud or Marianna or the Lady of Shallott.'

'I didn't realize you knew so much Tennyson.'

'Yes, it's fearfully unfashionable, isn't it? So why are you looking so Tennysonian?'

'I've been feeling,' she improvised, 'fearfully depressed. I don't know why.'

He shook his head. '*Povera* Eleanora! I really do sympathize. I have *the* most appalling glooms at times – you wouldn't believe. Drink up your nice port, and unburden your soul. Julian will be the great healer, like old Father Time.'

He put out his hand, and ran it over her hair. She was on her feet, at once, clutching him. She felt him stiffen, but held on tight. She raised her face, and grabbed his mouth with hers.

He pushed her back onto the sofa with such violence that she bounced. 'Oh Christ,' he said. He took a step back. His shoulders were hunched as if he were cold. She had never imagined that she repelled him, but that was the only explanation for his expression.

Visibly, he gathered himself together, with a rapid shake of his head. She sat up, back rigid, on the sofa. Then his shoulders slackened, and his features relaxed. He was himself again: whatever that was.

'Darling Eleanor,' he said now, 'you know how I adore you. This is frightfully mortifying for us both.' His voice was kind. He went on, 'I never imagined that you didn't *know*. I thought you were so sophisticated. My serpent of old Nile, casting your cold eye, and so on. I never imagined that you didn't understand – how shall I put it? – my position on the hormonic scale.'

She realized that her mouth was hanging open, and closed it. Looking at her, head on one side, he went on. 'Need I say more? Yes, from your expression, I fear I need. To be frank, darling, if I had to choose between you and Peter . . . you wouldn't be the one.'

His words were flowing now. 'Not a word to himself, as the Irish say. I don't know if *he* guesses, though I was so sure that you did. I've always thought he avoided thinking about it, perhaps. If he acknowledged it, he might feel he ought to be shocked. Our Peter definitely has a conventional streak. As it is, you and I can simply forget this little episode, as if it never happened. And of course when I said I'd choose Peter rather than you, I just meant because he's a he, not because I've got a *thing* about him. Fortunately, as he's so utterly hetero! Straight as the proverbial die, whatever that may be. It's part of his charm, of course, in a way.' She saw that he was enjoying talking about Peter. 'Really,' he went on, 'it's his quality of sheer sweetness that I like about him, not that he belongs to the right sex. Or the wrong one, as you'd say it was, for me. Of course no one could call *you* sweet, dearest Eleanor, and it's part of *your* special charm that one can't. It makes you so absolutely the ideal chum. But chums are chums, and lovers are lovers. *Chums and Lovers*. Rather an improvement on Lawrence's title, one feels.'

He was drawing on his resources to give her a chance to rally, to ease a restoration of the *status quo ante*. But was she capable of taking advantage of this? Her eyes roamed wildly. The harlequin on the table next to her wore a frightening black mask, and lounged in an attitude parodying that of a woman holding a child. But what the harlequin rocked in its arms was not a child, but a puppy (it had a muzzle instead of a face) which was swaddled in a flower-patterned shawl. Screaming, 'Ga-ah-ah-ah-ah,' she snatched the figure up and hurled it across the room. It smashed against the door.

At once, Julian was over by the fragments. He gathered them like pebbles till, realizing the damage was irrevocable, he relinquished them with a wasted gentleness that made her stop screaming and start laughing. At this, he stood upright, stepped towards her, and slapped first her left cheek, with his right palm, and then, her right cheek, with the back of the same hand. She had previously believed that people did this only in films. 'Cunt!' he exclaimed. She had never heard this word spoken, only read it, in an illegal foreign edition of *Lady Chatterley's Lover*.

Her face felt burning. Julian's was white. 'Hysteria,' he shouted. 'Bloody hysteria! Just what I've always hated about bloody women. Hysterics! Shrieking! Screaming! Baying bitches!'

She wished she could drink the glass of port on the table beside her. (She could have thrown that, instead of the harlequin.) But to drink the port, at this moment, was just not 'on'. 'Home,' Julian said. 'I'll drive you home. You're obviously not fit to walk.'

'I can – really.'

'No. Anyway, I feel responsible – to Peter.' He groped in his pocket, and found keys. She followed him to the front door, and went out ahead of him, then stood on the pavement, while he locked the door.

As he started the car, she heard the clamour of a fire-engine. Normally, one of them would have commented; neither did now.

'Julian, I'm –'

'Just be quiet. Not one single word, or I shall dump you in the gutter. Just shut up.'

His tone silenced her. As they drove, the fire-engine sound grew louder. It was almost deafening as they turned into the road up past the park to the crescent. Then ahead, against a swirling sky, she saw orange flames. 'The house. Our house. The one at the end.' Then she screamed, 'Teddy!'

'Nonsense,' said Julian, but he put his foot on the accelerator. A moment later, in a different tone, he said, 'Teddy will be all right. The old lady –'

'No,' she shouted. 'No.'

They reached the terrace wall. Through the heavy, choking smoke, she saw ladders, fireman, other hurrying figures, round the house aflame.

She stumbled out of the car, and up the steps to the terrace. Someone caught at her arm. Violently dragging herself free of the clutching hand, she pushed on. As she neared the house, the flames seared her, and she staggered back. Then, again, she flung herself forward.

Celia 1979

When, in the early morning, she vomited for the fourth time, all that came up was a trickle of yellow, bitter slime. She walked back along the veranda from the bathroom very slowly. In the courtyard the sodden tree-trunks looked as if they were coated with oil. It was still raining, and still dark.

Used glasses stood among empty bottles all over the kitchen table; she filled one with cold water from the tap. As soon as she had gulped down the water, some of it sprayed out of her mouth; then the rest gushed out, over the pans and dishes in the sink.

On every kitchen surface, as well as empty bottles and glasses, were dirty utensils. A crusted saucepan lay on its side on the draining-board. (There were stains of stew, as well as of plum brandy, down the front of her nightdress.)

Everything must be cleaned and tidied before Thalia arrived. Leaning against the sink she tried to calculate when that would be. Thalia came at eight on Friday morning. Could this be Friday? But with extreme relief she realized that today was Thursday. Yesterday she had forced herself to shower and dress and put on make-up, to look fit to go into Niko's shop for wine. When she opened the front door, she had recognized – from the silence, from a quick glance down the street – that it was Wednesday: early-closing day.

So she was reprieved until tomorrow. She looked at her watch. (Yesterday, in order to reset and wind it, she had turned on the radio for the first time since Saturday.) Now it was half-past six, and she could go back to bed. The thought of tea was repellent, and that of coffee worse. Later she would try to drink water again. Then, at eleven, she would make the long dreadful preparations for a visit to Niko. But today she would buy only three large bottles of beer, which would first refresh her, and then put her to sleep. When she awoke, probably late in the evening, she would have to embark on restoration: of herself and her surroundings.

As she entered the bedroom, dimly lit by the bedside lamp, the stuffy heat and reek of tobacco made her grimace. The electric fire had been on all night, but she was shivering now, so she did not turn it off.

The floor was littered with dirty, crumpled clothes. (How had she worn so many, when she had spent so much time in bed?) Also on the floor was the counterpane, under two odd shoes.

On the bed, the sheets were untucked, even at the foot, and the blankets twisted. Two flattened pillows lay aslant; the third was squashed into a lump on top of them.

Books were scattered all over the bed; others were beside it, some piled, some fallen. More were stacked on the bedside table, under the lamp, with a full ashtray, the two parts of an empty matchbox, a soaked packet with one wet brown cigarette in it, and three empty glasses, in one of which were several plum-stones. There was also a sheet of paper which she now picked up. The wavering writing was scarcely recognizable as her own, and she made out the words with difficulty: 'Foliage distortion impulse – insight obscured!!! Nietzsche?' She had no idea what this meant or might refer to.

Unable to summon force to tidy the bed, she subsided on it, and rolled over, pulling up the bedclothes round her. She could feel crumbs on the lower sheet; on the border of the upper sheet was a large smear of grease.

Now, more than anything she could imagine, she would have liked to fall asleep; this, she felt certain, was impossible. With a low groan she reached for the nearest book, face down on the blanket. It was *The Red Fairy Book*, open at the middle of a story called 'Dapplegrim'. She could not remember having read the earlier part, but she started with the first paragraph her eye alighted on, which began, '*He went down into the stable, and very sad and full of care he was.*'

*

On the previous Friday Thalia had found her crying, and – warm concern on face, in voice – had asked her why.

She had known she should not give Thalia the reason, but she could think of no other explanation, so she told her the truth: that she was crying because the cat had disappeared.

'*E gata?*' Thalia sounded incredulous. Celia had dried her eyes, smiled, and said, '*Einai tipota,*' which meant, 'It is nothing,' and was a lie.

The cat had been missing for three days. Before this he had never been absent for more than a single night, after which, in the very early morning, he leapt through the courtyard window, and then from the sill onto her bed. He landed with a wild expression in his yellow eyes and a smell of air in his fur. Then he settled on her chest, dabbing her neck with a paw, and purring deeply.

Had he been run over, poisoned, crippled by a hurled stone? Perhaps he had wandered a long distance, and was lost. Since his disappearance, she had constantly wandered round the courtyard, and stood by the wall, calling him. She even called him in neighbouring streets, though more quietly. Panicos, the name she had given him, was popular among islanders; puzzled males might emerge from buildings in response to her cries.

All Friday morning she had been aware of Thalia's glances. She felt sure that on reaching home Thalia would describe how the English-woman had been crying about a cat. Her family might laugh; they would exclaim; they would certainly jerk back their heads, close their eyes, and turn down the corners of their mouths.

Celia stayed up late that night. Now, in February, it was too cold to pace the hall. She sat in her bedroom by the electric fire, drinking wine and smoking. She left the back window and the shutters open: Panicos might still return. Even after she went to bed she stayed awake, listening for him, but there was only the rain and the occasional thud of a lemon, falling from a tree.

Next day, the Saturday morning bustle seemed particularly irk-some: the shouts, the revving of engines, the prolonged hoots from neurotic drivers. Preparing to do her shopping – always a special effort on Saturday, because Niko's shop was crowded with people to whom she was still an object of interest – she felt a design forming, loosely, like a cloud, in her mind. *Perhaps I won't*, she thought. *I needn't. I can choose. Perhaps I won't.* But she did.

She bought more food than usual; much more bread: the traditional round yellow loaf, a crusty white 'Germanikos', and sliced brown, for toast. She bought butter, eggs, tomatoes, onions, a bottle of brandy and two bottles of red wine.

As soon as she had unloaded these things from the pink transparent bags in which Niko had packed them, she took two proper, opaque shopping bags from the handle of the kitchen door. One was suede, and the other – very deep – was made of shiny black plastic. She always used these bags when she went to shops other than Niko's. He was so kind and obliging that she did not want him to know that she shopped elsewhere. Nor did she want him to know that she bought extra drink: islanders were abstemious and, from him, she bought far more than most of his customers did.

Into the black bag she put an empty gallon wine-jar of a kind formerly covered with plaited straw, but now encased in white plastic. Carrying the two bags, she made her way through the busy streets to a large supermarket. Here she exchanged the empty wine jar for a full one. She took a bottle of brandy from a shelf, then hesitated. *After all, it's the weekend*, she thought, and then wondered in what way weekends differed, for her, from weekdays. All the same she put a second bottle of brandy in her trolley, as well as various goods Niko did not stock: chilli powder, Worcestershire sauce, two tins of potatoes, two tins of carrots, and two tins of baked beans in tomato sauce.

Twice during the next few days she heard knocks at her door, but of course she did not answer. She drank, and also cooked herself several hot mixtures which she ate with large quantities of bread; thickly buttered whether plain or toasted. Drinking and eating, she read familiar books, all the time, except when she fell into sudden heavy sleep. Waking, she would immediately start to drink and to read.

It was in bright daylight that, after a long sleep, she turned on the radio to find out the time. It was two twenty-five; from the light she knew it was the afternoon. When she went to the kitchen she discovered that all the drink was finished. That was when she dressed and found that it was early-closing day.

Back in the kitchen she had searched all the cupboards. It was with a shock of relief that, at the back of a shelf, she unearthed the large jar of plums she had preserved in brandy the previous summer. When she had drunk all the liquid, she ate the brandy-soaked fruit.

*

'Dapplegrim asked "Do you hear anything?"
'"Yes; there is such a dreadful whistling up above in the air that I think I am growing alarmed," said the youth.'

She let her hand, with the book in it, flop down at the side of the bed. Her gaze travelled slowly round the room. It was essential to believe that, within the next twenty-four hours, before Thalia came, bedroom and kitchen would be cleared, bottles disposed of, dishes washed, bed freshly made, dirty clothes and sheets first put to soak in the bath, with detergent, and then washed and hung on the line. It was essential to believe this, but, at that moment, she found it impossible.

LAURA 1962

Ben had returned on Thursday. He telephoned her on Sunday, and she asked him to dinner the following Wednesday. She would have liked to see him sooner, but he had waited three days before telephoning her, so she left the same interval before the dinner. And he did not suggest an earlier meeting.

Preparing the meal, she was irritated by this recollection. In any case, she was in an irritable mood. Not hungry herself, she did not feel eager to cook, though if she could have prepared a luscious dish, she might have become absorbed in the task. But Ben, for reasons of health, preferred simple food.

Ben always took good care of himself. This reflection added to her irritation. So did the prospect of what awaited her at work next day. The worst job ever assigned to her, the first hint of it had come from Mr Johnson at the office Christmas party, more than two months ago.

*

'Slimes dams?'

She laughed, repeating what the man had said was the technical name for those glittering table-topped hills she saw each day from the crest of the city.

He had told her he was an accountant. He and she stood facing each other at the cocktail party. Not a breath of sex warmed the space between them. Encouraged by her laugh – at last he had found a topic – he told her more and more.

The slimes dams were composed of pumped liquid sludge. It was as the liquid settled out that they flattened. Originally alkaline and dark, they turned acid and golden when their pyrites contents oxidized.

'Not, of course, that, after the very thorough extraction process, they contain much actual *gold*. Only, in fact, about point two gram per ton. They are chiefly composed of silic –'

'Laura, you'll be in the office tomorrow morning?' The interruption came in the tone-deaf voice of 'her' client, Mr Johnson. He was, as usual, oblivious of everything but his personal obsession and, as usual, his smooth salmon-coloured face reminded her of his product. ('Excuse me,' said the accountant, and escaped.)

'Yes, I'll be at work.' She added, 'There's always so much to clear up before one goes on holiday.'

This addition, to Mr Johnson, was quite irrelevant. 'I'll be in first thing,' he said. 'I've got a new angle to discuss with you.'

Later, when she was in bed, waiting for her sleeping-pill to take effect, words spoken by the accountant recurred. *Alkaline, dark . . . becoming acid, golden.* But the gold was deceptive. Like the city itself. Pale shiny castle . . . it might crumble. Bleak escarpment . . . over black lake.

*

When she woke, essence of traffic was filtering up to the thirteenth floor, reminding her of *Rhapsody in Blue*, a musical compromise she did not care for. But the association would have delighted the inhabitants of this city, who constantly compared it to New York. (Instead of naming them after dead generals and millionaires, they should have numbered its long, grid-patterned streets, as streets were numbered in New York. The inhumanity of numbers would have been appropriate to the place. In the event, soldiers and moneymakers were the next best thing.)

The weekday rush suited the city which, at leisure, was uneasy. Quiet Sunday mornings seemed unnatural, as if the silence were that which follows a bombardment. And by seven in the evening the city centre, apart from a few hotels and a fistful of cinemas and restaurants patronized mainly on Saturday, was always closed and dark. People hurried home from work, ate at once, went to bed early. (There was no television.) Here, up on the hill, by half-past nine, most of the lights were out in the flats whose rear windows Laura could see from her bed. It was congruous, she thought now, that her bedroom, living-room and balcony should overlook the back of another block, instead of the city; that only the bathroom and kitchen – both with opaque, granulated windows – should face that view. People here had no 'eye-life' as Ben would have put it. The thought of Ben aroused a restlessness which urged her out of bed. In any case, it was time to get up: half-past seven.

The pill, slow in taking effect last night, had made her sleep later than usual this morning. She must be at work punctually, at half-past eight. Mr Johnson had said he would be 'in first thing', and – with his one-track mind – could have meant it literally; he might well arrive as the office opened.

Often Laura walked to work, which took half an hour. Today she would catch the bus. She peered up through the window at the sky. White and heavy it would press down on the town all day till, in the afternoon, there were mutters of thunder. Then – probably just as Laura left her office – lightning would crack the sky, and water would descend as if from a bucket. But by then she would be free: for three weeks. Tonight she was having dinner with the Ardens and tomorrow she was going to the farm. In the kitchen, switching on the electric kettle, she smiled. She crossed the hall to the bathroom.

It was a pity Mr Johnson was coming to the office. She had hoped to spend most of the morning in the studio with Max, working out the new campaign for Taylor's Toffees.

'Something madly austere, don't you think?' she had said to Max yesterday.

With a grunt of laughter he replied, 'Oh madly.'

'Not a toffee in sight.'

'Well, perhaps just one.'

'A *tiny* toffee.'

But now she might have to spend the whole day on Mr Johnson's 'new angle'. Writing copy for Mr Johnson took up more and more of her time; work was losing its saving element of fun.

Both in her previous London job and in her present one, fun lay in achieving a jaunty – secretly snook-cocking – smartness. Laura, unlike many copywriters, thought visually, and had a rapport with art directors; especially with Max. United, they battled – the account executive ('that spineless A.E.') an uneasy intermediary – with old-fashioned clients, and often won.

They had eliminated the beaming chef's-hatted pig, waving a Sampson's sausage on a fork.

'Cannibalism! How perverted!' Laura said. Max laughed, and the A.E. flinched.

The night-capped, candle-carrying, bearded dwarf, 'Old Snoozer', who personified Slumberest mattresses, was reduced to a small – almost unidentifiable – symbol in the bottom left-hand corner.

'Who wants to go to bed with an old dwarf?' asked Laura.

'Don't ask *me*, dear,' said Max, and the A.E. blushed.

Now they were determined to liquidate the freckled boy with the bulging cheek, from whose lips issued a balloon containing the words, 'Taylor's are Tops!'

'They aren't. They're toffees,' Laura said, Max smiled, and the A.E.

frowned: the 'Creative Side' was often so frivolous. But he managed to persuade them that, if they got rid of the boy, they would have – at least for a time – to retain the slogan. The loss of both at one blow would be too much for old Mr Taylor.

Might one perhaps find a copy approach that would make some kind of sense of a visual of a pretty Victorian spinning-top? The idea was Laura's. She and Max discussed it after the A.E.'s departure. A striking, simple visual, a short headline, a little wedge of entertaining copy: that was what Laura liked. Max, of course, liked it too. It was an art director's dream, but it was also an old-fashioned client's nightmare. What the client wanted to see was his product, as big as possible, accompanied by his symbol, his slogan and his logo.

Yet almost all client's packs were shrinking. Their friendly familiars – pig, dwarf, freckled boy – were being exorcized. When the A.E. fulfilled his function, and supported the 'Creative Side' – which often happened, for all A.E.s were terrified of Max – clients were converted to strange new beliefs: 'brand image', 'clean modern design', a 'coordinated campaign' with 'consumer-appeal' based on 'motivational research'.

Consumers! An odd phrase had recently come into Laura's mind. It recurred often: *Consuming, we have been consumed.* She muttered it now, as she finished brushing her teeth. Then she scowled at the thought that she was playing a decreasing part in the civilizing mission of the 'Creative Side'. The reason for this lay in C de C as – except in his presence – Mr Johnson's product was called in the agency.

C de C was short for Crème de Coolay. Packed in a plain glass bottle with a pale pink label, C de C provided 'everything a woman needs for true complexion beauty'. She could use it to 'cleanse away' (not 'clean off') 'dust' (never 'dirt') and 'stale' (never 'old') make-up. 'Smoothed' (not 'rubbed') 'in', 'with an upward and outward movement', it would 'nourish during the hours of sleep' while 'all through the day', it 'moisturized, at the same time providing an ideal foundation, and protecting against the harmful effects of excessive heat and cold, harsh sunlight and chafing winds.' And C de C 'cared' not only for the face, but for the hands and neck; indeed it would supply 'after-bath pampering for the entire body'.

In addition to its 'properties', C de C's origins were remarkable. It was not only 'a pure natural product' but 'the outcome of modern scientific laboratory research'. Could either of these apparently conflicting claims – Laura pulled off her nightdress – be disproved? On the whole she thought not. She sighed. She had a secret fantasy about 'exposing' C de C.

Lanolin – the grease extracted from sheep's wool – had first been used by Mr Johnson – whose uncle was a sheep farmer – to make an ointment for cows' inflamed udders. This was modestly profitable, but the market was restricted. Mr Johnson transferred his attentions from cows to women. ('Each to his taste,' commented Max to Laura.)

Nature – the sheep – had supplied the basic substance. Now science played its part. In Mr Johnson's laboratory (garage), modern research (a chemistry student) refined the grease to a fluid, and substituted a new scent for the original smell.

Mr Johnson in his Grail-quest for the appropriate texture (neither sticky nor runny) and the suitable scent (not heavy, yet not antiseptic), had a Guinevere in view. In his head was a woman. But it would be better – more refined, more appropriate – to call the person for whom he had created C de C a 'lady'.

'D,D,D,D,D,D' sang Laura, in her shower, on a note approximately two octaves above Middle C. 'Dull, dense, diffident, drab, dumb and dreary.' This seemed to her a comprehensive description of Mr Johnson's lady.

She was Mr Johnson's, but her importance for other people – including Laura – lay in the fact that she existed not only inside his small, flat-backed head, but also outside it, and apparently in such large numbers that it was not yet possible to arrive at a clone-count. Sales of C de C constantly increased, and faster and faster. C de C itself provided no explanation of this. The reason could only lie in Mr Johnson's approach to the lady he knew so intimately.

He knew that to sweep her off her feet – let alone assault her – was unthinkable; she was extraordinarily timid. Nor would it be profitable to try to seduce her; she responded to nothing even subtly sexy.

Laura stepped onto the bathmat, and reached for her towel. The lady must be wooed. But – Mr Johnson was determined not to shock or even to startle her – she must not be aware of it. It was from this premise that he advanced; on tiptoe.

He had first considered – at length, though it was so little – what the lady read; novels ending with a conjunction of closed mouths, matt-paged magazines of domesticity (bewildered and unnerved by *chic*, the lady found glossy fashion magazines 'silly'), the woman's page of the newspaper bought by her husband (she was probably a housewife) or her employer (she was perhaps a typist). Careful financially, why should she buy a paper of which she only read one page?

If Mr Johnson dreamed of persuading romantic novelists to insert references to C de C in their books, he woke to recognize the idea as too ambitious (though who knew what might be possible one day?).

Therefore he could conduct his chaste courtship only in the matt magazines and on the women's pages. In the first it must take the form of a beauty column, and in the second of a beauty hint, both purporting to be the creations of a woman journalist. (The name he chose was Linda Lawson.) Although the space was bought, the material that filled it must not appear to be commercial; it must not seem like advertising.

There had been debates on whether the initials of the product should be capitalized. Mr Johnson's instinct was for crème de coolay to glide – serpentine, unstressed – into the copy. On the other hand his lady was not bright. (He would not have known and loved her as he did if she had been.) At least to begin with, he must help her to identify the product, so that she could ask for it at the chemist's. Therefore, once in each advertisement – never more often – it should appear as Crème de Coolay. But its success was so great that Mr Johnson foresaw a time when it could always be in lower case.

Laura put on her clothes. She knew that she was lucky not to be involved in the constant wrangles, between the A.E. for C de C (c de c?) and various magazines and newspapers, about the size and positioning of the word 'Advertisement' – its appearance obligatory where advertising copy might be mistaken for journalism – and the thickness of the ruled border which must, in such cases, surround 'column' or 'hint'. However, her own problems with C de C seemed to her worse than these, and far worse than those involved in battling – at Max's side – against porker, dwarf and sun-blotched boy.

She saw herself as an aspiring actress, offered a big, safe, wholly unsympathetic part. What could she do but accept it? Now, starting to put on make-up, standing in front of a tall, late-Victorian chest she had found in a junk shop, Laura imagined Mr Johnson's lady. At a Dolly Varden dressing-table, in front of a triple mirror, she sat smoothing C de C into her insipid face.

Laura's scents and cosmetics were foreign and expensive. 'I'd sooner put prussic acid on my face than C de C,' she had said to Max.

'Warn me, won't you, when you do. I covered my eyes at *Phantom of the Opera*.'

'The Lon Chaney?'

'No – have a heart, dear! – the Claude Rains.'

There were several untouched bottles of C de C – presented to her on various occasions by Mr Johnson – in Laura's bathroom cupboard. Eventually she might have enough to drown the lady with whom she was constantly forced to *empathize*.

A steady flow of Linda Lawson material was needed, for Mr

Johnson felt that frequent repeat insertions made hints and columns seem too much like advertisements: as which, Laura felt, though he paid for them, he no longer saw them. She liked also to imagine that his lady had become – perhaps always had been – more than a mere concept in his mind.

In the room reserved for meetings between clients and agency staff – 'the brothel' as she and Max called it – she would face Mr Johnson across the veneered table (the A.E., seldom consulted, sat between them, at the end) on which a giant ashtray marked each place; Laura, like many others, chain-smoked at such meetings. Facing Mr Johnson, she would half close her eyes . . .

Yes, that glazed pink face had the precise tint and sheen of C de C. Mr Johnson *was* his lady; she was he. Now, blurred by smoke, Mr Johnson's lips pouted in a rosy moue; his little blue eyes widened; his thin grey hair puffed into a lacquered bouffant. Now, she pictured him in his bedroom at home. There were bouffant wigs on stands all round his dressing-table. (It was a Dolly Varden: pink-flounced; kidney-shaped; triple-mirrored.) Here each morning, each evening (perhaps after every meal, as Americans were said to brush their teeth), he sat on a (pink brocade) stool, *smoothing in* C de C. No wonder his skin had acquired such pinkness. (All his undies were that colour, too. They were dainty rather than glamorous, and he crocheted his own little pink bedjackets for winter.)

Eyes still narrowed, Laura would consider Mrs Johnson, whom she had met once, in Reception. (At first, Laura had thought she was a nurse, but then realized that her white uniform was what middle-aged women wore to play bowls.) Mrs Johnson was stringy and weather-beaten. Her face, much wrinkled, was no recommendation for her husband's product. But two C de C ladies under one roof might have led to nasty tiffs. Perhaps Mrs Johnson massaged him – using C de C of course – with her muscular, bowler's arms, so that he was pink and glazed all over. But at this point Laura would widen her eyes – she must concentrate on what he was saying – and he would resume his customary male form: male but not masculine, yet definitely not 'gay', even though Max, since she had told him of her fantasy, referred to him as 'she' or 'Lady Johnson'.

Laura put on a neat blue linen dress and white shoes with stiletto heels. (She would take no such dresses to the farm, and not a single pair of high-heeled shoes.) This was her office 'costume' – in the theatrical sense – always worn with stockings and frequently-renewed make-up. Dressed, she murmured, 'A Star is Born – Linda Lawson!'

She felt ashamed that she played the dreadful role so well –

consuming, we have been consumed – and that Mr Johnson was so keen on her performance. On the day when he had announced to the agency's managing director, in her presence, that she had a real flair for the work, she had known that her job was safe for the play's lifetime ('This show will run and run!'). She was secure, or you could say, 'stuck': not temporarily, as she had been with the slimes-dam man last night. She was permanently stuck with C de C.

She looked at her watch. Five to eight: five minutes for a cup of tea. She drank it in the kitchen where the utensils from last night's scrambled eggs (she had left the party early, though not as early as Max who had scowled in a corner for only ten minutes) were piled in the sink. Evelyn would wash up. Evelyn – Laura did not know her surname – came five days a week to do housework and the washing and ironing. Last night, Laura had put Evelyn's wages for the past week, and for two of the three weeks of her coming absence, in an envelope on the kitchen table, with a greetings card containing two pounds extra, as a Christmas present. During the two years Evelyn had worked for her, Laura had seen her only three times: the work was done as if by gnomes in a fairy tale. Communication – rare – was through little notes left on the kitchen table.

In the hall, Laura undid the bolt, the chain, the lock that drove a metal rod into the ground, the Yale. In the door was a peephole through which she could examine anyone who rang the bell. Outside, she fastened the lock that controlled the metal rod.

The opposite side of the passage was open above balcony level. At night – for anyone prepared to linger in this bleak corridor – there was a scintillant view of the city: a steeply falling flight of starry towers which now, in daylight, were revealed as ugly slabs and cylinders, though down in the city they were hazed. Everywhere giant cranes, yellow or orange, hovered and pivoted. And in the distance were those strange flat shining hills.

The entrance to her block was in a narrow street lined on both sides by high buildings: tall stalagmites keeping the sun from a cold canyon. Although the day was heavy with heat, her images of this southern town were invariably chill. She turned the corner into the main thoroughfare from the northern suburbs into the city: the noisiest street in Hillbrow, which was the most densely populated area in the world.

Life in Hillbrow had a transient mood. There were food and drink shops, a few coffee bars and tearooms. Otherwise it was composed of blocks of rented flats, occupied by single people, childless couples and recently arrived immigrants. It belonged more to the city than the suburbs, each of which could be labelled rich or poor, smart or dowdy. Hillbrow eluded such classification. It was like an airport or railway station.

Just as she reached the stop, a bus drew up: she boarded it, and found a free seat by a window. The bus started to descend the hill.

Most people wanted to leave this district: to acquire property, to move to houses with gardens. Apart from the fact that she could not have afforded it – though well paid 'for a woman', she was careless with money, spending everything she earned – Laura could not imagine herself buying a suburban house. She could not imagine herself 'a settler', the term by which a girl she had talked to on the plane from England had defined herself. A settler *here*?

From the window she watched feet fiercely tap the pavement. When a traffic light clicked from red to yellow, drivers began to jab their horns. But at this moment, lights just ahead turned from yellow to green, and there was still no movement. Peering ahead, she saw a long line of jammed traffic. The horns blasted until suddenly all the drivers, at the same moment, seemed to realize the futility of their efforts. In the hush there came, from a canvas-topped lorry next to the bus, a roar of singing.

'*Wosa, o wosa!*' Black singing. The voices rang. And all round her in the bus Laura became aware of white people tensing and stiffening. Those who carried bags and packages clutched them closely, as if making ramparts for their bodies. '*Wosa, o wosa!*' And she?

Submerged, she closed her eyes, bowing her head. But it was only a – deep-water – moment before the wave receded, the roar died away. Looking up she saw that the line of traffic on the right was edging forward. The lorry moved on. The voices were lost in an ugly, renewed rage of horns.

Now the bus too was inching forward. Inside it, everywhere, were little rustles and relaxations. She looked around her. Some of the passengers were murmuring, sniggering to each other. But what an eased look there was on every face. She flinched from the white chill of these people, of this city. Yes, it resembled its mine-dumps, its hardened slimes-dams: mounds of glittering detritus with a negligible contents of gold. White temple, ritually purified of blackness each evening: Johannesburg.

*

'But how can you possibly go to such an appalling place?'

That was the question she had been asked in London, when she had applied for the job. Replying, she commented on the fact that none of the nice people who asked it had ever visited the 'awful place'.

They would answer that they did not need to: by its own laws, pronouncements, actions, it was self-condemned. She said, 'I've never really been interested in politics.' She wanted to be *on the move*. This job in an overseas branch of the agency she worked for offered an escape from the restless but monotonous life she had been living since her divorce, two years before. Any change, surely, must be for the better?

If her desire for escape had been weaker, she would – even if she had managed to ignore the response of the nice people – have found a powerful deterrent in an opposite reaction. She would have acknowledged that people who had visited the country – and declared it 'wonderful' – were invariably coarse and callous: not 'nice' at all. Yet even they, extolling its opportunities, dismissing 'all the nonsense' talked about it, quoting statistics about the high standard of living of 'the natives' (the highest, they would announce triumphantly, in Africa) admonished her to 'take her time', to allow a year or more to pass before reaching a verdict, let alone pronouncing sentence. They had calculated, as she now realized, that for her, as for most other immigrants, custom and prosperity would dull the – almost inevitable – initial shock. But in her case, this hadn't happened. She felt sure it wouldn't. After all, she had been in the country for two years now.

The bus was approaching the stop opposite the agency building. She stood up.

*

In the corridor she passed Max, carrying a folder under his arm and scowling (the word 'frowning' was inadequate). His scowl was permanent at this time of day; Laura tried never to enter the studio before ten-thirty.

'Good morning,' she said.

'Morning,' he muttered. Although he did not smile, he raised his eyebrows, slightly relieving his face's expression of compressed fury. She doubted if he would have done this for anyone but her; there were few whose morning greetings he would have acknowledged in any way.

Max was a licensed prima donna. Because he was one of the best-paid art directors in the country, his 'temperament' was a source of uneasy pride to his employers. It proved him to be the genuine 'Creative' article. Max detested all clients and account executives. He was kept, as much as possible, apart from the former, but had been known to throw anything to hand – from a heavy ashtray to a jar of paint water – at the latter, when even mildly provoked.

That Laura was such an exceptional favourite of his puzzled people. He was believed to dislike women; and the objective of most copywriters seemed to him to be the disfigurement of his layouts with unsightly and unnecessary words. In this regard, Laura with her visual bias was an exception, but they had other things in common: both despised their work; each made the other laugh.

Max had confided in her that once, alone in the studio at lunchtime, after a morning session of photography for which the model had been dressed as a bride, he had felt a compulsion to try on the wedding outfit. Having locked the door, he had taken off his shirt and trousers. Then he had put on the white satin dress, forced his feet – fortunately small – into the white satin shoes, and draped the veil over his head. Clutching the streamered bouquet in both hands, he had gazed into the mirror. 'I felt terrific!' he said.

Laura now smiled, thinking of Max, with his squashed face and stocky little body decked in the bridal raiment. Max was Jewish. Laura wished she knew more Jewish people.

Jewishness was yeast in the pallid dough of this city; the cream of its grey skim milk. Johannesburg's reputation as the country's 'cultural capital' – though the imported concerts, plays and ballets seemed to Laura superimposed – rested entirely on Jewish effort and interest. The brilliant professional men were Jews. The faces, the names, the foods that sometimes gave her a brief sense of that romance she had associated – before coming to South Africa – with the word 'abroad' were all Jewish. Passing a ground-floor window on a Friday evening she glimpsed a de La Tour scene lit by Sabbath candles; or in the street she noticed a haggard noble-featured face. As for the food, when she first arrived – she had never seen a delicatessen before – she had lived on cartons of Jewish takeaway: gefilte fish, *latkes*, hot salt beef, rye bread, bagels, rollmop herrings, chopped liver with *schmaltz*, dill pickled cucumbers. (Could these great seafruit, spurting cold salty juice, be related to England's meagre shrivelled 'cocktail gherkins'?)

Passing the office next to her own, she was glad to see that it was still empty. Not having to say good-morning to her fellow copywriter, Antonia Kingsley, was a minor pleasure.

They might have been expected to be friends. Instead they had disliked each other instinctively and at once. They had met first not at the office but at the Inanda Club, a place Laura was determined never in any circumstances to revisit.

145

She had arrived in Johannesburg with various introductions. Two of these (both supplied by nice people, enemies of the 'appalling place') had led to friendships: with Richard and Alice Arden, whom she was dining with tonight, and with Peter and Susan Field, whose farm she was going to tomorrow. Other introductions, given by admirers of the 'wonderful' country, had invariably resulted in mutually tedious encounters. The first of these had been at a Sunday lunch at Inanda.

How passionately casual all the members looked in their 'country clothes', their spotted scarves and polished leather. Many wore riding gear; a few had actually been playing polo. In England, the aspiring bourgeoisie used horses as vehicles on which to approach the upper class. Here in South Africa, where there was none, they presumably used them to impress each other.

They were having drinks, Laura and her host and hostess, the Barlings – a middle-aged pair with a corgi; it would be a corgi – on the terrace, when Mr Barling hailed a passing couple. In a moment Laura was being introduced to someone who, by the extraordinary coincidence which had just struck Mr Barling, not only worked in the office where Laura would be starting work next day, but did the very same job.

Antonia Kingsley was attractive rather than pretty. She was a slim, beautifully dressed and painted blonde. Pressed, she and her extremely handsome husband, Tom – who had been playing polo – sat down. Mr Barling ordered drinks from a black waiter in white uniform, white gloves and a red sash. As this waiter turned to go, Mrs Barling called after him, 'And bring some water for the little master.' (Who was the little master? There was no child in the party. If there had been, Laura felt that this would have been a ridiculous way to refer to him.)

Antonia Kingsley was saying that work at the agency was 'super fun'. Did Antonia, Laura wondered, use 'fun' – in an advertising context – in the same way she did? Somehow she thought not; there had been no irony in Antonia's tone. Now the waiter returned.

He brought the drinks. He also brought a bowl of water, which he put down on the ground, for the corgi. *The little master.* Laura felt her face twist with incredulity and with disgust. Her eyes met Antonia's, but found no sympathy there; far from it: windows were slammed, and shutters fastened. This was not, she realized, because Antonia was stupid; far from it: Antonia saw what she was feeling, and rejected it. At that moment they became enemies, and remained so.

Even then, Laura sensed a clue to Antonia's attitude in her obsessive gaze at her husband, Tom, with his wooden perfection, like that of a hero of the First World War. Physically Tom was in this mould. But –

146

she became aware as he spoke, and it was later confirmed by agency gossip – he was very stupid: too stupid even to succeed in business.

To Laura, business seemed to require little intelligence. Some people believed that real brains were needed in order to succeed in it; she did not accept that for a moment. What about Mr Johnson, who was making a fortune? That was not the result of brains, but of monkey tricks. Business, Laura felt after several years' experience of it, was a chimps' tea-party on a giant scale.

The chimps looked smart and bright in their clean clothes. As they had been trained to do, they ate from plates and drank from mugs; the audience was delighted. But then the crowd dispersed. One animal gave another a pinch; it responded with a bite. Both rolled in the dust. Others joined them. Soon all were dirty and degraded.

With regard to handsome, stupid Tom, Antonia, dedicated to pleasing him, was terrified of her own intelligence. She kept it chained in a kennel: little slave rather than little master. She knew that in order to please him, all her opinions must be conventional.

For some time, Laura and Antonia had dull, stilted conversations in the office. This went on till Antonia started work on a campaign for powdered milk, aimed at Africans.

The agency business was in a state of confusion about the African – or, as most people said, 'native' – market. Although almost the whole African population lived beneath a – stringently defined – poverty line, it was a fact that an African market existed. The results of advertisements – at first inserted only in African picture papers – proved it. There was a market; so it must be exploited.

Early advertisements followed the pattern of old-fashioned advertisements aimed at whites: a large picture of the product, accompanied by a simple slogan. The ideas current in new advertising to whites were set aside: the idea that Africans might have complex 'motivations', might be susceptible to 'brand images' seemed ridiculous to clients, and to their advertising agencies. But then research turned up the information that Africans were buying products they could not afford, products only advertised in publications intended for whites. (Of course any advertised products were products Africans could not afford: maize flour, animal entrails and dried beans are not advertised.) Why, since Africans were not motivated as whites were, did they buy white products? It must be because they wanted to imitate whites. (Whites could understand *that*!) So advertisers began to insert the same advertisements in African papers as in white ones. But then an advertisement had been placed in *Drum*, showing a – white – child, cuddling a dog. To this, someone in the client's office objected, remarking that Africans thought dogs dirty, and certainly did not consider them lovable. So, while Africans wanted to be like whites, advertisers had to recognize that, at the same time, they had tastes, taboos, peculiarities of their own. It was all very tiresome. Here and there, little research projects sprouted. One Johannesburg agency – not the one where Laura worked – even employed an African sociology graduate to provide interpretations of his people, full-time.

It was common knowledge that most African babies who survived infancy did so as the result of prolonged breast-feeding. (Once deprived of mother's milk, they started to suffer from nutritional deficiencies.) This knowledge was of no concern to powdered-milk manufacturers now devoting their efforts to persuading African mothers that their products were 'better', 'more modern', 'easier to use' than breast milk. ('Easier to use' they were for women who had to leave their babies in the 'locations' while they worked all day in the city. Was this her maid Evelyn's situation? Laura wondered. It was not the sort of thing one could ask in a 'little note'.)

'It's so *wrong*,' Laura said to Antonia, about the campaign.

Antonia raised her eyebrows. 'Wrong? Why on earth? Look how many European mothers bottle-feed their babies.'

'But *white* children,' Laura said, rather offensively stressing her different choice of word ('European' seemed such an absurd description of white South Africans), 'get all sorts of supplements: orange juice and vitamins and so on. When they're weaned, their mothers can afford to put them on a balanced diet. African women can't. Besides, the breast milk is meant to give children an immunity to all those awful diseases you find in African areas.'

Antonia looked straight at Laura. She smiled brilliantly. 'None of my business, I'm afraid.'

That was Antonia's and Laura's last conversation. Yet Laura couldn't help wondering what she would have done if the powdered milk campaign had been assigned to her. (This was unlikely: Antonia was the specialist in 'hard-sell'. She wrote all the soap-account copy, and Max loathed her work. 'Nothing but subheads and screamers,' he said. A 'screamer' was the advertising word for an exclamation mark.) But would Laura have asked not to work on the campaign, if she had been told to? And would her request have been granted? Probably the answer to the second question was 'Yes', because of her usefulness to Mr Johnson. Perhaps there were advantages in being stuck with C de C.

It was quite easy to avoid Antonia at work, and they never met outside the office. None of her meetings with people of the Inanda sort had led to further ones. They had not found her interesting; she had detested their little pseudo-English world, from which they looked down on other people, especially (leaving out Africans, of course, who didn't count as people) Afrikaners.

Although they ruled the country, Laura didn't know a single Afrikaner. There was an Afrikaans copywriter in the agency, Mr Joubert (he was always called that, though the rest of the 'Creative Side' used first names). He was a sombre man, with a dark, pitted face, a little moustache, and a preoccupied frown (not a scrowl, like Max's). He reached the office, a secretary had told Laura, long before anyone else, and wrote for two hours. Apparently he had published more than thirty 'skiet-en-donder' (blood and thunder) novels. Laura could not connect his appearance with such books; she would have expected him to write gloomy stories set on isolated farms.

She was sure she would never get to know Mr Joubert; he spoke very little to anyone, except to one of the typists, who was Afrikaans too. Laura had been startled to hear him laughing heartily with this girl one morning. Perhaps he disliked English-speaking people. She wondered, if so, which he disliked more: English people from England, like her, or imitation ones like Antonia.

Mr Joubert was more a translator of advertisements written in English than an original copywriter. This was the custom in most agencies, though recently an all-Afrikaans agency had opened in the city, appealing specifically – and from a patriotic angle – to Afrikaans clients, of whom there were many more than there had been a few years ago. The English agencies were becoming worried; until lately, they had concerned themselves almost as little with Afrikaners as with Africans.

Laura did not feel the same desire for Afrikaans friends as for Jewish ones. Africans were the people she would most have liked to know. The Ardens talked nostalgically of the early 1950s when there had been multi-racial parties. That was all over now. Everyone – black and white – was too afraid of the government. It was a pity. The Africans were exotic and good-looking compared to most whites, who looked dull and lumpy. She thought of a family she had seen in a café in Hillbrow one morning: paunchy father, dowdy mother – she probably used C de C – and two whining washed-out children. They all seemed leaden, and, waiting on them, light and supple, was a slim handsome black waiter. How could people call Negro features coarse? she had wondered, comparing the waiter's face with the formless faces of those whites.

Sitting at her desk this morning, she realized that she hadn't told Mr

Johnson the truth, yesterday evening, when she had said she had 'so much to clear up'. There were only two folders on her desk: the one for Taylor's Toffees and another containing two 'hints' to show to Mr Johnson. One advised keeping half a lemon by the bathroom basin 'to soften and whiten wrinkled or sallow elbows, before smoothing in a few drops of crème de coolay'. Mr Johnson would be quite happy with that, she felt, but she wondered if she would get away with her second suggestion: 'New tip from Paris for a bright young beauty: follow your after-bath softening with crème de coolay with a light blush of rouge on the knees.' Would Mr Johnson swallow that? Laura could not resist occasional experiments of this kind. She wondered if he ever suspected . . . but no, she felt sure he would not imagine she might joke on such a subject. He would believe any excesses to be due to over-enthusiasm. Yes, she would risk the blushing knees. Mr Johnson was particularly pleased with her at the moment because of the new campaign she had originated: the 'Before and After' series. As the ads occupied double-page spreads in magazines, the agency, too, was delighted.

'Ellen, a housewife, finds new beauty' had been the first. 'Judy, a secretary, discovers new charm' was the second. Other subjects were planned: a receptionist, a nurse, a young mother. Each article, for they purported to be articles (and it was amazing how readers managed to disregard the ruled border and even the word, 'Advertisement'), was illustrated by two full-length photographs: the second larger than the first. Subtly, in true Linda Lawson style, the copy implied that C de C had played the key part in achieving the transformation which had taken place between the two. Laura, Max and the photographer dismantled a pretty little model, who giggled, for the 'Before' picture, and then reassembled her (though not quite to her normal standard of glamour, which would have been too 'extreme' for Mr Johnson's lady) for the 'After'.

The summons to the conference-room came at ten. She heard the tea-trolley in the passage just as Bob, the AE, 'buzzed' her, and she sighed. In the conference-room, tea would come on a tray, and she would have to pour it out for the men. Having renewed her powder and lipstick and combed her hair, she set off, with the two hints in their black folder, and also a notebook and ball-point pen, so that she could make notes on Mr Johnson's new angle, whatever it might be. She learnt as soon as she had poured out the tea: Mr Johnson never made small talk.

'I've been thinking,' he said, 'about the native market, Laura.' As usual he addressed her, ignoring Bob. He always called her 'Laura', though she called him 'Mr Johnson'; not that she wanted to call him by his first name, which was Bradley. She wondered if 'Mrs Johnson' – as Mr Johnson referred to his wife – called him 'Brad'.

'The native market,' she repeated blankly. Familiar though the term was to her, she did not associate it with Mr Johnson, and formed a picture of small heaps of decaying vegetables on dusty ground: a market she and Ben had wandered through when they went to Lourenco Marques.

'Yes, the subject's been on my mind for quite a time now. I've been worried, though, that advertising to the native might cheapen the product. In the eyes of Europeans, you know.'

He paused. Bob nodded keenly. Laura looked attentive.

'But then I realized that of course our European ladies never see the native magazines. So there would be no problem there, reely, hey?'

'No . . . but isn't Crème de Coolay a bit expensive for . . . them?' She wouldn't say 'natives'. Why didn't she say 'Africans' straight out? Because she was a coward.

Although C de C did not cost as much as most products imported from Europe or America, it was not cheap. Mr Johnson felt that his lady would not have believed in it if it had been.

'The native mind's a funny thing, Laura.' Gloomily she prepared to listen. 'The native mind' was a subject on which all white South Africans believed themselves to be experts, and on which they were eager to hold forth. As long as he didn't say that the natives thought just like children – people did say this, often – she felt she could bear it. 'You see,' Mr Johnson continued, 'if a native doesn't have to pay for a thing, doesn't have to dip into his pocket for it, he has no faith in it.' This was also his view of his lady, but he seemed not to make the connection. 'You should just see,' he went on, 'what they're prepared to spend on *muti*. Medicine that the witch doctor brews up from hell knows what.'

As opposed to simple sheep's grease. She was silent, trying to think why Africans should want to 'dip into their pockets' for C de C.

'The approach, you see, Laura, will be based on the fact that Crème de Coolay makes the skin fairer.'

'*Fairer?*' she asked. This was an entirely new claim.

'Yes, it gently lightens, you know. The natural ingredients have brightening as well as softening properties. As it clears away dullness, an increased fairness becomes evident.'

As always when he talked about C de C, he sounded as if he believed every word he was saying. It was without a trace of self-consciousness that he went on: 'You'll have noticed that in all the ads in the native papers, what they want when it comes to beauty is to look lighter.

Well, it's only natural. More like us, you know. But of course, we aren't going to show Crème de Coolay as a harsh bleaching cream – oh no, not a bit of it. My idea is that we'll follow the approach we used with Ellen and Judy – the 'Before and After' angle. In the second picture, of course, the native girl's skin will be seen to have lightened. You get the idea?'

'Yes,' Laura said.

After a moment, Mr Johnson's expectant look changed to a frown. It was obvious that he had expected a more enthusiastic response from her; Bob nudged her foot with his, under the table. But Mr Johnson's face cleared. 'Yes, it's quite a new angle, isn't it?' he said, evidently deciding that this originality had awed her. 'I'll leave it with you,' he said. 'You'll be able to think about it while you're away. When is it you get back, hey?'

'On the eighth of January,' she said.

'My word! That's a helluva long holiday!' Mr Johnson was one of those clients – she had met others – who felt that his product was – or ought to be – the most important element in the life of anyone connected with it. Evidence to the contrary tended to puzzle or hurt him; might, if forcefully presented, arouse strong resentment.

'Three weeks,' she said, adding defensively, 'it's my whole year's allowance.' She wondered what he did with his leisure. She couldn't imagine him being interested in anything but C de C.

'Oh well,' he said, 'Christmas always takes up a lot of time anyway. Might as well get your holiday over at the same time.' But Bradley 'Scrooge' Johnson must have realized he sounded grudging. Now he said, 'Well, Laura, enjoy yourself.'

She said, 'I've got two new hints here for you.'

He brightened, holding his hand out eagerly as she opened the black folder. He scanned the smartly typed sheets attentively.

The lemon elbows were on top. He nodded and smiled. Now, as he studied the blushing kneecaps, she saw the look of doubt she had anticipated. 'This rouge on the knees, Laura – you thought that up yourself?' Was there a shade of suspicion on his face that she might be, as Max would have put it, 'sending him up'?

'I saw it in *Vogue*,' she said quickly.

Affability returned. 'Oh yes, *Vogue*. Well, I'm glad you keep up with the fashions. Though perhaps, for our readers, this idea's, well, a trifle on the exaggerated side. All the same, I'll think it over.'

In the corridor, her first thought was that C de C wasn't actually harmful, in the way that weaning babies onto powdered milk was. But it was too expensive. In order to afford it, African women would have to make sacrifices ... sacrifices of things their children needed. *Consuming, we have been consumed.*

She headed for the studio. Perhaps Max would cheer her up. But when she reached his office, separated from that of lesser artists by a hardboard partition, he was bent over his drawing-board. His scowl as he looked up was fierce. It faded at the sight of her, but he said, 'That bloody oil company. Some stupid idea for an extra Christmas ad. Wanted yesterday of course. I'll spare you the details. But no time for toffees, I'm afraid, dear. They'll have to wait till Monday.'

'I'll be away.' Absurdly she felt a little hurt that he had forgotten.

'Oh yes, of course,' he said. 'Well, I'll stall on the toffees till you get back. Bugger this thing!' He straightened up, and produced a smile. 'Have yourself a ball,' he said.

'And you. Happy Christmas.' But did one say that to Jewish people? 'And a gorgeous New Year.' That was safe; although didn't they have a different New Year, too?

Returning to her office, she determined not to think of C de C again until she came back from the farm. *Consuming, we have been consumed.* Nor would she think of anything else that was unpleasant. Conscious of a cloud at the back of her mind, she reiterated, *anything.*

She spent the rest of the morning reading magazines. She did not have to do this furtively; it was part of her work. The agency subscribed not only to British and American 'professional journals' (*trade rags*: how could anyone describe advertising as a 'profession'?) but also to magazines, to see what the trends were 'overseas', and to keep in touch with what foreign advertisers were 'getting up to'. And indeed, in these magazines, the text seemed grudged: articles and stories followed little winding lanes through the fecund acreage of ads.

Turning from *Vogue* to the *Ladies' Home Journal*, she reflected that she preferred the former. It had a saving madness: pure fantasy for all except a small band of dedicated lunatics who actually followed its prescriptions. The sheer silliness of high fashion and *haute cuisine* seemed preferable to the leaden childishness of the American magazine: clothes like uniforms, imposing a schoolgirl trimness; food designed for giant babies. (Hateful minced meat was formed into loaves and patties, to be forced down with the aid of sweet tomato mixtures; canned fruits and vegetables were combined in casings of synthetic jelly; skyscraper cakes were layered with sickly fillings.)

She looked at her watch, deciding, though it was only just twelve, to go out for an early lunch. If she went out at twelve, no one was likely to notice if she did not return till two: almost everyone left the building at that time.

She spent ten minutes in a book shop, looking for a thriller to see her through until next day. On the farm she would read real books, of which Peter and Susan had plenty.

With the thriller in her bag, she walked to the East African Pavilion. She sat at a small table in a corner, and ordered curry. Ben disliked curry; that was one of the things she thought of when she felt antagonistic to him. People who disliked curry, like those – often the same – who recoiled from brains, sweetbreads, kidneys, tripe, seemed to her to resemble Mr Johnson's lady.

Soon the table was covered with small dishes. Reading her book, she tucked in, relishing the spicy food more than the thriller. She liked a thriller to concentrate on the criminal or on some 'outlaw' private eye, not as here, on a policeman; especially when, as in this case, the author tried to make him interesting by referring to his long sensitive fingers and two slim volumes of poetry he had written. What rubbish! She helped herself to more brinjal pickle.

*

It was half-past seven. She was waiting for Richard to fetch her. Her holiday had begun, but she paced in the flat.

Although she had lived in it for two years, she did not feel at home in it, and still prowled it suspiciously, like a newly transplanted cat. Its contents – books, pictures, furniture found in one of the town's few second-hand shops (a vast storehouse, echoing and melancholy, of furniture from the 1880s to the present day) – had been chosen with care. Yet often in the evening she found herself unable to settle in a chair and read or play records. The only way she could stop herself pacing was by going to bed; often as early as other inhabitants of the city whom she mocked for their dull ways.

Now, waiting for Richard, she wondered if what made her so restless was the fact that she could never escape the flat un-accompanied after dark.

Laura could not drive. She thought this contemptible, but felt she would never be able to handle one of those great unwieldy foes. All machines were her enemies. Richard Arden had twice taught her how to change an electric plug. Yet, when this necessity arose, and she undid the screws that held the plug together, she would gaze with incomprehension at the tangle of wires within, as if it were the nest, seen for the first time, of some dangerous creature. When domestic machines went wrong, she shook or struck them. Occasionally this worked, but not often. However if she had done it to a car, she was sure it would have taken revenge. Cars were notorious killers: murderers of innocent and guilty alike. Apart from these criminal propensities, they stank and made city life unpleasant. They had grinning mouths full of metal teeth. She remembered the traffic jam that morning – *Wosa, o wosa* – and stood still. *Wosa, o wosa*. The grinning machines had ground forward again, drowning the singing. She knew she did not really want to handle anything she hated and feared so much. If only – as in London – it were possible to walk. But even in Hillbrow – considered, paradoxically, an unusually safe area because of its dense population – that was impossible, at night.

In the suburbs, where servants lived in cells in the gardens, and maids smuggled in their husbands to sleep with them, every house was a fortress, every window burglar-barred. (Even so, it was said that nothing should be left by an open window: black thieves with fishing-rods would come by night; blankets might be removed so skilfully that the sleeper beneath them would not wake.)

In Hillbrow, in the evening, all blacks – except for a few night-watchmen – were swept away to their slum 'locations', crushed into wheezing buses and ramshackle trains on which people hung from the windows, and even balanced on the roofs of the carriages. (Fatal accidents happened constantly, and on payday, *tsotsis* – black gangsters with knives – pushed through the trains demanding money. It was easier to rob fellow blacks, unprotected by police, than whites.)

Hillbrow, at night, approached Verwoerdt's dream of racial purity, and whites tended not to commit random violence against each other. Yet still Laura could not walk alone at night. No woman did. There was always the possibility of an African invader, lurking in the dark dustbin alley between blocks, or even in the passageway of the flats. When Richard collected her, he would come upstairs. It would not be safe for her to meet him outside.

In London, she would have caught a bus to the Ardens. (Orange Grove, where they lived, was too far to walk to.) She would have been independent. Now the doorbell rang. Through the glass peephole she observed a miniature Richard.

*

Richard was a Professor of Psychology. He was forty-five, and Alice was thirty-one; a former student of his. In those days, she had been not only very bright and hard-working, but also a keen hockey-player. He had described her to Laura one evening as having been 'a great, big, gorgeous bouncing girl.'

Alice had smiled when Richard used this phrase, but Laura could see that she did not like it; the picture it conjured up was not truly feminine. Alice, Laura sometimes thought, was even more dedicated to being feminine than was the woman in Mr Johnson's head. The years she had spent being psycho-analysed in Hampstead and learning to become a child-therapist had also taught her the importance of fully accepting 'woman's role'. There was a conflict here which Laura could not have discussed with Alice. Wasn't it an indication that a woman had not fully overcome her 'castration complex' and her 'penis envy' that she should adopt a profession? Wasn't it an – 'immature' – attempt to 'compensate'? Alice always stressed that she was a '*child-*therapist'; Laura felt that this was because treating children seemed a more feminine activity than presuming to treat adults.

Laura was puzzled and fascinated by Alice's obsession with femininity. She fingered the exceptionally expensive cosmetics in black and silver jars on Alice's dressing-table. She examined the rows of clothes (all simple but made of silk, of suede, and with expensive names on their labels) in Alice's wardrobe. She looked at the row of copper saucepans, the shelves of herbs and spices, the stocked shelves of the store-cupboard in Alice's kitchen. Laura's own possessions were not only less expensive, but also lacked magical properties, which Alice seemed to find in hers. In regard to material possessions, Alice was guilt-free, as she was not in connection with her work. She felt at liberty to buy expensive clothes, to eat in expensive restaurants. (Her literary tastes were rich, too: her favourite contemporary work was the Alexandria Quartet.) *Consuming, we have been consumed.*

It was the same with time. She would frown when a patient was due, but not when preparing an elaborate dish in her kitchen. In fine weather she spent hours sunbathing on the lawn. On cold or rainy days she lay in the sitting-room, on a chaise-longue covered in yellow velvet, playing with her two Siamese cats. (When they caught birds, she seemed pleased. Triumphantly she announced, 'It is their nature.')

Alice intended to have children in another year or two. Laura was not sure that this was a good idea. Once, Laura had been talking to Richard, while Alice treated a little patient in her consulting-room. (The patient arranged toys and objects: Alice interpreted these arrangements and the comments that went with them, as an Ancient priestess had interpreted entrails.) But the children in the house next door made a noise, and Alice rushed out and told them that she was a witch, and if they were not quiet, she would send her cats in the night to scratch out their eyes. What would Alice's idol, Freud, have thought of that?

One by one, Laura had borrowed Freud's works, in their green bindings, from Alice. She tried on bits of case histories, as if she were trying on dresses. She spent hours discussing her childhood in Freudian terms with Alice, enjoying it as she would have enjoyed visits to a fortune-teller. Alice sometimes said that she felt guilty about talking at such a deep level to Laura when she was not doing it professionally. (Who was Alice letting down: Freud himself, or her fellow psycho-therapists? One of the things Laura found most suspect about analysts was their self-serving theory that it was psychologically necessary for patients to pay for their treatments. Why didn't they simply admit that they needed and wanted to make money from their work?)

Tentatively Laura suggested to Alice that individual analysis was a luxury. (That would justify the need-to-pay theory; everyone expects to pay for caviare and champagne.) Didn't analysis turn one inward instead of outward, away from the world not into it? Firmly Alice disagreed, speaking of the 'psychic energy' released by an analysis. 'Where Id was, Ego shall be,' she quoted fervently. Yet, observing Alice, who had been analysed, Laura thought her not an example of released energy but of energy channelled into acceptance. Why should one want to muster 'psychic energy' to make a *boeuf en daube* or to turn, on the lawn, from gold to copper, from copper to bronze?

'Freud is an artist without a medium or a style, poor fellow,' Laura said, alone with Richard, who laughed. His psychology was quite different from Alice's, taking the form of experiments on rats. He never expressed to Alice the view of analysis which he now produced for Laura.

'Freud is certainly not a *scientist*,' he said. 'Any more than that bogus old bullshitter, Jung, is. And it's not even as if their so-called therapy works. They admit themselves that they can't help really disturbed people: only neurotics need apply. And neurotics need to talk about themselves. Any listener will do. Freudian, Jungian, or a Roman Catholic priest in the confessional – really much quicker and cheaper.'

Alice returned, and Richard quickly changed the subject. He gave Laura a test which he said he always gave his first-year students. 'Where are *you*?' he asked. 'Point, and show me.'

Immediately Laura pressed her forefinger into the centre of her body, between breasts and navel.

'No, that's the wrong answer,' Richard said impatiently. 'You should have pointed to your head.'

'How can there be a wrong answer? Richard, what rubbish,' Laura said. They were off.

Afterwards, in the kitchen, Alice said to Laura, 'Of course, when *I* argue with a man, there always comes a point at which I retire gracefully.' Laura thought this sounded like the advice in the women's magazines in her office, but she did not say so. She was careful with Alice, as she wasn't with Richard, because she preferred him and did not want to show it: she never winced when Alice jarred on her.

There was no point, she found, in complaining to either of the Ardens about advertising. Richard thought her job was hilarious, and egged her on to tell funny stories about it, to 'do a turn' on the subject at dinner parties. Often she enjoyed this, and would become quite carried away, especially about C de C. Alice, she noticed, found this less amusing than other people did. Alice probably considered Laura's fantasies about Mr Johnson's secret life almost blasphemous; bizarre psychology was not meant to be funny. In any case, Laura suspected that Alice thought that being funny was unfeminine.

Alice, however, was interested, rather than disgusted, by the manipulative aspect of Laura's work. She viewed this with a kind of relish: 'Why don't you just sit back and enjoy it? There isn't anything you really want to do instead.'

Laura felt like answering 'Anything else in the world' but Alice would have thought that melodramatic, so she said nothing.

Alice said, 'Anyway, copywriting is creative, in a sense. You write within a form and with a purpose.'

'But *what* a purpose!'

'Quite a reasonable one, really, I should have thought. After all, people have to buy things and they need to know what's available.'

'It's all crap,' Richard put in, beaming. Laura beamed back. Alice did not beam, but said, rather sharply, 'Anyway, if you're doing the job, you just have to adjust to it.'

Adjust, Laura thought. *I'm not a radio*. She did not say this. She did not want to offend Alice. The Ardens were her only friends in the city. Max was just an office friend, and Ben was more than a friend. It was the Ardens who had introduced her to Ben. Ben and Richard talked about art.

At weekends, while Alice sunbathed on the lawn, Richard, on the back veranda, painted canvases of faces with empty eye-sockets and gaping mouths. Richard was narrow-shouldered, with skin so white that it had the blue tinge of watered milk. He avoided the sun, but he loved to watch Alice turning from gold to copper, from copper to bronze. He joked that if she became any darker, he and she would be arrested under the Immorality Act, the law that prohibited interracial sex.

Richard was obviously mad about Alice, sexually. Laura had seen him look quite desperate when Alice flirted with other men; Ben, for instance. Sometimes, though Richard and Alice were so happy together, Laura felt uneasy about their future. Richard was a tamed bird and Alice a predator. One day mightn't she, like one of her cats, *mangle* him? Because it was her nature.

Tonight Laura whirled in the Ardens' hall. 'Free! Free!' she exclaimed. Unclouded – almost – was the truth of what she mimed, what she said.

'Rustic bliss on the famous farm!' There was a trace of sourness in Alice's tone, and Laura thought she knew why. Alice felt that the Fields, whom she considered smart – Peter belonged to an old South African family – could well ask her and Richard to the farm for a weekend. Alice did not guess that, on the one occasion when the Ardens and the Fields had met, she – though not Richard – had jarred on them slightly.

*

The farm was Laura's refuge: an island floating in bare pale highveld instead of sea. On the farm, in the stone house above the waterfall, she did not feel South Africa to be appalling.

The Fields had three children, and Susan was now pregnant again. They were devout Catholics: Peter a born one, and Susan a convert. He was compact and sturdy; she had the fierce delicate beauty of a miniature eagle.

Susan's parents had recently been divorced. Her father had not earned enough money for the Inanda life her mother enjoyed. Now her mother had married a rich man, and her father had come to live on the farm in a large cottage down the valley.

Here he had made himself a little England. He called the cottage the Dower House. A file of nursery-rhyme ducks marched to and fro past his window, and he kept a fat spaniel and two yapping beagle pups. His drawing-room was full of well-polished silver rowing trophies, won at school and at Cambridge, and scenes of Jorrocks's sporting mishaps hung on the walls. Tea was measured from a caddy, in a shovel-shaped spoon, and made in a silver teapot. On the hearth of the open fire were bellows, a toasting-fork and a three-legged brass stand, called a trivet and intended to bear a dish of hot buttered crumpets or muffins, both unknown in South Africa.

He had bought a pony to harness to an old trap he found in a decaying barn behind the cottage. Once a week he drove it five miles to the nearest dorp.

This was Buffelfontein. It was not quite as ugly as most South African small towns, because magnificent trees were planted down both sides of its single street. These had been a present to the town from Peter's mother, thirty years before; although Afrikaners disliked trees, no one had cut them down. Yet a peculiarly Afrikaans melancholy permeated the place. A few pieces of rotting fruit lay in the window of the dreadful café, which otherwise offered only cases of soft drinks and cartons of cigarettes. Once, when she was standing by the Fields' car, waiting for Susan, the only sound Laura could hear in the dorp was the sawing of wood; she felt sure it must be for a coffin.

To the dark, dusty general store, which he called 'the village shop', Susan's father came to make his weekly purchases. He summoned a black child to hold the pony and, after doing his shopping, he had a drink in 'the village pub'. This was the gloomy bar of a small hotel where fishermen occasionally stayed. 'A pint of your best ale,' he would say, and the barman would produce a bottle of Lion beer. Sometimes a morose Afrikaans farmer would be resting a meaty arm on the counter, and would respond with a single grunt to any remark. ('Not very chatty, the locals hereabouts!') After downing a couple of brandies and water with furtive Calvinist desperation, the farmer would jolt off in his truck at a furious speed. (African labourers in the back, amongst sacks of samp and mealies, would have to cling to the sides.) 'Quite mad the way these yokels drive,' Susan's father would comment, back at the farm.

Where Laura had despised Inanda Englishness, that of Susan's father charmed her. He was part of the farm, and everything about the farm was charming. It was a place she hoped would never change.

Sitting with Laura on the pale grass in front of the house – there was the rush of the waterfall, the scraping of crickets, the whirr of a Christmas beetle – Susan spoke of the Fields' concern for their farm workers. Peter supplemented their diet of mealies and occasional meat with high-protein soup powder. He had just finished building a school for their children – who would otherwise receive no education at all – and was going to employ an African teacher. Laura suspected that Peter and Susan believed that the country could be run as they ran their farm.

She became part of the rhythm of the place. In the mornings when Peter was out on the lands, Laura and Susan talked, or Laura read while Susan organized the household. Sometimes they drove into the country or went shopping in Buffelfontein. Laura bought bright material from the Indian store just outside the dorp, and Susan made her two dresses. At lunchtime, Peter often joined them and the children for a picnic down by the waterfall.

Laura swam across the pool. It was patterned with the reflection of leaves and branches. The nearer she swam to the fall, the louder was the rush in her ears, and the colder the water. One day, Peter, taking her hand, guided her behind it, helping her up through the thin fringe of water at the edge. Then, backs against a wall of rock, they edged along, hand in hand, till they reached the centre, behind the fall's full curtain; drowning in its roar, gasping. Peter dived out into the pool, but Laura edged back the way they had come.

In the evening, when Elias, the African man-servant, had laid the table and lighted the oil lamps, and Sophia, the African nanny, had fed and bathed the children, and Susan had heard their prayers and put them to bed, Laura and the Fields sat drinking brandy and water. Susan wandered in and out of the kitchen, cooking the dinner. She was a good cook, and at dinner they always drank wine. Afterwards, over more brandy, they talked and played old 78 records on an ancient wind-up gramophone. They played African *kwela* and the thumping Afrikaans tunes of Nico Carstens, and 1930s' records, bought by Peter's father: 'She had to go and lose it at the Astor,' 'The Old Music Master' and 'The Bluebells of Broadway'. Sometimes they danced, separately or together, on the square of green carpet in front of the fire. (Although it was midsummer, the highveld nights were always cool enough for Peter to light the fire after dinner.) When they danced, the large brown dog called Jock, who dozed in front of the burning pine-logs, would rise and stalk off to the other side of the room.

Flopping into a chair, panting and laughing, Laura would suddenly feel exhausted.

Her room was in a separate building, up a flight of stone steps at the side of the house. Peter would hold the door open to give extra light as she climbed the steps, sometimes slightly unsteadily, holding her flickering oil-lamp. In the stillness of the night, the rush of the waterfall was like the sound in a shell. As soon as she was in bed, Laura extinguished the little flame of the lamp. With the smell of oil in her nostrils she would slide at once into a deep pool of sleep.

On the morning of Christmas Eve she woke late. Peter was on the lands, and Elias told her that Susan had gone early into Buffelfontein to buy something she had forgotten. After Laura had drunk a cup of thick black coffee from a metal percolator on the Aga, she walked up to the pine forest above the house. Here the trees were old and very tall.

Her feet sank into thick pine-needles; sharp green ones were loose on the surface of brown decaying layers. She sat down, and trickled new needles from one hand to the other. Light slanted down between the trees in long thin strips, as if through narrow windows. Laura felt an awareness of religion. It seemed to surround her, and she felt that it was because they were religious that Peter and Susan were good. Laura felt that she would like to be good, too, and now, in the pine forest, it seemed possible. She imagined a weight of guilt being lifted from her shoulders.

That evening she told Peter and Susan that she would like to go to church with them next day. Early in the morning they drove to the farm of a neighbouring family called the O'Reillys, who, Peter said, had lived there since the previous century. They were Afrikaans-speaking; all they had kept of their Irish origins was their religion. Three years ago they had built a big new chapel on their farm. The Bishop had consecrated it and now, every Sunday and on Holidays of Obligation, a priest came from a town twenty miles away to hear confessions and say Mass.

Laura was introduced to the O'Reillys outside the chapel. People were exchanging Christmas greetings. Inside, the priest entered the confessional. Mrs O'Reilly and one of her daughters went to confession, and so did Peter and Susan. Absolution, which Laura and the Fields had been talking about the night before, seemed a refreshing idea; but of what sins, she wondered, did Peter and Susan need to be absolved?

The Mass began. Laura looked round the chapel. It was built in the shape of a letter L, upside down, with the horizontal bar pointing to the right. The altar was where the two sections met, and it faced the one in which the congregation was sitting. From where she sat, Laura could see nothing of the section at the side of the altar, and she wondered if it were a Lady-chapel.

The time came when almost all the congregation except Laura filed up to the altar to take communion, returning with their heads lowered and their hands clasped. Then from the invisible section east of the altar, other people filed up: these were black.

Laura placed the idea of absolution in a scale, and weighed it against this newly built, Bishop-consecrated chapel. As the black men and women disappeared again, she realized that she must carry her guilt on her own shoulders. The marks of her actions must remain on her spirit, as the marks of time remained on her face.

When her holiday ended, she caught the evening train that stopped at a siding near the farm gate. Peter and Susan saw her off. She got into a carriage, and they left at once. They were going to stand on the lawn in front of the house and signal to her as the train laboured up the side of the valley.

An old woman was lying along the opposite seat, with her back to the carriage. The strings of her loosened corset trailed out from under a blanket. The train started. It chugged over the bridge across the river Springbokspruit, and then began, with effort, to chug up the steep hillside. As Laura pulled the window open, the old woman muttered crossly in Afrikaans. Suddenly through a gap in the trees, Laura saw the farm, brightly lit. In front of it the tiny figures of Peter and Susan danced with lamps, like glow-worms. Laura waved vigorously, though she was sure they could not distinguish her carriage from down there in Noah's Ark. Trees blocked the view again. The train gave a last shudder, and moved off, fast and smoothly across the veld.

Laura pulled up the window, and sat down. She opened the novel she had borrowed for the journey, but did not start to read. She thought, with a pang, that they would be back in the house now: Susan checking that the children were asleep, Peter pouring out a brandy, the dog undisturbed on the square of green carpet. She thought, with a pang, that they had returned to the calm of their living, as she must return to the anxieties of hers. One of these was grave; she now felt sure that she was pregnant.

She had hoped that, during her stay on the farm, it would prove to be a false alarm. But this had not happened. Seven weeks had now passed since her period, and her female mechanism worked with unfailing regularity; a variation of two days was the most she ever experienced. Now, as soon as she was back in Johannesburg, she must take action.

First, of course, she must be sure. She would go to see a doctor she did not know, giving him a false name and address. Then, if – when – her suspicion was confirmed, she must start the search for an abortion.

It was a good thing, she reflected now, in the train, that her religious impulse had been so short-lived. At the thought, her lips twitched in a smile. If the impulse had persisted, a 'conflict' – as Alice might put it – would have been set up. Now she felt a single-minded determination to go ahead, and to overcome every obstacle. For there would be obstacles. Abortion was illegal; it was censured and punished with the rigour of a patriarchal Calvinist society. (Of course, in this regard, the Fields' Roman Catholicism was just as rigid. That was why she had not mentioned her suspicions to Susan.)

A bottle of gin and a hot bath; pills to 'correct irregularity': she felt sure that both these methods were a waste of time. And she intended to have no dealings with that figure of female folklore (who undoubtedly existed): the old woman with a knitting-needle or crochet-hook. No, after confirming that she was pregnant, she must find a doctor. She would have to seek advice about this. From whom?

Alice was the first person she had thought of; but could she trust Alice not – in any circumstances – to tell Ben? Of course, Alice could not track him down now, somewhere in Europe, and by the time he returned, at the beginning of February, 'all would be over,' or so she hoped. But she did not want Ben to know, even then. He might feel he had to pay for the abortion, and the situation was her fault. She had assumed the responsibility for contraception, and the cream she had been using for years had failed her. Wincing from rubber contraceptives, she had always ignored suggestions that it was not entirely reliable.

It was her fault, the cream's fault, but certainly not Ben's fault. Surely Alice would not tell him, if Laura asked her not to, even though he and she were such friends, even though Alice viewed herself as the patron of Laura and Ben's relationship? Having 'brought them together', Alice liked to feel partly responsible for the fact that Ben was Laura's lover. *Laura's lover!* It sounded like a Victorian poem or a Pre-Raphaelite painting. Yet what other word was there? Boy-friend sounded coy, and plain 'friend' seemed to come from the lips of an Edwardian lady with a past, taking the waters at a German spa. (Laura giggled, and the old woman on the other side of the compartment shifted; her corset strings were a grubby pink.) But 'lover'? Ben had never said he loved her. She did not think that 'love' was part of Ben's plan.

Ben's life was a plan in two stages. He had published his – very well-received – study of South African art. That was the first stage, and now he had embarked on the second. He was doing early research – the research would take years – for the *magnum opus* in which he would formulate his philosophy of art. This book would be massive, magnificent, momentous, a masterpiece. (What a lot of ms! Laura giggled again. But Ben was the one person she knew whom she believed might produce a masterpiece. She believed this partly because of his obsession with it and partly because of his independence of people, including herself.)

His flat – in Hillbrow, but in an older block than Laura's; humanized by its architect's absurd Art Deco touches – was heaped with files, with manuscript, with bundles of papers. Books were piled everywhere, as well as filling the shelves.

He lectured at the university on History of Art. He was a friend of Richard's, though he did not own any of Richard's paintings. (Laura had one in her living-room.) In fact, there were no pictures at all on

Ben's walls; he said he found them distracting. On the other hand, stones, shells, fragments of pottery were everywhere: on shelves, tables, window sills. The flat was dusty, but not dirty, though he had no servant. (The kitchen was spotless, for he never cooked; at home he ate only fruit and wholemeal bread and honey.) He himself looked both clean and tidy. His clothes, which tended towards autumn tints, matching his own colouring, became him. He was a slow and fussy shopper.

He was precise. She remembered the week they had spent in Lourenco Marques. He carefully rubbed himself with oil, and always wore his dark glasses. He remembered to hang up his swimming-trunks at lunchtime, so that they would be dry in the afternoon. She forgot to put on her protective lotion, and turned red. She felt uneasy in dark glasses, so the sun made her eyes ache. She often had to struggle into a damp, sandy bathing-dress, which she had discarded on the bathroom floor.

Ben lay neatly on a geometric – and autumnal – towel. She sprawled on one from the hotel; it was too small. Ben never lit a cigarette till he had decided that he really wanted it. She smoked all the time.

'That gull – what marvellous calculation!' he exclaimed. 'Just before it touched the water, wheeling up in that perfect curve!' She had sensed a flash of white against a blur of blue. Until Ben spoke she had not known it was a bird.

The first time he took her out, after their initial meeting at the Ardens', they went to a matinée of Ingmar Bergman's *The Magician*. Afterwards they sat in Laura's flat, arguing about the film. She had seen the magician as a priest, but Ben saw him as an artist, and she began to come round to his point of view. Talking and drinking wine, she became aware of a stabbing sensation which, with astonishment, she recognized as desire. Standing to fill his glass, she wanted to topple towards him; in fact, she swayed in his direction. It was enough. Argument forgotten by them both – there was no question of 'retiring gracefully' – he took the bottle from her, and put it on the table. (She had felt a moment's doubt. In London, before going to bed with a man, she had always had several drinks so that she would feel less nervous.) Ben took her hand and led her into her bedroom. (Wasn't there something rather absurd about being led to bed?) He drew the blind down over the window. This blind, cream-coloured, with a raised pattern of concentric circles, had softened the still-powerful late-afternoon light. They undressed. He stroked her arms, and she was gone. 'I don't understand,' she said afterwards. 'You only touched my arms.'

'Sex isn't just here . . . or here . . . or here,' he said, indicating what she had believed were the only places where desires – like moody dogs in kennels – lurked until someone dragged them out. 'It's all over you.'

'Oh, I see,' she said, and fell asleep. Afterwards she felt so lotophagous, so stretchy.

It was never better than that first time ('The time with my arm and the blind,' as she thought of it). It was different. Sometimes she found him clinical: 'Have you had enough of this?' or 'Do you need some more of that?' Yet she enjoyed it. She would have gone to bed with him more often, but he was busy and had many friends. The only ones Laura knew were the Ardens, who invited them out together, as if they were 'a couple'. This, of course, they were not. Now Ben was travelling light, in Europe. He had sent her a postcard from Amsterdam. Now, outside the train window, lay mile after mile of empty veld.

*

She did tell Alice. Alice knew so many people. Surely, one of them could recommend a doctor? And, for Laura's purpose, a doctor had to be 'recommended'. She could not pick one at random from the telephone book, as she picked the gynaecologist who confirmed that she was pregnant.

Before telling Alice, she had not foreseen how much discourse would be involved. Alice felt obliged to deliver a lecture on possible damage to Laura's psyche. (It was her body that Laura was worried about.)

This lecture was interrupted by the arrival of Richard. Laura had always expected that Alice would tell *him*. She had not even thought of asking her not to, when she asked her not to tell Ben. (Alice had agreed to this before embarking on the lecture.)

Now, when Richard arrived, Laura herself told him the news abruptly. Alice resumed her disquisition, but Richard cut it short, saying, 'The decision is entirely up to Laura.'

'I only wanted to warn her of possible emotional repercussions,' Alice said. A few minutes later, however, she agreed to 'put out feelers'. Within two days she had heard of a Dr Karaolis who was known to have 'helped' many women.

'Karaolis – what an odd name,' Laura said.

'It's Greek.'

'Oh.' Laura would have preferred a doctor who was British-trained.

'There's only one drawback,' Alice said. 'He's so well known that there's a rumour that the police may be on his track.'

'Oh.' All the same, Laura rang up and made an appointment.

Except for a middle-aged receptionist with a foreign accent and hennaed hair, the waiting-room was empty. Within minutes Laura was shown into the surgery.

He sat behind a large old-fashioned desk, under a bright yellow reproduction of a painting of the Acropolis. He was a pale, plump, middle-aged man. She wondered if his gloomy expression were habitual. He did not smile even when he said 'Good afternoon.' He asked her to sit down, and when she had done so, said, 'And what can I do for you, *madame*?'

She had considered various ways of approaching the subject. What she said was, 'I'm going to have a baby,' which was absurd, because this was what she was determined not to do. 'Well,' she added. 'I mean . . .'

But he raised a hand to silence her, and suddenly she was astonished to see tears pouring out of his eyes. He felt for a handkerchief in his pocket, and mopped them, and then his forehead, which was sweaty. 'No, you must please go away,' he said. 'I cannot help you. No. It is too dangerous.' Then he looked frightened. 'I advise you to see another doctor about your baby,' he said. 'I am not a gynaecologist.'

Now she and he, under the Acropolis, were both crying. 'You must please go,' he said, and she stood up.

A week later she saw another doctor about whom Alice had heard a rumour. When he understood what she wanted, he showed indignation. Next Alice mentioned a woman. 'Not a doctor, but she used to be a nurse. She's meant to be very clean. A friend of mine went to her.'

Laura was terrified, but she nodded. 'The only thing is,' Alice said, 'that my friend will have to take you there. Otherwise this woman might think it was a trap.'

Alice's friend was a dark sturdy woman called Fay, married to a lawyer and now the mother of a child. It was more than three years since she had visited the former nurse. Together she and Laura set off in her car. The former nurse lived in a suburb called Saxonwold. 'I'm sure this is the street,' Fay said, turning a corner. 'And this is the house. At least I think it is. I'm not quite sure. In fact I'm not absolutely sure that this is the right street, after all.' They drove round and round Saxonwold. In the end, Fay, unable to recognize street or house, took Laura back to the Ardens.

*

A week later, Laura, Alice, Richard and one of the Siamese cats were in the Ardens' sitting-room.

'I got into a discussion on abortion at the university the other day,' Richard said. 'With someone I thought might know something. There was only one person he'd heard of who had done it, and then the circumstances were exceptional. The girl had had an affair with an African. The child might have been black. The girl could have been prosecuted.'

'What's this doctor's name?' Laura asked.

'He's called Fein. He's got a practice in the southern suburbs. But from what I heard I'm absolutely sure he wouldn't do anything for you, Laura. Another dead end!'

When she made her appointment with Dr Fein, she did not tell the Ardens. This time, the receptionist 'fitted her in' when she said it was urgent. The doctor's waiting-room was crowded with mothers and small children. She had to wait for almost an hour.

He was in his thirties: large, good-looking, slightly heavy. His manner was brisk. 'Yes?' he said. She felt intimidated.

She said, 'I'm pregnant, and I can't, I mustn't have the baby. Will you help me?'

'*I?*' he said. 'What could possibly have made you come to me? I'm a family doctor. I can only presume you picked my name out of the phone-book.'

'Someone at the university said . . .' She hesitated.

'Someone at the university is misinformed.' He looked angry.

'You see,' she said, 'the father's black.'

He glanced up at her sharply at this. Then his face became expressionless. He started to tap his fingers together, like a lawyer in Dickens. At last he said, 'I see. Well that does make a difference – to your situation, I mean. You're quite sure you're pregnant?'

'Yes, I had a test and everything.'

'Hmm. Have you tried anyone else? About termination?'

'There was a Greek . . .'

'Hmm. He was arrested two days ago, if it's the man I'm thinking of. You can understand why doctors are hesitant to break the law, whatever their personal beliefs.'

'Oh yes, I can.'

'Hmm. Well, you aren't allowed by the law to get married. And of course you can't have the child. Unless you leave the country.'

'Oh no.' Saying this, she was surprised that she meant it.

'What does he feel – the father?'

'Oh . . . he understands.'

'Naturally. Are you fond of him?'

'Yes.'

'What does he do?'

'He's a teacher.'

'Hmm. Well, something must obviously be done.' He paused. He smiled with some irony. 'It appears,' he said, 'that I'm the person who must do it.' Up till now, he had been tapping his fingers, lawyer-like. Now he clasped his hands together. At that moment, she loved Dr Fein, truly loved him.

'Well,' he said, 'we must set the wheels in motion. The technical term is a "D and C". The reason for it is that you have an infection. You must never tell anyone the truth. Do you understand? And you must never give anyone else my name, however drastic their circumstances. Even if they're in the same boat as you are now. Do you promise?'

'I promise,' she said.

'Hmm. As for "someone at the university", will you tell them – but, no, on second thoughts, don't tell them anything at all. Say . . . that I refused, if they ask you. Will you do that?'

'I promise.'

'You must realize that my life's work is at stake.'

Loving Dr Fein, she appreciated that he said, 'life's work', not 'career', the word a lesser man would have used.

*

Dr Karaolis's fee, she had heard, was two hundred pounds. This 'D and C' cost twenty; for the anaesthetist. Dr Fein did not charge her for the operation, and he booked her into a large new hospital. This – like other white facilities, including schools – was free, though hospitals and schools for Africans charged fees.

At the end of their first meeting (which – apart from a glimpse of his masked face before the operation, and the brief examination he gave her the day after – was their last) Dr Fein gave her a prescription for 'the Pill'. She had heard of it, of course, but, accustomed to her cream, had not thought of using it. Now she decided that there had never been an invention with such power to set women free.

She told the Ardens that she had found an abortionist – whose name she had promised not to reveal – through someone in her office. They were relieved.

She returned to work two days after she left the hospital. She did not feel ill, and a slight soreness was soon gone. She was not depressed.

'You're very quiet,' Richard said at her first dinner with the Ardens. 'It's the reaction,' said Alice. Laura felt irritated. She was not depressed. Soon after, she dined with the Fields, who were spending a night in the city. 'You look peaky,' said Susan. Peter said, 'Yes. What you need is a nice juicy steak.' It was kind of him, but the thought of the red meat appalled her, and she ordered Sole Véronique. She was not depressed. It was just that she could think of nothing to look forward to, though there was, of course, Ben's return.

*

On the Wednesday night when Ben came to dinner, she cooked cauliflower cheese because he was so fond of it. She had bought a wholemeal loaf, and she made a green salad. At the last moment, feeling that the meal looked dull, she prepared a mush of aubergines and garlic in olive oil.

He kissed her – lips closed – on arrival. A characteristic of his was never to make erotic gestures until 'bedtime'. He was paler than usual; it was winter in Europe. He said he was thinking of a long weekend in Natal, before term started. He did not say he wished she could come too. Of course he knew she could not, because she had just taken her holiday, so, even if he did not want her with him, he might safely have made the gesture.

He enjoyed the cauliflower cheese and the bread and the salad, but he left his small helping of aubergine, after one mouthful, saying it was 'rather rich'.

He talked about the pictures he had seen. Here he was, cool and pale, talking about art, when she had been through so much because of him. For, in a sense, it had been his fault. After all, it could not have happened without him.

Now he was eating an apple, although he had left his aubergines. Sometimes Laura would start to eat an apple, and stop half way, out of sheer boredom. She was very different from him.

At this point he asked her if she would like to go to the Film Society with him on Sunday, to see a programme of documentaries. She seldom enjoyed a whole evening of these, but she said, 'Yes'. He took his black notebook from his pocket, and made an entry in it.

'Coffee?' she asked, knowing he would refuse. He never drank coffee in the evening. She would have liked a cup, but she could not be bothered to make it just for herself, and she hated 'Instant'. She went into the kitchen, and opened a second bottle of wine – they had already

170

drunk one – but when she offered some to him, he said, 'No thank you.'

'Nothing Dowson about you, Ben,' she said, and then quoted, '*I called for madder music and for stronger wine.*'

'I love that line,' he said. 'Can't you picture the scene? "Waiter, do ask the band to play some *madder* music and, while you're about it, you might bring a bottle of some *stronger* wine."'

She laughed; against her will.

'And how is C de C?' he asked.

'Oh, for heaven's sake, don't let's talk about *that*. I'm expecting the worst day ever, with C de C, tomorrow.' Then she said, 'Far more significant things than C de C have been going on in your absence.' The need to tell had become irresistible.

'Oh? How intriguing. Why have you been so silent about them until now, instead of regaling me with them?'

'The subject wasn't really one for the dinner table, I thought.' That sounded exactly the sort of thing Mr Johnson's lady might say (though 'the subject' would never have arisen in her conversation). Laura said, 'I found I was pregnant. I had to have an abortion.'

'Goodness, how did *that* happen?' He sounded interested, but impersonal. She believed that she could see into his mind, and that he was wondering whether he or someone else had been 'the father'. She *knew* he was thinking that.

'My bloody cream didn't work.'

'Oh, *what* a silly girl. You must use something more reliable.'

'I always shall, from now on. I've got "the Pill".'

'Excellent!'

'Goodness, you're callous,' she said with a little laugh. 'Don't you realize how difficult it is to get an abortion?'

'There's a Greek doctor, I believe,' he said, absolutely ignoring the accusation of callousness. (How slippery he was; it was impossible to quarrel with him.)

'He doesn't do it any more. He's been arrested.'

'Oh. But you found someone?'

'Yes, I did. In the end.'

'And all's well that ends well. The kindly doctor – who was he? Or perhaps it was a she?'

She said, 'I'm afraid I promised not to give the name.'

'Oh. Pity. It's useful to know of someone in that line. One's always hearing of desperate damsels in distress. Anyway, I'm glad you got it sorted out.'

He wasn't going to ask about the cost. Knowing about Dr Karaolis –

what an odd coincidence! – he might well know what he had charged. Ben had no reason to believe that another doctor would have charged less, yet he did not offer to contribute. ('Oh, *what* a silly girl.')

But now he stood up and came over to her. 'Poor Laura. Come to bed and be happy. Nothing to worry about any longer.'

So there they were. 'A little more of that?'

'No . . . no, thank you.'

As usual he had a doze, and then got up to shower, dress, go home. 'Good night, sweet Laura.'

She pretended to be drowsy. He let himself out. As soon as he had gone, she got up to lock and chain the door. The time was quarter past eleven.

She showered. Usually she wanted to retain his stickiness, his warmth till morning. Tonight she wanted to wash him away.

Afterwards she put on a clean nightdress. (She always wore a nightdress. Ben said it was old-fashioned but, sleeping naked, she felt vulnerable.) Then she wandered to and fro between living-room and kitchen, carrying dishes which Evelyn would wash-up next day. She sat down in the living-room (she never sat in the kitchen, which had a white strip-light), in the armchair where she had been sitting when Ben said 'Poor Laura'. Now, under the dining-table, she noticed an object: the black book he always carried in his pocket: notebook, address book, diary.

She went to pick it up. Before returning to her chair, she poured herself a glass of wine from the almost full bottle she had put in the refrigerator. Sitting down, she took a sip, then put down her glass, and sat holding the notebook in her hand.

The book had a stout elastic band around it, for it bulged with cards, cuttings and scraps of paper on which Ben had jotted things he wanted to remember. (How did he ever find them again? She was reminded of the heaps of paper in his flat.) The book was his constant companion. She was astonished that, even this once, he should have forgotten it.

Carefully she removed the band. She turned the pages slowly; determined not to drop any of the enclosures. With his ability to find his way through what seemed to her a jumble, Ben might well notice if something were misplaced. The scraps of paper had names, addresses and telephone numbers on them, and the titles, authors and, often, publishers of books.

This was not a diary in the sense that it had dates printed in it. Ben added those as he went along, when noting engagements. For instance, *8 pm. 1.iv. '60* (how precise he was): *A & R*. That must have been dinner with Alice and Richard, before Laura had met him.

She turned to the most recent entries, for 1962. The last (7.15. 11.ii. '62: Fetch L. Film Soc.) was the one he had made this evening. (That must have been when he had dropped the book.)

She went backwards and forwards, turning pages. On many occasions single initials had numbers after them in brackets: usually 1, sometimes 2, occasionally 3. She wondered how to interpret this. Flipping about, she became aware that during the past year (their affair had lasted a year now) various Ls were treated in this way, usually followed by (1), but sometimes by (2). An interpretation occurred to her.

She remembered the date on which they had first made love, and she looked it up. Her suspicion was confirmed; her initial was followed by (2).

She remembered another date: the Fifth of November, last year. South Africans still keenly – and surprisingly, she thought – commemorated what they called 'Guyfox': the foiling of that attempt in 1605 to blow up the parliament at 'West-min-is-ter'. She took another sip of wine. After dining out that night, they had seen, from the balcony outside her flat, rockets and flares exploding all over the city. Afterwards there were sounds like distant gunfire: they experienced the affinity between sex and fireworks. It was the only occasion on which he had ever made love to her three times. 5.xi. '61. Yes, here it was: L (3).

All through the book, and all through the past year, there were other single initials with bracketed numbers after them. There was an E. There was a J. There was an S. Two recurred frequently: D and A. (A? Surely it couldn't be . . . But Laura remembered her own speculation: *mightn't Alice mangle Richard? Because it was her nature*.) D was the one in Laura's mind now. For today, before his engagement with her, he had seen D. At 3 pm: D (1).

She wondered if now, at home, he were searching for the book, in order to record L (1). She finished her glass of wine. Then – careless of burglars or prowlers – she undid the door, and went out into the passage. She tore all the cards, all the cuttings, all the pages of the book into tiny pieces, and scattered the flakes over the Golden City.

> *I'm dreaming of a white Christmas,* [she sang]
> *Just like the ones I used to know,*
> *With vampires kissing,* [she improvised,]
> *And children missing –*

At this point she broke off, and went back into the flat.

She was woken by two peremptory noises. Opening her eyes, she identified both after a few seconds: the alarm by her bed and the telephone in the living-room, ringing simultaneously. Her hand went out, and pressed the button on top of the clock. She stumbled through into the sitting-room, and snatched the receiver from the telephone.

'Hunh?'

'Oh, did I wake you. Sorry, but it's probably just as well. You have to go out early this morning, didn't you say?'

'Hunh?'

'It's about my notebook. The black one. You know?'

'Oh. Yes.'

'I did leave it at your flat last night, didn't I?'

'Hunh? Oh, yes. Under the table.'

'Ah! Thank goodness for that. If it were lost, I would be, too. I'll drop in for a second this evening and pick it up if I may?' It was during this speech that she remembered what she had done with the notebook. 'Hullo, hullo,' he said. 'Are you there, Laura? Will that be all right?'

She spoke quickly: 'No, not this evening. I'm going out. Directly from work. I may be late. I don't know what time. This evening won't do.'

'Oh?' He sounded inquisitive. There was a pause. He said, 'Well, when, then? It will have to be tomorrow. I'll call for it on my way to work. I've got an early lecture. I'll rush in at about 7.30. 'Bye.'

He rang off. She headed back to bed, running, and she skidded on the parquet floor, which a 'flat-boy', employed by the owner of the block, polished to a furious gloss each day. (He cleaned the corridors, stairs and lifts but, inside the flats, only the floors; other housework was left for the tenants' own servants.) Laura caught at the bedroom door to stop herself falling, and succeeded, but with a jar which made her realize how awful she felt. She had taken two sleeping-pills – normally she took only one – at two that morning, driven by her craving for sleep. Now she sat down on the bed, but realized that she must not get into it. The time was half-past six, and the photographer was picking her up at seven. She was going with him to fetch a model, because this model was an African woman, and he had not wanted to travel alone with her in his car. Even if she sat in the back, police might have stopped and questioned him, on the chance that he had contravened, or intended to contravene the 'Immorality Act'.

*

174

In the studio, the African nurse stood on a sheet of heavy green paper, rolled down from a wall for the photographic session. The nurse was doing this work, after night duty, for a fee which – a third of what a white model would have been paid – was the equivalent of her normal weekly wage.

Laura and the photographer, Joe, had picked her up outside the African hospital: an ageing barracks set among prefabs in a bleak yard surrounded by a high wire fence. The nurse, who was very good-looking, was still in uniform, but carried – as previously instructed – a bag containing two dresses: her best and her worst.

On the way back, they were caught in a traffic jam. Laura felt ill. She wondered if she would have to jump out of the car to vomit, but controlled the urge. In the studio, Max was scowling because they were ten minutes late. It was lucky that Laura was there. (Mr Johnson liked her to attend all C de C photographic sessions, 'to provide the feminine touch'.) If it had been Antonia, Max would probably have burst out in one of his rages. Now he merely gave his watch a long stare.

There was the business about the model's changing to be settled. Models usually changed in the ladies' cloakroom, but this was for 'whites only'. In the end Laura accompanied the model there. While she changed, Laura waited outside the cubicle, ready to explain the unusual situation. Happily, no typists appeared; any of them would have been horrified to see a native emerging from a white wc.

Back in the studio, Max studied Laura's captions for the three pictures Joe was going to take. Laura's hand, holding her own copy of the captions, shook, and Max, observing this, raised his eyebrows.

First, Joe photographed the model – un-made-up, and in a dismal dress – in shadow. 'Look *sad*,' Max said, and a glum expression was quite soon achieved. The caption said, 'Mary's skin used to be dull and dark looking. She was so worried that she spoke to a friend about it. Her friend gave her a kind hint.'

In the second picture, a close-up, a towel swathed the model's shoulders. 'Now pat some of this stuff into your face,' said Joe. Laura showed how it should be done (*with an upward and outward movement*) while the model held up the C de C bottle in her other hand. (Mr Johnson would never have included the bottle in an advertisement aimed at his lady, but he felt it was necessary for the native market.)

'Try to look *hopeful*,' Max said.

'Hopeful?' said the nurse.

'As if you hope something good is going to happen.'

The nurse bared her teeth. At last they got it right. The caption said,

'Mary's kind friend told her that Crème de Coolay would make Mary's skin look brighter and lighter. So Mary tried it.'

There was the changing business to go through again. Then the nurse's face was made up with pale foundation and powder. Joe fiddled with his light meter and made adjustments to the camera.

'A *real* smile this time,' Max said. Suddenly he beamed at the model. Instinctively she beamed back. The caption said, 'How surprised and pleased Mary is a few weeks later! That dull, dark look seems to have melted away. Mary's skin looks so clear and fair!'

The nurse was preparing to leave. 'How'll you get home?' asked Max.

'By the bus,' she said.

'You look tired. Been up all night, hey?'

She shrugged and nodded.

Max had already paid her fee. Now Laura noticed that he reached for his own wallet when he said, 'I think we can run to a taxi fare.'

Max is kind, thought Laura. For several minutes she had been feeling increasingly sick. Now the urge was irresistible. 'Excuse me,' she said, and then, hastily, to the nurse, 'Goodbye'. She reached the ladies' room just in time. When she emerged from the cubicle, a typist called Denise was working on her face in front of the mirror. It was nearly lunchtime. The photography had taken all morning.

'Eaten something that disagreed with you?' Denise asked.

'Yes, I think so.'

'Shame,' said Denise.

Laura washed her face and hands. She had left her bag in the studio, so she couldn't put on any make-up.

In the studio, Max was alone. 'You look like hell,' he said. 'Feeling ill?'

'Just a bit.'

'Very British. Very stiff upper lip. Why don't you go home? I'll tell everyone you were on the brink of death, and how brave of you it was to come in at all. The call of duty! But you must try not to be so sensitive, darl.'

'Sensitive?'

'Yes. If you live in South Africa, you've got to put up with this sort of thing. Selling whiteness!' He gave an angry laugh.

So Max attributed her condition entirely to the events of this morning. She felt ashamed. 'Selling whiteness,' he had said. *Consuming, we have been consumed.*

'You must toughen up, Laura. Or you'll go under,' he said now.

Go under. She said, 'Perhaps I will go home, after all.'

'You do that. I'll come out with you. I want to get a sandwich.' He put on his jacket. She picked up her bag.

The office was almost empty, but on the landing, waiting for the lift, were Mr Johnson and the agency's managing director, 'Robby' Robbins. They were obviously going out to lunch together.

'Hullo there, Laura,' said Mr Johnson. 'Did the photographs of the native girl go well?'

She said, 'To hell with you and your stinking sheep's grease,' and started down the four flights of stairs.

Max came after her, calling, 'Laura!' He caught up with her on the second floor. 'For God's sake,' he said, 'go back and say you're sorry. I'll tell them you're ill. We can make it all right again. Otherwise, sure as hell, they'll chuck you out. When the news gets around, you'll never get another job in advertising. That's for sure.'

'I've burnt my boats,' she panted, short of breath, and kept on going down. At the bottom of the stairs she turned and kissed Max's cheek. 'Dear, dear Max,' she said, and hurried away.

The mad exhilaration she had felt when she spoke to Mr Johnson had died on the way downstairs. Outside it was another typical Johannesburg summer day, grey and heavy. Up on the farm it was never like this, though the farm was only a thousand feet higher than the city. *If she were on the farm.* But she remembered the truth she had acknowledged as the train moved off across the veld: Peter and Susan resuming their lives, and she returning to her own. After the break between her and Ben, which 'side' would the Ardens take? she wondered. Which side would 'A' take?

She stopped at the chemist's shop near the top of the hill. Here she always brought her prescription for sleeping-pills, and the same middle-aged woman was always behind the counter. She greeted Laura. Then she said, 'There'll be a storm this afternoon, and then it will be nice and fresh again. That's the joy of Joburg.'

'Yes.' Laura smiled. 'And do you think,' she said, 'that you could let me have two bottles of the pills. I've got to go away on business suddenly tomorrow, and I haven't time to renew the prescription.'

'A business trip, hey? Where you going?'

'Durban.'

'Very hot this time of year. Steamy. But perhaps you'll be able to get to the beach. Combine business with pleasure, hey?'

'Yes.' She smiled again.

'I think that'll be all right about the pills. After all, you're a regular customer.'

'Yes, you can trust me.' She laughed.

Her next stop was at the bottle store near her flat. There she bought whisky, which was extravagant, but why not?

The flat was very clean and very quiet. There was a smell of floor-polish. Washing, beautifully ironed, was piled on her bed.

In the bedroom, she drew the cream-coloured blind. Now all she needed was a plastic bag. She had a new jersey, in a drawer, still in its wrapping. She took the packet out of the drawer, and then carefully peeled off the transparent tabs of sticky tape that sealed it. (Normally, she would have ripped it open.) She took out the jersey.

The woman she remembered hearing about had learnt that she had inoperable cancer. She had washed down a number of sleeping pills with most of a bottle of whisky, and had then pulled a plastic bag over her head. Now Laura prepared to follow her example.

Celia 1980

She had returned from her swim at half-past eight. Now she was waiting for Kosta's knock on the side door; the grey wooden door in the courtyard wall.

Every Sunday morning he arrived between nine and eleven. She wished he would come at precisely the same time each week. As she had no other engagements it would have been absurd to suggest this, but ever since she had given up cigarettes – six months before – even trivial waits, delays or uncertainties seemed hard to bear. This, for Celia, was the worst aspect of not smoking.

Until a month ago, she had gradually got into the way of opening the door first thing in the morning and leaving it unlocked till she went to bed. Kosta, on Sundays, had come straight in, as Thalia did on Fridays. Now, however, Celia undid the three fastenings – a bolt, a large twisted nail, and a long heavy hook, embedded in the wall of the house and fitting into a metal ring on the door – only when there was knocking, and after she had inspected the visitor through a crack in the door.

She realized that anyone determined to enter the courtyard could scale the wall; it was less than eight feet high. But that would be positive trespass, a definitely illegal violation of her privacy which she hoped the Arab would not be prepared to risk.

*

She had first swum six weeks ago, at the very start of May. She went down the street that led from her house to the sea, making a short detour to avoid a small decaying home for old people. (Its residents were few and childless; islanders considered it disgraceful to abandon aged parents.) Outside this home, a demented woman in an orange mesh scarf – from a distance the scarf looked like wild rusty hair – often stood begging. When Celia remembered to bring money, she found fulsome thanks and blessings embarrassing, and when she forgot, she felt guilty.

179

Reaching the sea-front she walked along it to a point where the road narrowed; here, though concrete blocks towered opposite, palm trees grew round the last old building on the edge of the sea. (A dispute over compensation was delaying its demolition, but the municipality was eager to give the road – and the whole front – a uniform look.) Just beyond this house was a pleasingly haphazard little pebbly beach. Fishing boats rested on the shore around a low stone wall.

Celia took off her dress; she left it, with her sandals and a black plastic bag containing her towel and underclothes, on the wall. Then she entered the water, which was cool at this time of year. She swam, close to the shore, as far as the Public Gardens, and then she turned and swam back. She dressed under her towel, in the extra privacy given by the little wall, and walked home.

A month before, just as she was taking her towel from her bag, a man's right hand came round her and clutched at a breast; his left hand grabbed and squeezed a buttock.

She sprang away, and swung round. She saw that the man, who wore a loose white shirt and trousers, was one of the many Arabs who, in summer, came to the island from the Gulf.

Seizing her towel, she struck him on the head with it repeatedly. 'Go away,' she shouted. Head bowed against the battery of blows, he shuffled off a few paces, then turned. From between full lips he thrust out a thick tongue.

'Off,' she shouted, and then, lower but more fiercely, 'Pig! Swine! Pig!' The tongue was retracted. Now his face was furious, and he clenched his fists. She sensed that he was going to hit her, but then he glanced towards the nearby road on which cars were passing, and up at the windows of the nine-storey block beyond. He assessed the possibilities, then wheeled and set off briskly – his walk was stiff, and his shoulders under the loose shirt were narrow – in the direction of the town.

She had always felt a horror of Islam: of its barbarous penalties, its fanatic prohibitions and, above all, the way it degraded women. (In London she had winced at the sight of shrouded muzzled figures, shopping at Harrods but denied identity.) That the man who had attacked her was an Arab gave the episode an importance for her which it might otherwise have lacked.

The Arab's shadow lay on her morning outings. Even while swimming she glanced frequently towards the shore. She no longer swam the last stretch – formerly her favourite – where the blocks of flats across the road gave way to the trees of the Public Gardens. In spite of the cars on the road it seemed lonely there. Might he, seething under the unforgivable insult – 'Pig! Swine!' – be lurking behind the kiosk at the gate, waiting to dash into the water, to swim out and to drag her under?

She knew the idea was ridiculous. By now he had probably left the island. It was unlikely that she would ever see him again. Yet she often imagined that she saw him turning a corner ahead of her, or that he dodged behind her, secretly following her home. It was absurd. Yet this was the reason why she locked the courtyard door.

*

Now she heard Kosta's knock, and felt the momentary reluctance, the retreat from a demand, which she always felt before his visits, although, during them, she often found that she enjoyed herself. She went to the door, undid its three fastenings, and opened it. She smiled down at Kosta. He smiled up at her.

Nine years old, he was Thalia's son. It was as a gift to Thalia – so dependable, so generous with fish caught by Andreas, with lemony homemade brawn and mint-flavoured Easter bread – that Celia was teaching Kosta English.

IDA 1967

Ida woke in the froggy light that came through the mesh on the window. She heard keys and the clink of metal. She swung her legs out of bed, and pushed her feet into her sandals. Standing up, she put on her blue dressing-gown. While she was fastening the buttons, the bulb that hung from the ceiling lit up; a matron in the yard had switched it on with a key. Now another key turned. Ida's door opened, and two matrons, Mrs Steyn and Mrs Potgieter, came in. Mrs Steyn was in her brown overcoat, ready to go home. Mrs Potgieter had just come on duty. Her dress was patterned with big purple flowers that matched tiny spots on her face. Ida and the matrons all said 'Good morning' together.

Mrs Potgieter gave Ida a tin mug, two-thirds full of black coffee, and Mrs Steyn gave her a tin plate on which were two fried eggs with hard centres, a slice of bread and a nickel spoon.

Ida said, 'I must go to the lavatory.'

'Right you are,' said Mrs Potgieter, 'but we will have to lock you up again, after. There was one brought in last night.'

'Yes, I heard her.' Ida answered.

'You must have – the row she kicked up!' Mrs Steyn said. Both matrons shook their heads and raised their eyebrows. Ida realized that she was doing the same, and stopped. She felt she had been elected to a respectable club that she did not want to join.

Mrs Steyn said, 'It won't be long now before she goes to court.'

Ida put the plate and mug on the shelf by her bed, and went past the matrons into the yard. She saw a mess of legs and hair in the cell opposite. She smelt morning air and then drains. It was Monday. The cleaners did not come at weekends, so no disinfectant had been poured down the gratings since Friday. There was a thick mess of vomit in the middle of the yard. She looked away, and went through the doorless doorway into the washroom.

Glass crunched under her sandals. Looking up, she saw that the light bulb was broken. She pushed open the chest-high door that divided the washroom from the lavatory. It was like half a saloon door in a

Western movie, and she muttered, 'Sheriff of Lone Canyon – put your hands above your head!' The lavatory bowl was filthy; she tried not to retch. As usual, the first time she pulled the plug, nothing happened. She pulled it again, and it flushed. In the washroom she turned on the tap, and held her hands under it. Shaking the water off them as she crossed the yard, she glanced up at the colourless sky above the wire. The matrons were waiting just inside her cell, which smelt of sleep.

Mrs Steyn said, 'See you this evening, chummie.' She often called Ida 'chummie'. Ida believed that Mrs Steyn thought this was a word English people used a lot.

'Goodbye, Mrs Steyn.' The two matrons went out, and Mrs Potgieter closed and locked the door. Ida sat down on her bed, picked up her plate, and dug the spoon into one of the staring eggs.

She heard keys again, then heavy footsteps and a man's voice. The policemen were doing their first round. The girl in the other cell called out, '*Sies*, these fuckin' eggs are cold.' The spyhole cover on Ida's door was raised, then dropped. As always, she felt self-conscious, as if she were being photographed. The girl shouted, 'Do you boys calls this blerry muck breakfast?' and one of the policemen laughed.

The girl would be gone in an hour, and Ida wondered why she bothered to complain. Anyway the food wasn't really bad. Because this was a police-station, not a jail, there was no special diet for prisoners. They ate the same meals as the policemen.

The sweet, chicory-flavoured coffee was nearly cold, but she drank it all, except for the mud at the bottom of the mug. She reached for a cigarette, but then there was a knock on the door, and the spyhole cover was lifted. A voice said, 'Hey!' Ida stood up, and went over to look through the circle of glass.

The face of the girl outside was so young that it was still a soft moon shape. It was blurred and silly, smudged with traces of bright make-up. Ida could not smell the girl through the door, but she felt sure that she smelt of scent and sweat, that she smelt used but young.

'What's your name?'

'Ida – and yours?'

'Marie. Got a *stompie*, Ida?' Marie's teeth were white and crooked; the fourth on top on the left was missing.

Ida had learnt in jail that a *stompie* was a cigarette stub. She said, 'I've got cigarettes.'

Marie looked surprised. 'You have? That old bitch took my smokes off of me when I come in. I thought always, when they search you, they take your smokes off of you, though sometimes you can smuggle in a *stompie*.'

Ida said, 'It's because I'm here all the time that they let me have them.'

'Oh? Then you're not going to court today?'

'No.'

After a moment Marie asked, 'Why they lock your door, man?'

'Because I'm not allowed to communicate with other prisoners.'

'Communicate?'

'I'm not allowed to talk to them.'

Marie laughed. 'Well,' she said, 'you're talking to me. What you in for then?'

'I'm political.'

'Political. Why they want to keep you locked up here for that? You're on remand, then? I thought always they sent the remands to the jail in Roeland Street.'

'I'm not on remand. I haven't been to court.'

'You haven't? I thought always they have to take you to court. That's one thing I thought I knew about the fuckin' law. Court next morning, or on Monday, if they picks you up over the weekend.'

'Usually they have to,' Ida said, 'but there's a special law for politicals.'

Marie shrugged and sighed. 'It's peculiar,' she said. 'How long you been in, then?'

'A hundred and forty-four days.'

'Thirty, sixty, ninety, one-twenty. That's nearly five months, man. You been in this dump all that time?'

'I was in Pretoria for three weeks at the beginning.'

'*Ag*,' said Marie. 'Pretoria. Was you in the cells there, too?'

'No, in the Female Prison.'

Marie whistled. 'That's where they take the women to be hanged. The last white woman they hanged was a poisoner. People say a person who poisons has got a cold heart.'

'Mmm.'

'So do you like it better here in Cape Town? Or is Pretoria your home town?'

'I like it better here. No, I'd never been in Pretoria before.'

'Man, since it's not your home town, I can say it – true as God, that place is a fuckin' dump. It's dead from the ground up. My auntie stays there. So how long you still got to do?'

'I don't know. They can keep me as long as they like.'

'Well, it's peculiar,' Marie repeated. She shrugged again, shaking back her dark-rooted yellow hair. Ida could see that she was getting tired of the conversation, and said, 'I'll fetch the cigarettes and matches.'

'They let you have matches? Hell, man, why don't you burn the place down?' Marie giggled. Why didn't she get a false tooth? Perhaps she was too poor. Pulling three cigarettes out of the packet, Ida wondered how much prostitutes earned. It would be rude to ask, she decided, extracting three matches from their box, and then tearing a small piece of strike off its side. She wrapped the matches and strike in a tissue.

Marie was lounging against the door with a bored look, propping the spyhole cover open with one finger.

'If you kneel down I'll push them through.'

'Thanks a lot,' Marie said, letting the spyhole cover fall back into place. Ida knelt down. She called, 'They're coming.' She flicked the cigarettes under the door. Then she pushed the little packet after them, but it stuck, for Marie said, 'And the matches, man?'

Ida lowered her face sideways to the floor. The packet was nearly through. 'Pull with your finger-nail,' she said. She clenched her fist, feeling tense. She was listening for the sound of keys. Marie's finger moved along at the edge of the door. Her nails were bitten down. Ida jabbed at the packet with her own nail. '*Ag, ja*,' Marie exclaimed, and pulled the packet through with her fingertip.

Ida stood up, She waited by the door, but Marie didn't raise the spyhole cover again, so she sat down on the bed. As she lit a cigarette, she heard keys. She hoped Marie would put out her cigarette and hide it quickly. If anyone found out that Ida gave cigarettes to other prisoners, she would not be allowed them any more.

Mrs Potgieter's voice called, 'Hurry up there. You'll be going to court just now. Are you ready?'

Marie said, 'I want my things. I want my handbag.'

'You will get them at the court,' said Mrs Potgieter.

'But I want them *now*. For my make-up and my comb.'

'Well, I can't give them to you *now*,' Mrs Potgieter said in a satisfied tone. 'It is contrary to the regulations. You will have to tidy your hair with your hands. As for the *make-up* – far better just to wash your face.'

'The water is cold.'

'Cold water never did anyone an injury that I have heard of.' Mrs Potgieter's voice became fainter as she said this, and now Ida heard the yard door slam.

'Fuckin old *hoor*,' Marie remarked, but not loudly. She sounded subdued. Ida wondered if she were worried about going to court. She probably had a bad hangover. She had been very drunk the night before. She had sworn a lot, first telling Mrs Steyn that she only worked as a matron in order to sleep with the policemen, and then – contradictorily – that she was a *koeksuster*. *Koeksuster*, actually a kind of braided doughnut, was Afrikaans slang for a Lesbian.

'Feeling in girls' bras and panties!' Marie had shouted.

It was extraordinary that Ida had never been searched. She remembered how Stella had been made to jump naked, with her legs apart, so that if she had hidden anything inside her, it would fall out. But when Ida had been arrested, they told her to pack her suitcase, and then took her to the airport. It had been late at night when they reached the Pretoria Female Prison, and the only wardress on duty took her straight to her cell. When she was brought back to Cape Town, the matron – it had been Mrs Steyn – did not search her because the Special Branch men said they were going to move her in a few hours. She wondered why they had changed their minds. Perhaps the cells everywhere else were full.

If she had known she would never be searched, she would have hidden a pen in her clothes. She should have tried it, anyway. She had nothing to lose. Except the pen. She remembered Charles saying 'You have nothing to lose but your brains.'

The police van rattled into the covered passage outside her window. There was a roar as the driver revved the engine, and then silence. After a moment, a door banged, and a man shouted in Afrikaans. Keys jangled, and she heard Mrs Potgieter yelling, in the way she yelled only at the Coloured and African women. Ida could not remember how many had been brought in during the weekend; about fifteen, she thought. Each one was brought into the white prisoners' yard to fetch two blankets from a cupboard between the cells. These blankets were called Non-European blankets, but were the same as the European blankets, which were stored in Ida's cell.

One weekend, so many African and Coloured women were arrested that there were not enough blankets in the cupboard. Ida said, 'What about all the blankets in my cell?' But Mrs Potgieter exclaimed, '*Sies*, no! Those are the European blankets.'

Ida had once asked Mrs Steyn what the Non-European section was like, and Mrs Steyn said it was exactly the same as the European one, except that there were no beds or mattresses. Ida wondered how the women managed to sleep on the cement floor, especially in winter. They must often have had to lie in the yard because they were too many to fit into the two cells.

Now there were keys, and then footsteps outside Ida's cell. '*Kom, kom, kom,*' Mrs Potgieter called briskly.

'All right. I'm coming.' Marie's voice was sullen. There was the tapping of high heels, and then the yard door slammed. Ida hoped that it would be several days before any more white prisoners were brought in. Often there were none between Monday and Thursday; most were arrested at weekends. What Ida hated most was when they were arrested on Friday. Then, because there was no court until Monday, she had to spend the whole weekend in her cell.

Mrs Potgieter had told Ida a story about a woman who had spent ten years in jail. 'And when she was released,' Mrs Potgieter said, 'she took an axe, and she chopped down all the doors in her house. True as God, she did. She would not have a door in her house after that day.'

Of the three elderly matrons – they were not 'wardresses', as in a prison – who did regular eight-hour shifts, looking after the women's cells, Mrs Potgieter was the ugliest and the simplest. Ida had a feeling that the other two looked down on her; especially Miss Maree, who would come on duty this afternoon.

Even though Mrs Steyn called her 'chummie', she was Ida's favourite. She would never have done what Miss Maree had done twice: brought friends to stick their heads into the yard and gape at Ida as if she were in a zoo. Mrs Steyn was calm and dignified, which Ida found soothing. Mrs Potgieter was not soothing, but Ida liked listening to her stories.

There was a shout outside, and then the sound of the police van backing out of the passage.

Now Ida made her bed, tucking in the corners neatly. Next she folded the paper bag in which, during the weekend, she had put empty cigarette packets and other rubbish. She transferred cigarette ends from the tin lid she used as an ashtray into another bag, already half full of those she had saved for the cleaners since Friday, and she buried three new cigarettes among them. She put the two bags by the door. Then she sat down on the bed and lit a fresh cigarette. She looked around the cell.

Above her bed was the window, barred outside, and covered inside with close green mesh. On two hangers stuck into the mesh hung four of Ida's cotton dresses. Opposite the window was the door. Words were scratched on its grey paintwork.

Marie and Ria
Dinky
Cynthia 23 days in goal + 7
Christy and Shorty

Aletha Roach (This name was scraped in enormous letters. Each time she looked at it, Ida thought that it must have taken a long time to do.)
Mary 4 day inside
Leonie Theart (As usual, Ida wondered whether 'Theart' rhymed with 'heart' or 'hurt'.)
Vicky was here for runaway from Durbanville
I love Piet de Koker (Ida imagined Piet de Koker with a blond crewcut and absolutely blank grey eyes.)

Along the wall on Ida's left was the wooden shelf piled with European blankets. ('European blankets, European blankets, European blankets,' Ida said aloud. The words sounded odder each time she said them.) At the end of this shelf by her bed, she had cleared a space where she kept her handbag, her Bible, her spongebag, and extra food, when she had any; it was always finished by Monday. Every Thursday she was allowed to dictate a shopping-list to a young policeman. He bought cigarettes, matches, soap and toothpaste, fruit, biscuits and chocolate. The matron paid him, in Ida's cell, with money from Ida's purse, which was kept in the matron's sitting-room. At the same time she paid in advance for the laundry Ida gave him: a pillowcase containing two sheets and a towel. This procedure had been worked out at some length with Major de Wet of the Special Branch.

Opposite Ida's was another bed, on which were her towel, two cartons of cigarettes, a packet of matches, and some of her underclothes; the rest were packed in the red suitcase under her bed. Ida sometimes compared herself to this suitcase; an object lugged about from one place to another. Then she would think: *And the Special Branch unpacked me.* It still sometimes surprised her that Ida-as-suitcase had been so full.

*

She had enjoyed the peaceful years when she worked in the bookshop. She was good at the job. The bookshop's owner, Miss Rubinstein – skeletal, always tired, often ill – gave her more and more responsibility; for ordering as well as for selling. She had, Miss Rubinstein once told her, a 'feel' for the business.

She liked the shop itself: the packed shelves, the heaped tables, the dimness. (Why were bright lights inappropriate in a bookshop?). It amused her to observe the people who came in to browse. She found it a challenge to try to answer customers' questions, and often still more of one to interpret their distorted memories of titles and authors. She felt a sense of satisfaction as she wrapped books she had sold in bags marked *Forward*, which was the shop's name.

She also appreciated being able to take new books home in the evening to her 'flat': the upper floor of a small pre-war house in the rather dilapidated district of Cape Town named 'Gardens' after a large park through which she walked to work, except in heavy winter rain, when she went by bus, which took ten minutes.

The flat suited her. She had been delighted to find it, after spending six months in a drab residential hotel. When she first moved in, two students from the university were living downstairs, but they left at the end of that year, and new tenants did not replace them. The landlord, an old man, was not much interested in this property – which would never command a high rent – and was not prepared to spend money on it. Ida had painted the upstairs rooms herself.

The very best thing about her life was her lovely affair with Charles, her 'married man'. Yes, he was married but, as he told Ida, 'Sally and I lead our own lives.' This was proved true, Ida often reflected, by the fact that Charles spent so many evenings at her flat.

His wife was rich. They lived in Wynberg, on the Indian Ocean side of the peninsula; the fashionable side. They had two sons at an expensive Anglican public school. They could never have afforded such a life on his journalist's salary, even though he was a very well-known 'liberal' journalist: indeed he was a 'name' throughout the country, writing for a national Sunday paper, as well as for the better of the two local dailies.

How lucky Ida was to be having an affair with charming Charles. 'Charming', that vague word, was in this case an exact one: Charles was precisely what an earlier generation would have called 'a charmer'. He looked like the 1930s film-star, Leslie Howard: fair, sensitive, handsome, and utterly, utterly English. Charles *was* English. (Leslie Howard – as Ida was astonished to read in a magazine – had actually been Hungarian.)

Charles, 'brilliant but lazy', had just missed a First at Cambridge. After gliding round the world, alighting briefly here and there, he had finally found his perch in Cape Town; a large bird in a little aviary. Ida understood all this perfectly, but it made no difference to the way she 'adored' Charles; not in the religious sense of the word, but in accordance with its cocktail-party usage: 'I simply *adore* him!'

Ida 'adored' his long legs and his fine, fair hair. (Charles was forty; it was surprising that such fine hair had not thinned, and that traces of grey simply merged in the fairness.) She found him altogether attractive. She not only 'adored' him sexually. She also 'adored' his company. They had read the same novels, and they laughed at the same jokes. They had, as the phrase went, 'so much in common'. That phrase, however, was usually applied to a prospective married couple, which in this case was inappropriate. Although Charles and his wife sounded so indifferent to each other, and although he seldom referred to his children, Ida felt convinced that Charles would never abandon the 'way of life' he shared with his family. It was lucky she didn't mind. (She always had a sense of luck in connection with Charles: as if she had picked a winner with a pin.)

They had started with 'so much in common', but Charles introduced her to something new.

Ida was squeamish: she turned the page when she saw a police atrocity headlined in her newspaper. She deplored 'the government', but was bored by reports of new 'Acts' and their endless 'clauses'. And though, of course, she had always loathed apartheid, one couldn't feel indignant *all* the time. Charles could. Ida began to pay attention to politics because she wanted herself and him to have *everything* – apart from marriage – 'in common'.

He did not 'enlighten' her for missionary reasons, for her 'good'; but because the subject was always present in his mind: a substratum. It underlay chatter and jokes; nothing wholly removed him from it, she thought sometimes, hearing him sigh or seeing him frown, even though, while he did so, his arm was round her, her head was on his shoulder, and he had just lit a cigarette for her between his own lips. He was thinking about politics again: she knew it; just as she knew that politics was what made him drink a little too much. He admitted that he did this. He called drink an 'occupational hazard', but Ida thought his reason for drinking lay deeper: in a rage he felt every day of his life. This rage was in constant conflict with his work, which must always be restrained and judicious, both for legal reasons – there were numerous laws under which he could be charged if he 'went too far' in criticizing the government – and because of the policies of the business group which controlled the newspapers he wrote for. Mightn't the rage, Ida sometimes wondered, also be in conflict with his 'way of life'? However he always said that he was not a socialist: 'In England, I'd be a dear old fuddy-duddy Liberal.'

*

Ida heard water splashing on the cement in the yard. Then there was the sound of a broom sweeping. This reminded her of autumn, and she wondered why. Autumn leaves rustle drily, and the broom made a wet sound. She tried to remember when she had last heard leaves being swept, but all that came into her mind was the whirr of a lawnmower and the smell of cut grass.

Keys jangled. Mrs Potgieter opened the cell door. Every time she saw her, Ida was struck by how tiny her eyes were.

'Are you ready to move?' she asked. What would happen if Ida said 'No'? *The entire structure would collapse.*

'Yes,' she said, picking up her cigarettes and matches. She saw that there was only one cigarette in the packet. Although she 'knew' she would only be in the small cell for a very short time, she took another packet from the opened carton on the second bed. Going past Mrs Potgieter out of the cell, she saw that one of the cleaners was pouring disinfectant into the drains. The vomit had been cleared away, and the cement floor of the yard was wet and shiny.

She went into the small cell, and Mrs Potgieter shut the door and turned the key. This cell had already been cleaned. The blankets were in a neat pile on the floor, and the mattress – there was no bed – had been propped against the wall. It was covered with big uneven stains because drunk prisoners wetted it so often. When this happened, the cleaners put it in the yard to dry.

Ida was very glad that this was not her cell. It was so small that if the mattress were on the floor, it would almost cover it. One weekend, three prostitutes had shared this cell, and Ida had asked Mrs Potgieter if she would like her to swop with them. Mrs Potgieter said, 'Ag, no. You stay put. Don't worry about them. Brought in off a Jap ship, the constable tells me. How white girls can do that I just don't know. But it isn't illegal for them to do it with Japs, you know. It was only the fuss they kicked up that got them arrested. It's illegal with Chinks, of course, but there's this trade with the Japs. My husband told me. It's this pig-iron. The Japs buy it from us, or we buy it from them, and so they have been made honorary whites.'

On the day the three prostitutes had gone to court, the walls of the cell had been scrawled with ball-point writing. (How had a pen eluded the search?) It was still there.

> *I love Sugimoto*
> *I love Jap ships*
> *. . .* (a name had been scratched out) *loves Japs*
> *In jail we are all hoors*
> *For you my love – Jeanette*
> *East or West the Japs are best*

Now Ida could hear the cleaners in her own cell. It was odd to have servants in jail. In Pretoria, it had been African women who did the work. Here it was Coloured men.

The key turned, and Mrs Potgieter opened the door. She stood back for Ida to enter her cell, which now smelt as strongly as the yard of disinfectant. Ida stood in the doorway. Mrs Potgieter crossed to the outside door, which was open, and went through it, shouting to one of the cleaners in Afrikaans. Now there was only one cleaner in the yard; the old thin one. He trotted into the small cell and brought out the four blankets which were piled there. Ida stood back for him to bring them into her cell. When he had put them with the other European blankets, Ida quickly pulled three cigarettes from her new packet, and held them out to him. He took them with a hunch of his shoulders and a twitch of his lips. He pushed them into the front of his patched khaki shirt, and scurried off. Although he moved so quickly, Ida felt that he was too old to be a convict, and wondered what crime he had committed.

She stood in the cell doorway again, looking round the yard. The young cleaner came in through the outside door, stooping, carrying a steaming aluminium bucket. The third convict, the big trusty, who didn't work himself but gave orders to the others (he 'supervised', in the way reserved for whites in the outside world), slouched in. The trusty had big shoulders and a heavy yellow face. He leant against the frame of the outside door while the other two ran in and out, bringing piles of Non-European blankets, and stacking them in the cupboard between the cells. When at last they closed the cupboard, he waited for them to leave the yard, then swung round after them. His body had a threatening quality.

Now Mrs Potgieter put her head into the yard. 'Well, I'll leave you to your bath,' she said to Ida. The door slammed. The key turned. Ida walked into the centre of the yard.

Looking up, she could not see the sun yet, though it gave the blue sky a gilt tinge. Against the sky, the barbs on the wire were dark, thorny stars.

When Ida had first arrived, there were many objects on top of the wire: two twisted metal coathangers, the foot of a nylon stocking, a sheet of newspaper, a ball of greaseproof paper, a coffee carton and two small dangling lengths of rusty chain. Now there were only the two chains and a tattered fragment of stocking. Ida wondered where the other things had gone. She could not remember exactly when they had disappeared. Had they been carried away by the South-Easter two weeks ago? At that time there had been a madman somewhere in the building who had called on God continually. At night it was hard to distinguish between his howling and the howling of the wind.

'Well, chummie,' Mrs Steyn had said to her, 'you tell me you don't believe in God. Yet even that cracked old Coloured realizes that there is a Supreme Being.'

Now Ida went over to the far wall, behind which was the washroom. Touching the bricks she could still feel the night's coolness in them. She stood, stroking the cold dead bricks which later in the day would feel warm and living. Standing very close to this wall, she could just see the top storeys of an office building. She wondered if the people in it could see her: an ant pressed against the side of a wire-covered matchbox. A seagull swooped down past the building, and she flapped her arms. Then she realized that her bucket of water would be getting cold. She fetched her clothes and towel and spongebag from the cell, and went into the washroom.

She poured half the bucket of water into the basin, and tested it with her finger. It was still hot, though not very, and she added cold water from the tap to make it go further. Then she washed carefully all over. She had not had a bath since leaving Pretoria four months ago, but she did not think she had become dirtier. She dried herself, and put on her clothes. Her cotton dress had a fresh smell.

When she had brushed her teeth, she rolled up the end of the toothpaste tube; this was something she had never done before she went to jail. Then she took her spongebag back to the cell, and fetched the clothes she had worn the day before, and the packet of detergent the policeman had bought for her. She used the rest of the hot water to wash the clothes, and then rinsed them in cold water. She hung them up in the yard to dry, from a convenient knob under the window of the small cell.

She wondered if Mrs Potgieter would bring her a cup of tea, as she usually did. When occasionally she did not, Ida believed it was not because she forgot, but to remind Ida that the cup of tea was a favour. Ida fetched the empty bucket from the washroom, and put it down with a clang by the outside door. That was when she realized that she had not washed her hair.

It was Monday, and she always washed her hair on Monday. But now there was no hot water left, and besides she suddenly felt tired. Of course she could wash it on Tuesday. *The entire structure might collapse.* She fetched her bottle of shampoo from the cell, and washed her hair in cold water.

After she had dried and combed it, back in the cell, she took her make-up out of her handbag. She used the little mirror inside the lid of her powder compact, noticing the two lines – the Pretoria lines, as she thought of them – that slanted down her cheeks. Perhaps they would fade; though surely time accentuated lines rather than eliminating them? Her wet hair was flat now, but when it dried it would be thick and fuzzy. It needed cutting; she thought her face looked like a ferret peering out of a bush.

Her mouth red, powder on her nose, her eyebrows darkened with brown pencil, she stood in the doorway of her cell. Now there was a square of sunlight at the top of the washroom wall, but the cement floor was still too damp to sit on. She paced up and down, but as usual tired of this quickly. The yard was so small – eleven paces by eight at its longest and widest – that walking made her feel more caged than sitting or standing.

She thought that when – if – she was released, she would explode into the world like a firework, leaving a trail of sparks behind her. But she remembered her friend Sharon saying that, when she had been released, after being detained in the 1963 State of Emergency, she had felt tired and weak and had often cried for no reason. So even whites, who did so little in jail, apparently could not 'store up' energy there. She thought of the African prisoners on Robben Island, breaking stones all day in the quarries, and sentenced, if they flagged, by secret tribunals, to lashings, or to periods on starvation diet in solitary. She wondered what happened to the stones those prisoners broke. Were they brought to the mainland, or were they used to extend the prison so that it could hold more and more prisoners?

The key of the outside door was turned. *Tea*, thought Ida, but Mrs Potgieter merely thrust in her fat freckled arm, picked up the bucket, and then slammed the door again. Ida's annoyance about the tea – so absurd, so childish – mingled confusingly with her indignation about the prisoners on Robben Island. But immediately, the key turned again, and the door opened. Mrs Potgieter came in. Steam curled up from the flowered cup, which she carried on a matching saucer.

'Oh, thank you,' said Ida, hurrying forward to take it, though she knew Mrs Potgieter would not put it down on the ground, as the wardresses had put her food in Pretoria.

As Ida took the cup from her, Mrs Potgieter smiled benevolently. Her tiny eyes glittered in her spotted face. Ida imagined her at home, sitting on her stoop, and telling her husband how good she was to Ida; but perhaps he would disapprove.

Mrs Potgieter said, 'I'll be back for the cup.' As she left, Ida returned to the washroom wall. Now the sunlight formed a rectangle just above her head. Gulping the sweet strong tea, she felt it first in her throat, then in her chest. Stella, serving her sentence in Barberton Female Prison, would never have tea like this: tea with milk and sugar; tea in a cup with a matching saucer.

*

Stella came into the bookshop for a History textbook. It was out of stock. Ida told her she would obtain a copy in a day or two.

Stella looked very young. There was something endearing about her appearance. She was pretty, but rather absurdly so. Her eyes were blue and round as marbles. Her nose turned up at the end. Her primrose hair curled like a Cupid's, and her mouth was that Victorian dream: a perfect Cupid's bow. She was slightly bandy-legged, and this was emphasized by the high-heeled shoes she wore. Her clothes were extremely conventional. It was September – early spring – and she was wearing a grey pleated skirt and a short-sleeved pink angora jumper.

The shop was empty. After Ida had written down Stella's order and her name (she did not give an address; she said she would call for the book), they began a conversation. Stella was at the university, writing a thesis on the history of African mineworkers. However, she was thinking of transferring from Cape Town to Johannesburg, as she and her present supervisor did not get on. 'He has a thoroughly incorrect approach,' said Stella. 'He is hostile to any but a totally bourgeois interpretation of events.'

These words, in conjunction with the nose, the legs, the pink angora, inclined Ida to laugh, but instead she nodded. She did not want to hurt such a young girl's feelings. She asked Stella if she lived at home with her family. Stella said that both her parents were dead. 'I have one sister, who is married and lives in Durban, but I never see her.' Stella paused, then added, 'When we were small, my sister was the "good little girl", and I was the "naughty disobedient child".'

Ida was touched by this intimate admission, after so short an acquaintance. She said, 'Is that why you never see her?'

'Oh no. I don't believe in those individualistic psychological explanations. It's because her husband disapproves of me so much. He's a *businessman.*'

'Why does he disapprove of you?'

'Oh,' Stella said, 'because of my being arrested, and so on.'

'*Arrested?*'

'Yes, for my political work. Demonstrations, etcetera.'

'Oh,' Ida said. She would have asked more, but at that moment a man came into the shop and approached her desk. Stella said, 'I'll come in for the book on Friday.'

*

Now the sun was overhead. Ida stroked her hair, which was warm and drying rapidly. All the wetness had vanished from the cement. She went into her cell, to fetch her Bible, her cigarettes and matches, her tin-lid ashtray, and three of the European blankets. She folded two of the blankets lengthways, and rolled up the third to make a pillow. Then she lay down on her back, and looked up through the wire at the sky in which the sun now hovered over her. Like a swan, she thought, remembering the myth of Leda.

*

When both Stella and the other customer had gone, Ida looked at Stella's name on the book order-pad. She decided to ask Charles – he was coming to see her that evening – whether he knew anything about her.

'Oh God, yes.' Charles was sitting in the faded blue armchair, with his long legs extended. She was on the divan, feet curled under her. He took a gulp of his whisky and soda. Insisting – rightly – that she could not afford to provide it, he brought his own whisky to the flat. Ida was sipping a glass of wine; she detested the taste of whisky. 'One of the Comrades,' Charles said, in a weary voice.

'The "comrades"?'

'Yes, one of the few surviving communists that they haven't rounded up. In fact I don't think she's even banned. Very surprising.'

To be banned meant, among other things, that one was confined to a particular district. A banned person might not meet more than one other person at a time, and might not meet another banned person at all. Charles often angrily mocked this piece of legislation.

'But surely they couldn't ban her?' Ida said. 'She's so young.'

'Twenty-six or so, I suppose.'

'*Really?*'

'Yes. She's been at it for about five years I think.'

'*At it?* You don't sound very sympathetic.'

'I'm not, really. You know I loathe communism almost as much as apartheid. In fact sometimes I think it's a toss-up between them, my darling girl.'

She liked him to call her 'my darling girl,' even though – or perhaps

196

because – she wasn't a girl, but a woman. But now she persisted: 'How do you know she's a communist? You can't have any evidence. Being a communist is illegal.'

'Oh, of course she'd never *say* she was a Party member. "A Marxist approach" would be the most she'd ever admit to. But one always knows who they are – the Comrades. By what they read, for instance. Anything that's too personal will be dismissed as a "mishmash". They admire pedestrian novelists whom you've never heard of – and the very bad books fairly good writers produced in the 1930s. Dos Passos, Steinbeck's *In Dubious Battle*, Hemingway's *For Whom the Bell Tolls*. All Americans. And of course they detest America. But they love early American proletarian heroes. Sacco and Vanzetti. (Though, actually, *they* were all right. Anarchists. Rather fine.) The Scotsboro Boys. Someone called Joe Hill. There's a dreadful song about him.' Charles sang the words, '"I dreamed I saw Joe Hill last night,"' but then he broke off. 'Can't remember any more. Anyway, the ghost of this trade unionist, Joe Hill, tells them what matters is to *organize*. And Comrades always take *that* advice. How else do you identify them? Well, they call fellow-travellers "progressives". And of course everything Russia does is absolutely wonderful. Oh, by the way, there's another absolutely infallible sign. They never talk about "Russia" – or even the "Sohviet Union". They say the "Sovyut Union". You watch out for that with your new friend. "Sov" to rhyme with "of".'

Ida laughed. She said, 'Angel, she's not my friend. And, of course, if, as you say, she's twenty-six, she's far older than I thought. All the same, there was something rather touching about her. I thought of asking her round for a drink.'

'Touching! As touching as Frankenstein's monster – though, actually, poor bewildered thing that he was, he was much more touching than your Stella. If you do ask her round for a drink – though I strongly advise against it, as the Special Branch probably follow her everywhere – make sure it's when I'm not about.' He finished his whisky, put down his glass, and smiled. 'Now, come here.'

She liked taking orders of this kind from him, getting up from the divan, going over to the chair from which he now held out his arms to her: 'My darling girl.' Oh yes, she adored him.

When Stella came into the shop on Friday morning, Ida regarded her with keen curiosity. This time, with the same grey pleated skirt as before, she was wearing a white blouse and a pale blue cardigan. A *communist? Could* she be? Ida had never, to her knowledge, met a communist, but this was not her idea of one.

'Hullo,' she said. 'Your book has arrived. How are you?'

'I've got terrible backache, absolutely terrible,' Stella said. 'I'm sleeping on a sofa in the house of some Coloured friends.' (Wasn't that illegal? wondered Ida.) 'I moved out of my own flat after a bullet came through the window the other night.'

'A *bullet*? But who possibly . . . Haven't you complained to the police?'

Stella smiled, stretching her Cupid's bow. Apart from the indentation in the upper lip, her mouth was thin. 'But it was one of theirs, of course,' she said.

Now she took out her purse and paid for the book. She was turning to go when Ida said, 'Come and have a drink some time. How about . . . tomorrow?'

For Charles never visited her on Saturday. Saturday was his night 'at home', or, more probably, out with his wife. South African couples always went out on Saturday night.

Stella, rubbing her lips together, was studying Ida. Then she said, 'Yes, well, I think that would be quite nice. I won't be able to stay long, though. Where do you live?'

Ida had red wine in the kitchen cupboard and white wine in the refrigerator, and she had bought a bottle of sherry. (She decided that it was the pink angora jumper which had made her think Stella might drink sherry.) And there was Charles's whisky. That was what Stella chose; asking for it neat, with two cubes of ice.

While Ida prepared the drinks, Stella, who was wearing the pink angora again, with a white crimplene skirt, pale brown stockings and white high-heeled shoes (Ida was in jeans, a batik tunic and flat sandals), wandered round the room. (Surely the furnishings were simple enough, even for a communist?) She paused in front of a Victorian aquatint of a very large dog pulling an even larger – and apparently completely dry – boy in a blue velvet suit out of a river, while a woman clasped her hands together on the bank. Under the picture was engraved its title: *'He's saved! He's saved!'* Showing no reaction of any kind, Stella moved on to the bookcase. If what Charles had said was true, there would be nothing to interest her there. Not even a Steinbeck or a Hemingway.

Stella looked slowly along the shelves; then – as a last resort? – she pulled out a book whose title and author were illegible, worn away. It was Evelyn Waugh's *A Handful of Dust*. Having opened it, and glanced at the title page, Stella at once replaced it. She said, 'When I was eighteen, I nearly became a Roman Catholic.'

'Really?' Ida handed Stella her whisky, gesturing towards 'Charles's' armchair, and then sitting down on the divan.

Stella remained standing, but took a swallow of her drink. 'Yes,' she said. 'I admired their discipline so much.'

'Oh.'

'I even thought of becoming a nun,' Stella went on. 'I could have accepted the whole system. The only trouble was that I couldn't believe in God.'

Ida laughed, but Stella remained perfectly serious. She said, 'I can only stay for a few minutes more. I have an appointment.' She did not enlarge upon this. Ida supposed that the appointment was political. Stella had said in the shop that she would not be able to stay long, but Ida had not imagined quite such a short visit as this.

She said, 'Oh I'm so sorry you have to go,' and noticed that Stella's glass was empty. Her own was still almost full. 'A drink?' she asked.

'Just one more,' Stella said. She was still standing.

'Won't you sit down for a minute?'

'I haven't time,' Stella said. She went on, 'I'm afraid I can't ask you to visit me. I'm still sleeping on my friends' sofa. I don't feel like going back to my flat.'

'Goodness, I should think not. I'd be *petrified*.'

Stella downed her second whisky in one draught (the way the Russians were said to drink vodka). Ida said, 'You must come round again.'

'That would be quite nice,' she said. But apparently she wanted to come, for she added, 'I'll call at the shop next week. Perhaps we could arrange something then.'

'Yes,' Ida said. 'Of course.' When Stella left a minute later, Ida, seeing her off at the front door, watched her set off – click, click, on her high heels – in the direction of Upper Orange Street. Her bandy-legged walk made Ida smile.

'I'm afraid I gave her two huge shots of your whisky,' Ida said, describing the occasion to Charles the next evening: Sunday; so peaceful.

'*My* whisky, indeed! How absurd you are. But all the same I wish someone else instead of that dreary Comrade had drunk it.'

'Charles, you're being unfair. Honestly, she really is pathetic. So withdrawn, and lonely, too, I think. I'm sure you'd feel the same if you met her. Of course I'd love to find out what you think of her "in the flesh".'

'In the flesh,' Charles repeated, and laughed. 'As opposed to the spirit, do you mean?'

'Seriously, won't you meet her just once. To please me,' she added, and suddenly felt like a pouting, wilful Dickens heroine. But he didn't mind. In fact he smiled: *indulgently*; yes, that was the word. She added, 'I'm sure you could draw her out better than I can. Actually I don't know what she and I would have talked about yesterday if she'd stayed much longer. But she'd probably blossom like a flower under the influence of your charm.'

'Flattery will get you absolutely nowhere.' But ten days later, Charles and Stella were in Ida's living-room together.

Together! What happened was that, as soon as they were introduced, and drinks poured – Charles had brought a new bottle of whisky – he and Stella began to argue. Ida, apart from refilling their glasses, contributed nothing at all.

Camps! That had been the culmination. Stella, speaking of a new Bantustan, had called it a great concentration camp for reserves of cheap labour. Ida felt sure that if she herself had said this, Charles would have agreed. To Stella, he said, 'Yes, almost as bad as the camps in Russia, except that the climate's better here. And of course, from those camps, one can't escape even to work.'

'I thought we were talking about South Africa.' Stella had a point there, Ida thought. Now she went on, 'Everyone admits that there were bureaucratic distortions and infringements of socialist legality during the Stalin period in the Sovyut Union' – Charles glanced at Ida – 'but deformations of that kind have been corrected.'

'Oh, don't talk that nonsense to me. Perhaps things have slightly improved, but people are still being herded into camps quite as bad as the prisons here. The African prisons I mean. Prisons for whites are far better here. Of course in both countries, people are arrested for so-called offences which would be perfectly legal in any civilized country.'

'*Civilized!*' said Stella. 'I suppose you mean capitalist. I suppose you call capitalist, imperialist Britain and America *civilized*. Without their backing, apartheid couldn't survive for six months.'

Capitalist! Imperialist! The words embarrassed Ida. Everything she read, everything people – especially Charles – said inclined her to dismiss them as meaningless jargon. Yet, she suddenly wondered now, could they be totally meaningless? Hadn't Charles himself often admitted that South Africa was dependent on Western support, and shown regret that this support was given: given, he said, for reasons of 'commercial interest' and 'defence policy'. Might these be other words for 'capitalism' and 'imperialism'?

But now Charles was comparing the officials who had enacted Stalin's policies to 'Nazi automata' and Stella was defending them on the ground that they had been 'subject to Party discipline.'

'What a revolting idea, and what a revolting phrase,' Charles drawled.

'Yes, I imagine you would think so.' Stella stood up. 'I'm afraid I must go now.' She put down her glass; she had drunk four strong whiskys, but showed no signs of having done so. 'I'll see you in the shop some time, Ida.' She nodded curtly to Charles, who stood up, smiled, and said, '*So* nice to have met you.' Ida went to the top of the stairs with Stella, who smiled, and said, 'I'll let myself out.'

She went back into the living-room. Charles was still standing. Now he was pacing up and down.

'Christ!' he exclaimed. 'So that's your poor little creature! An absolute monster. She admits there were "infringements of socialist legality" under Stalin, does she? Well, you can be sure she wouldn't have admitted it at the time. She wouldn't have been any more disturbed by Stalin's atrocities then than a devout Spanish Catholic would have been by Torquemada's. You told me she'd thought of becoming a Catholic, but couldn't believe in God. Well, now she's found an atheist religion, and it's just what she needs. Christianity would never have suited her, anyway. Much too much emphasis on love.'

'You're contradicting yourself,' Ida said. 'What about Torquemada?'

'No contradiction there. Like most official Christians, Torquemada ignored what Christ himself actually said. He ignored that noble imperative to love.' Charles lingered on this last phrase in a way that made Ida suddenly wonder if he would become a Christian one day. She didn't like the idea. The thought of a man who 'knelt down and prayed' was abhorrent to her. She did not understand how any woman could marry a professional kneeler; a clergyman.

Charles said, 'No, it's quite essential for Stella to be able to dismiss love as "bourgeois humanism" or "bourgeois idealism". Even in this country – crawling with cruelty like a corpse with maggots – it isn't suffering that stirs her. There's no compassion there. It's hate that drives her. The last straw' – Ida had never heard him sound so vicious – 'was when she started talking about Party discipline. Did you hear that tone in her voice: the tone of the man who wants murderers hanged "to protect innocent people", who believes children should be beaten "for their own good"? I know them. They pretend to be calm and judicious, but actually they only have one motive: they're thrilled by the idea of punishment. Punishment! Whenever I hear someone advocate it, I detect that undertone I heard in Stella's voice tonight. Unmistakable. A note of sexual relish.'

Now, at the table with the drinks on it, Charles stopped pacing. He held up the wine bottle with a questioning expression. She shook her head. He poured himself a whisky and soda, returned to the armchair, stretched out his legs. He gave a little smile. 'Of course,' he said, 'I can see that she's rather sexy.'

'*Sexy!*'

'Mmm. Those demure clothes, and the Victorian mouth and the golden curls. And behind all that – just the opposite.' He smiled again. 'But don't worry.'

'Worry?' Ida realized that she was frowning, and stopped doing so. 'I'm not *worrying*.'

'Oh. I thought you looked cross, darling girl. Anyway – ugh! I'd rather go to bed with a mamba. Do me a favour – never let her cross my path again. If you see her – I can't imagine why you'd want to – count me out.'

Ida shrugged. At that moment, she felt she didn't really want to have anything more to do with Stella.

*

Now a clear picture formed in Ida's mind of Stella, moving her restless lips, as she stared through a barred window in a cell at Barberton Female Prison.

She heard keys, and sat up, turning to face the door as Mrs Potgieter opened it. Two policemen came in on their mid-morning round. One was a middle-aged sergeant who was always polite – even friendly – to Ida. He said to Mrs Potgieter, 'So the young lady is on her own again?' Mrs Potgieter nodded, and he said to Ida. 'Good morning. Is everything all right with you?'

She wondered what would happen if she answered 'No'. *The entire structure would collapse*. She said. 'Yes, quite all right, thank you.'

The sergeant smiled. 'That's OK then,' he said.

His companion was a young policeman Ida had not seen before. She saw that he was looking at her furtively, as if she were a banned book. She remembered the Special Branch man sniggering as he removed her copy of *Ulysses*.

The sergeant said, 'It is certainly a beautiful day.' The young policeman gave him a look which suggested that he suspected him of fraternizing with the enemy.

She said, 'The last days of summer.' She smiled at the sergeant warmly. She wanted to annoy the young policeman with his flat freckled face and his blank eyes.

'True,' the sergeant said. 'It won't be long before winter's here.' She glanced again at the young policeman. *White bastard*, she thought, though it was absurd for her to use 'white' as a swear-word.

She saw that the sergeant could think of nothing more to say about the weather. Nor could she. He said, 'Well, we must be on our merry way. Bye-bye for now.'

'Goodbye.' Ida said. Before following the sergeant through the door, the boy shot another look at Ida. She could sense him thinking that he wouldn't make things easy for her kind. She suddenly wanted to stick out her tongue at him, and to put her thumbs in her ears and flap her fingers, but all she did was twitch the corner of her upper lip.

Mrs Potgieter closed the door. Ida felt her upper lip fluttering as if a moth were trapped under the skin. The twitch she had intended as a sneer was continuing of its own volition. She pressed it firmly with a finger, and it subsided. She stretched out again, but this time face down.

*

Next time Stella came into the bookshop, Ida asked her to supper during the following week. She did this partly because of Charles's remark about her being 'sexy'. (Ida wanted to try to see Stella 'through Charles's eyes', though she knew this was an impossible undertaking.) Also, looking back at the argument between Stella and Charles, she wanted to *let Stella have her say.*

Stella had it, and continued to do so on other occasions. At first, Ida watched Stella on the first level. *Sexy?* The turned-up nose, the bandy legs, the thin Cupid's bow, the flowered cotton dresses which, now that summer was coming, were replacing the skirts, blouses and cardigans. But of course that was just the point Charles had made: the contrast between that staid yet ridiculous prettiness and: what? The mill in Stella's head; to which cartilage as much as filament, bone as much as flesh were grist. *To be ground into Marx-mince*, for Ida to fork around, taste, swallow; for Ida to accept or reject. Soon Ida quite disregarded 'Stella-as-sex-object'. Soon she was wholly concerned with 'Stella-as-mind-mill.'

The philosophers have tried, in various ways, to interpret the world. The important thing, however, is to change it. Marx's idea was a noble one; Ida couldn't deny that. *To change the world*: wasn't that nobler than the 'noble imperative to love' which Charles had spoken of, and which had never influenced human affairs at all? *To change the world*:

no one, reflected Ida, had even tried to do that; before Marx, before Lenin.

Man's dearest possession is life. And since it is given to him to live but once, he must so live as to feel no torturing regrets for years spent without purpose; so live that dying he may say, 'All my life and all my strength were spent on the finest cause in the world – the liberation of mankind.'

Those words of Lenin's were noble, too. And, like the idea of changing the world, their heroism was disinterested. For Marxists, unlike Christians, did not try to live good lives from any vulgar hope of heaven or fear of hell. They were not, as Christians were, immobilized by tortuous efforts to change themselves; it was the world they were concerned with. Nor did their spokesmen manipulate the oppressed – through hope of heaven, fear of hell – into accepting their lot, but urged them to overthrow their oppressors.

How pure this was! And yet: mightn't it be *too* pure? Wasn't there a possibility that, lacking either hope-and-fear or introspection, one might become ruthless, might justify any means of achieving (noble) ends? As – Ida would remark to Stella – had happened in what, taking the middle ground (after all, to talk about 'Russia' was like calling America by the name of a single one of its component States), she had begun to call the Sohviet (*not* Sovyut) Union.

Stella would reply that in a country as isolated as the Sovyut Union had been (treated as an enemy by all the world), an atmosphere of suspicion was bound to have developed. Yes, there had been 'distortions'; there had been 'infringements'. But now 'all that' lay in the past.

Strongly Ida would express her conviction that this was not the case; that persecution still continued. The battle raged between them. Yet, after one of these evenings, whichever 'side' seemed – to Ida – to have – provisionally – prevailed, she would re-endorse Charles's view of Stella's essential indifference to human suffering.

Even if there had been 'distortions' and 'infringements' under Stalin, Stella wasn't really concerned about the victims. Ida had lent her a book by a woman – a member of the Communist Party, too – who had spent twenty years in a camp in Siberia. Stella said she had read it, but Ida, having found a bus ticket, marking a place half way through the fourth chapter, had not believed her, and said so. 'Anyway,' Stella said, 'that woman didn't sound like a communist to me. She didn't seem to have a Marxist attitude. Really, she sounded like some kind of idealist. In the circumstances prevailing at that time, I might have sent her to prison.'

On another occasion, one of the children in the Coloured family

Stella stayed with had been cheated by a shopkeeper. 'Never mind,' Stella had said to the child. 'After the revolution, we shall bring him before the People's Court.' As she recounted this to Ida, Stella's Cupid's bow stretched in its smile. Then her lips resumed their usual in-and-out movement.

Yet, Ida wondered, was this repugnant quality of Stella's necessarily part of her communism? Mightn't it be simply part of her?

One evening Stella took Ida to meet a banned friend of hers called Sharon. Sharon lived quite near Ida, in an old block of flats in the Gardens district. She had many bright cushions and peasant mats and carvings. Soon after Stella and Ida arrived, the doorbell rang. As Sharon was allowed to be in the company of only one other person, Stella hurried into Sharon's bedroom and shut the door. Sharon said quickly to Ida, 'It's just you who are visiting me. Stella's having a nap.'

Ida felt nervous, but the caller was only a Jehovah's Witness, offering leaflets about the end of the world. Sharon got rid of him, and called to Stella, 'All right. You can come out now.'

Sharon, who was in her thirties, had been a teacher until her banning order prohibited her from entering any school. Now she worked in a shop. 'I was better at teaching than selling,' she said with a laugh. She sat curled in a big armchair, crocheting brightly coloured squares. As she finished one, it dropped from her hands like a leaf from a tree, and she immediately started on another.

Sharon spoke of a trip to Moscow she had made seven years earlier. 'In the Sovyut Union,' she said, 'children don't compete like animals in a jungle. In fact the Russian word for education literally means "to make human beings human".'

Yet Sharon was different from Stella. She spoke caustically of photographs she had seen in museums, in which Trotsky and other out-of-favour figures had been excised from groups of revolutionaries, and she condemned Stalin outright. 'We must never let such terrible things happen again,' she declared indignantly to Ida who could not help wondering how 'we' would stop them. Stella was frowning, and now Sharon said, 'You mustn't listen to Stella. She's a real old-fashioned Stalinist. It's strange, as she was a mere child when he died.'

When Sharon went into the kitchen, Ida went over to her bookcase. It held a mixture of political works and romantic novels. Sharon, returning with a casserole, saw Ida examining a book-jacket on which a doctor seemed about to embrace a nurse. Putting the casserole down on the table, she said, 'I like stories with happy endings.'

After supper, Sharon, though continuing to talk, did ballet exercises with one hand touching the wall. She was small and rounded, though not fat, with handsome features and a long chestnut plait swinging over one shoulder. She laughed, describing the things that kept happening to her old car: sugar in the engine, paint poured over the roof, 'Red Jew cunt' scratched on the door. 'It's true,' she said reflectively. 'Left-wing, Jewish and a woman – I could hardly be less acceptable to the *volk*.'

Shortly before going home, Ida mentioned an article she had recently read in a magazine. It said that, gradually, climatic conditions were being created on the planet, Earth, which would make it impossible for life to survive there. Ida couldn't remember if the article had said that Earth was getting too hot or too cold. She plumped for cold, and neither of the others contradicted her. 'So what is the point,' Ida asked, 'what is the point of trying to change things?'

'If that is going to happen,' Sharon said, 'it won't be for thousands and thousands of years. By then we shall have explored other planets, and we shall have enormous space-ships.' Sharon tossed her plait, as she declared, 'We shall transplant the human race.'

Ida told Charles about her visit to Sharon.

'Oh my God,' he said. 'Another dyed-in-the-wool Comrade! Jailed, banned. She was an actual paid-up member of the YCL when it was legal.'

'YCL?'

'Young Communist League. You must familiarize yourself with the terminology, darling.' He said 'darling' in a tone different from his usual one.

Ida was always careful to keep Charles and Stella apart. But one evening he called unexpectedly when Stella was there. He stayed for a drink, and within minutes he and Stella were arguing. Suddenly Ida felt enraged. 'I wish you'd both shut up,' she said. 'I don't agree with either of you. I don't like capitalism, but I don't like communism either.' She was surprised by her own desperate tone.

Stella's voice, in contrast, was bland. 'So your answer is "A plague on both your houses"?'

'Yes,' Ida said. She paused. 'I suppose it is.' She glanced at Charles; he, unlike Stella, looked angry.

As soon as they were alone – Stella left early – he said, 'But you can't really *mean* that, can you? You can't seriously put the two systems on a par?'

'Don't know,' she muttered. Nowadays she hated talking politics with Charles. His rage against the system seemed – when he was with her – to have been transferred ... Yet, at that moment, seeing her bowed head, he exclaimed, 'My darling, don't look so dejected,' and embraced her. After he had gone she wondered if they were now happy only in bed. But soon – at any rate for Charles – there was good news.

Stella had been trying ever since Ida had met her to arrange her transfer to the university in Johannesburg. Late in November she heard that she had succeeded. She was to leave in February for the start of the new academic year. 'Wish it were sooner, but all the same let's have champagne,' Charles said. Ida laughed. Lately her discussions with Stella had seemed repetitive. Perhaps she would not miss her very much.

She missed Charles when, early in December, he and his family went to Natal for two weeks. To cheer herself, the night after he left, she put on a record he had given her. This was a series of dialogues, improvised – to music – by a young American actor and actress. In one – to a limpid Chopin accompaniment – a father, broken-voiced, bade a poignant farewell to his small daughter, before being taken away to jail. The child appeared to respond with equal emotion – 'Daddy! Daddy!' – but, as the door closed behind him, remarked brightly, 'Oh well, there he goes again!'

Ida had thought the record funny. She had played it to Sharon, who often came to see her these days; but the dialogue between father and daughter had made Sharon *cry*. Ida had thought this preposterous. Now, listening to the record again, she tried to put herself in Sharon's place. Many of Sharon's friends were serving long prison sentences; others, summarily detained, had had no chance to say goodbye to their children. Sharon herself might – on some pretext, or none – be arrested at any time. Ida saw now why the record had not amused Sharon, and for her, too, it lost some of its charm. She did not think that she would soon replay it. In any case, two days later, she was denied the opportunity.

Almost always, when she arrived home from work, Ida put on a record. Her collection was small but various. Her choice depended on her mood: Bach or Billie; Mozart or Monk; Elgar or Ella. On this particular evening, missing Charles, and after a tiring day at the shop, she was not sure whether she wanted to be soothed or enlivened. Approaching the record shelf, she found it empty.

The records must have been stolen. Yet nothing else had gone. She went into the bedroom, where a pair of garnet earrings lay on the dressing-table. What an odd robbery this was. In England, she would have informed the police next day. (She was not on the telephone at home.) Yet everything she had heard about the South African police disinclined her to become involved with them.

Next morning she asked Dora, her maid – who arrived before Ida left for work, and stayed until lunchtime – if she knew anything.

Dora, a large dreamy woman, looked startled. 'The records? They took them to renew, like Madam wanted.'

'To *renew*?'

'Yes, they came yesterday morning. A white *baas*, with a Coloured boy to carry the records. The white *baas* said you wanted them renewed. Isn't that right?'

Angry about the theft though she was, Ida couldn't help savouring the choice of word. *Renewed*: it sounded so convincing; anyway, it had convinced Dora. 'I'd better tell the police,' she said.

Dora, whose face was normally inexpressive, looked alarmed. Ida wondered if the police might suspect Dora and interrogate her roughly. She did not get in touch with them.

Charles was still away when Stella took Ida to meet the Ellistons, so – at least temporarily – she was spared his comments. Even before she became interested in politics, Ida had heard of Bill Elliston.

He had been an MP in the days when the Cape Coloureds had the vote. (They had always elected communist representatives.) Before that, he had worked full-time for the Party, and his wife, Rachel, had done secretarial work for it. Now, for a long time, the Coloureds had been disenfranchised and the Party had been illegal. For the last three years Bill and Rachel had both been banned. He could not find a job, and she did free-lance typing at home. They lived with Rachel's widowed mother in a small well-kept house, full of large, well-kept furniture in Oranjezicht. This district, though only a few minutes uphill walk from seedy Gardens, had a suburban quality inappropriate and uncongenial to the Ellistons.

Stella did not come into the house. She introduced Ida to Bill and Rachel by shouting from the doorstep. The government conceded that, in terms of a 'banning order', a married couple counted as one person. This sounded mystic; what it meant was that the Ellistons were able to entertain a single guest.

Stella left. It was kind of her to have brought Ida; she had said it would be nice for her and the Ellistons to meet. Had she any other motive? Ida occasionally conjectured that Stella might regard her as an item on the agenda of her 'political work'.

However, in the warmth of the Ellistons' welcome, their eagerness for her to enjoy her meal, she sensed no trace of calculation. They ate in the big kitchen. Rachel's mother who had eaten earlier, now sat in the living-room. If she had been present, the occasion would have 'constituted an illegal gathering'.

Bill was solid and muscular, Rachel pale and gaunt. He was vigorous and lively. She seemed serene until Bill's account of some political injustice made her eyes flash and her hands tighten.

The Ellistons talked politics all the time. They spoke a different language from Ida's. (They used a vocabulary similar to Stella's, but not in Stella's stilted way.) Suddenly Ida felt that her own speech was frivolous, and that Charles's – even at his most serious – was too. Ida wondered if she would be able to learn the Ellistons' language.

But wouldn't she always speak it with a foreign accent? At one point, Bill actually used the word 'comrade' – 'an old comrade of ours' – and she thought, for a second, that he was joking. Previously she had only heard this word used to express the sinister or the ridiculous; Charles usually managed to imply both at once. Ida tried to understand its meaning for the Ellistons; it seemed not quite the same as that of either 'friend' or 'colleague'. Was it something less, or something more? Ida tried to imagine herself speaking of 'my comrades'.

Now Bill was talking about how the Special Branch had taunted a young Indian whom they were interrogating. They had made him strip, suggested he was impotent, and sneered at the size of his penis. Bill said, 'If they'd done that to me, I'd have lifted it up and pissed right in their faces.' Bill, Ida decided, was 'earthy'.

But although the Ellistons were so friendly, so natural – and, in Bill's case, so earthy – their lives awed her. Ida felt herself starting to idealize them. By the end of the evening, as well as liking them, she saw them as symbolic figures, larger than life.

Charles, she reflected, after she had met the Ellistons, seemed light-weight in comparison. Yet, when he returned, her first reaction was to feel that she still adored him.

'And you,' he asked, after making love, 'what have you been doing? Giving your Marx a last polish before the departure of the Marquise?' This was a name he had for Stella – short for the Marquise de Sade – and Ida felt he used it to annoy her. At once she told him about her supper with the Ellistons.

She had expected an outburst. Instead, he sighed. 'You know,' he said, 'you'll get into real trouble sooner or later, if you spend all your time with people like that.'

'But I don't spend *all* my time with them. Look at me now!' She gestured to her naked body, but he didn't smile. *He worries about me,* she thought. Wanting to distract him, she said, 'The most extraordinary thing happened while you were away. I had a musical burglar.' When she finished the story, she said, 'Wasn't it odd?' But he was looking horrified.

'Hasn't it occurred to you,' he said, 'that your living-room may be bugged?'

'*Bugged?*'

'Yes – bugged, taped . . . whatever you want to call it. That would account for the records being taken. You're always playing records, and nothing interferes worse with bugs.'

'But that's absurd.'

'*Is* it? With Stella here all the time. And Sharon Lensky. I wouldn't put it past you to have asked the Ellistons.'

She was silent. She had, in fact, invited the Ellistons to supper in a few days' time. But, anyway, the whole idea was ridiculous.

'I'd advise you,' he said, 'to avoid political discussions in that room. Though do you have any other discussions nowadays? Perhaps you'd better keep clear of it altogether.'

Certainly, after that, she could feel that he was uneasy in the living-room. He headed for the bedroom with his drink. But the bedroom wasn't a good place for sitting and drinking, or for eating. It was too small, and rather dark.

She mentioned Charles's suspicion – outside the house – to the Ellistons, to Sharon, to Stella. To her surprise, they all thought it possible. Bill said, 'You must never talk any real politics in there.' Real politics? She thought she talked them all the time. Yet Bill, Rachel, Sharon, Stella, all – on their separate visits – continued to express strong opinions in the living-room. She realized that by 'real politics' Bill meant something different. Charles came round one evening with a batch of new records. That was sweet of him. Now, with music playing very loudly, he and she again ate and drank, though – perforce – talked less, in the sitting-room.

Three weeks before Stella was due to leave for Johannesburg, she told Ida that an old aunt of the Swarts – the family with whom she stayed – had been ill. Now the aunt was coming out of hospital, but still needed looking after. The sofa Stella slept on was wanted.

'I don't know where to go,' Stella said. 'The room I've fixed up in Johannesburg isn't free yet.'

'I suppose you could come to me,' Ida said, without thinking. 'There's the divan. Probably more comfortable than the Swarts' sofa.'

'Could I really?' Stella, unusually, sounded grateful. (Stella seldom expressed thanks; Ida had decided that she thought them bourgeois.)

'Mmm,' Ida said, but she was already regretting the invitation. Charles's reaction was sure to be unfavourable.

'To *stay* with you?' he said when she told him. 'To *stay*? You know, there are times when I think you must be mad.'

'She's got nowhere to go – and it isn't for very long. Only till the twelfth of February.'

'Nowhere to go? She's not a complete pauper, surely? Why doesn't she move into a boarding-house? Hasn't that bugging business affected you at all? Be sensible, darling. Tell her to find somewhere else.'

Ida hesitated. He was probably right.

'One thing I *can* tell you – if Comrade Marquise comes to stay, *I* shan't come here.'

'That sounds like blackmail,' she said. 'I don't care to be blackmailed.'

He left at once.

*

The key turned. Mrs Potgieter came in, alone. She leant an elbow against the wall. 'I came for your cup,' she said, but Ida decided that this was the pretext for a chat. Mrs Potgieter often found one when she felt bored.

'Won't you have a cigarette?' Ida said. Mrs Steyn always refused. Miss Maree occasionally took a few dainty puffs at a cigarette, and then stubbed it out. Mrs Potgieter usually accepted. 'I love a smoke,' she had told Ida. 'But I do not buy them. My husband does not think it is nice for a woman.'

Now she said, 'I don't mind,' and moved across the yard. Ida stood up, holding her cigarettes and matches. Mrs Potgieter took a cigarette, and so did Ida, who then lit them. 'Thanks,' said Mrs Potgieter, and then, 'Ah!' as she inhaled.

Ida sat down again, and put the cigarettes and matches by her Bible, to which Mrs Potgieter now pointed. 'You read your Bible a lot?' she said.

Ida nodded. 'It's the only book I've got.'

'It is good to have the time to read the Bible. My late father-in-law was a great Bible-reader. But that was the only book he read. He had no use for the others. He was a man of great faith, my father-in-law. And they say that faith can move mountains, don't they?'

'Mmm,' said Ida.

'Well, once in the great drought, he was on trek in the wagon. And he moved over the border from the Free State to the Colony – this was called the Cape Colony in those days, you know. But the Colony was just as dry as the Free State.

'My father-in-law was very tired. He had been on trek for very many days. So he stopped at a farm and asked the farmer if he could rest for a few hours on his land. But the farmer said that he had not grass enough for his own cattle, let alone my father-in-law's.

'So then my father-in-law said to the farmer, "I am sure that it will rain if you will let me rest here." Well, the farmer laughed, but all the same he told my father-in-law that he could rest there for one hour – for one hour only. Then my father-in-law went to the wagon, and he prayed to the Lord. He prayed, and in twenty minutes there was a cloud in the heavens the size of a man's hand. He went on praying, and all the time the cloud became greater and greater. He went on praying until the cloud covered the whole sky. And I tell you, on the hour exactly, *op die kop*, the rain came down in thunder. Yes, now that is the faith that can move mountains, wouldn't you say? And also, once, when he was a very old man, he prayed for money. He had not a penny in the house but, next morning when he woke, there was a pound note on the window sill.'

'How nice,' said Ida. 'Like Father Christmas. I wonder who put it there.'

Mrs Potgieter shrugged. Then she pointed to the cup and saucer. Ida handed them to her; Mrs Potgieter stubbed out her cigarette in the saucer. Then she set off for the door. Ida wondered if she had offended her by talking about Father Christmas, but at the door she swung round, beaming. 'Oh well, you know,' she said, 'it has rained frogs, so it can rain money.'

As the door closed, Ida looked up at the sky. *It has rained frogs, so it can rain money*. She remembered hearing at kindergarten that manna, the food which had fallen from the sky for the Jews, had been like flakes of the finest white bread. Ida, knowing nothing of Marie Antoinette, had thought, 'If bread, why not cake?' She had preferred cake in those days.

*

Until Stella came to stay, Ida had not known her at all.

Stella slept badly. In the morning, Ida, before she left for work, would – as Stella had requested – go into the living-room to wake her, but would almost always find her staring at the ceiling. Because of back-ache, she slept with a plank – rather inconveniently removed from Ida's bookcase – under the mattress of the divan. On this she lay like a stone figure on a tomb.

Stella was often hungry, but when given food, would usually only eat a few mouthfuls. Even so, soon after, she might dash to the bathroom to be sick. At other times she would double up, feeling a stabbing pain in her stomach. Doctors could not explain these symptoms. She did not have an ulcer.

Odder still were the lumps that came and went on the back of her head. Ida, at Stella's invitation, had felt them: three large round knobs under the primrose hair. Next day they had gone. Stella said that a doctor who had felt the lumps had done various tests. Finally he said that, as they were not painful, she should forget about them.

Ida formed a theory that these phenomena were Stella's humanity asserting itself. Of course she did not mention this to Stella, to whom anyway she found it difficult to speak. It was unfair to blame Stella for Charles's absence, but she felt that the rage she suppressed about the disorder Stella created was justified. Who would have guessed that someone so neat-looking and so obsessed with discipline would be so chaotic?

Stella sat at the living-room table on which her papers were untidily scattered. Her clothes were all over the room. Her suitcase was always open in the middle of the floor; she ignored a suggestion that she might keep it in Ida's bedroom.

She made herself mugs of instant coffee all day, taking a fresh mug each time. She never washed the dirty mugs, and when an ashtray started to overflow, she tipped its contents into the waste-paper basket. Ida, coming home to the smell of cigarette butts, and to overlapping brown rings from the various coffee mugs on the table, would clear up in grim silence, while Stella talked. On Sunday, Stella would sit watching Ida make up the divan; a task performed, on weekdays, by Dora.

Ida wondered why she did not shout at Stella, why she still felt that odd compassion for her, still found her inexplicably touching. A week before Stella left, she provided grounds for sympathy. In her stiff, detached way she told Ida that she was in love with – no; she said 'committed to' – a man serving 'Life'. This sentence, in South Africa, for political prisoners, was precisely that; unlike other convicts, they received no remission.

Poor Stella! On the day she left, Ida, returning to the flat, cleaned and tidied by Dora, sighed: partly with compassion, partly with relief, partly because the empty rooms reminded her of Charles, the weight of whose absence now dropped over her like a large stifling blanket. Half an hour later she heard his car draw up outside.

He had come back; he had remembered the exact date of Stella's departure – only mentioned once – and had returned on it. She next thought of the weeks during which he had stayed away. (He had not even telephoned her, at the shop.) Then she ran downstairs to open the front door.

'All clear?' he asked.

'All clear!' she answered.

*

Now, in the yard, the sun pressed on her head and shoulders. She rested her chin on the brown blanket in which she could see threads of white and purple and grey.

*

Picasso had been through first a 'Rose' period, then a 'Blue'. Ida, after Charles's return, was bolder; she combined a 'Pompeian red' with a 'Vandyck brown'. The first colour seemed appropriate for passion (an embarrassing word and a new experience), and the second for cookery (to which she now devoted inordinate time and care). Giving Charles her all in bed and at board, she compensated for her infidelity of spirit.

It was not merely that she was seeing Sharon and the Ellistons far more often than she admitted to him – she did not mention them unless he asked her, when she answered vaguely – or that she never argued with him, even when he tried to provoke her. Far more important was her private obsession. Just like a bird, nest-building from scraps and fragments, Ida was making her own Marxism.

Ida had a trait which posed particularly acute problems for a Marxist: she was a stranger in the world of facts. Therefore she lacked economic material; she picked up odds and ends dropped by Sharon and the Ellistons. Economics were essential to Marxism, but she was prepared to take 'all that' (surplus value, and so on) on trust. After all, Bill said that many Marxists had not read *Das Kapital*.

It was the same with statistics. When she read those which demonstrated Western support for South Africa, they wholly convinced her. (Surely they would convince anyone?) But afterwards, when she tried to remember the figures, they had melted from her mind. However, their detritus, in the form of her belief, remained.

Far more in tune with her requirements were those noble passages about changing the world and about the liberation of mankind. These never failed to move her; and to them she added other chips and cuttings from Marx and Lenin.

But the debris she made best use of came from less orthodox

sources: authors who had never been Marxists, or who had long ago recanted:

MacNeice: *A life beyond*
            the self but self-completing . . .

Although, perhaps, a Marxist might find it more satisfactory, here, to change 'but' to 'so'.

> *Give those who are strong a generous imagination*
> *And make their half-truth true and let the crooked*
> *Footpath find its parent road at last.*
> *I admit that for myself I cannot straiten*
> *My broken rambling track –*

There, however, Ida halted. For the Marxist position – the position she desired to adopt – was surely that one *could* straiten one's track, *could* find the parent road? And besides, 'half-truth' was not really permissible.

Connolly: *It is closing time in the Gardens of the West, and from*
            now on the artist will be judged only by the resonance
            of his solitude or the quality of his despair.

That had always been one of Ida's favourite quotations. Although 'negative', which Marxists disapproved, it applied, after all, specifically to the West. Mightn't one infer that things would be better in the Gardens of the East?

Weeping, Ida had read *One Day in the Life of Ivan Denisovitch*. Yet the fact that it had been published in the Soviet Union – she no longer cared how 'Soviet' was pronounced; Charles was so petty – implied that things had changed.

Bill was in two minds about this book. 'I can't help wondering,' he said, 'If it's constructive to rake up what's all over and done with. I can see, of course, that it's well-written. And, as it's been published over there, it must be true.'

'But of course it's *true*,' Ida said. 'Everyone's always known that.'

'*We* didn't. Hadn't any idea till Khrushchev's speech at the 20th Congress. We were so used to the distortions of the capitalist press that we didn't believe a word of it till then.'

'Didn't it make you feel like giving up politics altogether?' asked Ida.

'Never! Not a chance! Give up fighting Fascism because of our own internal problems? I was far too busy. Though I know one woman – a very staunch comrade, too – who had a nervous breakdown. Fortunately just one session of electric shock treatment put her right.'

'Shock against shock?' said Ida. 'I don't believe in shock treatment.'

'Well it worked for her. At least it's scientific. Not like all that psychological mumbo-jumbo. Anyway, you can understand from that comrade's breakdown what a blow the 20th Congress was. Stalin had been my hero, since I was a boy.'

Bill sounded wistful. How could he have idolized such a monster? He had explained. He had not believed the capitalist press. And didn't she herself notice, more and more, how it – even Charles's 'liberal' paper – distorted things?

Ivan Denisovitch remained one of the most significant components of Ida's Marxism. She added another novel: Malraux's *Man's Fate* (though Malraux, of course, had stopped being a communist years ago). She lent it to Bill, but he did not share her enthusiasm: 'A bit of a mishmash,' he said. (She hated it when Charles's old jokes rose up like this to confront her.)

Thus Ida, on solitary evenings, worked at her Marxism. She had a tit-bit, a treat, which she always saved to the end. It came from the French communist poet, Louis Aragon. Ida said it aloud: '*My body is a roulette wheel and I am betting on red.*'

This red, of course, was a different red from 'Pompeian red', and if she had quoted that line of Aragon to Charles, he would have asked her what it meant. Even though she *knew*, she would not have been able to formulate an answer.

As months passed, the things – apart from the making of her Marxism – which she couldn't share with Charles grew in number. She undertook errands for Bill: she carried notes between him and Sharon – who, both banned, were not allowed to communicate with each other – and she posted letters for him to addresses in England. Bill felt – despite the 'bugging' possibility, now seldom referred to – that Ida was unlikely to be under the same surveillance as he suspected himself to be.

She was writing, too; for a cyclostyled newsletter, not specifically Marxist, though its approach was more 'analytical' than that of most other anti-apartheid material. This newsletter was posted to various influential people, one of whom was Charles. Ida had seen it among some papers he was carrying, and – afraid of sounding artificial, and thus arousing his suspicion – had not dared to ask him about it. He had not referred to it himself. If he had thought it communist in tone, she felt that he would have produced one of his diatribes. Bill said that Ida's tone was exactly right for the newsletter.

The Ellistons were having supper with her on an April evening. They had just arrived. She was in the kitchen, fetching drinks, when she heard a loud knocking on the front door. 'I wonder who that can be,' she called to Bill and Rachel, as she passed the living-room door. Anyway, she thought, as she went downstairs, it was not Charles. He and his wife were dining out that night. The knocking continued; it was extraordinarily aggressive. Opening the doors, she was faced by what seemed a crowd of men, all wearing suits. Most of them were wearing hats as well. A bulky man with a military moustache – his hat was of checked tweed, with a fishing fly stuck into the band – handed her a piece of paper. 'We have a warrant to search your premises,' he said in an Afrikaans accent. It was only then that Ida realized that they were 'the SB'.

At once they clattered up the stairs, moving closely, in a pack. Though they seemed many more, there were five of them; two carried large empty cardboard boxes. Bill had come out of the living-room, and now stood on the landing.

'Good evening, Mr Elliston,' said Tweed-Hat, in a jolly voice.

'Good evening,' Bill answered in a flat tone.

There weren't many places to search. There was the living-room, where Rachel sat primly upright on the divan, giving a mere nod when Tweed-Hat greeted her as he had greeted Bill, and the bedroom, the landing, the kitchen and the bathroom, half way up the stairs, which she had originally shared with the downstairs tenants. The men were all so large that they made the small flat seem tiny. But they were comic, in a way, she thought, especially the man in the silly hat.

On the landing, the only furniture was a bookshelf, a filing-cabinet and a table, on the edge of which Bill was now sitting. As Tweed-Hat pulled open the top drawer of the cabinet, Ida's attention was caught by the expression on Bill's face. He was looking at Tweed-Hat just as a little boy would look who was waiting in anxiety outside the headmaster's study. And sitting there, on the edge of the table, he was swinging one foot as a little boy might; a nervous, sheepish little boy. But the comparison was absurd, she thought immediately, between Bill, of all people, who had survived 'outside' so long – 'Billy the fox,' he had once designated himself with a twinkling eye – and a child. Then the comparison and her reaction to it were both lost, forgotten, as she watched Tweed-Hat ransacking her so-called filing-cabinet.

It was, in fact, a filing-cabinet – an old grey metal one, without a key – but nothing in it was 'filed'. Into it, Ida, an inveterate keeper of papers for long periods (at the end of each such period, she would spend a day sorting the papers, and would throw most of them away), dropped letters, clippings from newspapers, magazines containing articles that had interested her, postcards of pictures she liked, notes she had made on various subjects at various times. Tweed-Hat was piling all this into a cardboard box.

Apart from the entire contents of the filing-cabinet, they took away very little: two copies of the *New Statesman* and *Ulysses*, which one of them said was a banned book. It was not, she told him firmly – she had learnt that in the bookshop – but he shook his head obstinately, and took it all the same, sniggering to one of the others, and muttering in Afrikaans. He had obviously heard that it was 'dirty'. Annoyed though she was, Ida coldly smiled. He would be disappointed; he would certainly never persevere as far as Molly Bloom's soliloquy.

As quickly as they had come, they left, carrying their plunder.

The Ellistons and Ida looked at each other in silence for a moment. Then Bill said, 'Well, how about those drinks, my girl?' Fetching them, she looked at the casserole in the oven; it was bubbling gently.

Bill, drink in hand, was informative about the various 'SB men', three of whom he knew. 'That big bugger in the hat is Major de Wet, the head of the Cape Town SB,' he said. 'He's the one who broke Wilson Kunene's ribs.'

Comedy turned sour. The chill ran down her spine. But Bill talked on, and soon she was talking too. Even Rachel, usually quiet, was talkative after this extraordinary event. Although, of course, the event had not seemed so extraordinary to the Ellistons as it had to her; over the years, their various dwellings had been searched many times.

After the hectic talking came a sudden tired quiet. The Ellistons left early, soon after they had eaten. Ida sat on the divan, thinking about the search. In retrospect, the big, jostling SB men frightened her more than they had at the time. Yet she also felt exhilarated . . . that she had, as foxhunters say, been 'blooded'. But she didn't care for that. 'Baptized' was preferable; she had been baptized politically.

She would not have told Charles about the search, but when he came round next evening, he had already heard about it on the journalistic grapevine.

'I told you so,' were – tiresomely – his first words. 'I told you something like this would happen. I thought you'd cooled off those bloody Comrades, but apparently I was wrong. Don't you understand that they're putting you in danger – and me as well?'

'You?' She raised her eyebrows.

'Don't be stupid, Ida. Can't you see that, in my position – I'm sorry to sound pompous – I just can't afford to associate with someone the Special Branch are watching all the time. Particularly when the association is – what shall I say? – illicit. I am *married*, you know. I could be compromised. They might try to blackmail me, especially in view of my liberal opinions. They could even try to get me out of my job. Newspaper proprietors are as nervous of them as everyone else is, you know. Can't you understand?'

She stood looking at him. Yes, she could see that he might be in difficulties. But he interpreted her silence as hostile.

'Unlike you,' he said, 'I've got a lot to lose. I suppose that, with your drab little job, you feel nowadays that you've got nothing to lose but your chains. Personally I'd say that you've got nothing to lose but your brains, which are shrinking every minute under the Comrades' influence.'

This speech of his had made a fatal change. 'Oh yes,' she said. 'You've got a lot to lose. Your *un-drab*, great big job, your chance to express your wishy-washy liberal ideas. But that isn't the *main* thing, is it? It isn't nearly as important as your precious *way of life*. Sally wouldn't like a fuss, would she? And that would never do, because what would happen to your lovely unearned Wynberg Wonderland?'

While she was speaking, he had paled and become rigid. (She herself was flushed and shaking.)

'Well,' he said, 'Ida, I'm afraid you have to choose between the Comrades and me, and it seems that you've already chosen.'

She realized that what she had just said had affected him so strongly that he could not refer to it. But on she went. 'You talk about the SB blackmailing you, but it's you who are blackmailing me, with your talk about choices. I told you before that I won't be blackmailed. Yes, I've chosen.'

She turned away abruptly, because there were tears behind her eyes. A blaze of feeling – 'Pompeian red' – almost drove her round towards him. She heard him going down the stairs.

She knew that he would not come back. What made her certain was what she had said, about his *way of life*. That would stay in his mind, irritating it, like grit in an oyster: material for a black pearl of abhorrence. Could even unconditional surrender interrupt the process that had already begun? But that question was rhetorical. *We shall never surrender.* Which reminded her of *We shall fight on the beaches.* A picture of Cape Town's beaches – white bodies browning on the sand – made her smile. (Though on those very beaches, there might be fighting, one day.)

> *Now, if thou wouldst, when all have given him over,*
> *From death to life thou might'st him yet recover.*

'Pompeian red' against black pearl? *We shall never surrender.*
She was glad of her job. (She wondered how women who did not

219

work coped with suffering.) It was in early May, a fortnight after she and Charles parted, that Ida, on her way home, bought an evening paper, and read on the front page that Stella, and various other Johannesburg people, had been detained under the 180-day clause.

Ida went straight to Sharon's flat. Sharon made coffee. 'What do you think solitary confinement *does* to people?' asked Ida. (Would Stella become stronger? Or would she break down?)

Sharon thought before she answered. 'You probably remain yourself – only more so.' Ida had not expected such a strange answer from Sharon. She turned it over in her mind.

Next day, she borrowed one of two Bibles in the bookshop, and took it home. She knew that a detainee was allowed a Bible; this had been established in court.

Now, except at work, Ida saw no one but Sharon and the Ellistons.

Sharon gave her warm companionship and hot chicken soup. She gave her gossip about the former love-affairs of people who were now in jail or in exile. Love-affairs, to Sharon – who had not had one since she received her banning-order – were a subject of absorbing interest, but although she had not met him, she thought that Ida was well rid of Charles. (Now the black pearl had only a rim of 'Pompeian red'.)

Sharon could be perceptive; she could also be crude. If ever the subject of religion cropped up, she would sing an awful little song:

'I don't care if it rains or freezes.
I am safe in the arms of Jesus.
I am Jesus' little lamb.
Yes, by Jesus Christ, I am!'

Ida would wince. Atheist though she was, she could not bear this song. And she was unable to talk about books to Sharon. Peering gloomily along Ida's shelves, Sharon would ask, 'Haven't you got *anything* light?' Authors who amused Ida – Waugh, Powell, Trevor, Spark – seemed cynical and obscure to Sharon. Certainly none of them was 'light'.

With the Ellistons she listened to music. Or there was talk, but never gossip. Gossip was about love; talk was about battle. On the field of politics, setbacks were temporary and victories famous. The soldiers, led by astute generals, were all heroes.

Her flat was not raided again. Sometimes she wondered if she were being followed, but, glancing round casually, would see no one. (Her glance was casual because she did not want a follower to think she suspected him; to think she thought there was a reason for his presence.) Looking out of the window in the evening, she would sometimes feel almost certain that, on the corner, she saw the shadow of a man cast by a street lamp. She would slip back, from between the curtain and the window, into the room, to make her Marxism. She had a new and favoured fragment: *Freedom is the recognition of necessity.*

Two months after her detention, Stella was released from solitary confinement, taken to court and charged with being a member of the Communist Party. The others who had been detained at the same time were also charged, apart from one who had agreed to become a State witness.

Now that Stella, on remand, was able to receive letters, Ida wanted to write to her, but Bill said she would be foolish to draw attention to herself. Soon Sharon had a letter from a friend in Johannesburg who had visited Stella in prison. On her way to court to be charged, just after her release from isolation, Stella sat in the back of a police car. It had stopped at a red light, and Stella had opened the door and sprung out. She had run along a crowded pavement (touchingly bandylegged, thought Ida; pathetic in her invariable high heels). In a moment, the two SB men who had been sitting in front were after her. One of them brought her down with a rugby tackle, and they dragged her to the car. That night, back at the prison, she had been made to jump naked, with her legs apart.

Shortly before Stella was charged, three Africans had been hanged for killing an informer responsible for sending six men to life imprisonment on Robben Island. The story of their death was brought to Bill – Ida did not know by whom – in a letter from a white political prisoner, just released after serving five years in Pretoria Central. Bill read this letter to Ida in the Ellistons' garden, where it was getting dark, but there was still enough light to read by.

'. . . It was through his laugh that I first became aware that Ncgobo had arrived in the condemned section. Isolated in my tiny cell in the adjacent block, I was sensitive to every variation in the murmur of life. Ncgobo's laugh burst into my world with shattering certainty. Soon I heard on the prison grapevine that he, Mvusi and Simelane were in the "last week" cell.

'I marvelled at Ncgobo's daring. No one laughed aloud in Central prison. It was absolutely forbidden. And Death Row, although there were more than sixty Africans there, was one of the quietest parts of the Prison.

'There was more than laughter. Every day, in the "last week" cell, those three men *sang*. They sang traditional and Freedom songs. They sang in the unison of long-practised harmony. In the early evening the singing seemed to express a special power. The iron gates did not clang so often at that time. There was only a skeleton staff on duty. And I could sense that, all through the Prison, men were listening, lying on their mats in their cells.

'On the last evening it was late at night when the singing ended, and the Prison fell into an almost unbearable silence.

'I was already awake when the singing began again in the early morning, floating through the barred windows, echoing off the brick walls of the exercise yard. And then suddenly – the *shout* of Ncgobo roared down the passages. He must have been standing on his stool with his face close to the barred vent in the cell wall. He shouted three times, "*Amandla Ngawethu*." And then it was Mvusi's turn, and then Simelane's, as they too defied all prison rules to shout '*Amandla Ngawethu*."

'Soon after that, I heard the door of their cell being opened. And then the three men began to sing. The singing seemed to fill the whole prison, and then it gradually faded away into the depth of the condemned section.

'Since my release, I have seen a last message which Ncgobo smuggled out of prison. In it he said that, at the beginning of that last week, Captain Pretorius and two policemen came to see him. They asked him if he knew that his Appeal had been dismissed, and he said that he was not interested to know from them what his lawyer would tell him. They then said there was still a big chance for him to be saved if he would give evidence for them in another case. He refused.

'Captain Pretorius then asked him if he would make the *Amandla Ngawethu* salute, and sing as he walked the last few paces to the gallows. He said "I promise that I will," and, as he put it, "after a few more jokes of that nature, they left."

'Well, Ncgobo kept his promise . . .'

Bill broke off. Tears were running down his cheeks. Ida was crying, too. Yet from her streaming eyes, she looked at Bill with a wild and hopeful joy. *So there were heroes, after all.*

The men had killed. But unless one was an absolute pacifist, it was possible to believe that killing in a just war was justified. Ida believed that the war against Hitler had been just, and she believed the same about this one. *Amandla Ngawethu:* Strength is Ours! Ida had made her Marxism; the bird had built its nest. In the Ellistons' garden, she said to Bill, 'Is there any possibility, nowadays, of a person joining the Communist Party?'

He looked at her. Then he said, 'So you want to become one of us?'

Next time they met, he said, 'You realize that you will be working in a white world. This is a bad time in the history of our movement. We shall re-organize. The masses will re-group. Meanwhile we must do what we can.'

She had not expected to have contact with Africans. (Did Bill, himself, have any, at this time?) But she had not expected to meet no new people at all. She joined a group – it was called a 'group', not, as in books, a 'cell' – but it consisted only of Bill, Rachel and herself. They had Party names: Bill was 'Tom' and Rachel was 'Rosa'. Ida chose 'Diana'; she had no idea why.

They had meetings every fortnight. Sometimes they walked. Sometimes they went for drives in the Ellistons' car. Always, of course, they remained within the Magisterial District of Cape Town, to which Bill and Rachel's banning-orders confined them. At these meetings they analysed the situation; but really these analyses were not very different from the conversations they held in Ida's flat or in Rachel's mother's house. Ida paid a monthly subscription: a tenth of her salary.

The work Ida did – apart from her articles for the newsletter – was not discussed at group meetings; only by her and Bill. She continued to take messages between him and Sharon. She posted his letters. She now also opened a bank account for him, under a false name, and paid – in cash – the monthly rent for a flat, under this same name.

Ida hurried along a pavement, after dark. She wore a scarf over her head, and trod so softly that she could not hear her own footsteps. She also frequently glanced behind her.

The block of flats, San Marino Court, was built into a cliff. She looked quickly to left and right before turning down the steps. The sound of the sea came closer. From each outdoor landing, she could see the white sands on which white people lay in the daytime – *we shall fight on the beaches* – but which were now deserted. She reached the bottom, turned left, and went through an archway to the flat where Bill was already working the duplicating machine, with the radio playing very loud.

The leaflets he was duplicating were different from the newsletter, and went to a different mailing-list; though the two lists overlapped. These leaflets exhorted people to action, and bore the name of the Communist Party, so producing them could earn one years in prison.

Ida learnt to fold a batch of leaflets cleanly with a ruler, so that they could be easily slipped into envelopes. She learnt to shake talcum powder into rubber gloves, so that they did not stick to her fingers. She learnt that, to moisten many stamps, she must use a sponge – something she had previously thought of as an affectation – because otherwise her mouth became dry.

She had come by bus. After Bill and she had finished work – often late at night – he drove her back, leaving her a short distance from her flat. Sometimes, before they left, they walked along the beach. Ida took off her shoes, and let the little waves lap over her feet.

All this time, Stella's trial dragged on. She and her fellow accused were not convicted of being members of the Communist Party until late November. The man who had not been charged, and who had been a State witness – 'a bloody traitor,' as Bill called him – was largely responsible for her conviction.

On the day in early December on which Stella was sentenced to three years' imprisonment, Ida had a drink with Bill, after work, at a hotel in the centre of Cape Town. (Hotels were good places to meet; you could sit with your back to the wall, and make sure that your neighbours did not look like SB men.) She had a message from Sharon to deliver to him, which she handed over.

Then, sipping her drink, Ida spoke hesitantly: 'Sharon once said that, in detention, one is probably oneself, only more so.'

'Sounds a bloody silly idea to me.' Ida was surprised by Bill's vehemence. 'If there's one kind of crap I can't stand, it's psychological crap.'

Ida said, 'I had a dream last night. I dreamed that men were asking me questions. And I wouldn't answer, so they called this robot over. He was huge, and he came over to me with this stiff walk, as if he had been wound up like a toy. He had enormous arms. He swung one of them back, and it was like the piston of a train. That remorseless backward movement – and I couldn't help it – I wanted to sit up straight, but I cringed away. And then I woke to find myself pressed back against the pillow, with my fingers clutching at the edge of the mattress. Oh Bill, I was so frightened.'

He was smiling at her with a fatherly kindness. She went on: 'But I can't help thinking . . . well, that if I was so frightened in a dream, how would I be, that is, how would I manage, if it happened in real life. I mean –'

He interrupted her. 'It's no good thinking about that, my girl. No good at all. If they pick you up, all you remember is that, if they ask you questions, you just answer, "I have nothing to say." Like in the army all you give is your name, rank and serial number. Ida, it is like going to war. You don't think about it beforehand, but when the time comes, you put your bloody knapsack on your back, and you're bloody *off*, and that's that.'

She remembered Bill talking on an earlier occasion about 'psychological mumbo-jumbo'. So his advice was: *Don't dig!* And perhaps he was right. After all, he had been to war. He had fought in North Africa and Italy against the Nazis when she was only a child.

'Must go now.' He finished his drink. She waited in the lounge a moment or two longer, so that they would not be seen leaving the hotel together, and then caught a bus home. She was too tired, that evening, to walk through the park. Anyway, it was getting dark.

When she reached home, it was dark. *Don't dig!* Suddenly she wished that there were tenants on the ground floor. She let herself in, shut and locked the door behind her, and went upstairs in darkness, sensing more darkness waiting at the top. She thought of Stella's bullet, and the things that had been done to Sharon's car.

On the landing she switched on the light, and stood under it, re-reading the newspaper report of Stella's sentence. Next to it was an account of another case, involving two young white men. One was twenty-two, and the other twenty-four; both were motor mechanics. In the evening, it had been their custom to borrow a car from their employers' garage, and drive round the outskirts of Johannesburg. When they came across an African, alone, they would get out of the car, and beat him unconscious. One night, a man had died from the beating. That was the night they were unlucky; for they were caught, and charged. Now they had each been sentenced to two years in prison with one year suspended.

Ida went into the kitchen. Pouring out a drink, she thought again that Bill must know what he was talking about; that he had been to war. But when he had gone to war, he had been with others; he had not gone alone when he put his bloody knapsack on his back. And why did he disapprove so much of 'digging'. Could it be something to do with the Stalin period: a habit of evasion? Was 'not digging' in some sense an alibi?

But then she thought of people who spent all their lives 'digging'. Wasn't that a worse alibi than 'not digging'? One could 'dig' and 'dig' in order to avoid activity, to avoid commitment: Lenin's 'years spent without purpose' that led to 'torturing regrets'.

She made herself a cheese sandwich, which she ate standing in the kitchen. Nowadays she never cooked, except for Sharon and the Ellistons, and then simply; no 'Vandyck brown'. *Now, if thou wouldst . . . We shall never surrender.* She saw a sudden image of the robot, swinging back its arm.

A week later, she was arrested.

*

Hearing keys, she rolled over and sat up, as Mrs Potgieter came in with a tin plate of lunch and a tin mug of coffee.

'You were resting?' Mrs Potgieter asked, and Ida nodded.

'It is good to rest sometimes. One cannot be busy all the time. Once I knew a woman who never stopped working. When she had nothing else to do, she would sew, sew, sew, or knit, knit, knit – even in her lunch-hour, while she ate her sandwiches. One time I asked her why she never took a bit of a break, and she answered' – Mrs Potgieter deepened her voice – ' "The Lord might come and find me idle." '

Mrs Potgieter and Ida both laughed. Ida took her plate and mug. 'Well,' Mrs Potgieter said, 'I will leave you to your meal while it is still hot.'

It wasn't hot, but it was still warm. It was curried mince with rice; one of the police-station cook's better dishes. All the food here was incomparably better than it had been in Pretoria.

*

Bill was taken to Pretoria on the same small government plane as she was, but they were seated well apart. She smiled at him often till she saw that it was an effort for him to smile back. He looked old.

From the government airport they were driven off in separate cars. The last she saw of him was his back view – he looked smaller as well as older – as he went off across the tarmac between two big SB men. He did not look round.

It was very hot during her first eighteen days in the Female Prison. She walked up and down her cell; it was the condemned cell. A white prisoner with an Eton crop (she was in for theft; the only other white prisoner was a brothel-keeper) had muttered this information through the spyhole.

The spyhole had no cover, and its glass was missing, too. This made it easier to talk to passing prisoners. It also meant that Ida had to give away most of the small loaf of coarse brown bread – baked in the prison, and issued at breakfast – which was the only food that tasted clean. African women prisoners, who received no bread, just porridge and beans, would come to the spyhole asking for it, and Ida would break off pieces and push them through. She passed cigarettes to the two white prisoners. She was allowed to smoke, but they were not. She did not know how they lit the cigarettes she gave them. She could get a light only when a wardress came round, and this made her chain-smoke, except when she forgot, and stubbed out her cigarette. Then she often had to wait an hour for another.

Because Ida's was the condemned cell, it was – the prisoner with the Eton crop told her – the best. It was the largest, and the only one with a proper window. This window was high and barred, but sometimes Ida climbed on her wooden chair to look out. She could see a stretch of gravel where cars were parked, and beyond this a swimming-pool where the prison staff and their families swam in the afternoons. Children splashed and shouted, and a dog yapped.

Sometimes Ida read Miss Rubinstein's Bible for half an hour or so. (She wondered how Miss Rubinstein was managing without her, in the shop.) She would have expected to read more, but she kept falling asleep. During those first twelve days she slept far more than she usually did.

In the morning, African women prisoners cleaned her cell and polished the floor while a wardress stood in the doorway with a leather switch in her hand. The wardress never used this switch in front of Ida, but sometimes, when the door was closed, she heard the sound of it striking against flesh.

As well as cleaning the prison, the African women did the laundry of members of the government. Ida during her exercise hour, walked up and down between the lines of clothes. Once she saw the name of the Minister of Justice on a pair of sagging underpants.

She was not able to spend the whole hour walking. She had to fit in her bath, and the washing of her clothes. In the yard was a big wash-house with six bathrooms in it, but only one bath plug, which seemed to be in a different bathroom each day. During her first week in the prison Ida used each bathroom in turn. Later she always (after she had found the plug) used the same one. This made her feel safer.

At meal times, the wardress opened Ida's door and put her food down on the floor, just inside, but, after a day or two, Ida waited by the door when she heard the food-trolley coming, so that the wardress had to hand her her plate and mug. Apart from the bread, the food consisted of lumpy porridge without milk, a sort of stew, and a weak black chicory liquid, which was slightly sugared.

On the nineteenth day, when Ida came back to her cell from the yard, her lunch was waiting. The greyish-brown stew had a wrinkled skin on top, and she could not bring herself to taste it. She still had a small piece of bread – she had eaten a lump of it for breakfast, and then pushed some though the spyhole – and she was eating that when a wardress came to tell her that she was wanted in the office downstairs.

She thought that perhaps the British consul had come to see her again. He had visited her a week before, and had said he would return when he could. Now she felt surprised that they had let him do this so soon.

He had seemed very nervous on his first visit. He was a small man with a ginger moustache. He saw her in the chief wardress's office, and he thanked this woman effusively when she brought them coffee.

As soon as they were alone, Ida asked him if he were trying to arrange her release. 'We are in constant touch with the authorities,' he said. Then he asked her if there were anything she wanted, and she answered, 'Books'. He said that he was sure he could get her a Bible. When she told him she already had one, he was silent. Then he asked her if she smoked, and when she said 'Yes', offered her a cigarette. As he lit it for her, he asked if she were allowed to smoke in her cell, and she told him how she could have cigarettes, but no matches. At this an eager, boyish look brightened his face. He glanced quickly round the office. Then, with a big wink, he took a box of matches out of his pocket, and pushed it across the table towards her. But just then footsteps sounded in the passage outside, and he snatched up the matches and stuffed them back in his pocket. The chief wardress and another, younger one came in. The consul stood up and repeated his thanks for the coffee. That was when he said he would come again as soon as he could, and he and Ida said goodbye. Then the younger wardress took Ida back to her cell.

Now she wondered if he had any news for her. But it was not he who was in the chief wardress's office. Two SB men were there, one of whom had travelled with her on the plane from Cape Town. He now signed a receipt for her, and gave it to the chief wardress. Then the two men took Ida out to a large black car in which a chaperone was waiting. The chaperone was a young Afrikaans girl in a full-skirted, flowered summer dress. She wore wrist-length white net gloves, and white high-heeled shoes with peep toes.

People were walking about in the streets as if nothing extraordinary were happening. Ida remembered how Stella had run through the Johannesburg crowd. The car stopped outside a big building in the middle of the city where Ida, the chaperone, and one of the SB men got out, and the other drove off. Ida wondered what would happen if she screamed, 'Help! Help!' She decided that it would be embarrassing. In any case she felt sure that all the whites in Pretoria were her enemies.

It was dark in the building. The SB man said something in Afrikaans to an old yellow-faced doorkeeper, who sat just inside the door in a glass-fronted box. Then the SB man and Ida and the chaperone walked down a long passage with doors on both sides of it. One of the doors was open, and Ida saw a fat man talking on the telephone at a desk in a room with a bright green carpet. At the end of the long passage they went through a large office where several girls sat typing. None of them looked up. This office opened into another where men with rolled-up sleeves were putting papers into filing-cabinets.

Beyond this, yet another passage led to a room furnished with chairs, tables, a cooker, a refrigerator and two camp beds. Here several men were sitting, drinking tea. The chaperone remained in this room. She was taking off her white gloves as the SB man led Ida into a room beyond. This was very big indeed, and quite empty, except for a small pegboard cubicle built into the far corner. Into this cubicle the SB man ushered Ida.

It had a window, which faced straight onto a red brick wall. Next to the window was a small wash-basin with taps. A table had a wooden chair behind it, backed against a radiator, and there were three more chairs on the other side of the table. The SB man told Ida to sit on the chair by the radiator. She did so, and he left the cubicle. At once she stood up and went over to the window. When she found she could see nothing outside except the high brick wall, she sat down again.

A few minutes later, one of the ugliest men Ida had ever seen came in. He was squat, with a bulge of flesh around his waist. He wore shorts and an open-necked shirt, and rubber sandals on his thick feet. He had a big face like raw meat, long red arms and short red legs. The close-cut hair on his round head looked like coarse fur.

'Good afternoon, Ida,' he said. She raised her eyebrows at his use of her first name, but he did not seem to notice this. 'I am Captain Pretorius. I expect you have heard of me.' *Ncgobo kept his promise.* Yes, she had heard of Captain Pretorius. She said nothing. He smiled. 'Anyway,' he said, 'I know a lot about you. I know about that bank account you opened for Bill. I know about the flat, Number One, San Marino Court, and what you did there. I also know that you are a member of the Communist Party – Party name: Diana.'

Ida had always imagined that if the SB interrogated her, they would ask her questions to which they did not know the answers. Not only was she shocked and astonished by what Captain Pretorius had said, but she felt it was unfair that they weren't starting on an equal footing. She said, 'I have nothing to say.'

'We'll see about that.' Captain Pretorius left the cubicle. Staring at the brick wall outside the window, Ida felt that his visit ought to be erased. They should start again; she with her secrets, and the SB with their questions.

A young blond SB man came in. He leant on the table opposite her, and said angrily, 'You wanted to poison the Minister of Justice.'

'What nonsense!' she exclaimed. This absurd remark was more the sort of thing she had expected.

'Nonsense, hey? I can quote your very words. You said you would love to smuggle some poisonous mushrooms into his kitchen.'

Now Ida remembered laughing as she said this to the Ellistons, who had brought her mushrooms they had picked on Table Mountain.

She said, 'But that was a joke, of course.'

'Not a very funny one,' the young man said as he left.

So her living-room had been bugged. Yet she knew that none of the things Captain Pretorius had mentioned had ever been discussed there.

For the rest of the afternoon, different men – a different one each time – kept coming in, quoting things she had said in the flat, and going out. As daylight faded, the bricks outside seemed to darken moment by moment. One of her callers asked if she were counting them.

She said that she wanted to go to the lavatory. Evidently the young chaperone had gone off duty, for a woman with short grey hair came to fetch her. As they went through the room where the SB men were sitting, one of them called out, 'Don't let her lock the door!' There were still two men in the filing room, but the typists' room was empty; there were covers on the typewriters. Near the street door, which was closed now – there was no one in the glass-fronted box – the woman turned right and opened a door into a room with wash-basins in it under a horizontal mirror. As Ida went into one of two lavatories at the back, the woman said, 'Leave the door ajar.'

When she got back to the cubicle, the divisions between the bricks in the wall were hardly discernible, but Ida went on staring out of the window. This was partly because the cubicle door was open and, if she looked straight ahead, a naked bulb in the large room shone straight into her eyes.

An SB man came in, and switched on a fluorescent bar in the cubicle ceiling. It blinked, and then steadily glared. Now all she could see in the window was her own reflection. This man asked her what kind of sandwich she liked, and she said 'Ham', because of the protein, which she hoped would sustain her. 'Plain or toasted?' 'Toasted, please. And could you get me some cigarettes? I have money at the prison.' He left, saying nothing, but when he brought the sandwich, in a paper bag, he also brought cigarettes and matches. He went out of the room, and came back with a cup of coffee. Then he left again.

Ida had finished the sandwich and coffee and was lighting a cigarette when six men came crowding into the cubicle together, like football players coming onto a field. They were all yelling, jeering and swearing loudly; she could not have answered the questions they were shouting

230

at her even if she had wanted to. Suddenly, as if a whistle had sounded for 'Time', they all jostled out. She was sweating, and she wiped her forehead with the back of her hand.

Captain Pretorius returned a few minutes later, carrying a stack of cardboard files. Another man brought a second stack, which he dumped on the table before going out.

Pretorius sat down, and he and Ida faced each other across the table. He said, 'I have your life story in here.' He opened one of the files, and Ida saw that it held neatly bound sheets of foolscap. It looked like the typescript of a play, with the speakers' names in capitals, and the dialogue in ordinary type. 'Each of these files covers one evening,' Pretorius said, and then, 'I'm surprised you never guessed your flat was bugged.'

I did, Ida wanted to say. Instead she said, 'I want to go back to the prison. It is illegal for you to keep me here when I refuse to answer questions. I shall complain to the British consul. In fact, I demand to see him now.'

Suddenly, Pretorius's raw red face became purple, and he hammered on the table with his fist. He shouted, 'Fuck the British consul. The British consul can go and get stuffed. You won't even see the British consul's prick until long after you've told us everything we want to know.'

'What language!' Ida said.

'Language, is it? There's worse on some of these tapes. You weren't so fucking fussy about Bill Elliston's language, were you? And you and that married man of yours had some pretty funny conversations. Hot stuff! Until you fought with him over your Commie pals. Whew, he and Stella were certainly at it hammer and tongs. And you, as usual, were the referee.'

The referee? She was interested by the idea.

'Though that Charles sounds to me like a fellow-traveller himself.'

'Nonsense,' she said vehemently, 'no one could be more anti-communist than Charles.' But she was letting him draw her out, and she must not do that.

'Huh – all your friends were communists or fellow-travellers. All rubbish, all shit. I suppose that now you are going to complain about my language again, hey, Ida? All shit, I said. Shit, shit, shit.'

From being purple, and hammering on the table, suddenly, his colour fading, he was quiet. She realized that she could hear frogs croaking, and thought that there must be a park or garden somewhere near. She realized also that she had been aware, at intervals, of the faint, distant chime of a clock. Now two struck, and the sound of the hour seemed a positive thing. She told Pretorius that she wanted to go to the lavatory. This time, a big dark-haired woman was on duty. Their footsteps made the wooden floors of the dimly lit passage creak. When she had used the wc, Ida splashed cold water on her face.

Back in the cubicle, two other men were sitting at the table with Pretorius, who now said in an ironic voice, 'May I present Lieutenants van Schalkwyk and du Plessis.' To her annoyance, Ida heard herself say, 'How do you do.' Van Schalkwyk's hair was shiny with cream. He had a pale unfinished-looking face, but that of du Plessis was like a clenched fist.

The three of them asked her question after question about conversations in the files, and to each Ida answered, 'I have nothing to say.'

Just after the clock struck four, du Plessis left the cubicle. He came back a few minutes later, carrying a wooden truncheon. He leant it against the wall under the window, and sat down again. Ida felt a powerful intuition: she should comment on the truncheon. She should *bring it out into the open*. Instead, she pretended not to notice it.

The questions went on. Suddenly she noticed that a paleness was growing outside the window. Soon she could again distinguish the pattern of the bricks. Then she realized that the frogs had stopped croaking, and that instead she could hear the awakening calls of birds. She thought, *I have come through*, and as if they heard and acknowledged this, the three men got up and left the cubicle.

She wondered if they would take her back to the prison soon. Sitting, watching the bricks turn red and hearing the birds, she murmured aloud, *'This city now doth like a garment wear the beauty of the morning.'* A shiver of exaltation ran over her body. The big dark woman came in, bringing her a cup of coffee, and said, 'It is going to be a fine day. You can tell from the voices of the birds.'

After this, Ida was left alone for a long time. Traffic was starting, and she could no longer hear the clock. She drank the coffee and smoked two cigarettes.

The young girl was on duty again, for now – wearing another flowered dress – she came in to collect Ida's coffee cup. Soon after, one of the young SB's brought her a plate of breakfast. There was a fried egg in the middle of the plate, with a circle of chips around it. The rim of the plate was covered with shredded lettuce, on which four circles of beetroot were placed like three, six, nine and twelve on a clock-face.

The young man who had brought it lounged against the wall by the window, talking to her while she ate. He asked her about her job in the bookshop. 'Must be rather slow work,' he said. 'Don't think it would suit me. Is the pay good?' She could see that he wanted to know what she earned, but all she said was, 'Not bad,' although she did not particularly object to him. 'Well, cheerio,' he said, as he took her empty plate – she had eaten even the beetroot – away.

She stretched and yawned. She thought that they would take her back to the prison soon, now that they realized it was no use keeping her here. Her legs ached. She looked down at them, and saw that they were black with dust.

She stood up, and went through the big empty room outside the cubicle to the doorway of the SB room. There were only two young men in there, one of whom was the one who had brought her breakfast. They were talking to the girl chaperone, whom Ida told that she wanted to go to the lavatory.

The short-sleeved men were back at their filing-cabinets, and the typists were drinking coffee. In the washroom, a girl was powdering her face in front of the mirror. Ida went into the lavatory, and locked the door. What would happen if she just stayed there? Nothing but embarrassment; she would merely make herself ridiculous. When she came out, she washed her face and hands. Then she smeared soap on her finger, and rubbed her teeth with it. It tasted vile; sweet but very harsh.

She felt refreshed. When she had been back in the cubicle for a few minutes, Captain Pretorius came in. His hair was damp. He had shaved, and he was wearing a clean shirt.

'Good morning,' he said, and then, 'Yes, Ida, I can see that you think the morning is good. In the morning the sun rises, and your spirits rise. But in the evening, when the sun sets, then your spirits fall. And the evening will come, Ida.'

She had a sudden sense that she was not in control. It was Captain Pretorius who controlled things. But that was nonsense. She had held out so far; she could go on doing so. She felt that an unexpected crack had appeared in her, but that she had repaired it.

Pretorius was sitting down now. He said, 'Of course, I am just doing a job. Yes, this is just a job to me. I worked for the last government, and I will probably work for the next one. I am not a politician, Ida. I would not be such a fool as to give the money I earn to the Nationalists, as you gave money to the Communist Jews. You know, Ida, I am surprised that a refined English person like yourself should let herself be made use of by the Jews. By Sharon Lensky, and by Bill Elliston who has a Jewess wife. They were just making use of you, you know. They were not your real friends.' He paused. 'Ida, I am really your friend.'

Ida smiled. Pretorius was a fool, after all. Did he really expect her to swallow that?

233

'You smile, Ida, but it's true. Look at us now. We are talking like friends. You know, very often my detainees become good friends of mine after they are released. They drop in to see me. And I help them to become rehabilitated.'

'Rehabilitated?'

'Yes, I help them to get jobs and to make new friends – real friends. You, of course, would not need a new job. You could get your old one back just like that – if I said the word. Or I could even find you a better one. Yes, if you cooperate with me, Ida, I will cooperate with you. You don't want to spend years in prison, do you, Ida?'

At this moment, the girl chaperone came in, carrying a small tray, covered with an embroidered cloth. On it were a cup of coffee, a bowl of sugar, and a large chocolate-iced cake. On the plate under the cake was a paper doily.

'My mom made the cake especially for you, Captain,' the girl said. She looked at Pretorius archly as she cut him a slice. (Could Pretorius conceivably have a wife? Ida found this hard to imagine.)

'And a very fine cake it looks,' he said. 'But, *poppie*, won't you bring this lady a cup of coffee, too, and give her a slice of the cake?'

'Oh yes, Captain,' the girl said, and went to fetch coffee for Ida.

When Pretorius and Ida had eaten their cake and drunk their coffee, he offered her a cigarette. She took it. Then his red hand, with his lighter in it, shot out towards her, and she had to stop herself shrinking back. She held the cigarette tightly between her fingers so that it would not shake as he lit it.

'So Ida,' he said, 'you'll be making your Statement soon, and saving us both a waste of time. Then you'll give evidence in court, and all your troubles will be over. You'll begin a whole new life.' He stood up. 'Yes, you'll be making your Statement soon,' he repeated.

'I have nothing to say,' Ida said but, leaving the cubicle, he did not turn round.

A few minutes later, the two lieutenants, van Schalkwyk and du Plessis, came in, and sat down opposite her, side by side.

Van Schalkwyk smiled at her. He said gently, 'Now you are going to make your Statement, Ida. See, I have a pen and plenty of paper. You don't have to write it down yourself. I'll do all the work for you,' he said pleasantly.

'Yes, you'd bloody better get on with it,' du Plessis said. 'We're just about sick of wasting our time. We're just about losing our fucking patience.' A flush rose up his neck, not a reddish purple like that of Pretorius, but mauve tinged with grey.

234

She looked away from him, and Van Schalkwyk's glance caught hers. He shrugged apologetically.

'You're too soft with her, Piet man,' du Plessis said. 'Too bloody soft with her. Leave her alone with me, man, for a bit.'

Van Schalkwyk looked hesitant.

'Yes, you go along, Piet. I'll soon get her talking.' Ida managed to stop herself asking Van Schalkwyk not to go, and he left.

Du Plessis stood up, resting his hands on the table, leaning towards her. She noticed the muscles on his arms. He said, 'Start talking,' and Ida said, 'I have nothing to say.'

He took two steps over to the window. Now he was standing by the wooden truncheon. Ida felt her thighs trembling. She was afraid that the trembling would spread all over her, and that du Plessis would notice it. She tensed her body. Looking down, she saw that the muscles of her calves were knotted with cramp. She pushed at the table, to give herself more space, but it would not move, and she realized that it must be fixed to the floor. She thought: *Everything is calculated.*

'Admit that you are a member of the Communist Party,' du Plessis suddenly shouted.

'I have nothing to say.'

'In that case,' du Plessis said, 'I can see that we shall have to use other methods.' Ida clenched her hands in her lap. *It would happen now.* But he turned abruptly, and went out of the open door.

Ida tried to work out what she was afraid of. She imagined du Plessis bringing the truncheon down on her shoulders or her head. The picture seemed unreal. *That wasn't it.* Yet she was trembling. She stood up, went over to the window, and stared out at the bricks. Then she looked down, and held out a finger to touch the handle of the truncheon. Just before her finger reached it, she heard a sound behind her, and jumped round. Van Schalkwyk had come in. Had he seen that she was about to touch du Plessis' truncheon? Blushing, she turned back to the window to hide this.

'Come on, Ida,' van Schalkwyk said. 'Sit down.' She returned to her chair, and he sat down again, opposite. He stared at her, and then slowly shook his head. 'Ida,' he said, 'I fear for you.'

'Fear for me?'

'Yes, I am afraid of what *they* will do to you.'

Ida was suddenly aware of high, distorted choral singing. Could it be coming from a radio? But it was such strange singing: like, she thought, singing in a dream. That was when she realized that it was a hallucination. She recognized this fact, and yet the singing continued. Sitting listening to it, she thought: *So reason is powerless.*

Van Schalkwyk said, 'Please, Ida. Please cooperate. I am so afraid of what they will do. I am afraid I won't be able to hold them back much longer.'

The singing had stopped. The tone in which van Schalkwyk spoke – anxious, *concerned* – suddenly touched her. She felt tears at the back of her eyes.

'I want to help you, Ida.' Van Schalkwyk gazed at her sincerely. Suddenly she knew that this spaniel sincerity was unnatural, but – extraordinarily – she did not want to know it.

He rolled a ballpoint pen across the table to her. She picked it up and stretched out her hand to put it back in front of him.

'Come on,' he said again. 'Take it. I've got plenty of paper for you. It's easy when you make a start.' He rolled the pen towards her again. 'Just take it,' he said. Again she put it back in front of him.

'You've stood out a hell of a long time,' he said. 'Much longer than most people – really you have. Now come on – give it a go!'

He put the pen in front of her. This time she didn't pick it up. The business with the pen was beginning to embarrass her. She remembered once having gone to bed with a boring man because it seemed too silly to go on refusing.

'Now Ida,' van Schalkwyk said, 'come on. Be a sensible girl.'

With no idea that she was going to say it, she said, 'If I wrote, would you keep *him* out of here?'

'Du Plessis?' he asked quickly. 'Yes, of course. He'd never bother you again.'

'It's no use,' she said. 'I can't do it. I have nothing to say.'

'Oh now, come on. For your own sake. Surely you're tired by now? And you've stood out well. You've done as much as you can.'

'I see it all quite clearly,' she said in a cool voice. 'I've read about this sort of thing. This is the way they always brainwash people – they use *two*. Du Plessis is the brute, and you are the kind one: the one who softens me up, and makes me break down. You see – I understand the whole thing perfectly.'

A lightning-flash of anger crossed his face. Then it regained its normal look. A hangdog look, she thought. This was what the word 'hangdog' meant. Van Schalkwyk was like a sloppy, cringing dog.

He said, 'If you really believe that – what you just said – then there's nothing I can do to help you. You'll be on your own.'

She started to cry. She stood up, and went over to the window. The tears burst out of her eyes, and she could not see the bricks. Her whole head was filled with tears, and they were pouring out. She had no handkerchief, and she brushed violently at her eyes and nose with her hand. Sobbing, she said, 'I must go to the lavatory.' Van Schalkwyk sighed, but then he gestured towards the door.

Pretorius, du Plessis and four other men were sitting with the grey-haired woman. Ida was crying and crying. The grey-haired woman took her through the room where men were filing, and through the room full of typists. She went on crying, but no one looked at her. When they reached the open front door, she suddenly thought of 'making a dash for it'. But then she remembered Stella. In any case, it was too late. What did she mean by that? She had no idea.

She sat on the lavatory seat, crying and blowing her nose on paper, till her tears dried up. She wiped her eyes. She came out, and washed her face and hands.

On the way back, she remembered Ncgobo singing on his way to the gallows. Pretorius had asked him if he would sing then, and if he would make the *Amandla Ngawethu* salute. He had promised to. *Ncgobo kept his promise.* Walking along the passage, Ida thought: *But he was a hero.* How did people become heroes? Ida decided that it was probably a whole lifetime's work. Ida felt the softness of her own life behind her. It was as if an old feather bed were tied to her back.

A toasted ham sandwich and a cup of coffee were waiting for her in the cubicle. When she had finished them, van Schalkwyk came in. He said, 'Well, Ida, are you ready to make your Statement?'

She decided that she would write something down: nothing important. Then they would take her back to jail before she became too tired to know what she was doing, before she lost control.

She said, 'I will write if you leave me on my own.'

Van Schalkwyk put lined paper and the ballpoint pen in front of her. He went out, saying, 'That's my girl!'

Immediately, she began to write. It flowed.

'I have never been a member of the Communist Party, and I have no evidence that any of my friends are communists, though some of them have left-wing views. I am interested in politics and have often discussed them, but I have never been politically active.'

She started a new paragraph. 'I have always been opposed to apartheid.' Writing quickly, she filled a sheet and a half of paper with the reasons for this. Then she took the paper through into the SB room, and handed it to Pretorius. He said nothing. She returned to the cubicle, where the grey-haired woman brought her another cup of coffee.

She heard the singing again. It went on – high and blurred – until, after what she supposed was about ten minutes, Pretorius came in. He had the Statement in his hand. He stood looking at her. Then he threw it on the table. 'That's not a statement,' he said. 'That's just a load of shit.' The reddish purple welled up in his face. He yelled, 'How long do you think you can play around with us?'

'I've written everything I know,' she said.

'Everything you know! Everything you know! *We* know what you know. We know the very day you joined the Communist Party.'

'What nonsense,' she said. 'I've never been a member of the Communist Party.'

'We have it in writing.'

She shrugged and raised her eyebrows.

'In writing,' Pretorius repeated. 'Yes. Signed by Bill Elliston. He recruited you, didn't he? I have it in his Statement.'

'Bill would never make a Statement to you,' she said.

'Oh, is that so?' Pretorius laughed. 'Do you think old Bill is Superman? What do you think we were doing all the time when you were sitting in the prison? Playing patball? No, we were getting Bill's cooperation. Why do you think we brought him up here from Cape Town? For his health?' Pretorius laughed again. 'Then, after he'd made his Statement, we flew him down to Cape Town again, so that he could show us over Number One, San Marino Court. He's in Cape Town now. We've even let him see his wife. Yes, you can be sure that he fully cooperated with us.'

'I don't believe you.'

'How do you think we know you joined the Party. How do you think we know about San Marino Court? You never talked about those things in your flat.'

'I have nothing to say.'

'Nothing to say, nothing to say.' He mimicked her in a falsetto. Then he resumed his own voice. 'You've plenty to say.' He picked up the two sheets of paper from the table, and tore them in half, and dropped them on the floor. 'But none of it's here. A load of shit,' he said, as he left.

Had they followed Bill to San Marino Court one night? Could they have put some kind of tracking device in his car?

Van Schalkwyk came in, and sat down, shaking his head. 'Oh, Ida,' he said, and then, 'I suppose it is a shock to you about Bill?'

'What about Bill?'

'That he made his Statement. Everyone makes a Statement, Ida. There is no one who doesn't. So why are you tiring yourself out for no reason? Come on, now! You know that stuff you wrote wasn't the truth. I think it's better if you answer some questions, and we take down what you say. That way we can get all the details. Then you can read it all, and see if there's anything you object to. If there is, then of course you don't have to sign it.'

But now Ida knew exactly what she was going to do. She said, 'All right, then – show me Bill's Statement.' She said it triumphantly. She could feel her heart beating fast. 'If you show me Bill's Statement,' she said, 'then I'll make one.'

'I don't know about that.' Van Schalkwyk looked doubtful. She thought: *So I was right*; and as she thought it, she realized that she had gambled; that she had shifted the responsibility for her actions onto Bill.

Van Schalkwyk went out, saying, 'I will have to see.' She thought: *I wonder what they will try to cook up now.*

After a few minutes, Pretorius came in, followed by van Schalkwyk and du Plessis. Ida pretended not to notice du Plessis, just as she had pretended not to notice the truncheon the night before. Pretorius was carrying a file. She wondered if it contained more transcripts of tapes. He came round the table to stand beside her. She leant away from him, as he bent over, opening the file, which he placed on the table in front of her. On the top page of a document fastened with green tape was typed: *Statement of William Elliston.*

'Well,' Pretorius said, 'we have decided that there is no reason why you should not see this. The part concerning you, that is – the rest is no business of yours.' He flipped over the pages, licking a fat pink forefinger. Ida glimpsed Stella's name. Then he flattened a page with his broad palm. 'Here you are,' he said. She saw her own name. She followed the typed words as Pretorius read them aloud.

'It was at the end of that month that I recruited her into the Party. She took the name of Diana. There was no group for her to join, so she met only with me.' It was the omission of Rachel's name that made Ida start to believe what she saw and heard.

'She did various errands for me. She paid the rent of the flat at Number One, San Marino Court, hired under the name of W. P. Johnson, at the offices of Messrs Bingham and Bailey in Kerk Street. She opened a bank account for me under the same name at Barclays Bank DCO in Adderley Street. She took part in the preparation of Communist Party leaflets at Number One, San Marino Court.'

Pretorius closed the file. 'That is all you need to see,' he said. But then he turned to the end and showed her Bill's signature. Under it another signature was scrawled above the typed words: *Witnessed: J. Neethling, Commissioner for Oaths.*

'What did you do to him?' Ida said.

'Do to him? We did nothing. He was prepared to cooperate with us.'

239

She felt sure they had tortured him. Then she thought that, if Bill had made a Statement, no one could blame her for making one. She could blame herself, of course, but that, at the moment, seemed irrelevant.

It was dark again. Pretorius sat in front of her, between van Schalkwyk and du Plessis, writing. She went to the lavatory, accompanied now by the big dark-haired woman She ate another toasted ham sandwich and drank coffee. They brought her cigarettes which she smoked one after another as she answered their questions. As Pretorius wrote, she could hear the frogs croaking again, and the distant clock.

She tried to leave things out. She did not mention Rachel. She did not tell them that she had carried messages between Bill and Sharon; apparently Bill had not told them that. Any such tiny omission made her feel as if a little shock of life had been delivered to her passive body.

It was four in the morning when they stopped. The dark woman brought a camp bed and a blanket into the big room outside the cubicle. Ida lay down, and the woman switched off the light. Ida was sure that she was too tired to sleep.

Some large animal leapt at the woman on the lawn. She was down! Her husband, the vicar, writing his sermon, saw from the library window what had happened. Clumsily he hoisted himself over the sill, and stumbled towards her in his dark clothes. Blood was pouring from her wounds onto the grass. The beast was gone, and a band of horsemen was disappearing down the drive. Was the beast theirs? Was it hunting with them, or were they hunting it?

'There is something wrong with this place,' said the vicar. He was sitting in a deckchair, sucking at his pipe. He and Ida were drinking tea out of thin china. He said, 'I really don't know what we can do about it.'

'Couldn't you,' Ida said, 'being a clergyman, exorcize it?'

He looked puzzled. He cupped his hand behind his ear. 'I beg your pardon? I don't think I quite understand.' And now the thud of hooves was making the ground tremble.

'Couldn't you . . .' The horses thundered round the bend in the drive. They crashed through the rhododendrons. Ida couldn't get the words out. The beast was ahead of the riders. *Was it hunting with them, or were they hunting it?* Now the great creature was bounding towards her. She could not speak. She must. The beast was on her –

She was awake, pushing herself up, the words on her lips, so that she said them aloud – 'Exorcize it' – in the large empty room into which early light was seeping.

The girl came in. Today she wore a spotted dress, not a flowered one. She took a cup of coffee into the cubicle. Ida got up, and followed her. Ida sat down at the table and took a gulp of coffee. Du Plessis entered the cubicle, carrying a towel, razor and soap. He was wearing grey trousers and a white singlet. He went to the washbasin by the window, turned on the taps, and began to shave. She saw his muscled arms and the tufts of black hair in his armpits. She smelt his sweat, and shivered with loathing. While he shaved, he and the girl chatted in Afrikaans. When he had finished shaving, they left together, but Ida called the girl back, to say that she wanted to go to the lavatory.

As they went through the empty offices, Ida realized that she was beginning to stink. Her feet and legs were black with dust, under which were mauve blotches. She looked at herself in the washroom mirror. Under her eyes were dark wrinkled patches, and her lids were swollen. She saw that she had two new lines; one down the centre of each cheek. As she stared at her face, a tic started at the corner of her mouth. This face seemed to provide an excuse for what she had done. Pitying herself, she gave a deep sigh.

'Tired, hey?' the girl said brightly.

'Yes,' Ida said. 'I am, rather.'

Nothing changed in the smooth tanned face under the stiffly set hair. The girl said, 'As a matter of fact, I'm a bit tired myself. My boyfriend and I went to bioscope. I didn't get to bed till after twelve, and then I had to be up early.'

They were walking back along the passage. Ida remembered a record of Freedom songs she had heard at the Ellistons'. The African women had made an extraordinary trilling sound, like mad birds. The doorkeeper's glass-fronted box was empty, and the front door was closed. Ida imagined a great crowd outside, singing and trilling. She imagined the door bursting open, the crowd surging in. She imagined how the girl's face would gape with fear, and how her blank eyes would widen. Then a scream would come from the pink open mouth. The flowery smell of her cologne would be overpowered by the smell of the sweat of her terror as she was struck down and trampled on. *And the women would trill like mad birds as she died.* Ida's heart was thudding with joy.

Back in the cubicle, she was again brought fried eggs and chips, decorated with beetroot and lettuce. She ate it all, telling herself she must keep up her strength, but then asked herself what strength, and why.

Pretorius came in, holding a file. He said, 'Of course, what you have told us isn't enough. You have only confirmed the things we knew

241

already. Now you're going to start telling us the things we do not know.'

He went out. So they weren't going to take her back to the jail now. Du Plessis came in, and stood with his fingertips on the table. 'Talk,' he said.

'But I've told you everything.'

'Talk, I tell you.' He went over to the window, picked up the truncheon, and swung it in his hand. *Now it would happen.* But *what* would happen? Her mottled calves were knotted. Her hands were clenched in her lap, but she managed to unclench them as du Plessis came and stood beside her with the truncheon held in front of him in his hand. She could tell him about Rachel, about the messages she had carried between Bill and Sharon, about an address she remembered on a foreign letter. She remembered the name of a student who had distributed the newsletter at the university. She could smell du Plessis' hateful sweat again. With his free hand, he aimed a punch at the wall, arresting the swing just before he touched it. He moved from foot to foot like a dancing bear. She begged herself to wait for it to happen, to take the chance to see if she could bear it; just the chance.

Du Plessis stopped moving. He went over to the window, and put the truncheon down where it had been before. Then he left the cubicle, starting to whistle a tune.

Now she would never know. Or would the test be repeated? One of the younger SB men came in and gestured her to follow him into the room where people were sitting. A middle-aged man in a blue suit was waiting there. Pretorius read her Statement aloud, then said, 'Sign here.'

Should she demand to read it through herself? Should she refuse to sign? The Statement, she knew, was inadmissible as evidence in court. She signed her name and the man in the blue suit witnessed it. The young man who had fetched her took her back to the cubicle, and she expected du Plessis to return. But a few minutes later, Pretorius came in, saying, 'Well, we're taking you back to the prison now. You need a bath.' He looked at her with distaste. He said, 'We'll come for you again in a day or two.'

The street was dazzlingly bright. People walked in it just as they had done two days before, but everything had changed for Ida. She and the girl, who was wearing her white net gloves again, got into the back of the car.

Back at the prison, the chief wardress signed a receipt for her. The SB men went away. Ida said to the chief wardress, 'Captain Pretorius said I could have a bath,' and was ashamed of having cited this authority.

'Yes, you can have your bath and your exercise now.' Ida was sent upstairs with a young wardress, to fetch her things.

She lay in the bath, washing her hair, washing her body. The water became black, with a pale scum on its surface. When she got out of the bath she noticed that the purple marks were still on her calves. She washed the clothes she had been wearing, and again the water was black. Outside, she hung her washing on the line. There was a tree in the middle of the yard, and she sat down on the patch of grass under it. Previously she had always made herself spend her exercise-hour walking and usually reciting poems. Now, sitting under the tree, she said aloud, *This City now doth like a garment wear the beauty of the morning.* She began to cry, but quietly. The sun was hot on the grass. The clothes she had washed swayed in a warm breeze. The leaves rustled above her, and into her head came the thought that she would never be fond of herself again. But once more she spoke aloud: 'I shall never give evidence.' That was what she must hold onto, now. She wondered when the SB would come to fetch her for further interrogation.

But they never did. Three days later, they took her back to Cape Town and left her at the police-station.

*

She heard keys, and looked up, expecting to see Mrs Potgieter, but it was Miss Maree, wearing a brown dress, who opened the door, and Ida realized that Mrs Potgieter must have gone off duty.

Miss Maree was standing back, holding the door open. Lieutenant Steyn of the Cape Town SB came into the yard. Trying to move easily, Ida stood up. She did not like the idea of sitting on the ground with Lieutenant Steyn looming over her.

He came towards her, glancing sharply round the yard. One of his eyes was bigger than the other, and his body too was somehow off balance. His glance lighted on her empty plate and mug. She hoped that this evidence of her good appetite would irritate him. She knew that he was very annoyed that Major de Wet had given permission for her to spend all day in the yard, when there were no other prisoners, instead of just one hour for exercise. Now he looked angrily at her comfortably arranged blankets, her Bible, her cigarettes and matches.

He had a sheet of yellow paper in his hand. Still without speaking, he held it out to her, and she took it from him. It was printed, but various words were typed in on dotted lines. She looked at it without being

243

able to read it. She remembered that the same thing had happened when she had been handed the warrant for her detention.

She glanced up. Lieutenant Steyn was watching her with his uneven eyes. Beyond him, in the doorway, two uniformed policemen appeared, making their afternoon round, but at the sight of Lieutenant Steyn they retreated. She looked down at the paper again, and forced herself to make sense of it. She saw that it was a subpoena. The trial of William Elliston, under the Suppression of Communism Act, would begin in Pretoria, in the Supreme Court, on the 10th of May. That was the day after tomorrow. Ida was to be called as a witness.

Looking up, she said, 'I don't know why you're bringing me this. I told Major de Wet that I refuse to give evidence.'

Major de Wet had laughed and shrugged. 'Well, Ida,' he had said, 'that's entirely up to you. Of course I can understand you not wanting to split on your friends. But you realize that you'll get a year for refusing to give evidence – that's automatic – and then you'll be charged under the Suppression of Communism Act. That will probably be another five years.'

She did not believe it would be five. Stella had got three. She would count on three. So that would be four years altogether. But the words, 'I can understand you not wanting to split on your friends' had made an extraordinary impression on her. She would never have imagined that one of the SB might say them. After referring to the five years, he had smiled good-humouredly. *He had broken a man's ribs with an iron bar.* Yet she felt almost a liking for him. That was when she had asked him if she could spend all day in the yard, when there were no other prisoners. He had frowned, then laughed and said he didn't see why not, looking up at the high walls and the overhead wire. Lieutenant Steyn was different from Major de Wet.

Ida said, 'I haven't changed my mind. I won't be giving evidence,' and Lieutenant Steyn looked savagely round the yard and then up at the sky. She knew he longed to order that she should be locked in her cell. Two months earlier, he had come in one morning when she was sitting in the yard. 'What is she doing here?' he had yelled at Mrs Steyn, who was on duty. 'She should be locked up. She is only allowed an hour's exercise in the yard.' Mrs Steyn was silent. It was Ida who had told him that she had Major de Wet's permission, but he had not believed her. 'If you've been lying to me, you'll be in big trouble,' he said. 'Lock her up while I check,' he had shouted at Mrs Steyn. ('Same name, but he's no relative of mine,' Mrs Steyn had said drily, disparagingly, after he had gone.) Ida had been locked in her cell for two hours before he sent a messenger down to say that yes, she was allowed in the yard. She was sure that, by making him look foolish, this episode had intensified his dislike for her. Well, the dislike was mutual.

Now their glances met, and she saw him recognize that she had read his wish to lock her up and that she knew he was unable to countermand Major de Wet's instructions. She smiled. His face became red. He said loudly, 'Well, if you don't give evidence, then you must take the consequences. Anyhow, pack up your stuff. You will be flying to Pretoria tomorrow.' Then he left, moving rapidly, but stooping, his right leg dragging slightly. Miss Maree followed, pulling the door shut, and turning the key.

Standing in the yard, Ida became aware of something fluttering against the front of her dress. She looked down and saw that it was the sheet of yellow paper. She hoped her hand had not been shaking like that when Lieutenant Steyn was there. Holding the paper in both hands, she sat down and read the English version carefully. (The subpoena was printed in both English and Afrikaans.) She did not learn more than her previous glance had told her.

She thought about the flight to Pretoria next day. Would she be called as a witness the day after? No, surely not on the first day of the trial. Would they tell her when she would be called? It might not be for weeks. Would they keep her in the Female Prison, until the day — whenever it came — when she went into the witness-box, and said 'I cannot give evidence'?

She scrambled to her feet, dropping the paper, and ran for the washroom. As she pushed open the half saloon-door to the lavatory, she thought, *The Fastest Gun Alive*. She vomited undigested mince and rice into the lavatory pan. Then she leant against the wall, wiping her sweaty forehead with the back of her hand. She pulled the plug, and nothing happened. She pulled it again, and it flushed. In the washroom she splashed cold water on her face. Then she ran some into her cupped hand, and rinsed her mouth. As she went back into the yard, Miss Maree came in through the outside door. She had now put on a white overall that made her look like a nurse. The other matrons wore their ordinary clothes on duty. Ida believed that Miss Maree thought herself too good for the matron's job, and wore the white overall to distance herself from it.

She had brought Ida a cup of tea and a piece of sponge cake. Picking up Ida's lunch plate and mug, she said, 'I'm sure I don't know why Mrs Potgieter can't clean up before she goes running off duty. As you will have noticed, when I am on the morning shift, I always make quite certain to remove your cup and plate before I leave. Really, I don't

245

know what the Lieutenant must have thought, seeing the dirty things lying here. He probably got the impression that I do not do my work properly.'

Ida said, 'Oh, I'm sure he didn't.' Then she said, 'Well, they're taking me to Pretoria tomorrow. The trial starts next day. I'm going to refuse to give evidence.' She wanted to hear herself say the words, even though only to Miss Maree.

Miss Maree was shaking her head. She said, 'Now, why don't you do what they want? They are all such big men.' She gave a small shudder. Ida sensed that Miss Maree was repelled by men. She talked about *manmense* and *vrouemense* (men-people and women-people). Ida had at first addressed her as 'Mrs' Maree, but had been indignantly corrected.

Ida knew there was no point in talking politics to her. She said, 'Bill Elliston is a friend of mine.'

Miss Maree shrugged. 'In this world, it is everyone for themselves when it comes to the push, you know. And after all, it's not even as if he's a relative. He's a Jew, isn't he?'

Ida said nothing. Bill was not Jewish. But when Ida had first arrived at the police-station, Miss Maree had been very cold to her, until one day she had asked her if she were 'a Jewess'. Although Ida had no Jewish blood, she had felt guilty when she said 'No'. Ever since then, Miss Maree's manner had been friendly. Now Ida could not face announcing that Bill, too, was not a Jew. To have done so would have made her feel anti-Semitic.

Miss Maree went on, 'The Jews all stick together. They don't worry about anyone else. Of course, blood is thicker than water.' Then she said, 'Well, I'd better not stay talking here. The Lieutenant might come back.'

'I don't think he will,' Ida said.

'No, but one never knows, does one?'

Ida smiled. 'No,' she said.

The door closed; the key turned. Ida wondered if she would be sick again if she ate the cake and drank the tea. She didn't think so, but she ate and drank slowly. When she had finished, she went to her cell. She thought that she would wear a green suit, the smartest outfit she possessed, for the trial. She pulled her red suitcase out from under the bed and opened it. The green suit, folded on top, was rather crushed, but there was no point in hanging it up, as she would have to pack it again for the next day.

She was shutting the suitcase when she became aware of a penny whistle, outside among the traffic, playing an African *kwela* tune. The music came nearer and nearer till it was just outside, at the end of the short passage to the street.

Suddenly Ida imagined the whole world waiting at the end of that passage. The sun shone in an open, unbarbed sky. There were birds and gardens. (*There was 'Pompeian red'*.) Major de Wet, with his good-humoured smile offered her a key to the door at the end of the passage. But if she took the key, her hand would be stained with rust, with blood. If she opened the door, the sky would cloud over, the flowers would fade, the birds would stop singing. ('Pompeian red' would turn to grey. In any case: *We shall never surrender.*) And Ida would be ash blown through the wasteland – not a world at all – that she would find beyond the door at the end of the passage, where now the music was very faint, and soon was submerged in the traffic.

She heard the keys, and went to the door of her cell. Miss Maree stood back. It was another prisoner, Ida supposed. So she would have to be locked up. It was another prisoner, but not a white one. It was a very old Coloured woman. Her hair was yellow-white; her skin was yellow. She wore a ragged black dress, and on her feet were brown, down-at-heel men's shoes. Miss Maree chivvied her along to the cupboard between the two cells. The shoes were much too big for her, and she shuffled slowly.

Miss Maree pulled open the cupboard door, and pointed inside. '*Twee komberse,*' she said sharply. Slowly the old woman reached inside, and dragged two blankets from the middle shelf. She clutched them awkwardly to her chest as Miss Maree closed the cupboard.

Ida picked up her teacup and saucer, and handed them to Miss Maree. 'Thanks,' she said, and 'Thanks,' Miss Maree said, as she took them. The old woman watched, equally remote from them both.

'*Kom, kom, kom,*' Miss Maree yelped impatiently. Infinitely slowly, the old woman moved towards the door. Miss Maree strode ahead of her, and stood by the door, tapping her foot. '*Kom, kom, kom,*' she repeated shrilly. At last the old woman reached the door. Miss Maree stood back for her to go out, making an angry urging movement with the cup and saucer in her hand. She turned, and made an exasperated grimace at Ida before pulling the door shut, with a jerk.

Ida was still sorting through her clothes and rearranging the contents of her suitcase when her supper arrived. She ate a long piece of *boerewors*, a pile of boiled butter beans and a slice of bread, and drank the mug of black coffee. She took her things into the cell, in which the light had now been turned on, by Miss Maree, with the key that operated a device just inside the yard door. Then she went into the yard again. Little stars were pricking through the greyness above the wire. She decided to get ready for bed. The sergeant on night-duty that week was a tiresome, fussy man who liked Ida to be already locked up when he made his first round.

She went into her cell again. She undressed, and put on her nightdress and dressing-gown. She took her spongebag and towel to the washroom. It was dark. Looking up she saw that the broken bulb had not been replaced.

She went to the lavatory – *There's trouble at the Double S Corral* – and then washed, and brushed her teeth. The police-station was very quiet. Monday nights were seldom busy. She wondered if prostitutes took the evening off to wash their hair and mend their clothes.

After she had put her spongebag and towel in the cell, she lit a cigarette and paid a final visit to the yard. She did not know when she would next have as much freedom as this yard gave her. She stood in the middle, looking up at the stars. The sky was black now. The key turned, and Miss Maree and Mrs Steyn came in. 'Hullo, chummie,' Mrs Steyn said, and Ida said, 'Hullo, Mrs Steyn.'

Miss Maree looked at her watch with a frown. Ida said, 'Do you want to lock me in now?'

'Perhaps it would be just as well. Before I go off duty, and before that Sergeant Niehaus makes his rounds. You don't want the light off yet, do you?'

'No, not just yet.'

'Just call when you do,' said Mrs Steyn.

'Goodbye, Miss Maree,' Ida said. 'I'm sure I'll be gone when you come on duty tomorrow.'

Miss Maree hesitated, and then held out her hand. Ida shook it. 'Goodbye to you,' Miss Maree said. Ida went into the cell, and Miss Maree closed the locked the door.

Ida was alone in the glare of the naked bulb, which she hated. But if she asked for it to be turned off too early, the night seemed very long. This was the time when she usually read their book, the Bible; the book she was allowed. But she didn't feel she would be able to concentrate on it tonight. Looking at the names on the door, she felt she should carve hers there too. It was her last chance. But what could she use? When she wanted to cut her nails, she had to ask to borrow the matron's scissors, and the matron stood and watched till she had finished. She supposed she could use the nail of her forefinger to scratch her name, and she started, in a space opposite the name 'Dinky'. It was very slow work. Perhaps she might scratch only her initials. At that moment she heard keys and voices. Quickly she sat down on the bed, picked up the Bible, and opened it. The spyhole cover was lifted, and she imagined Sergeant Niehaus peering in, but she did not look up. The cover fell back into place. In a moment she heard the outside door slam.

She went back to the door, and started scratching at the paint again. The grating sensation was unpleasant, and her fingernail was beginning to wear down. She finished her first initial, and decided that would have to do. She said aloud, to convince herself, 'Oh I am feeling so *tired*,' and after a moment actually found herself yawning. She decided that she would call Mrs Steyn to put out the light.

'Mrs Steyn,' she called, and after a moment Mrs Steyn called out, 'Right you are.' A minute later Ida heard the outside door open, and then Mrs Steyn's steps in the yard. Mrs Steyn unlocked Ida's door, and stood in the doorway. 'Did you want your light out?' she asked.

'Yes please,' Ida said, and quickly got into bed. She liked to be in bed before Mrs Steyn finally locked the door and then put out the light.

The bed creaked. 'Not much of a mattress, that one,' Mrs Steyn said.

Ida laughed. 'I've got used to it,' she said. 'Before I came to jail, I'd never slept on a mattress without springs.'

'No? Oh I did for many years. When we were on the farm, my late husband and myself, we had the old kind of bed made of feathers. But my husband suffered terribly with his chest. Sometimes at night it was as if he was fighting for each mouthful of breath. Then the doctor said it might help if we got a spring mattress, instead of the feathers. Well, my husband couldn't bear to spend his money on a mattress. In the end, it was me that bought it – from the egg money, you know. It was the first in the district – yes, it was really quite a wonder. People would call, and the women would want to feel the bed.'

Mrs Steyn yawned. 'Well, chummie,' she said, 'let's hope tonight is quieter than last night. Honest, if a daughter of mine was to lead the life of those girls, I think I would die of the shame. But mine is a good girl – she married when she was only seventeen. She and her little boy are coming to visit with me next month – she only has the one child. That is a great sorrow to her. Well, she and I will share the big bed, and there is a fold-up bed in the lounge for my grandson, so we shall be quite comfortable. And I am fixing up a swing in the back yard.'

'A swing?'

'Yes – oh it was my dream when I was a child, to have a swing. But I never got one – my father was not interested in fixing up things like that for us children. I suppose I would never have thought about one, if we had not been to the city, to see relatives. And after Sunday dinner, us children and our little cousins went out to the park. I remember well that it was a Sunday because at home we would never have been allowed to play in the park like that on the Sabbath. Though of course there was no park where we were, only the veld and the railway siding. For my father worked on the railways, you know, and we lived in a railway house. But people are less strict about Sunday in the city. And oh, I shall never forget that swing in the park. My cousin pushed me, and I went up, up, till I could see the tops of the trees and the roofs of the houses. 'Again, again,' I kept calling, for I felt that I could never have enough of it. But of course my cousin soon got tired of pushing me, and the others had to have their turn on the swing too, and being the eldest girl, I had to see to them all, you know. But afterwards I was always thinking about that swing. Well, my husband and me, we only had the one child – I tell my daughter perhaps it's something in the blood – and when she was a little girl, I was quite set in my mind that she should have a swing. And I made my husband get the kaffir boy to fix one up behind the house, though my husband grumbled about taking him away from his proper work. But then, do you know, my daughter did not seem to care for it. She was scared I think. She would always rather be playing with her dolly. I suppose many girls are that way.' Mrs Steyn sighed. Then she said, 'How about you, chummie? Did you like to swing?'

Ida hesitated. 'I didn't like to go too high.'

'Ah. More like my daughter you were. But I am sure the little boy will enjoy it. Yes – to see the tops of the trees and the roofs of the houses.' She was silent. Then she shook her head briskly. 'Well,' she said, 'you've got everything you want?'

'Yes, thank you.'

'I shall be seeing you in the morning with Ouma Potgieter. But now I'll say that I wish you all the best, the very best of luck.'

'Thank you. Good night, Mrs Steyn.'

'Good night then, *bokkie*.' The door closed. Ida thought how much she preferred '*bokkie*' (little buck) to 'chummie'. She heard Mrs Steyn fiddling with her bunch of keys until she found the one that turned out the light.

To see the tops of the trees and the roofs of the houses. Ida, lying in the dark, remembered a garden where someone had pushed her in a swing. At first she had not minded. Suddenly she had begun to scream with terror: 'Will I fall? Will I fall?'

But her childhood was over, and now it was time to *compose herself to rest*. Each evening she used this expression. It gave her a feeling that her life was under her control. She whispered, as she whispered each night, 'I am a Communist, so I am not alone.' But she was alone in the picture she summoned up in order to *compose herself to rest*.

There were buildings. There was a dirty old city, but then a great wave submerged it.

The floods became calm and still. She drifted over them on a raft. Far below she saw the towers of the drowned city, and she heard the chime of a drowned church bell. The raft scraped on a shore.

She wandered over a great stretch of sand. She picked up pieces of driftwood and broken shells. She handled them, then dropped them back on the sand. She looked towards the far rim of the sea.

There it was, in the distance, the great ship, with the materials for the new city, with the builders who would teach her a new language. She ran to the edge of the sea, waving and calling . . .

But next day, on the plane, when the engine trouble started, she did not think of the ship or of the builders of the new city. She remembered, 'Will I fall? Will I fall?' The memory was a sign, an omen that she would fall: not from a swing, but from the sky. One of the three SB men, who had been in the pilot's cabin, came out to talk to the others in a low voice. Oil was leaking onto the wing. They were all frowning. The only one of them she knew was Lieutenant van Schalkwyk.

Elias, the African prisoner, sat calmly. Van Schalkwyk had brought him to the government airport shortly before the plane took off. He had been weighed after Ida and the unknown woman chaperone who had come in the car which fetched Ida from the police station. 'You are lighter than both the white madams, Elias,' van Schalkwyk had said to him. Elias, who was small and slight, did not smile. Ida had never seen him before, but she felt sure he was political, because the SB were transporting him by plane. She wondered if it were in connection with Bill's trial.

The silence, the stillness, the blackness of Elias made him an island, but when the engine trouble started, Ida decided that he was the only person on the plane whom she wanted to die with. She planned how as the plane hurtled down, she would rush across and put her arms around him. As the plane went down, she and Elias would shout *Amandla Ngawethu!*

But then she changed her mind about dying. She and Elias would not be killed. They would crawl free of the wreckage, and just as they were clear of it, the engine would explode.

When the debris was discovered, people would think that she and Elias had died with the rest, but they would have escaped. *Where?* Ida looked down through the window. She clung to the arms of her seat, for the plane was bucking like a colt. Far below was bare brown country.

Ida imagined herself and Elias – two tiny figures, one white, one black – in that desolate landscape. They would have to separate, of course. A black man, a white woman, wandering alone together, would be arrested on sight. She sent them off in opposite directions. They grew smaller. Once they turned and waved. Then all she could see was the great brown distance between them. A terrible noise was coming from the engine of the plane, and now it gave a final enormous shudder.

Celia 1981

Last night she had again forgotten to close the fastenings of the side door, so that now she had only to raise the latch. In the hot quiet street she pulled the door shut behind her. She could not lock it from outside, but she did not need to. Although recently a camera had been stolen from the seat of an open car in the tourist district, that would not have happened in this part of town.

As she crossed the road, a breath of air – like a soft little scarf – brushed her arm. At that moment the street lights went out.

It was day, but only just. Trees and telegraph poles were dark; walls were bleached, like the road and pavement. There was a tinge of rust in the neutral sky behind the café.

This summer she followed oblique routes to the sea. Now a cock crowed loudly in a courtyard. Next month the cicadas would rasp all night; at present, in July, they did not start until mid-morning. At lunchtime yesterday, Celia's cat, Chloe, had trotted along the veranda, making the sound of a muffled alarm-clock because there was a live cicada in her mouth.

As the sky paled, everything else took on colour: walls yellowed; tiles reddened; leaves greened. Celia turned a corner. There was a tremor in the air. As she advanced, it became a throb, then a thrilling shiver. Opposite the littered steps and battened shutters of the former Post Office – prospective site of a car park – grew a singing tree.

She knew three such trees in the town; all palms, they were agitated each dawn and dusk by the twittering and darting of birds she could not identify. Becoming familiar with plants, she was still ignorant of birds; a week ago she had ordered a book about them.

A garbage stink came from plastic bags – toppled on the pavement, and raided by cats – but on the corner of a narrow street, a patisserie, though closed, smelt irrepressibly of vanilla.

She went along this street, which led to one of the town's two remaining stone churches. Three others, lately demolished, had been replaced by brightly stuccoed concrete: tumorous domes and bandy arches; pygmy pillars and monster towers.

In this soft-coloured church square, edged with jacarandas, an ancient man occupied a small wooden cabin, painted blue; outside, he burnt rubbish in a rusty tin. He talked loudly to himself; sometimes, but not today, he broke off to shout '*Kalimera*' to Celia.

There was a smell of bread in the street beyond the square. Behind a window, a bearded man in khaki shorts worked at a roaring oven. Outside his shop stood two *koulouria* wagons: small glass chapels, framed in white wood and mounted on wheels. Soon, elderly men would trundle them along the streets, pausing to sell small warm loaves to passers-by.

After the smell of bread came the smell of jasmine. A green torrent, fleckered with white foam, poured over a wall, but, remembering Beauty's father, stealing a rose from the hedge and suddenly confronted by the Beast, she always felt furtive when she picked a sprig. Alternately sniffing the flowers and twirling the sprig between finger and thumb, she turned down beside the Public Gardens to the sea. Ahead she could see the red sun just above the horizon. By the time she reached the highway it was a circle in the sky. Now the highway was the same width all along the front. Last autumn they had pulled down the last house on the edge of the sea.

This year, Celia always swam opposite the Gardens. Leaving her bag, sandals and dress on the pebbles, she waded out; the water was a little cooler than her skin. She swam past two fishing-boats – *Zoe* and *Athena* – and past a pink bobbing line of buoys. She swam out a long way. There was a ship in the distance. On her left, the red sun had turned yellow, and on her right, last night's moon was a grey wafer in the sky.

The town was busy when she re-entered it. Shops were opening. People were sweeping their patches of pavement with wet brooms. Strong savoury smells came from inside houses; at midsummer, women did all their cooking early in the day.

Heading for the market, she reached a modern street she hated. Behind her, a shopkeeper opened his door, and a jangle of bouzouki music came out. Across the road, in front of a nursery-school – its windows decorated with cartoon animals, and its yard full of gaudy swings – an old man sat on a canvas stool. His bicycle was propped against the curb. Attached to its handlebars was a row of plastic windmills: acid green and electric blue.

The warm breeze rose. The windmills whirred. The bouzouki music blared. Children swarmed in the school yard like bees.

Suddenly Celia danced three steps. She laughed. Her eyes filled with tears which, as she walked on, she brushed away.

Each morning, she bought a *koulouri* from a bald man with a white moustache whose wagon was parked behind the market. She deliberated before making her choice. The *koulouria* were of various shapes. Long ovals were coated with sesame seeds. Rolls held pats of melted cheese. Chunky squares were studded with black olives, and there were flat sweet buns with a flavour of tahina. Today she chose olive.

With her *koulouri* wrapped in a square of paper in her bag, she went into the market. She did not want to buy anything: simply to immerse herself – though more briefly than in the sea – in its sights, its smells, its sounds; in its stir.

Nowadays she bought almost everything from Niko. She went to the supermarket only for Chloe's tinned catfood. Earlier this year she had not paid Niko's account for three months. She had also been two months behind with the rent, and had owed Thalia six weeks' wages. When she apologized, Niko, the landlady, Thalia, each in turn, had said, '*Then peirazi*' ('Never mind'), but she had longed for her cheque to arrive. When it did, it was smaller than the previous one. She supposed that the next would be smaller still.

When she reached home, Celia made coffee and ate her *koulouri*; around the olives the bread was dark and moist, with a rich taste. She ate it carefully: sometimes the baker removed the olive pips; sometimes he did not.

ANDREA 1972

As soon as she heard the front door slam behind him, she started to play the Game. Tonight there was no reason to shrink him. She simply twisted the key in his back, to start him down the steps; knees bent, and toes turned outwards. Then, at the speed of an old silent film, she sent him skimming over the pavement: Charlie Chaplin, without the hat and stick. Rusty was down at the end of the terrace in a moment, and whizzing across the Holloway Road, where a night lorry missed him by inches.

The pub on the corner had closed two hours ago. Now – hey presto! – she opened it, brightly lit it, filled it with yelling people, and spilt stale beer on the bar and tables. How astonishing and delightful this unique 'opening-time' seemed to Rusty, and how eager he was to take advantage of it. But – just as his hand touched the door – she jerked him back. How he struggled – legs kicking, arms flailing – till a twist of her key sent him spinning – all his struggles in vain! – round the corner into Upper Street.

> *Knees up, Rusty Flynn!*
> *Would you like a gin?*
> *Or would a whisky make you frisky?*
> *Knees up, Rusty Flynn!*

He was almost out of sight when a brass band – concealed in the dark garden in front of Compton Terrace – blared:

> *Tidderly-umpty* – pause – *ha ha!*

And he vanished.

*

Flynn, the mechanism: she had thus perceived him first one evening when he was enacting his full laugh ('full' in the sense of a 'full English breakfast' or a performance of the full text of *Titus Andronicus*). Head jerked back and then jerked forward; that was what initially

256

reminded her of a clockwork toy. The mouth was open wide, but emitted no sound; the head inched down spasmodically till almost touching the splay knees, when it started the return journey: a reverse series of jerks. Half way up . . . straight . . . finally tilted over the chair-back, for the consummation: *'Hwar . . . hwar . . . hwar . . . hwar . . . hwar!'* The creaking sound – Rusty's rusty laugh – like the movements preceding it, had the character of a machine.

At that time she had not yet invented the Game. The Game started on a subsequent occasion, after she and Rusty met in one of his pubs (she had told Oliver she was visiting Sarah), and then went together to a shabby house where he rented a room.

The ginger cat must have come in through the open staircase window outside which ran a narrow gutter. The ginger cat sat, front paws tucked under, in the centre of Rusty's room, and immediately he jumped at it, roaring. Up leapt the cat. It raced – its whole body flattened – round the room, close to the wall, and Rusty after it, with the roar that was a bigger – and even uglier – brother of his laugh. But the cat could not escape, because Andrea was standing in the doorway; so round they went again, the cat cringing, and Rusty roaring and jerking his arms up and down. This time, however, Andrea had pushed the door wide open, flattening herself – like the cat – against the wall. The cat was through the doorway, down the stairs, and out of the window. Rusty stopped running, stopped roaring; but then – hands resting on his knees – he started his laugh.

Later that night, at home (in bed with Oliver), she invented the Game, and played it for the first time.

She positioned Rusty in the centre of his room (precisely where the cat had sat). Next she shrank him (making him only slightly smaller than the cat; he was more fortunate than it had been). Then she inserted the key in an aperture between his shoulder-blades, and wound him up. Now the moment had arrived to open the door, and to admit the cat.

They were off: Rusty ahead, and Ginger after! Sometimes Ginger was skittish, swatting Rusty with a playful paw. Sometimes Ginger crouched, swaying hula-hula hips before a pounce. Rusty just kept on circling the room: round and round, time after time. His small arms and legs pumped in a frantic rhythm. Gradually, however, he was covering less ground. The movements of the little limbs slowed. *The mechanism was running down.*

A rattle came from Rusty's tiny mouth, and Ginger prepared for the decisive spring.

Frowning judicially, Andrea hesitated. Then firmly she stepped between the cat and its prey. Restraining Ginger with her left hand, she used her right to give a casual little twist to Rusty's key. It was enough: he was out of the door, down the stairs, over the window-sill, and into the gutter. It was an appropriate place for him.

*

Tonight, after she had spun him past the pub and off down Upper Street, Andrea abandoned the Game. She visualized Rusty's actual return home. Back in his room, he would pop two 'sleepers', as he called them, between his lips, like a child indulging in a couple of 'sweeties'.

Tomorrow, when he woke, he would swallow the other pills (perhaps he thought of those as 'wakers'), which he pretended that he no longer took. From drunken indiscretions and from his huffish rage that doctors no longer prescribed them – 'an assault on liberty' he declared this – she knew he lied. She supposed he bought the pills from a 'dealer', but wondered how he could afford to, with his pathetic earnings from seedy part-time jobs. (Typical was his sub-editing of an obscure monthly trade journal.) However, his rent was low and his clothes were shabby, so he could spend every penny on what he put into that rapacious orifice in his face: not food – he ate little – but the 'sleepers' and 'wakers'; the 'three' Guinnesses at midday; the (un-counted) evening pub drinks (and, if he were 'in funds', he would take a quarter bottle of whisky home at closing-time); the cigarettes he sucked rather than smoked. (Once, glancing sideways at him in a cinema where smoking was prohibited – another 'assault on liberty' – she saw his empty lips suck-sucking just as if they held an actual cigarette.) Sometimes, when he kissed her – he was fond of kissing – she saw herself as one more oral device to 'turn' the addict 'on'. Perhaps – apart from the imaginary one she twisted between his shoulders in the Game – the key to Rusty fitted between his lips: 'Flynn, the mechanism' was really 'Flynn, the mouth'.

At first she had tried to justify her connection with him to herself by the fact that he had once been a poet. In her teens she had bought *Devlin's Valley* (1949), his first book. She had not bought its successor, *Black Throne* (1958) until after she met him, six months ago. She had found it in a second-hand bookshop. Like *Devlin's Valley*, it was out of print, which seemed all that the two books had in common. The poems in *Devlin's Valley* – most of which concerned his Irish childhood – had a tortuous lyricism. Those in *Black Throne* reminded her of a Lowry painting she had once seen in a gallery. Examining it closely she became aware that all the little stick-like figures were maimed or twisted in some way; even a tiny dog limped, three-legged.

The poems also recalled to her how Rusty's eyes lingered on a newspaper-seller with a red empty eye-socket or a shopkeeper with hairs sprouting from her chin. He had told her how, between 1954 and 1960, he had looked after a woman who, paralysed from the waist down, was confined to a wheelchair (*Black Throne?*). This could have been interpreted as praiseworthy, but when Rusty said, 'I did *every-thing* for her,' his tone revealed that, the more menial, the more disgusting the task involved, the greater was his relish for it. He also liked to dwell on a time when he had been employed as a lavatory (*Black Throne?*) attendant; again she heard the note of relish.

'Why are you so attracted to degradation?' she once asked him.

He seemed pleased. 'Degragation!' he exclaimed. (He meant 'Degradation!', but he was drunk.) 'Degragation! Yes, that's the ticket!'

'A season-ticket,' she replied coldly. 'For *A Season in Hell*, perhaps?'

'*Hwar, hwar, hwar.*' But he was flattered. Inevitably, he idolized Rimbaud.

All his friends – though she thought the term 'boon companions' more apt – seemed to travel on those season-tickets. After two visits, she refused ever again to enter the particular Soho pub where they forgathered. A temple of 'booze and baccy', its congregation was composed of men whose purple faces looked as if they had been stamped on, and who spoke in hoarse voices. (Was this hoarseness a by-product of alcohol itself, or had it developed from a determination, when drinking, to shout down similarly resolved associates?) All of them boasted about the 'great works', in one medium or another, which they were producing in lonely attics. Andrea felt as convinced that they were all lying as she did that Rusty was when he talked about his 'work'. He had produced nothing since *Black Throne*, fourteen years ago; his poetic voice, she felt certain, had long ago croaked – she heard the caw of a dying rook – into silence. (He told her that he had originally been nicknamed 'Rusty' – his actual name was Patrick – because of his red hair – now a mixture of salt and powdered ginger – but Andrea thought that now – voice, character, talent; all rusted – he was totally 'Rusty' in a way he could never have been when young.)

The only evidence he ever gave of 'working' was an absurd 'hobby' – she felt a pleasing consciousness of how he would have detested the bourgeois word – which he pursued on Saturdays, when he visited a rich eccentric in Hampstead who owned a giant computer. On this Rusty wrote 'computer poetry'. Although, in Andrea's view, he was an extremely 'dated' person, he liked to believe himself *avant garde*; according to him, 'computer poetry' was 'the poetry of the future', and was therefore 'alive'. It was ironic, she thought, that the only thing she had ever heard him describe as 'alive' was produced by a machine. Usually he spouted about death: the death of the family, the death of society, the death of 'art as we know it'. In any case, she believed that the true reason for his trips to Hampstead was the prospect of free drinks. She had once met him after a 'session' in the computer 'lab', and he was reeling.

Now, lying in bed, she realized that she was evading the issue, which was that to expose herself to Rusty's degradation was similar to exposing herself to radiation. Might not even she, who balanced her life so skilfully – good job, happy marriage, and her new project, the 'Book of Shame' – be contaminated? She recognized the risk and acknowledged that there was only one way to avoid it. *She must give him up*.

It ought to be easy to do this, when she despised him so much. Yet there was a conflict, which she summed up in the words *'Those sunny caves! that dome of ice!'*

Usually, when the strange craving Rusty aroused in her had been satisfied, she fell asleep easily; not tonight. She got out of bed, and went – barefoot on the thick soft carpet – over to the window. She looked out at the lamplit plane trees edging the park across the road.

Now, in November, there were still leaves on the plane trees; last year she had seen the last one flutter down on Christmas Day. Now, at two in the morning, everything was quiet, except for the perpetual, pervasive hum of London: this city where – only twenty minutes by underground from its centre – she lived in such a delightful environment. In this regard – as with her job and her marriage – she enjoyed the best of two worlds. Now, suddenly, she shivered, though the room was centrally heated to an ideal temperature. She wished that Oliver was with her. However, he would be back from his business trip very soon: the day after tomorrow. Looking forward to this, she returned to bed. *She would give up Rusty*. In a few minutes she was asleep.

*

Next morning, on the underground, travelling to work, her attention, as usual, was divided between her *Guardian* and her fellow-passengers. Some news item about conquest or cruelty, arousing her indignation, would make her lift her eyes from the paper, and start to compose a letter to the editor, even though she knew that she would never write – let alone post – it. Staring into space, she would be distracted by the exotic people who, since her arrival in London five years ago, had startled and exhilarated her: people in trailing robes and shaggy coats; in cheesecloth, in Eastern or African materials, in denim. Men and girls alike had the bushy or flowing hair which it was one of the trademarks of the middle-aged to deplore. Andrea, however, was on the side of the hairy; and she had enjoyed the musical, *Hair*, which many people of her age – forty next week! – found disgusting. How delicious was the mildness of the young and hairy in comparison with the violence in her newspaper.

*

In her office, conquest and cruelty gave place to mutilation and murder, when she returned to the novel on which a decision must be reached that day. She looked at her watch: nine forty-five. She had at least an hour. Guy, the paperback company's chief editor, never reached the office before half-past ten, and needed to spend at least twenty minutes lying back in his chair, smoking, before embarking, with a groan, on the business of the day.

Adrea hated the novel, which was about a necrophile child-killer. Although he was eventually shot by a policeman – whose own (ordinary but very active) sex life was described in irrelevant detail – his death was not cheering; too much blood-saturated vileness had preceded it. However, for a book of its kind, it was well-written: considerably more than literate. It was convincing; therefore, she felt, it could do harm. What she had to find was a 'commercial' reason for rejecting it.

No moral objection could cut any ice with Guy. She had managed to persuade him to reject a collection of photographs of supine women, scantily clad in leather, with Alsatian dogs standing over or sniffing at them, on the grounds that the production costs, in terms of the size of the market, would be too high, and also that an important chain of booksellers would refuse to stock it.

Guy had been convinced by these arguments, but he had shown regret. He had a zest for what was bad, in both moral and artistic terms. Nothing delighted him more than a prospective bestseller that was appalling in both style and contents. Was this because he liked to feel superior to the people who would buy the book? Andrea did not think so. She believed that he positively enjoyed – a resemblance to Rusty here? – the degradation of literature. Concomitantly, he had a nervous horror of books which were good in a literary sense; these tended to sit, unread, on his desk for weeks.

None of this meant that he was stupid. On the contrary he was extremely clever. And he was a true 'whizz-kid': modern to the core, and still – though holding an important position – well under thirty. Even his very regular blond good-looks did not appear old-fashioned. (His shoulder-length hair helped here.) In the same way his Arthurian-Victorian name was magically transmuted into the American collo-quialism for 'man'. Guy also had charm; even Andrea admitted that. When he smiled – this was rarely – he had the gift of making the person he smiled at feel privileged, and his very shiny dark blue eyes – the eyes, Andrea had noticed, either of children or of the insincere – positively glittered. Often, though she felt guilty later, she would giggle toler-antly with him at some particularly crass big bad novel, which had dropped onto her desk like the corpse of an enormous rodent: stinking of corruption, pullulating with sentences like fat white maggots. Enjoying Guy's company, Andrea felt like a person dedicated to economy for a high purpose who cannot resist indulging in some pointless luxury.

It was at eleven that she went into his office, carrying the novel and the report she had just typed. Almost every woman publishing-editor – for instance Georgina, Guy's assistant – refused to have a typewriter in her office, in case she was mistaken for a secretary. Even – especially? – if she could type fluently, she would write out her report, and then hand or dictate it to a typist. Andrea, who had taught herself to type with two fingers years ago, thought this ridiculous; she always typed her reports.

Guy sprawled behind his desk. (This morning he did not have his feet on it.) Georgina sat in one of two chairs facing him. Georgina was a large pink-faced ex-deb whose main interest in life – apart from Guy – was being 'with it'. Today she was wearing denim dungarees: a favourite outfit in which she bobbed along behind Guy like a blue balloon behind a sacred image.

'Here's that book,' said Andrea, putting it, with the report tucked inside it, on Guy's desk, and sitting down next to Georgina.

After a moment he extended his hand and pulled out the report. As he read it – his face expressionless – Andrea ran through a few of her favourite fantasies about him.

Guy! He would toss a coin to a friend begging in the gutter; provided he had the loose change handy. *Guy!* He would avoid treading on a rare butterfly; it might make a mess of his shoe. *Guy!* If he had been a Roman emperor, he would have brought the gladiators to a halt, because he lacked the energy to make either the 'thumbs up' or the 'thumbs down' sign. *Guy!* Under the handsome mask, the smartly shabby 'gear': straw; but mightn't it be too damp to make a good bonfire?

'You don't think we should do it, then?'

'Hmm? Oh . . . No, I'm not keen.'

'Reely?' said Georgina, who had only recently learnt to pronounce the word in this way. (It was not 'trendy' to speak in an upper-class accent. Guy, who had been to a well-known public school, spoke 'mid-Atlantic' English.) Now Georgina looked at Guy, trying to gauge his reaction before venturing one of her own.

Guy said, 'I thought it was quite a gripping read.'

This was inauspicious. Any book that could hold Guy's attention must be readable; as, indeed, Andrea herself had found this one.

Georgina chimed in. 'Yeah. I thought it was sup . . . great.' She was still finding it difficult to abandon 'super', formerly her favourite adjective.

'I thought the policeman was a pretty tedious character,' Andrea said judiciously. She had. Besides she felt that this was the most promising denigratory approach.

'Lots of sex, though,' said Georgina.

Guy's telephone buzzed. When it did this for the third time, he extended a languid hand and raised the receiver. 'Yeah. OK,' he said, and sighed. 'Tell him to come up.' He put down the receiver. 'Visitor,' he said. Andrea and Georgina rose. 'Gotta decide by five this evening whether to make an offer.'

'My feeling's "Yes",' said Georgina.

'I don't think it's worth a lot,' said Andrea. (This was true. She did not think the book was a potential bestseller. Its success would be minor.) 'I don't feel it's really very commercial,' she added. This was the perfect exit line. Everyone in the company agreed that Andrea had an instinct for what was 'commercial'.

*

She was glad (after she had dictated a few letters expressing interest in forthcoming books, and read a chunk of another novel – historical; of the type known in the trade as a 'bodice-ripper') when it was time to go out to meet her friend Sarah at the wine-bar where they had arranged to lunch. Although one was called an 'editor', there was little real editing to do in a paperback house; it had already been done by the staff of the hardcover publisher. Andrea often wished she was a real editor, instead of an assessor of the prospects for hardcover books in paperback. Yet something in her nature responded to the restlessness, the sudden crises of the paperback world. What was she going to say today to Sarah, who had recently suggested that Andrea should join her in a new publishing company she was starting: a company which would be staffed entirely by women, and would publish only books by women authors? Sarah was a keen feminist. So, in theory, was Andrea. Why, therefore, did she not decide at once, to work for Sarah; or, rather, to work *with* her, for Sarah was determined that all decision-making should be collective. Sarah was a keen socialist. So, in theory was Andrea. What, then, held her back? Did she have a frivolous feeling that working with a band of serious 'sisters' might be claustrophobic? Certainly she was not influenced by the prospect of an initial cut in salary. (Oliver was Managing Director of a successful company which published books about business.) Was she hesitating because she didn't want to become *involved*, to the extent that would be necessary? Suddenly she shivered.

I know thy works, that thou art neither cold nor hot. I would thou wert cold or hot. So then, because thou art lukewarm, and neither cold nor hot, I will spue thee out of my mouth.

She could hardly quote that to Sarah – so positive, so militant – even though she thought of Sarah as her best friend. Sarah was the only person who knew about her affair with Rusty, whom she had considered awful when Andrea brought him round for 'a' drink at her flat. Gulping Sarah's gin, he had held forth about freedom.

Sarah yawned. 'Oh really,' she said, 'I'm not interested in the sort of vague bourgeois freedom you're talking about.'

'Bourgeois? Bourgeois?' Rusty almost spluttered. 'You call the freedom of man *bourgeois*?'

'Oh, the freedom of *man*,' said Sarah.

'Oh well, the freedom of women, too, if you like. Though I've never met one of the breed' – he chuckled – 'who really wants it.'

Andrea drew in her breath with a sort of snarl. Sarah merely looked at her watch.

'Anyway,' Rusty drivelled on, 'what I'm talking about is the freedom of the spirit.'

'But *please*' – Sarah gestured towards the gin bottle – 'feel free with it. Help yourself.'

Afterwards, Rusty had referred to Sarah as a 'bull-dyke', which she was not. She had once, she told Andrea, attempted a Lesbian relationship, as a matter of principle: 'It didn't work out. It wasn't her not having a prick that I minded. I just couldn't stand her having tits.'

Andrea – nearly forty – had blushed before she laughed.

Today in the wine-bar, Andrea and Sarah drank a bottle of Beaune, and ate bread and ripe Brie. Andrea far preferred wine-bars to pubs.

'So have you reached a decision?' Sarah asked her.

'Not quite.' *Because thou art neither cold nor hot. . .*

'You'll have to hurry up, you know.'

'Next week. I promise.'

'Is it Oliver who's holding things up?'

Oliver, though he thought the all-woman publishing house unlikely to succeed – in some ways he was rather a chauvinist – wanted Andrea to do as she wished. 'Try it, if you think you'll enjoy it.' But wasn't that patronizing? He would never have said it to a man.

'No, it's not Oliver.'

'Oliver's not too bad. Especially for a man of his age. When does he get back?'

'Tomorrow evening.'

'Have you been seeing that dreadful old drunk while he's been away. No need to scowl at me like that! I know he wrote a few good poems a hundred years ago, but now he's just a bore.'

'Not *just* that. Anyway – yes, I saw him last night. But I've decided that I'm definitely going to give him up.'

Sarah laughed. 'For Lent?'

Andrea laughed. 'No. For good.'

'I'm glad to hear it. It's so risky, anyway. Dear old Oliver would never forgive you if he found out.'

'No.'

'And the Book of Shame?'

'Oh, it's making progress.' Sarah was the only person – except Oliver, who found the idea amusing – who knew about the Book of Shame, as Andrea called the bestseller she was attempting to write.

'Can't think why you bother. It's not as if you were short of money. If you want to write, why don't you try to write a *real* book?'

'Oh, I don't know.' *Because thou art neither cold nor hot . . .*

*

The afternoon was Andrea's worst time of day. Thank heaven for the long lunches of publishing. It was half-past three by the time she returned to the office from the wine-bar. She could not face the 'bodice-ripper'. Instead she paged through a book on Zen. (Wasn't

Zen a bit *passé*? It was Georgina who was keen on the idea. Bobbing along in pursuit of Guy and fashion, she sometimes lagged a little.)

Guy wandered (he always wandered; she had never seen him hurry) into her office at twenty-past five. 'I've decided to make an offer for that book,' he said.

'Oh.'

'Three other paperback houses are interested, you know.'

'Oh.' Publishing often reminded Andrea of dances at which, if a girl seemed to be in demand, every young man automatically pursued her, whatever she looked like. All the same, Andrea felt depressed. Sarah's company – it had no name yet – would never dream of publishing a book like this one, with its mutilated, murdered children. And wouldn't it be wonderful to escape from Guy? At that moment he smiled at her.

'I'm probably making a big mistake,' he said. 'You know how I rely on your judgement.'

Whenever she felt most anti-him, he would say something like that. 'Time for a drink?' he asked.

'Sorry. I've got to rush.' It was true that she was sorry. She would rather have had a drink with Guy than with Jane.

*

Jane and her husband Geoffrey, who was a lofty Civil Servant, lived near Andrea and Oliver. Stepping off the escalator in the underground, Andrea saw that no ticket-collector was on duty. She kept her ticket to use again; she would alter the date on it. Oliver had once found her absorbed in this task, and had been horrified. 'But *why*?' he had asked. Why indeed? 'Oh, just for fun,' she said.

Jane was one of 'the wives'. By this Andrea meant that she was married to a friend of Oliver's.

The wives were all about ten years older than Andrea. (Oliver was twelve years older than she was. His first wife had died seven years ago.) Their children were grown-up, or nearly so. (Oliver had a married daughter of twenty-five, Davina, with whom Andrea had a cordial relationship.) None of the wives worked, except part-time in 'voluntary organizations', as charities were called nowadays.

The wives had anxious faces, carefully made-up. Their hair was tinted; their legs were waxed; their eyelashes were dyed. They seldom ate the foods they enjoyed. There was a spectre abroad. Nowadays, large numbers of men – including public figures – were getting rid of their old wives and marrying new ones the age of their daughters.

Hence tints, and treatments, and expensive clothes. The wives would not have been able to afford these in earlier years – when, in any case, they would have been unnecessary – and felt a residual guilt, which led to secret economies. Hanging on a well-off wife's washing-line, Andrea had seen frayed, faded briefs and a brassiere with stretched elastic, and in her bedroom, an old down-at-heel pair of slippers. Perhaps, Andrea had thought, in order to 'keep' their husbands, the wives should have concentrated more on their underclothes. But it was too late for that. Being a well-turned-out helpmate was really the only hope.

'I don't know how you manage,' Jane said this evening, in an irritated tone. 'Running a home as well as working must be a dreadful strain.' The wives knew that Andrea, though younger than they were, was not young enough to be a threat; 'threats' were hardly ever over thirty. And Oliver had been a widower when he met her; she had not 'stolen' him. It was Andrea's job that the wives resented; as if, in some way, it were a criticism of them.

'Oh no,' Andrea said, hearing a responsive hostility in her own voice. (Just as she aroused hostility in housewives, so they aroused it in her.) 'Mrs Berry comes in three times a week, to clean. She's very good. I find that's quite enough.' Now, however, she remembered that Jane had a 'daily'.

Jane, whose red hair was a little too bright for her lined face, was pouring out drinks in the tentative, measuring way of wives in their husbands' absence. (Geoffrey usually worked late at the Treasury.) She held up the glasses to the light to see if she had poured out tots that were too large or too small. 'I'd hate to have to rush home from work to cook the dinner,' Jane said. 'And it must be so difficult to shop in one's lunch-hour.'

'Oh no. I do almost all the week's shopping on Saturday. And we eat quite late. Anyway, I couldn't bear not to work.'

'I suppose, ' Jane said, her voice now reflective rather than unfriendly, 'I've never really been interested in doing things on my own. Just for myself, I mean.'

Andrea saw that not only did Jane believe what she was saying, but that it was true. What a gulf yawned between them! 'So really,' she said, 'you've always lived for others.'

Jane looked at her sharply, but recognized that she was not sneering. 'Yes,' Jane said, 'I suppose so. *Lived for others.*' Repeating Andrea's phrase, she – an intelligent woman – put it in italics and produced the brief ironic smile she felt was necessary in order to avoid giving the impression of a 'martyred' attitude.

*

Living for others: Andrea thought about it all the way home. She believed women did it because they wanted those others to be theirs. They were binding husbands and children to them with what they hoped were invisible threads. Andrea had seen Jane prodding at Geoffrey as if he were a splinter embedded in her thumb, picking at him as if he were a scab on her elbow, scratching at him as if he were an insect-bite: all metaphorically, of course. And the metaphorical prodding, picking, scratching were expressions of 'caring', of 'concern'. If Andrea had been a man she would have wanted to slap away that – metaphorical – caring hand, and say, 'For Christ's sake, let me alone.' All Geoffrey did was to give a huge shrug, as if to shift this weight of woman off his back. Then he subsided, tolerant, calmed by having momentarily eased the burden of 'caring', of 'concern' off his shoulders. Observing the scene, Andrea had wondered why men ever married. This was something she could not have told Sarah.

All the same, combining outside work and domesticity was not as easy as she liked to pretend to 'the wives'. (Why did she want – need – to devalue their efforts?) Often she felt as if she were running in a long-distance race; there was a constant demand for stamina.

'We've stopped making it. There was too much demand,' the local baker of a special wholemeal loaf had told her, and she had burst out laughing. But, one day, might she stop manufacturing stamina? Because there was too much demand.

Opening the front door, she immediately sensed the emptiness of the house, which made her feel restless, rather than – as one might have expected – serene.

She had drunk two gin and tonics at Jane's. Now she made a pot of strong coffee and took it with her favourite cup – a large Edwardian one, found on a junk-stall, and picturing a lady in a feathered hat, peering through a lorgnette – into the room where she worked, which faced onto the garden. (This consisted of a small lawn, three trees, and two flowerbeds, and was – thank heaven – Oliver's responsibility.) She drew the curtains. She hated uncurtained windows after dark; interior reflections seemed like things moving outside.

She poured out coffee, lit a cigarette, switched on the Anglepoise lamp, and sat down at her typewriter.

Marina looked into the great, gilded mirror. Gazing at her reflection, she saw herself transformed. The tulle was like a white cloud from which she emerged with startling vividness. Her shining hair clustered in soft curls about her neck. The string of pearls brought out a corresponding glow in her skin, and between her coral lips her teeth were very white. Her eyes sparkled, and a sudden gaiety took possession of her. She twirled in front of the mirror . . .

Andrea kept on typing.

Marina reached the top of the great staircase, involuntarily smoothing her hair before she started down. The marble banister was cool beneath her fingers. She was half way to the hall when Stephen came out of the library.

For a second she paused. Then she continued her descent. How long the stairs seemed! Stephen now stood by the bottom step. His face was very brown, his eyes were very blue above the expanse of his white waistcoat, stiff white shirt, white tie.

'Good evening, Mr Demarest,' she said.

'Good evening, Marina. Tonight all the women are bedecked and bejewelled, but you are the only flower I've seen.'

Those blue eyes in the brown face! 'The only flower I've seen'! Marina's hand tightened on the banister. It was at that moment that she recognized that she was in love with Stephen Demarest.

At last! Yet Andrea sighed. She still had such a long way to go. The book must of necessity be fearfully long: almost all bestsellers were. Marina had to be spirited, for all heroines had to be; and Stephen, like all heroes, must be masterful. Andrea calculated that the first kiss ('A ripple ran down Marina's spine') could not occur for another fifty pages. There must be a further two hundred before Stephen carried Marina across the room 'to the great bed with its oyster-coloured satin sheets.' And even after that, various disasters and misunderstandings must precede the obligatory happy ending.

She was finding it difficult to concentrate tonight. It was easier when Oliver was at home. Of course she had to cook dinner, but she often found that relaxing, like their pre-dinner drink, and their chatter during the meal. After dinner, Oliver sometimes worked, or he sat and read, or did *The Times* crossword, or occasionally, when there was an exceptionally good programme, watched television. Whatever he was doing, the consciousness of his presence seemed to help her, sitting at her typewriter, to 'churn it out': this absurd stuff which might conceivably make her independent both of her job and of him.

He must never guess that such an idea could enter her mind. She knew that, though he took an interest in her job and encouraged her writing, he believed that, without either, she would still be 'fulfilled': by him.

'Personal happiness. That's all that really matters in the last resort,' he murmured to her one night, after making love. He gave a happy sigh. Andrea sighed too. 'Decoration,' she murmured back, involuntarily, and felt real terror as she heard herself voice the word. However, she was lucky: her whisper had been so soft that he misheard it. He said, 'Yes, dedication. You're right, darling. Happiness is what one's ultimately dedicated to.'

Ultimately?

She first met Oliver – as she later met Rusty – at a publishing party. She felt immediately at ease with him, and he was attracted by her, and asked her out to dinner.

Oliver was so safe: safe in appearance, with his balding head, his genial spectacled face, his rather bulky figure (all his clothes, even his London suits, had a countrified tweedy look); safe in manner, which was bluff and affable. Yet, beneath appearance and manner, were sensitivity, kindness, devotion. (Although, occasionally, he broke out in short sudden rages which surprised her, within minutes he would be ashamed and apologetic.)

To her, he meant safety. What, she wondered, did she mean to him? She decided that he found her 'daring' (career-woman, sceptical, critical, sometimes caustic). She was certainly daring in comparison to his wife – dead four years before he met Andrea – who sounded fragile, misty, saintly; though perhaps this was the nimbus which death alone creates. Andrea had heard of people being jealous of dead predecessors; she could not imagine experiencing this herself. Her feeling for Oliver could undoubtedly never have given rise to anything of that kind.

She remembered the Spring afternoon when he had first taken her to his cottage in Kent: *their* cottage now, of course, officially. It was on the edge of a small almost theatrically unspoilt village, set – in more senses than one, she felt – in a countryside of lush grass and trees that were swollen with leaves. There were sheep, too; their lambs looked as if they had been newly washed in detergent, and were skipping and baaing as if under contract to do so. The cottage was deep in climbing plants, in shrubs and bushes: all so very green, so soft-looking, so moist. Even though the sun was shining brightly that day, she was conscious of moisture everywhere. Above her were big soft clouds: those English clouds that seem always yearning to dissolve in tears of rain. Underfoot were thick damp grasses and rich almost steamy soil. Everywhere, among the leaves, birds gargled and insects buzzed.

Perversely, she had longed for something drier and harsher; for less opulence of vegetation. She still felt that; she always thought of the cottage as Oliver's. (Didn't she feel the Islington house was his, too?) All the same, she had appreciated how gentle and restful the place was: just like Oliver.

She had married him. *Because thou art neither hot nor cold . . .*

It was six months ago that she had met Rusty: not at a large party, crammed with important authors and publishers, like the one at which she had met Oliver, but at a modest one, given by a 'highbrow' publisher (as was indicated by the word 'Press' in the title of his company). This publisher had printed both Rusty's books of poems, but had only asked him to the party – she learnt later – on the basis of a chance meeting in the street. Delivering a verbal invitation, he had escaped with grace from an encounter with a failed author. (This was Andrea's interpretation, not Rusty's.) He had added, 'I'll send you a card,' but had forgotten to do so (Rusty's interpretation, not Andrea's). Rusty however – the prospect of free drink firmly in mind – had remembered.

He behaved unusually well that evening, probably because the 'free drink' consisted of a weak 'cup'. Andrea, in conversation with him, had remembered his early poems; and Andrea had always revered poets. She was also attracted by his quickness, his slightness, his furrowed, haggard face. (His looks were the complete opposite of Oliver's.) She invited him to lunch the following Sunday, and he accepted. 'What time?' he asked.

'About one.'

'Oh dear me! I would have thought around pub closing-time would be better.'

That had been the first warning: disregarded. If only she had said, 'Well, don't come then,' and turned away. Instead, genuinely puzzled, she had frowned. Pub closing-time? That was two o'clock, wasn't it, on Sundays? (She and Oliver never went to pubs in London.) Why did he want to wait until then? Anyway, what cheek! It had amused her. 'Oh well,' she said, 'I'm sure we won't be eating before two, if you *prefer* to arrive then.'

'Hoity-toity,' he said, looking at her with what she now saw as his Irish con-man's stock-in-trade 'twinkle', but which then – combined with the expression 'Hoity-toity', which she had previously only seen in print – made her laugh. 'Well,' he said – stooping, he kissed her hand – 'one o'clock it shall be, proud beauty.'

Lunch had been disastrous: Rusty at his worst, drunk and pontificating. 'Really, what an awful little man,' Oliver said, when at last he departed. 'Yes, I'm terribly sorry,' she replied. Yet, when Rusty telephoned her at the office during the following week, she agreed to meet him for a drink. Why hadn't she faced the fact that when she did so, she had known what the outcome would be?

She stood up and put out the Anglepoise lamp. She was feeling very restless. She ate a cheese omelette and drank a glass of white wine. She did not feel she could bear to write any more tonight. She decided to read.

Recently she had felt afraid that the books she read at work, the book she was writing ('Why don't you write a *real* book?' Sarah had asked today) would make her incapable of reading anything good. To find out, she had started to re-read *Anna Karenina*, and to her relief had become absorbed in it. Now she reached the point at which Anna 'succumbed' to Vronsky.

That which for nearly a year had been the one absorbing desire of Vronsky's life, supplanting all his former desires; that which for Anna had been an impossible, terrible, but all the more bewitching dream of bliss, had come to pass. Pale, with trembling lower jaw, he stood before her and besought her to be calm, himself not knowing how or why.

'Anna! Anna!' he said in a choking voice. 'Anna, for pity's sake! . . .'

But the louder he spoke the lower she drooped her once proud, gay, but now shame-stricken head, and she crouched down and sank from where she was sitting to the floor at his feet. She would have fallen on the carpet if he had not held her.

'Oh God, forgive me!' she said, sobbing and pressing his hands to her breast.

She felt so sinful, so guilty, that nothing was left to her but to humble herself and beg forgiveness; but she had no one in the world now but him, and so to him she even addressed her prayer for forgiveness –

'All that fuss about a fuck!' Andrea – who hardly ever swore – shouted aloud, and she hurled the book away from her. But then she crossed the room, and picked it up, and smoothed its crumpled pages before she closed it. She had such a dreadful grinding sense of depression. She looked at her watch. The time was half-past ten: half an hour before closing-time.

She would go now to tell him that she had given him up: 'for good', in both senses of the phrase. She knew exactly where to find him: in the ugly pub – two minutes' walk from the house he lived in – which was always his last 'port of call'.

Arrived there, she opened the door, and felt the customary stuffiness, smelt the stink of beer and tobacco, and dirty winter clothes. (Why, when they could afford beer and tobacco, should the English be unable to afford dry-cleaning?) Loud voices roared from red faces. Peering through the fug, she could not see him, and felt an inexplicable sense of relief. (Did she not want to tell him it was over? She was sure she did.) Then she glimpsed him, leaning on the bar, talking to old Maggie, the barmaid, with her turret of dyed yellow hair and fingernails varnished dark green. (Where Rusty saw Maggie as a 'character', Andrea saw her as a superannuated whore.) It was a blow to see him; worse than the blast of pub that had met her at the door. He must have felt the gorgon glare she fixed on him, for immediately he looked up, straight across the room at her. His face lost its boisterous grin. With a nod, a word, a wink to Maggie, he drained his glass, and slunk – yes, he looked doggy, subject, abject – towards her.

'What a surprise! Delightful! But I'm afraid I can't offer you a drink m'dear. Closing-time, you know.'

'That's quite obvious,' she said, for the pub was now loud with the sound of a buzzer and voices shouting, 'Time!' 'But I don't want a drink. I want to talk to you.'

'Oh, well, well. By all means. Wish I could get you a drink, though. Looking a little – grim, perhaps aren't you?'

'I can't talk in here.' She could feel her face expressing her loathing of the place.

He looked nervous. 'Well then, shall I see you home?' (After all, it was after closing-time.)

'All right.' She turned, and he hurried ahead to push open the door for her. She was in command. Yet half an hour later the situation was reversed; he was in her bed. The craving was satisfied. Her detestation of him was intensified. Her despair was complete when downstairs she heard first sounds, then footsteps, than Oliver calling, 'Andrea, darling! Surprise!'

Rusty scrambled out of bed: quick, lean, white, nimble. He was bundling into his clothes as Oliver opened the bedroom door.

Oliver's first look round the room was bemused. Then his skin seemed to stretch over the bones of his face. Strangely, he hardly seemed aware of Rusty. His eyes were fixed on her. Taking advantage of this – of course – Rusty grabbed his shoes, and with them dangling from his hand, slipped past Oliver and out of the room. The little rat! Not that she wanted him to stay. But if only a great cat were there to pounce on him now, or perhaps a terrier to break his back with one snap of its teeth.

Oliver took a step forward, then halted. Andrea heard the front door slam. Now Oliver advanced until he was standing beside the bed. She was sitting up, pressed against the – uncomfortable – brass bedhead, the sheet pulled taut and gripped under her armpits, as the stiff fingers of his shaking hands stretched out towards her neck.

Celia   1982

The worst moment of the day had occurred in the morning when Chloe, mewing, was taken away, in a wicker laundry-basket, by the elderly English couple who had been willing to adopt a spayed and pretty cat.

In the afternoon the packers had removed the twenty-three tea-chests. Twenty-two – one more than when she had arrived – held books; and – as before – a single chest was labelled 'Misc. Household Objects'.

She had given everything else, except what belonged to the landlady, to Thalia. Inevitably the two plain divans, the rush-seated chairs, the old refrigerator and stove, the cheap kitchen equipment would not be to Thalia's taste; however, if she had no use for them, she could always sell them, for a small sum. Andreas was coming to collect them – and the electric water-heater – early next morning. Celia would be leaving at noon. Now, this evening, for the last time – holding a glass of wine, but no cigarette – she paced the hall: from veranda to front door; from front door to veranda.

*

It was on the veranda that it all began, five years ago. Sitting there, that afternoon, she had read those extraordinary lines of Gissing: 'The past is no part of our existing self; we are free of it; it is buried. That is the release time owes us for doing his work.' Could that, she had wondered, possibly be true? Was it conceivable to exorcize the past in such a way? The title of the thriller she had bought that morning, *Pale Grey for Guilt*, had raised another, but related, question. Could the grey miasma of guilt ever be dispelled? Then *The Road to Xanadu* fell to the ground, and when she picked it up she saw that couplet about death, and as she closed the book her glance alighted on its subtitle: *A Study in the Ways of the Imagination*. That was when the five women rose, as one, in her mind, and then dropped apart from each other: *the five women who were dead.*

275

Over five succeeding years – always recollecting those lines from Gissing – she had pronounced the women's names. She had remembered and re-created their lives. She had asseverated their deaths. Doing this had changed her. She recalled what she had been like when she arrived on the island: how the bustling market seemed a place of mourning; how a moment's contact with the arm of one of the women she had designated 'sheep' filled her with disgust.

Considering Charlotte – from her beginning to her end – she regained, though still cynical and solitary, some humour; she took a positive action when she adopted the kitten, Panicos. Eleanor, however, produced a contrary effect. Not the disappearance of Panicos, but Eleanor's existence and its termination were the true cause of that hopeless, hateful drunken bout. It had been Laura's life and death that enabled her to move tentatively into the world – to swim and to initiate Kosta's English lessons – though she was haunted by a ridiculous fear of that Arab who had once grabbed her on the beach. However, Ida's living, Ida's dying were what gave her boldness. Ida enabled her, in spite of increasing money worries, to rejoice: in swimming out to sea; in the liveliness of the morning town; in the stir of the market; in the simple delight of an olive *koulouri*.

It was a month ago that, one morning – contemplating Andrea's fate – she heard a gentle knock on her front door.

Her landlady, Kyria Maroula, stood on the doorstep. Normally this old lady – always dressed in black, though her husband had died more than twenty years ago – beamed on Celia. Today her expression was sorrowful and timid. She hesitated when Celia invited her into the house, though usually she seemed to enjoy a cup of coffee and a chance to practise her English, which was good; it was much better than Celia's Greek.

'Do come in,' Celia repeated. Kyria Maroula did so, but with an odd air of reluctance, and lingering just inside the door.

'Won't you have some coffee? Do come out onto the veranda.'

'No, no, Mrs Celia. I cannot stop.' She looked almost frightened. Celia wondered what could be the matter. Thanks to a recent windfall, no rent was overdue.

'It is about the house,' Kyria Maroula said.

'The house?'

'I have had an offer. From a development person. He will pull the house down.'

'Oh no!'

'Yes. He will build flats. Three floors of flats. And he will give me one for my daughter's daughter. She wants to get married, and you know a Greek girl must own a house or flat if she is to marry.'

'Yes, I know that.' Celia was trying to disentangle a strange confusion of emotions.

'I am so sorry, Mrs Celia.'

'Well, after all, it's your house, Kyria Maroula. You can do what you like with it. But it's so beautiful. Wouldn't your grand-daughter rather live in this house than in a flat?'

'Oh Mrs Celia, she would be ashamed to live in such an old place.'

'Yes, I see.' Celia felt sad that the house was to be pulled down, but she had other feelings too, which she did not understand. 'Well,' she said, 'I must move out, of course.'

Kyria Maroula still looked worried. 'There is something else. There is a part in the lease about a three-months' notice. But the developing man can get builders in a month's time. Often it is hard to find builders because they are all so busy. There is so much building going on in the town. He may not want to make the agreement if he cannot start next month. I do not know what to do. Perhaps, Mrs Celia, we can make some arrangement . . .'

'No,' Celia said. 'No, Kyria Maroula. I can move at the end of the month.' She was surprised by her decisive tone, but still more surprised when, stooping forward – she was taller than Kyria Maroula – she put her arms round the black-clad shoulders and, pressing them firmly, gave Kyria Maroula the island salutation: a kiss on the left cheek, followed by one on the right. When she stepped back, she saw tears in Kyria Maroula's eyes.

'You are a good person, Mrs Celia.' Now the tears were falling. 'I think that you must have led a very good life.'

'*What?*' Celia spoke so vehemently that Kyria Maroula looked startled. However, wiping her eyes, she repeated, 'Yes, Mrs Celia. A very good life.'

Celia was moving into a kind of trance. She dragged herself out of it to say, rather weakly, 'Are you sure you won't have coffee?'

'No, no. I cannot stop. I have an engagement. I will come back. Perhaps tomorrow morning, at this same time. Would that be suitable for you?'

'Hmm?' Celia said, and then, 'Oh yes. Yes, of course.'

'Goodbye, Mrs Celia, and thank you. Thank you so much.'

Smiling vaguely, Celia nodded. As soon as she had shut the door, she turned, and paced towards the veranda. A *good* life? No. Certainly not that. Yet she had lived *a* life. Celia stood on the veranda step, but did not see the courtyard. Celia was seeing the course of her own life.

A desert is a region without water and without trees. Imagine a stone hand pushing up through that desert sand.

After the car knocked her down that snowy night in Oxford, her multiple fractures took over a year to heal. And meanwhile her mother's tests proved negative. Her mother – like Betty's father – died slowly of cancer. And she, after scraping her second-class degree, did the easiest thing. She married 'loyal Thompson': Peter, as she always called him after the end of her friendship with Lissa.

The fingers of the stone hand contract into a loose hollow fist. A lizard basks on the stone, enjoying the heat and the hardness, but a terrified bird hovers and flutters round the hand.

Although she had flung herself a second time towards the wall of fire, the firemen had dragged her back again. Teddy's death – oh, Teddy! – and its circumstances did not, of course, draw her and Peter closer, but drove them further apart. It was during the proceedings leading to their divorce that she moved to London and found her 'amusing' job in advertising.

The lizard continues to bask, but now the bird makes little darting rushes at the fist. From the opening between finger and thumb comes an old dead smell.

Sitting on her bed in her flat in the 'Golden City', she faced the paraphernalia of death: the pills, the whisky, the plastic bag. She lay down, intending to close her eyes and think for a moment, but she fell immediately into a deep sleep. When she awoke, three hours later, she found that (in spite of the end of her affair with Ben, her wrecked career – which, in any case now repelled her – and, she recognized now, the depression caused by her abortion) life seemed preferable to death. She decided to make a break of a different kind. She moved to Cape Town; she took the job in Miss Rubinstein's bookshop.

Now the bird darts under the thrust of the thumb. The hollow inside is very dark and very cold. If the fist closes, the bird will always be trapped.

After the plane had given that last enormous shudder, it steadied. As the engine sound returned to normal, Lieutenant van Schalkwyk mopped his forehead. They reached Pretoria safely, but she was not called as a witness in Bill's trial. So that she and others should not be imprisoned for refusing to give evidence against him, Bill admitted all charges, and received a sentence of seven years. She herself was never charged. The Consul had been more active on her behalf than she imagined; in any case the authorities rightly considered her of little significance. She was deported to England, where for a time she became involved in exile politics. 'As long as one remains a monk, one goes on tolling the bell,' according to Mao Tse Tung. When she left the monastery, she entered the world, and she became worldly.

The lizard does not stir, though now the fingers of the fist clench as if they are preparing to crush the bird.

Just before Oliver's hands reached her throat, he withdrew them. Holding his arms rigidly against his sides, he turned and left the bedroom. Where her first divorce had been sad, her second was sordid. Oliver cited Rusty as co-respondent. However, except in connection with legal proceedings – the case was undefended – she never met Rusty again. She moved to a small flat in another part of London. She refused the job in Sarah's publishing house – which was an almost immediate success – and continued to read for Guy. Slowly, over four years, she completed the massive Book of Shame. She had no affairs. Indeed she felt a growing horror of all company. On many mornings she had to force herself to go to the office. When the Book of Shame was sold for a lot of money, she was pleased, but she did not want to be involved in its publication. It was at this time that she decided to move to the island.

The clenching movement of the fist halts. Now a close scrutiny reveals cracks in the stone. The lizard gives a small wriggle of unease.

She had named the women in order to distance them from her. She had told their separate stories in order to lessen the cumulative weight of guilt. She had killed them in order to absolve herself.

The hand splinters into fragments of stone. The lizard is crushed but the bird soars free.

Charlotte, Eleanor, Laura, Ida, Andrea: now their initials sprang together to form her own name. Now the diverse episodes of their existence conjoined to tell a single story. Now, by restoring them, she restored herself to life.

*

Now, on her last night in this house which in a few days' time would be a heap of rubble, she reflected that Gissing's idea was preposterous. Yet without following the path it indicated, could she have gone further? Of course something else had helped her: the island; its safety, its busyness, its cheerful, healthy kindness.

In a sense, she dreaded tomorrow's return to the country where she had been born: to its random violence; to the desolation of its worklessness; to private indifference, and public faces as stern or flaccid as those of Ancient Roman statues.

Yet did she really want to remain on the island? In that confusion of feeling she had experienced when Kyria Maroula spoke to her, had not one element been relief? Might not the island's rules come to seem more and more alien to her: its houseproud neatness, its gregariousness, its contempt for the past; especially that last? In the box labelled 'Misc. Household Objects', apart from the addition of a few pieces of rough pottery and a striped rug, were the relics she had brought with her, and which she had kept in her bedroom: treasures from her mother's mantelpiece at the Manor House; one Sheffield urn, rescued from the fire's debris (her 'harlequin set' had been destroyed on the same night as Julian's harlequin); a photograph, taken from the pine-covered hillside, of the Transvaal farm, perched above its waterfall; an absurd Victorian picture called, 'He's Saved! He's Saved!'; an Edwardian cup depicting a lady with a lorgnette and a feathered hat.

In any case, she could not afford to stay on the island, even if she had wanted to. Her last royalty cheque had been tiny. It was her 'windfall' – an unexpected late sale of foreign rights – that had enabled her to settle her bills, to buy her ticket, and to pay for the transport of her tea-chests. The only way she could have stayed on the island would have been by writing another Book of Shame. She was incapable of that, just as she was incapable of ever again earning her living by writing advertising copy or by reading trash. *So what was she going to do?*

She had arranged that, when she arrived in England, she would stay with Sarah while she looked for a room and a job. She wondered why she felt so sure that – especially in a country with so much unemployment – she would be able to find work. Was it because she had always worked? (These five years of 'not working' had been the hardest work of all.)

Many people would feel that her age was against her. It was strange that – fifty later this year – she had the sense that she had only come half way. Half way where? To a hundred? No that was not at all what she meant. Yet the phrase 'half way' constantly recurred.

'In a sense,' she had read in her bird book, 'migratory birds seek perpetual summer. However, this is at the cost of repeated punishing ordeals which many of them do not survive.'

Now Celia prepared to take wing: not as raptors, gliding, are carried on the high warm currents of the great thermals; but as small migrants, storm-baffled, frozen, forced down towards demented waves, must pit themselves – perpetually – against Nature.